The Stars for a Light

CHENEY DUVALL, M.D.
BOOK ONE

The Stars for a Light

Lynn Morris

HENDRICKSON PUBLISHERS

The Stars for a Light

Hendrickson Publishers Marketing, LLC
P. O. Box 3473
Peabody, Massachusetts 01961-3473

ISBN 978-1-59856-738-0

Second Hendrickson Edition Printing — April 2014

Cover Photo Credit: Mike Habermann Photography

To my Dad,
because I couldn't have done it without you.

And to my Mom,
because neither of us could have done it without you.

A Note to Readers

A warm welcome to all of our faithful readers and, we hope, to new readers of the *Cheney Duvall, M.D.* series.

My father taught me how to write. Without him, Cheney never would have lived. But somehow by about the third book, it had become mostly my creation (and my anguish!), and Dad has turned the series over to me. It's been awhile since I've "revisited" Cheney and Shiloh, but with this new release of the series, I've gone back down the long road I traveled with them. To give you some idea of how much this series means to me, I would like to give you one example of how *Cheney Duvall, M.D.* changed my life.

I received many, many letters asking me if Shiloh Irons was based on a real person, if I knew this man (and if he had any brothers at home!). It's true that he was, in one way, based on a real person. That person was my brother Alan; my physical descriptions of Shiloh's height, weight, and physique were his. As far as Shiloh's persona, that was a creation (or a dream) of my own.

I dedicated one of my books to "my pretty sister" and my "Norse god of a brother." These weren't my words. This was an inside family joke. A good friend of ours is a poet, and he wrote one about my sister Stacy and my brother Alan, and those were his descriptions. I wasn't in the poem, so I finished the dedication "from the short one with the good personality," and it still is true. I'm average, average, average. Stacy is five feet ten, slender, and beautiful. Alan was six feet five, 220 pounds, and muscular.

In 2007, at the age of forty-eight, my brother Alan died. In our wrenching grief, our entire family was brought closer to the Lord. We found that only he is our comforter, only he gives us peace, and only he gives us joy. That was four years ago. But for the first time since then, I can now revisit Cheney and Shiloh, along with the inescapable memories of my brother, with pleasure and even with smiles and laughter. I still miss him; but I know I will see him again. I hope that my faith in the Lord, even in times of sorrow, comes through in every one of my novels.

Lynn Morris

Counsel is mine, and sound wisdom: I am
understanding; I have strength.

Proverbs 8:14

Contents

PART ONE: A TIME TO EVERY PURPOSE

1. The Steamship *Continental* 3

2. Shiloh and Dev 19

3. A Stitch in Time 37

4. A Time to Keep Silence and a Time to Speak 55

PART TWO: SONGS IN THE NIGHT

5. One Hundred Petticoats. 69

6. First Night 85

7. Back and Forth 99

8. Earth and Air, Water and Fire 117

9. Prayer Meeting, sans Prayers 133

10. Captain Weldon's Ball 145

11. Cargo Deck: Crew Quarters 163

PART THREE: SHADOW OF THE ALMIGHTY

12. A Matter of Fists 175

13. Havana 187

14. Guns, Gold, and Women 203

15. Train Ride to the End of the World 215

16. The Terror by Night 231

PART FOUR: HE DIVIDETH THE SEA

17. *Vomito Negro* 249

18. Murder at Sea 265

19. Now . . . in the Hour of Our Death 281

20. End of a Voyage 299

THE VOYAGE OF CHENEY DUVALL

The planned route from New York to Seattle

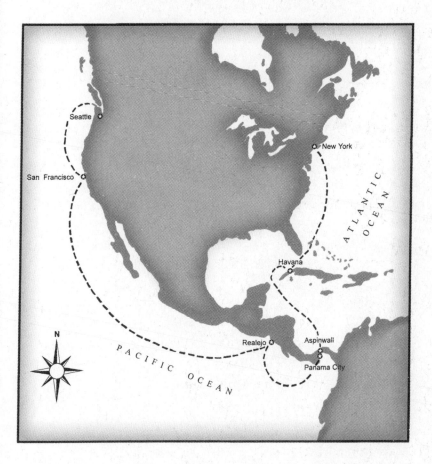

PART ONE

A Time to Every Purpose

To every thing there is a season, and a time to every purpose under the heaven.

Ecclesiastes 3:1

1

The Steamship Continental

"Whoa, there, ye good-for-nothin' flibbertigibbet—"

The affectionate tone of Jack Gaines' voice softened his gruff words as the small, leathery Irishman led the skittering, nervous team pulling the luxurious black carriage around to the street in front of the Duvall home.

"Crazy beasts," he groused as the black Arabians shied and pranced in harness. He laid a calming hand to a glossy arched neck. "But then maybe yer in the right household for it."

He shook his head toward the house, which sat dignified and stately on a slight rise, far back from the street. The massive Doric columns gleamed white and pristine on the portico of the imposing two-story mansion.

"You'd sure never guess all the goin's on, what with young ladies becomin' doctors and gallivantin' off to who knows where. . . ."

At that moment the great oak door opened and Cheney Duvall, M.D., walked across the spacious porch, hurried down the steps, and strode briskly toward the carriage at the end of the white brick walk. "Uh-oh," Mr. Jack muttered to the horses, watching Cheney's thoroughbred's pace. "She's lookin' right sassy this mornin', of which I know we're gonna do some sashayin' today!"

The young woman coming toward the carriage was an unfashionable five feet ten inches tall, and walked in long, determined strides instead of the tiny, mincing steps affected by proper Victorian women. A slender, lithe figure, twenty-four years old, she wore a crisp blue-and-green plaid taffeta dress and a small green bonnet. A matching parasol and reticule hung from her left wrist, and in her right hand was a somber black leather doctor's bag that seemed incongruous with her stylish appearance.

It was neither her clothes nor the trim figure that first drew the eye, however, but the thick, curly auburn hair shining with fiery red glints in the early afternoon sun. Tendrils and wisps of it escaped from the bonnet to frame her oval face in glowing color. She held her head high; dark, heavy brows arched above sparkling sea-green eyes; clear, smooth cheeks flushed with new excitement. She had a small nose and a wide, generous mouth and had inherited her mother's beauty mark, a small mole high on her left cheekbone, almost under the eye. Although her face was too strong to be called beautiful, her carriage and countenance emanated energy and vitality.

But to Mr. Jack she just looked sassy, and he eyed her warily as she reached the carriage and jumped in. "Mr. Jack," she ordered, "take me to Lower Manhattan, to the docks. We have to find the S.S. *Continental*." She pulled her voluminous skirts in after her, pushing them down impatiently.

Helping her shove her skirts in, folding up the steps, tucking in more rustling taffeta so he could close the door, Mr. Jack muttered, "Yessiree, Miss Cheney. I do see as how yer dressed to go down an' visit with them dock rats this mornin', an' I'm sure an' certain that there silly leetle bag has the makin's of a tea party. . . ."

Cheney paid no attention; she was accustomed to Mr. Jack's dire monologue. Settling back in the black velvet seat, she drew a deep breath and blew it out with a most unladylike "Whew!" as the carriage started with a jerk. The last two days had been a blur of frantic activity and sleepless nights, topped by a frustrating morning wait. *What if she doesn't get here?* Cheney leaned her head back and closed her eyes to collect her thoughts.

The elegant carriage, though well-sprung, jounced and joggled slowly down the cobbled streets. It was two o'clock in the afternoon of April 29, 1865. The specter of war had dissipated three weeks earlier at Appomattox, only to be replaced by the black days of Abraham Lincoln's assassination. But New York's heartbeat did not falter for distant wars and dead presidents; the city streets still resounded with strong and raucous rhythm.

A delicious smell wafted into the carriage and Cheney lifted her head, sniffing appreciatively. A young boy shouted, "Bread! Fresh bread right here!" Calls rang out all up and down the streets, a chorus matched with the percussion of carriages and wagons and horses clattering on the cobblestones. Mixed voices, loud and muffled, singing and cursing, English, German, Irish, female, male, filled Cheney's ears. Once, Mr. Jack yelped sharply, "Here now, boy! Get outter the way 'fore ye get kilt, or worse!"

What's worse than getting "kilt"? Cheney thought with amusement. Mr. Jack had been with her father as long as she could remember, taking care of Richard Duvall's beloved Arabians. Neither Jack nor anyone else knew his date of birth or parentage. Cheney surmised his age to be about sixty. Although small, he was wiry and strong, with shrewd blue eyes that belied his simple speech and manner. Either he didn't grasp the fact that Cheney was now a doctor or, more likely, he chose to ignore it—but he still treated her like the wayward child she had been years ago.

The weak sunlight suddenly disappeared. Cheney craned her neck out the window to scan the sky. Tattered, soot-colored clouds were scudding across the sun. A wisp of cool wind smelling of sea salt and fish touched her upturned face. They were close to the docks.

Leaning back in the seat again, Cheney reviewed the turn her life had taken. It seemed almost impossible that her interview with Asa Mercer had been held only two days before. She had desperately replied to a small, insignificant ad in the *New York Herald:* "Physician needed for extended sea voyage. Average pay, excellent chance for travel. Apply: Asa Mercer, Belvedere Hotel, Manhattan." But her time with Asa Mercer had turned out to be highly satisfactory for both of them.

For Cheney, it had been exciting and gratifying to actually be offered a position. After the last two months of applying and interviewing for seven different positions, then being summarily rejected because she was a woman, she had almost given up hope. But now, in just two days, she would be on her way to Seattle with Mercer's Belles!

When Cheney had graduated from the Women's Medical College of the prestigious University of Pennsylvania and become a full-fledged, documented, accredited physician, she had just assumed that she would immediately find a suitable position. Instead, she had faced a series of rejections ranging from subtle to outright rude, and she had been crushed by them. For all her obvious talent and advantages, Cheney was very insecure about being a physician, so Mr. Mercer's offer to her felt like a cool drink of water in the desert. He was actually *glad* she was a female doctor!

Asa Mercer had indeed been excited with the idea of hiring a woman physician for his voyage from New York to Washington Territory—and with very good reason. For the second time Mr. Mercer had contracted with northern women—war widows, poor women, and a few older, unmarried women—to travel to Washington, where the ratio of men to women was nine to one. He was a respectable, earnest young man who had successfully completed one voyage such as this in 1864 with eleven women, and all had been married within a year. This time more than two hundred women had responded to his territory's call, and Asa Mercer had conscientiously decided to provide a physician for the three-month voyage.

He had not even thought of a woman doctor, however, until Cheney came for her interview, but he was extremely delighted. After questioning Cheney and scanning her credentials, he had told her enthusiastically, "Of course! You're the perfect woman's doctor, and obviously you are a lady of intelligence and good breeding—the perfect chaperone!"

The horses had slowed to a cautious walk. These streets weren't fashionably cobbled or bricked, but plain mud—and they stayed mired because of the vast amount of traffic going back and forth to the crowded confusion at the port. The carriage passed a stalled wagon, piled high and covered with a dirty canvas. The horse—a huge Clydesdale—had slipped down, tangling his harness, and now was crouched in the mud with all fours under him. Two shabby young men were yanking on his bridle and yelling. The horse just looked bored.

As Cheney peered ahead, she could see the long, wide wooden dock, the pier of the S.S. *Continental*. The steamer sat majestically, unmoved in a choppy gray sea. Long and sleek and painted black, the vessel seemed immense to Cheney, although Mr. Mercer had described the ship as a mid-sized side-wheeler. Two towering masts loomed fore and aft, with a fat red smokestack in the middle. The side paddles looked crude—two huge wheels stuck in the exact middle of the hull on each side and covered with black canvas.

Mr. Jack pulled the carriage up smartly, close to the huge gangplank. Immediately Asa Mercer's head popped into Cheney's window. His brown hair was mussed, with a stubborn cowlick in back, and his slender, earnest face wore a harried expression. "Dr. Duvall! It is so good to see you again!" He opened the door and pulled down the carriage steps, adding breathlessly, "But I was surprised when I got your message that you'd be here today. There's still two days before we sail, you know."

Cheney descended from the carriage and opened her tiny blue-and-green-striped parasol, glancing around the docks with frank curiosity. "Yes, I know, Mr. Mercer, but I want to make sure the infirmary is well-stocked and sea-ready before we leave New York, so I thought I'd better take care of that today."

Asa Mercer blinked. "Yes, yes, of course, Miss—I mean, Dr.—" His eyes focused on a point beyond her shoulder; abruptly he shouted, "No! No! Not that one—!" and dashed off to two burly dock workers who were slowly trudging up the gangplank with an enormous dome-topped trunk between them.

"Nervous feller, ain't he?" Mr. Jack remarked. Cheney turned to the small man. He was planted firmly behind her with her black bag in his left hand and her tiny, gold-tasseled reticule clutched gingerly between two gnarled brown ringers in his extended right hand. He was holding the drawstring bag out to her as if it were a tiny little snapping turtle. She took the tiny purse and reached for the valise, but like a grownup withholding candy from a child, he hid the case behind his back, a stubborn look on his face.

He opened his mouth to speak, but Cheney said hurriedly, "Now, Mr. Jack, I told you that I have a lot of work to do here today. Thank you for your help, but I want you to go on home and come back later tonight."

Still hiding the valise from her, he said grimly, "Nope, Miss Cheney. Ye ain't got no business flittin' around these wormy docks by yerself, and I ain't got no business leavin' ye here."

Cheney snapped impatiently, "Nonsense! I have no intention of flitting anywhere—and if I do, Mr. Mercer is here!"

Mr. Jack snorted with derision and looked meaningfully at Asa Mercer, who was talking loudly to the burly dock workers and waving his arms vigorously.

"And besides, Mr. Jack," she went on with a note of pleading in her voice, "I need you to go home in case my nurse gets there. She's on her way right now, and she's going to come to the house. When she gets there, I'd like you to bring her down here right away."

Mr. Jack's face lost some of its severity, but he still remained reluctant and suspicious. A low grumble of thunder rolled through the air above them and Cheney added slyly, "Besides, it's going to storm, and I know you don't want to get Mr. Richard's carriage and horses mired up to the seats down here in Lower Manhattan, do you?"

Mr. Jack glanced up at the gray sky; the clouds overhead were light and not really menacing. Then he looked out to sea, where a well-defined, ominous black mass sat low on the horizon. "You sure are right about that, Miss Cheney," he agreed, though hesitant. She had hit his one vulnerable spot: his highstrung Arabian horses.

"All right," he relented, with one final dark glance at Asa Mercer. "But don't ye be out here a-prancin' about with Mr. Flibbertigibbet. I'll come to yer cabin, you hear? I'll come find you!"

Patting his arm affectionately, Cheney laughed and took her valise. "Yes, sir, Mr. Jack. Come back about nine o'clock, please." She turned and hurried toward the gangplank.

Mr. Jack scrambled nimbly back up to the driver's seat, muttering, "Sure, and there she goes *a-runnin'* again, like she don't know ladies don't be *a-runnin'* in public, like that idjit parysol's gonna help a person what ain't got sense enough to get outter the rain. . . ." He snapped the reins smartly and made a clacking sound. The jittery horses reared a little, then started off down the big wooden pier.

I really do wish Mr. Jack could have stayed! Cheney thought nervously. *He's always been there for me, never failed me. . . .* Then, with a shake of her head she set her jaw and started up the gangplank, only to be halted by the sight of Asa Mercer running down toward her. He was twenty-five years old, slender and tanned and rumpled. Cheney had known as soon as she met him that he was dutiful and conscientious. He was also boundless energy in perpetual motion, and that, combined with his ever-present cowlick, made him seem very young, but she liked him.

He was still about ten feet from her when he started talking, his voice raised a few octaves. "The infirmary is stateroom 12 on B Deck, and your stateroom adjoins it on one side, number 10, and the nurse's is on the other. Is she here yet? And we're not going to get any blue mass." He stopped short in front of her, looking over her shoulder. "You didn't let your carriage go, did you?"

Cheney shook her head to clear it after this confusing flow of information and questions. "One thing at a time, please. Which stateroom did you say? And why didn't we get any blue mass?" Blue mass, a bitter concoction of quinine sulfate, licorice, myrrh, and oil of sassafras, was essential for the treatment of malaria.

"Staterooms 10, 12, and 15," he repeated, his eyes darting up and down the dock, then explained, "The rest of the infirmary supplies got here early this morning, but the apothecary sent a note that he didn't get the quinine he'd ordered and can't get any more until next week."

"Oh, for heaven's sake!" Cheney exclaimed in frustration; "we *have* to have quinine." She stared into the distance, obviously deep in thought. Medical supplies had been funneled to the armies as fast as they could be manufactured—or, as with quinine, imported—for the last four years. Cheney had counted herself extremely lucky to find one apothecary to fill her order completely, and the fact that he hadn't received quinine as ordered didn't really surprise her. But she knew she couldn't waste any time trying to find some; it might take all of the next two days to gather enough for two hundred women. The fact that part of their journey would be through Panama made quinine an absolute essential.

"All right, Mr. Mercer," Cheney said decisively. "I'll go right now to the apothecaries that are close by the docks. If a shipment has come in recently, the shops might still have some."

Asa exclaimed with frustration, "Yes, but that's the problem! I can't leave right now! Some of the ladies' luggage has arrived, and it's piled every which way on the dock." He gestured to a huge clutter of trunks, cases, and boxes off to the left of the gangplank. "I've been working with the captain and gotten the stateroom assignments straight. Oh yes! Here's a diagram of the staterooms; this way, you'll know where everyone is in case of an emergency—heaven forbid." He handed Cheney several sheets of paper showing layouts of the various decks. She leafed through them and located her stateroom, filing the location away in her mind with the confidence of one accustomed to memorizing long lists of symptoms and treatments. She wanted to peruse the skillfully drawn diagrams more closely, but Asa Mercer was still busily telling her things, so she folded the plans and put them in her tiny reticule.

"But this luggage *must* be loaded before it storms," he went on in a harried voice, "and right now the shore gangs are busy with this shipment from Duvall's."

A smile flitted across Cheney's face. She had already noticed the cargo being loaded from her father's factory, Duvall's Tools and Implements. Almost all the ships going west carried shipments of the shovels, pickaxes, hammers, and plows from Duvall's. Asa Mercer, however, hadn't connected the name, and he continued. "So as soon as they finish with this, I'll have to be here to direct the loading, and I imagine I'll be doing some loading myself."

"Yes, I see, and it's all right, Mr. Mercer." Cheney spoke with calm authority. "I'm perfectly capable of walking a block or two by myself."

Mercer's boyish face grew anxious. "No. I can't let you go walking around the docks by yourself!"

Cheney lifted her chin stubbornly. Only two months after her graduation, and she was already sick and tired of this attitude. "If I were a male doctor," she challenged, "there would be no question of it!"

Turning quickly from her, he walked away a few paces, considering. He reached up and smoothed down his cowlick, his back to her; then he came back and faced her. "You're right," he admitted ruefully, pulling a large gold watch out of his pocket, "and it *is* only three-thirty. But you need to hurry. It's going to storm soon."

The black mass on the horizon was growing. It was taller than before, with huge, silver-gray, puffy tops. The dark clouds were advancing steadily, eerie lights flashing within them. Continuous low thunder rumbled in the air.

"Yes, it is," Cheney agreed, though undaunted.

Swinging around in a little circle, Asa Mercer said, "Now, where would an apothecary—?" But Cheney had already walked about ten feet away and was busily talking to the nearest burly dock worker. Asa skittered quickly up behind her.

"Thank you." Cheney smiled to the man, turned to Asa Mercer, and stuck her doctor's bag into his hand. "Add this to that mound of luggage over there, please. There's an apothecary two streets past the end of the pier, down the first side street on the left. I'll be back soon. Don't worry," she said crisply and struck off at a quick pace, her face determined.

Watching her go, Mercer thought, *Well, she can sure take care of herself!*

⊰❈⊱

Cheney walked swiftly down the street, her skirts billowing around her. The wind was picking up, and cool wet drafts brushed her face. The sky was getting darker and darker, the clouds thickening and slowing. People were beginning to pull their coats around them and anchor their hats as they rushed along.

Cheney, however, really wasn't paying attention. Her brow was furrowed as she navigated the muddy quagmire that was supposed to be the street. *I must get ahold of some quinine*, she thought anxiously, *and what about the nurse? I wonder why she hasn't arrived.*

Mr. Mercer had asked her if she could engage a nurse for the trip, and Cheney had assured him that she would find one, even though it was only four days until their departure. Immediately she had wired her friend and mentor, Dr. Henry Vallingham, the president of the University of Pennsylvania:

NEED NURSE BY MAY 1 STOP SEA VOYAGE 6 MONTHS $50 PER MONTH STOP HELP STOP

The next day—yesterday—she had received a wire from Dr. Vallingham:

SENDING BEST NURSE I'VE EVER HAD STOP WILL REPORT TO YOUR HOME APRIL 29 STOP GLAD TO HELP STOP

Cheney had waited for the nurse all morning, but no one had come. What if something had gone wrong with that, too?

Ahead on her left was the side street, which she eyed with hesitation. A dark little tavern named Mathilda's Lantern squatted on the corner, its blackened oak door propped open and a rough-looking bunch of sailors lounging around outside. Harsh voices and raucous laughter drifted on the wind and enveloped her in embarrassment. She gulped, ducked her head, straightened her shoulders, then hurried around the corner, ignoring the murmurs and catcalls that followed her.

Immediately she saw the apothecary's storefront about halfway down the small muddy street, on the right side. Cheney sighed with relief. By now she could feel the unmistakable moisture in the wind, and she tried to hurry, but she had to pick her way carefully through the sticky, stinking mud. Raising her skirts as much as she dared, she struggled over to the small shop. Her stomach hurt, and she suddenly remembered that she hadn't eaten since breakfast—and then scantily. Cheney was healthy and strong; she had always scorned the affectations of ladies who picked at their food, cinched in their corsets, and then complained of the vapors. But her meals had been few and hurried in the two days since her appointment, and she knew it was affecting her stamina.

She opened the apothecary's door and stepped in. A little gray-haired man with sleeve garters looked up from a worn desk that held a gas lamp, already lit, and a litter of mortars and pestles, bottles, little piles of powders, and small pieces of paper with prescriptions scribbled on them in Latin. Iron-colored eyebrows lifted at the sight of Cheney. With pleasure in his voice he said, "Yes, ma'am. How may I help you today? Some rose water? Belladonna? Candy, perhaps?"

Cheney smiled at the strange little man. "I am Dr. Cheney Duvall. How much quinine do you have?"

His face changed at Cheney's businesslike tone, and he stood and bowed deeply. He was very short and bowlegged. "I'm honored to meet you, Doctor. Unfortunately, all I have is four five-gallon kegs of quinine water. It's been very difficult to get quinine sulfate for the past few years," he said regretfully.

"Yes, so I understand," Cheney murmured absently. Quinine water was much less palatable than blue mass, and it was impossible to tell the strength of the mixture, so the dosage was a matter of pure guesswork. But it was certainly better than no quinine at all.

Outside a long, loud growl of thunder sounded as Cheney weighed the option and the little apothecary patiently waited. "All right," she said finally, "I'd better take all of it. Can you have it delivered—no, never mind, I'll send someone to pick it up. I'll pay you right now, though, so you won't be tempted to let it get away from you."

They negotiated a price, and Cheney quickly paid him, picked up the receipt, and stepped outside. Her eyes widened at the alien landscape.

The street was deserted. In just the few minutes she had been in the shop, the weather had grown dark and menacing. The wind, salty and wet, was blowing hard and carrying with it the sound of low, ominous thunder, almost continuous now.

Cheney checked her purse and silk parasol hanging on her right arm, then lifted her skirts and started unflinchingly down the muddy street. She was trying to hurry, but it was still slow going. She reached the wide street that ran straight down to the pier and saw with relief that the door to Mathilda's Lantern was closed—all the unshaven patrons were inside. Hastily turning the corner, Cheney stopped to look around in the eerie light. There was hardly anyone left of what had been a busy, congested throng of noisy people. *Of course,* she thought, *I'm the only ninny still outside with this storm coming on!*

Cheney couldn't see the pier yet, but she headed in that direction. Watching her feet, she tried to stay out of the muddiest and deepest ruts. Suddenly she bumped into something and stopped short—two feet appeared in front of hers!

Her head shot up and she saw a man, much shorter than she, square in front of her, and off to her left another man, large and completely bald. At first she thought they were black men, then realized they were covered from head to toe with soot. Coal stokers. Her nose wrinkled. *The last trip must have been a long one, from the smell of it—or them.*

"Excuse me. Let me through, please," she said impatiently, stepping to the side.

The small man thrust out his hand and grabbed Cheney's upper right arm, grinning at her, his breath foul, his teeth broken and black, his features sharp and sly, ratlike. "No, missy. You ain't excused." The large man grabbed her left arm. The small, ratty one continued. "You're comin' wid us. Right now."

Cheney looked wildly behind her and up the street. Not one soul in sight! The murky air, the dimly lit gas lamps, and ghoulish tendrils of dirty gray fog forming and floating around them added to the nightmare. Stark fear shot through her.

"All right, lady," one of them said as they started hauling Cheney off to her left, toward a dark alleyway that gaped between two buildings. She frantically fought to jerk free. The shorter one just grinned—a death's head mask, face blackened, eyes red, mouth open.

Cheney's eyes widened in horror and she opened her mouth to scream. A huge, grimy hand from behind her clamped over her face and jerked her backward. Her feet flew out from under her; the small man let go of her arm. The stinking giant was dragging her toward that huge alley. She dropped everything and clawed at the iron-like hand over her mouth, kicking her feet against his legs.

The ratty man was walking slightly behind them, facing Cheney, looking down at her, laughing. When they reached the black, stinking alley, he leered at her and croaked in a voice of poison, "Now, we're gonna get to know each other—" Then, inexplicably, he stopped, and his mouth opened in a perfect black O.

Slowing down, Cheney thought wildly. *We're all slowing down because of the shadow, the big tall shadow—* In the middle of his little speech, the rat man's feet had suddenly left the earth. He rose slowly, almost majestically; Cheney's eyes followed his movement upward. Then, with no sound, he flew across the alley, hit the brick wall about three feet up, and bounced to the muddy ground, a shapeless black hump.

The iron grip around Cheney's mouth and waist suddenly let go, sending Cheney sprawling in the mud. She scrambled up, turned, and started backing off, wheezing painfully. The big giant, a thick black shadow, was crouching and holding something in front of him. She caught a flash of silver. *A knife!* As her eyes grew accustomed to the dim light, Cheney could see another man, also crouched, both hands out, empty, weaving them in time to the snaky movements of the knife. Without taking his eyes off the blade, he yelled, "Run, woman! Run!" and grabbed the man's arm above the knife.

Cheney whirled, pulled up her muddy skirts, and sped off at top speed. She'd never run so fast in her whole life. Both shoes had come off. Her bonnet was a soggy mess hanging down her back, her hair disheveled, streaming in every direction, whipping in front of her face, getting in her mouth. She didn't care. She just ran.

Nearing the pier, she could see the welcome lights of the S.S. *Continental*. Desperately she struggled toward the ship, the haven, homing in like a lost little pigeon. Her stockinged feet barely touched the rough boards of the pier as she skimmed toward the gangplank. Lightning flashed like an explosion, thunder rolled into a loud roar, and she felt the first cold drops of rain mix with the tears that poured down her face.

Cheney reached the gangplank and raced to the top without losing a second's momentum. It, too, was deserted. She stumbled down the tiny little stairwell and ran through the dark, narrow hallways, searching for the room number Asa Mercer had told her. Finally she found a door marked 10 and flung it open, slammed it behind her, and crumpled in a heap.

Slowly she raised up, her back against the door, and sobbed. Then her knees began to shake.

Horrible! Horrible! Those dirty, stinking men—awful! Cheney couldn't think clearly. She pulled her knees up and dropped her head on them, crouching on the floor, crying helplessly. She sobbed convulsively and thought she was going to throw up. But having had little food, she only gagged.

After a while—Cheney didn't know how long—her sobs subsided and she straightened up, leaning back tiredly against the door. Spotting a pitcher and bowl on a tiny table by the two-tiered bed, she pulled herself to a standing position, leaning dizzily against the door, and almost passed out from nausea and weakness. But she stayed conscious and took two unsteady steps to the washstand. Picking up the spotless white cotton cloth lying in the bottom of the bowl, she poured the tepid water into it and scrubbed her face and hands and neck until they were red.

Tired. I'm so tired! she thought dazedly. *And so dizzy!* She looked vacantly around the small room and collapsed on the bottom bunk, sitting on the edge and staring into space.

Cheney lost track of time. Every once in a while she shivered. She simply didn't know how long she had sat there, eyes open but unseeing. When a knock sounded at her door, she jumped in shock. A businesslike voice asked, "Dr. Duvall?"

Cheney rose and stared at the door, fear pulsing through her again and bile rising in her throat. Her eyes wide, she looked frantically around the room for a weapon. There was nothing.

The quiet knock sounded again, and a polite voice repeated, "Dr. Duvall? Please, I need to see the doctor. This is the right stateroom, isn't it? Number 10?"

"W-why? Why d-do you n-need to see the doctor?" Cheney had calmed down a little at the reassuring tone of his voice, but she still couldn't think straight.

"Well—umm, ma'am—I'm bleeding."

The calm, almost offhand words hit Cheney as if someone had dashed a bucket of cold seawater in her face. This was it! *She* was the doctor—Cheney Duvall, M.D. And the doctor was cowering in her stateroom like a cornered little mouse while a man was standing outside in the hallway bleeding. He had naturally come looking for a doctor, not a mewling kitten. Cheney shook her head, trying to get her thoughts under control. She realized that she had to open that door. It was her job.

She turned and fought down the nausea as she walked to the door. Clinging for support, she cracked the door a little bit. Outside in the dimness of the hallway stood a very tall man, his features obscured in the dark shadows. Cheney's heart lurched with fear, and she drew a sharp breath through her teeth.

*It's him! He's here! He followed me, and now he's going to—*The shadow of the man began to fade as darkness edged her vision.

Then she fainted dead away.

Shiloh and Dev

There is too much noise here, and I want it to stop. So foggy . . .
loud fog . . . Where . . . ?

Her eyes were still closed, and Cheney thought vaguely that
it was unusual for her to see the fog with her eyes shut. With
an effort she opened them, but her vision was clouded and ob-
scure, and her thoughts were floating, bits of information that
seemed to have no connection with her body. *Boxes . . . "Bren-*
nan's Apothecary" . . .

For a moment logic intruded upon her disoriented dream,
and Cheney realized she was still on the ship, in a bed, but not in
her stateroom. The ship was heaving back and forth sickeningly,
and the noise that made Cheney cringe came from a crashing,
blowing storm outside and the answering creaks and screeches
of the ship. The *Continental* was pitching heavily in what must
be a roiling sea. Cheney's head pounded, chilling nausea swept
over her again, and the corners of her vision began to turn a
dirty gray.

Infirmary . . . must be in the infirmary . . . boxes from the
apothecary's . . .

A tall man ducked through the stateroom door, knelt by the
small bunk, and took her cold hand. "I'm gonna take you home,
Dr. Duvall," he said in a calm voice that somehow carried over
the clamor of the storm.

"Doesn't matter . . . just a dream . . ." Cheney muttered, and
her eyes closed again. The persistent screaming of that cold, dark

sea called her. She started floating downward, and the murky green depths closed above her.

⁂

It was blessedly quiet and she was blissfully warm. Cheney roused out of a deep sleep and looked around her.

She was in her own room and her lamp with the pink tas-seled shade glowed softly on the table by her bed. Her mother sat in a large wing chair close by, and a man stepped out of the shadows behind her. Drowsily she thought it was the dream man again; then she saw with some dismay that it was Devlin Buchanan. He leaned over her with a small whiskey glass, saying, "It's all right, Cheney. Drink this."

She drank the small amount of liquid and mumbled, "Lau-danum." He smiled down at her, the sharp planes of his face strangely shadowed, and then he slowly faded from her sight.

⁂

"Where's Dally?" Cheney yelled unceremoniously down the stairs. "I need some hot water!"

A few moments before, Cheney had awakened with a start and grabbed the ornate ormolu clock on her bedside table. Nine-thirty already! Impatiently she had thrown back the covers and scrambled out of bed, groaning a little because she felt sore all over. But Cheney was young and strong, and the nightmares and weakness of the previous night were already dissolving in the clean-washed April morning.

A statuesque black woman appeared at the bottom of the stairs carrying a huge steaming pitcher wrapped in thick snowy towels. With grand deliberation she started up the steps. "I'm already a-comin'," she muttered. "Ain't no need in shoutin' the house down."

Dally was a very large woman, taller than Cheney's father, with big hands and feet and long legs and arms. She had been given her freedom by the Duvalls three months after their marriage, and had been offered the position of housekeeper at the same time. Dally had accepted with great dignity and was still there, treating the entire Duvall family like helpless infants.

Now Cheney whirled and flounced back into her bedroom, followed by Dally with the pitcher of scented hot water. A refreshing aroma of rosemary and chamomile filled the room. Dally set the pitcher down on a mahogany washstand that was cluttered with small colored bottles, jewelry, various medical supplies, and one glittering scalpel. She put her hands on her hips and surveyed the room with exasperation. "Well, Miz Doctah Cheney Duvall," she said sarcastically, "I sho' hope none of your po' patients done crawled up in here and died! 'Cause it'd take me 'til kingdom come to find 'em in all dis mess!"

Wincing at Dally's vehemence, Cheney looked around her bedroom. It was disastrous, she scolded herself. Four huge round-top trunks stood open, the top trays carelessly thrown down beside them. Dresses, petticoats, crinolines, jewelry, parasols, corsets, and assorted mismatched shoes spilled out of all four. Medical supplies, instruments, and books lay on top of every horizontal surface in the room. The doors to the massive armoire stood open; nothing hung *in* it, but various articles of clothing were hung *on* it. Ordinarily Cheney was meticulous, trim, and methodical; now the condition of her bedroom seemed as tumultuous as her thoughts had been for the last two days.

"Oh," said Cheney in a small voice. "Well, I'm packing."

Dally snorted, then turned to leave the room. At the door she quickly stepped back to allow Cheney's mother to enter. Irene Duvall glided in with a soft rustle on a faint waft of sweet perfume. Sailing out soundlessly behind her, Dally's deep voice echoed a warning from the stairs, "Don't you fall in no hole or git buried under a pile of somethin' in thet room, Miz Irene."

Cheney and her mother smiled with amusement; Dally never left a room without an exit line drifting back to the occupants.

Irene Duvall's face clouded a little as she looked up at her daughter, searching her face. Irene was a small, classically beautiful woman. At forty-three, she had one solitary white streak in her deep auburn hair, and her face was still as smooth and unlined as a woman half her age. Cheney had inherited her mother's beauty mark and sea-green eyes, which were now narrowed with concern.

"How are you feeling, dear? Better?"

"Yes, Mother, much better, but who—how did I—?"

"Just—don't worry about that right now," Irene interrupted gently, sitting Cheney down on the bed and stroking her tangled mass of auburn hair. "We have a lot to talk about, but I want you to come downstairs now and eat something. Dally's fixing a late breakfast."

Cheney nodded vigorously. "Oh yes! That sounds marvelous. I'm starving. Can we have peaches? And Dally's Double Cream? And tea instead of coffee?"

Irene Duvall's face cleared of worry. Smiling, she rose and walked toward the door murmuring, "Yes, you do feel better, don't you, Cheney? Well, hurry up and come on down. Everyone is waiting for you." She stopped at the doorway and looked around the littered room. "Dally has to take this afternoon off, dear. Tansy is having her baby."

Cheney groaned, "Oh no! However am I going to get all of this packed? I have so many things to do today—like finding out about the nurse!"

"You certainly do," Irene answered with a soft irony that Cheney didn't quite understand. "But don't worry about the packing. I'll take care of it for you."

"Oh, Mother! Will you really?" Cheney ran and hugged her so boisterously that the diminutive Irene Duvall staggered a little. "That would help me so much! Thank you, thank you!"

A deep voice interrupted. "Well, if that's the reward, I'll pack your bloomers and ditties too!" Cheney's father emerged from his bedroom across the hall to stand behind his wife. Even leaning heavily on his cane, Richard Duvall managed to hold himself erect and straight-shouldered. He was a tall man with the features of an aristocrat: silver hair, clear gray eyes, and a clean-cut face.

Cheney threw her arms around him and said, "Good morning, Father! Everything's all right now. I feel fine! Now, will you two please leave so I can get dressed for breakfast. I really am starving."

Cheney's parents smiled at her, both of them searching her face carefully. Richard Duvall nodded, "She's better," and the two turned toward the stairs.

Cheney quickly stripped and threw a small towel into the warm water on the nightstand. Wringing it out and breathing deeply of the clean smell, she began to scrub herself mercilessly. Then, wincing at unexpected pain, she looked in the mirror and saw dark bruises on her neck and shoulders. Her eyes narrowed, and she reached for a high-necked white cotton blouse lying on top of one of the trunks. *Those men! Was it real? A nightmare? But how in the world did I get home last night? Seems as if—was some man carrying me? Mr. Mercer? No, that's not it. . . . Was Dev here?* Hastily she dressed and crammed her hair into a delicate crocheted white snood, questions and thoughts darting like hummingbirds back and forth through her mind.

Sighing, she finally headed for the stairs to the dining room. *Well, one thing I know,* Cheney thought fiercely as she hurried along, *I'm not telling Mother and Father one thing about those awful men last night! My parents worry enough as it is.*

Reaching the foyer, she turned down the hall toward the big double doors of the dining room. In the doorway she jerked to a stop and gulped. "You!" she blurted.

The dream man! her mind shouted in sharp confusion. *He's— the tall shadow man! In the alley! Or my dream?*

He was standing at the heavily laden sideboard, looking at the dozen or so shiny silver bowls set there. "Who—who are you?" Cheney asked weakly. "What are you d-doing here?"

The young man watched her gravely, but Cheney thought his eyes looked amused. Richard and Irene Duvall stood at the other end of the long sideboard, drinking tea from delicate pink china cups. Cheney's father set his cup down and made his way slowly around the long, shining mahogany table to the door where Cheney stood. "Cheney," he said gently, "come in—there's someone I'd like you to meet."

"What?" she asked in obvious confusion, "M-meet him? Haven't I already met him? I m-mean, he was—I w-was on the ship, and he—I mean—" As her father reached her he held out his arm; Cheney clutched it with both hands, her eyes beseechingly on his.

"Come in, Cheney," he repeated, patting her hands, "and we can all tell our stories." He led her back around the table. "This is Mr. Shiloh Irons. He's your nurse, and he's also the man who saved you yesterday, down on the docks, and then brought you home."

Cheney stopped in midstride and said in a strangled voice, "He's who? And he did what?"

Shiloh Irons stepped forward. "I'm Shiloh Irons, Miss Duvall. It's a pleasure to finally meet you. I sure chased you around a lot yesterday." Cheney nodded automatically in greeting as he continued. "Then when I found you, I had to carry you around a lot. Glad to see you're feelin' better." He returned to the sideboard and leaned casually against it, watching her with the ghost of a smile on his face.

Dally came through the door from the kitchen and looked at Cheney. "Shut yo' mouth, Miz Cheney," she said, setting a silver bowl down on the sideboard and polishing it busily with a clean white towel. "Ladies ain't s'posed to have they mouths open in public. You ever seen Miz Irene standin' aroun' with her mouth gapin'?"

Cheney's mouth wasn't actually gaping; she was still standing motionless, her green eyes wide and round on Shiloh Irons, her lips parted just a little. Just the same, she closed her mouth, swallowed hard, and shook her head slowly. "I'm . . . I'm . . ." she faltered.

"You's hungry," Dally growled, "jes' like ever'body else. So ya'll come on and eat. This here's all they is." She planted herself at the end of the sideboard and looked accusingly at everyone.

"Thank you, Dally," Cheney's father said. "Let's say grace now, everyone, and then we can eat—and talk." They bowed their heads, and Cheney unconsciously stepped a little nearer to her father. She didn't quite understand his close and personal relationship to the Lord; she herself didn't feel that God was a person she could just speak to as if He were in the room. But that was how her father always prayed, and it always calmed and quieted Cheney somehow, deep in her spirit.

"Our Father," Richard Duvall prayed, "thank you so much for the delicious food we have here, and thank you again for Dally, who takes such good care of all of us. And Irene and I want to thank you again for this guest, Mr. Irons, whom you sent to take care of Cheney last night. Bless him, Lord, and keep him, we pray. Amen."

Loudly and fervently Dally echoed, "Amen!" and looked knowingly at Cheney, who ignored her.

"Did you say you're my *nurse?*" Cheney demanded, her eyes now sternly fixed on Shiloh Irons. She was getting her second wind.

"Cheney, I'm hungry, and you need to eat," Richard said firmly. "So let's get some food and sit down." Gently he disengaged his arm from Cheney's grip and started toward the buffet. Dally had laid out pink china plates in front of the bowls and trays of food. "Help yourself, Mr. Irons," he told the young nurse, winking at him. "Don't be shy."

"Thank you, sir," Shiloh said, and began piling food on one of the plates. Cheney's mouth tightened but she followed them to the buffet and started helping herself. Irene Duvall did the same.

Cheney gave the nurse a sidelong look as he helped himself to large amounts of food. He was about twenty-two or twenty-three, she guessed, and easily three or four inches over six feet. He was exceedingly lean and lithe and gave an impression of agile strength. Long legs were encased in tan breeches with a yellow stripe down the sides, tucked into knee-high boots. Longish blond hair waved over the collar of his plain brown shirt. His eyes were a startling sky-blue and they were surrounded by small marks of scar tissue; there was one deep scar, shaped like a perfect V, next to his left eye.

Cheney said evenly, "Well, Mr.—Irons, was it?"

"That's right, Doc. But call me Shiloh."

"All right, Shiloh, and you can call me Dr. Duvall." Moodily Cheney plopped a big helping of thick cream on some sliced peaches. "I thought you were a woman."

"And I thought you were a man," he answered easily, dipping into the deep silver bowl of peaches with awkward movements and completely covering the one empty space left on his plate.

That's all I need! Cheney thought with irritation, noticing that he was using his left hand, *A left-handed, clumsy male nurse.*

Shiloh ambled over to the massive dining table, put one filled plate down, and unabashedly returned to the sideboard to fill another one. "Guess you have a lot of questions, huh, Doc?"

"Yes, I do," she answered as they all drifted back to the table with heavily laden plates. Dally carried Richard's to the head of the table. Cheney sat on Richard's right; Shiloh and her mother sat right across from Cheney. "When Dr. Vallingham said he was sending me the best nurse he'd ever had, I thought he meant from the hospital at the university. They were all women. Is that where you met him?"

"No, I met him when I was in the Confederate Army."

"You were in the Confederate Army?"

"Yes, afraid so."

"Well," Cheney snapped, her eyes narrowing just a little, "that's very interesting, considering Dr. Vallingham was *not*. In fact, he wasn't in any army. He's a Quaker!"

"So, Cheney," her father said lightly, "are you saying that you think this man is making up this story? That he has somehow done away with the real nurse and has come here to impersonate her?" The twinkle in his eyes as he looked at Cheney turned the ridicule into gentle teasing.

"Well, no, of course not," Cheney said hastily. "It's just that I—I—just wondered, that's all—"

"It's all right, Doc," Shiloh said, his eyes filled with amusement. "You sure have the right to ask me as many questions as you like, and I don't mind explainin' everything to you. And don't let your father tease you—believe me, he asked me a couple of hundred questions last night."

"Very true," Duvall agreed.

"Anyway, what happened was," Shiloh went on matter-of-factly, "I met Dr. Vallingham at Chimborazo in Richmond—the biggest Confederate hospital in the South. I'd taken a little lead in my leg, so I was sent there. Dr. Vallingham brought a team of Quaker doctors down from the North. You gotta believe me, they were welcome! We didn't have enough of *nothin'* by then, especially doctors. We all thought they'd come to treat the wounded Yanks—but they treated us all alike—Federals and Confederates.

"I wasn't hurt badly," he continued, "so I started helpin' with the nursing. When the doctor said I was the best nurse he'd ever had"—Shiloh's face colored a little—"he must have meant that 'ever took care of him.' He got sick while he was there, and I was his nurse."

"But how did you meet him after the war?" Cheney asked.

"That was after the war—when he was sick, I mean. See, I left my musket at Appomattox and went straight back to Chimborazo—thought maybe I could help. And Dr. Vallingham was still there. Almost worked himself to death. Like I said, he ended up in bed himself with some kind of fever, and I nursed him for about four days—until he was well enough to go home."

"But, Mr. Irons," Cheney's mother asked with concern, "did you say you went straight to Chimborazo after Appomattox? Don't you have any family to go home to?"

"No, ma'am, no family or home. When I was a baby, they found me on the steps of an orphanage in Charleston. I was wrapped in a plain gray blanket in a wooden crate stamped Shiloh Ironworks, which explains where I got my name."

"Long way from Shiloh, Tennessee, to Charleston, South Carolina," Richard mused.

"Yes, sir, it sure is. But—were you at Shiloh, sir?"

"Yes, I was," Cheney's father answered with a deep sigh. "I was on General Grant's staff." All eyes—except Richard Duvall's—went to the cane leaning against the table. Cheney's father looked into the distance for a moment; then he casually took a bite of bacon. "Got winged while we were sitting around at Petersburg," he told Shiloh, munching unconcernedly.

Colonel Richard Duvall had volunteered for Grant's regiment in 1861, even though he was not a man of war. Originally serving as a nominal member of Grant's staff, Colonel Duvall had quickly proved himself a shrewd military tactician, much like the general himself. Either a stray bullet or a sharpshooter's bullet—it was never clear which—had blazed into a staff meeting at the siege of Petersburg and grazed Colonel Duvall's left thigh, chipping the bone. It was not a serious wound, but at fifty-three he had found it difficult to regain total use of the leg. He still depended much on the cane.

Shiloh glanced at the two women, whose faces were almost identical masks of grief as they stared at the cane. "Funny," he drawled, "only injury I got fightin' was catchin' a musket ball in my left leg, too. Hurt like everything, but it sure coulda been worse." Cheney and Irene came out of their dark reveries and looked at him with renewed interest. "Anyway, sir, what I was getting at is that you've seen Shiloh, Tennessee. I was there, too—Twenty-Second Alabama Regiment. And there sure aren't any ironworks there, or anything else, 'cept trees." He shrugged. "So I figured that wherever I got my name from, it wasn't Shiloh, Tennessee."

Cheney got up abruptly and went to the sideboard. She filled her plate again and returned to her seat. Dally, standing silently by, rolled her eyes to heaven, but Cheney ignored her. "What did you do before the war?" she asked Shiloh. "I mean—you were raised in an orphanage? Did you have a trade, or something?"

"Umm, kind of . . ." He hesitated, his eyes sliding to Irene, whose own green eyes took on a mischievous spark.

"Oh, deah," she whispered in gently exaggerated Southern Belle, "am I going to swoon? Were you a train robber or a saloonkeeper?"

"No, ma'am, not quite that bad," he grinned. "Just a fighter."

Cheney's green eyes widened and she started to speak, but before she could say anything her father snapped his fingers and pointed to the young man. "That's it! I thought I'd seen you somewhere—and the name! Of course! I saw you fight in New Jersey several years ago—Shiloh Irons and Duke Watts!" He glanced at Irene Duvall, whose eyebrows had shot up, and he grinned like a child with his hand caught in the cookie jar. "Sorry, my dear. I'm afraid I found myself at the fights with some of our New Jersey buyers." He looked back at Shiloh speculatively. "But you're so young—you couldn't have been more than—"

"Seventeen, sir," he answered; "started fightin' when I was sixteen." He took a sip of hot tea, and Cheney noticed that the delicate pink teacup looked strange in his hands. They were strong and rawboned, and some of the knuckles were outsized.

"How in the world did you go from being a prizefighter to a nurse?" Cheney asked with a tinge of disdain in her voice.

"After I caught that musket ball in my leg, I couldn't keep up with the regiment," Shiloh answered. "That's when they sent me to the hospital." He and Richard Duvall exchanged glances of mutual recognition and understanding as he continued. "But I couldn't just sit around watching, so I started helpin' the doctors when they brought the wounded in." His eyes grew remote and sad for a moment; then he faced Cheney squarely. "After I learned a little, I kept on nursing even after I was able to march again. I'm a good nurse, Miss—Dr. Duvall."

Silence fell in the room as they ate. All three Duvalls were thinking that this man was, indeed, a good nurse; in one way or another he had ministered to each of them in the last twenty-four hours. He had earned immediate respect and trust from Richard Duvall, whose judgment of men was shrewd and generally accurate; and Richard's mind had been eased somewhat when he realized that Shiloh Irons would be with Cheney on this dangerous sea voyage. Shiloh had treated Irene Duvall with gentleness and understanding, and had expertly soothed and quieted her anxiety at seeing him on her doorstep with a dripping, limp, and pale Cheney in his arms.

And he was practically an avenging angel to me, Cheney thought as she moodily poked holes in a biscuit with her fork, wondering why she felt so irritated by this turn of events. *He's just not what I expected, that's all.*

Abruptly Dally started removing plates off the table. "Well, I knows you're through 'cause Miz Doctah Cheney done et two platefuls, and now she's playin' wid her food, so please ever'body move on." She busily cleared and cleaned, and the four diners stood with chastened faces. "My Tansy's gonna have that gran'baby o' mine any minute, Miz Irene, so we'll be gittin' along now."

"Yes, Dally, let's go," Irene said. Just as conscientiously as her own mother had tended to the two-hundred-plus slaves on the plantation where she had grown up, Irene attended the births and deaths in Dally's family. "I'll just go get my things."

Richard and Shiloh drifted in the direction of Richard's study, talking quietly.

"I'm coming, too, Dally," Cheney broke in hurriedly. "I *am* a real doctor now, you know, and I want to make sure Tansy's all right."

Dally picked up a stack of dirty dishes and sniffed, then turned toward the kitchen. "No thank you, Miz *Real* Doctah Cheney! Mistah Dev's there right now." Faintly her voice floated down the hall after her. "An' I ain't never seen Mistah Dev eat hisself into an early grave like some other doctahs I know. . . ." Dally alternated between berating Cheney for being too skinny and for eating too much; the fact that the two were mutually exclusive bothered her not one whit.

Cheney was dumbfounded. Devlin Buchanan, M.D., was much sought after by upper-class New York families—particularly the ladies of the families. Regardless of that, two years ago Dr. Buchanan had eliminated obstetrics altogether, referring that part of his practice to a just-graduated physician he knew and respected. And now he was attending Dally's daughter? After considering it for a few moments, Cheney realized that Dev, as he was affectionately called by the family, probably did this because of his heavy sense of obligation to Richard and Irene Duvall.

Irene turned to Cheney, saying softly, "Yes, darling. Dev has taken care of Dally's family ever since he returned from England. He and Rissy are staying with Tansy this morning until Dally and I get there, and then he's coming over here to check on you." Rissy was another of Dally's daughters, the same age as Cheney. When Dev had returned from England, he had promptly engaged Rissy as his housekeeper.

Cheney's eyes widened at the news; she hadn't seen Dev (except for last night, which didn't count) for a week. Without another word she turned and hurried from the room. Irene heard her clattering up the stairs and smiled to herself. Gathering up a light cloak and a mound of gifts for Dally's family, she went to find Dally and Mr. Jack.

Cheney flew into her bedroom, slammed the door, ran to the dressing table, and looked at her reflection in dismay. Her hair had escaped the snood and now waves and curls framed her face in glorious disarray. She snatched up a silver brush, then threw it down distractedly. A glittering diamond and sapphire pin caught her eye and she grabbed it. Pinning it at the neck of her demure blouse, she noticed that her hands were shaking.

With disgust she sat down on the elegant little chair in front of the dressing table. Deliberately she took three deep breaths and severely told her reflection, "It's just Dev. You've known him all your life. Calm down."

It really wasn't that simple, however. Richard and Irene Duvall had taken Devlin Buchanan as their ward when he was only six years old and had completely supported him and his young widowed mother. Cheney, who was only an infant when he came, didn't know the whole story even now. But she and Dev had studied together with the same tutor until Dev was eighteen and she was twelve. Dev's mother had died that year. Again, Cheney didn't exactly know what happened, but the Duvalls had sent Dev to England, where he had graduated from the prestigious Hospital of University College in London. Then he had spent two years at St. George's Hospital, where he had specialized in surgery.

When he was twenty-four—six years ago—Dev had returned to New York just as Cheney was leaving to attend the Women's Medical College in Philadelphia. *It was different when he came back,* she reflected. *It was so easy before—he took care of me, just like a brother—*

It had been Dev who cured Cheney of her stutter. She had begun to talk at an early age—fourteen months—but every word she said was painfully stammered. When she was eleven Dev had started working with her, encouraging her to speak very slowly, to think about the words and to picture herself saying them whole, to mouth them a certain way. *He was so handsome, even then—seventeen—and so patient, taking so many hours with a stuttering, skinny little girl!*

It had also been Dev who first led Cheney to think that she could become a doctor. He had written her from England, telling her what he had heard of women physicians and urging her to consider becoming a doctor. In a way, it was he who had planted the seed of what she had become.

When Dev had returned from England, he had established a very successful practice in Manhattan and had remained close to Richard and Irene Duvall. At the same time, he had maintained a relationship with Cheney. He had visited her in Philadelphia, sometimes encouraging her, sometimes cajoling her, sometimes pushing her to the brink of anger with his criticism, which Cheney now recognized as a very effective motivator for her. On her visits home to New York, they had seen each other socially, attending parties and soirees, sometimes with her parents, sometimes by themselves.

Generally, Dev treated her with the same grave, formal courtesy and respect he afforded all women. But occasionally they would lapse into the close, unselfconscious affinity they had enjoyed as children. And occasionally, especially recently, there was something else. Something different—exciting but confusing. Dev was a complex, intense, private man, and Cheney's feelings for him were now ambivalent and hard for her to define.

The brass bell at the front door sounded; Cheney jumped from the chair and rushed onto the landing. Then, steadying herself, she walked down the stairs with great decorum and answered the front door.

Dev Buchanan stood there, looking elegant in a long black frock coat, spotless white shirt, and simply tied black cravat. His dark eyes swept over Cheney appraisingly; then he smiled just a little. "Well, Cheney," he said in his deep, commanding voice, "may I come in? Or am I to examine you on the front porch?"

"No!" Cheney exclaimed in confusion. "I—I mean," she stammered and opened the door wide, "of course you can come in. And, no, you're not going to examine me. I'm fine. Is Tansy all right? Is the baby here yet?"

Dev stepped in, removed his hat, and walked over to a wide mahogany table that stood at the far end of the foyer, centered beneath the curving marble double staircase. Setting his hat on the table, he turned and held out his hands, smiling. Cheney quickly moved across the room and placed her hands in his, returning the smile. "You do look much better, Cheney," he said appreciatively, his glance sweeping over her again. "Let's go into the drawing room to talk."

The large, airy drawing room opened directly off to the right of the foyer. It was elegant and cozy at the same time, with two large burgundy velvet couches facing each other in front of a massive fireplace. Two big wing chairs stood in an intimate reading corner, directly across from a gleaming buffet. Sunlight streamed through the windows and lit up an arrangement of deep red roses on the low table between the couches.

Cheney and Dev sat together on one couch. Dev turned toward her slightly and took her hand. "Tansy hasn't had her baby yet," he told her, "and it looks as if it might still be a while. Now, what about you? You certainly look better than you did last night!" His eyes went to the glittering pin at her neck; he had given it to Cheney for Christmas. "And the pin looks beautiful. This is the first time I've seen you wear it."

"Oh, I've worn it," Cheney teased. "You just haven't been around to see it."

"Nonsense, I've only been gone for a week," Dev unsmilingly corrected her, releasing her hand. He had gone to Massachusetts to lecture at Harvard University. Because of his specialization in surgery—which was not yet available as a specialty in America—Devlin was often asked to address medical students at colleges throughout the northeast. "And when I come back, I find out that you're planning to steam off to Washington Territory with some sort of—wife broker and a giant male nurse—" Cheney opened her mouth, but Dev held up one hand to silence her. "Once you get over being viciously attacked down on the docks, that is!" He took her hand again and shook his head with obvious disapproval.

"Dev, if you'll just let me explain," Cheney said tremulously. Dev had the knack of making her feel like a wayward, erring child. "This—position, it's not—like that. Mr. Mercer and his ladies are perfectly respectable, and the nurse is, too, even though he's somewhat—unorthodox. And you know what a terrible time I was having finding a suitable position. I was beginning to feel as if I shouldn't have become a doctor after all, that it was just a waste of my time."

Devlin Buchanan's face had grown tense during this speech. He let go of Cheney's hand and stood abruptly. He paced up and down in silence, his head down, his hands crossed behind him, obviously thinking hard.

Cheney watched him with a mixture of admiration and confusion, seeing again how handsome he was. Dev wasn't much taller than Cheney, but he was slim and always immaculately groomed. His jet-black hair shone, never a hair out of place. He had dark, almost black eyes, a straight nose, and a strong jaw with a set mouth that could be severe. Incongruously, deep dimples showed when he smiled, but that was rare. Devlin Buchanan was one of the most sought-after men in New York; even the most sophisticated women fluttered around him like pastel-colored moths around a flame.

He stopped pacing and turned to Cheney, his hands still behind his back. The enigmatic expression on his face made Cheney nervous, and being nervous always made her feel awkward and coltish.

"Cheney," he began with some difficulty, "I have something to tell you—and something to ask you."

"Y-yes, Dev?" she asked with a touch of anxiety.

"I want to tell you that I am very proud of you. I know how difficult it is to become a doctor, especially for a woman, and I like to think that I've encouraged and helped you." He came to stand close in front of Cheney, and she craned her neck, looking up at him. "I've done that because I have the utmost confidence that you'll be an excellent physician, Cheney." His look, so grave and serious, made her feel a little flustered.

"Well, thank you, Dev. That means so much to me, coming from you." Praise wasn't earned easily from Dev Buchanan, and Cheney warmed at his words. But she was still uneasy at his tense attitude and strained tone.

"Now I have something to ask you." He frowned and began fidgeting with something he was holding. The room grew very quiet, a loaded silence, and Cheney searched his face.

Suddenly he went down on one knee and held out a tiny blue box. Taking out a flashing sapphire and diamond ring that matched the pin at her neck, he looked at her with intense dark eyes and murmured, "Cheney, will you marry me?"

3

A Stitch in Time

"Whoa, there, Romulus! Whoa, Remus!" Mr. Jack called loudly. The glossy black Arabian stallions pranced and tossed their long manes disdainfully, but they stopped with the carriage door centered perfectly at the end of the long brick walk from the Duvall's front door.

Richard Duvall and Shiloh Irons moved toward the carriage, Richard talking with great animation, making gestures and pointing to the horses. Shiloh listened, nodding, looking critically at the team as he and Richard drew near. Mr. Jack nimbly jumped down, snatched off his hat, and bowed as Richard Duvall reached him.

"Good morning, Jack," Richard said warmly. "This is—oh, but I forgot. Of course you met Mr. Irons last night."

Mr. Jack bowed to Shiloh, saying, "Yessir, Mr. Richard, I did have the pleasure of makin' Mr. Arn's acquaintance last night."

Shiloh laughed. "That's a nice way to put it, Mr. Jack! Helpin' me return a stolen carriage in the middle of a howling storm! I'd say we got acquainted, real quick."

With great dignity Mr. Jack replied, "I don't recall nothin' about no stolen carriage, Mr. Arns, an' I'll tell you right here right now how much I 'preciate you escortin' me an' these here fancy-pants horses back from the depths o' hell. Of which," he took a deep breath and continued, "I had to go to on a errant for Mr. Richard. An' also for rescuin' Miss Cheney from the jaws o' death." Mr. Jack nodded with satisfaction; he'd been practicing this speech all morning.

What had actually happened was that Shiloh had stolen a buggy that was hitched outside a noisy tavern near the S.S. *Continental.* Knowing he had to get Cheney home and warm and comfortable fast, he had simply driven off in the first unattended carriage he saw to find the address Dr. Vallingham had given him. Then, after he had gotten Cheney home and settled in, he had taken Richard Duvall aside and candidly told him what he had done. Without hesitation Richard Duvall had called Mr. Jack and instructed him to follow Shiloh to the docks, drop the carriage, and bring him back. Mr. Jack had never blinked; he and Shiloh had left immediately and returned in record time. Shiloh doubted the owner ever knew the carriage was missing.

"You're welcome," Shiloh said with a smile. "And it's Shiloh."

"Mr. Shiloh, yessir."

"Now, Mr. Jack," Richard Duvall said, "we have something very important to ask you." He spoke with urgency and Mr. Jack turned his attention on him with great earnestness. "Please explain to Mr. Irons—and me—how in the world you ever trained my saddle Arabians to a yoke?"

❧

The sounds of the three men laughing and talking outside filtered into the house with the sunshine, but it failed to lighten the heavy silence and tension in the drawing room. Cheney searched Dev's dark, brooding eyes and forgot to breathe. The words seemed to echo in the stillness: *marry me . . . marry me . . . marry me.* Then Cheney's thoughts began whirling and tossing.

Finally she drew a sharp breath and said so softly that her words were almost inaudible, "Thank you, Dev, for asking me.

It's the greatest compliment a man can pay a woman." She hesitated, trying to find a way to make her answer more palatable, then saw there was none.

"But I have to say no, Dev." She reached over, folded his hand with the ring inside it, and held it with both of hers. "I just can't get married yet. I'm a doctor now, and I want to *be* a doctor, not just be *named* a doctor."

His expression hadn't changed, he didn't move a muscle. In the same low tone he said, "Cheney, I love you. Marry me. Please."

The intensity of his gaze and the impact of his words felt like a physical blow to Cheney. Her hands tightened on his clenched fist; then she bent and laid her cheek against it for a moment. Looking back up into his face she said tremulously, "N-not now, Dev, not y-yet. I c-can't."

"Yes, you can." Dev stood up in front of her again, crossing his arms, his eyes not leaving her face. "Cheney," he said gravely, "I've loved you for a long time, since we were children, I think. And I really believe you will be a wonderful doctor; that is why I encouraged you as I did."

Cheney started to say something, but he held up his hand and shook his head. "No, just wait. Listen to me, please. This was something I had thought of way before you went to medical school; then when you went, I began to, ah, consider certain possibilities. For you, and for me." He began to pace again, darting looks at Cheney in determined punctuation. "I want you to marry me, Cheney. It's perfect. Forget about this trip, about going to Seattle. You can practice here, in Manhattan, with me."

Cheney jumped up, her face troubled, and swept by Dev, her whalebone crinoline hitting his legs. She stared out the window blindly. "This is a lot to consider, a lot to think about, Dev," she said in a low, pained voice. "All I can say right now is that I've taken this job, and I'm proud that I have it. I've been so afraid that I couldn't do it. That I *can't* do it—"

Her voice broke a little, but she straightened her shoulders and finished in a stronger voice. "This is something I have to do, Dev. I'm going to Seattle, and I'll be back in six months."

Dev stood impassive for a moment, his brow furrowed. He hadn't anticipated these negative and conflicting emotions from Cheney, and he couldn't quite comprehend the problem. He had thought he knew and understood Cheney through and through, but he didn't understand this.

Finally he said evenly, "All right, Cheney. You'll be gone for six months, but I want you to think very seriously about your life—a life with me—while you're gone." Moving to the window, Dev put his hands on her shoulders, which were taut and stiff. "I do love you, Cheney, very much. I believe that you're facing a life of hardships, obstacles—insurmountable difficulties—beginning with this job. I'd just like a better life for you, and I think I'm the man to give it to you."

Blindly staring out the window, Cheney didn't speak for a few moments. Dev's words saddened her; ever since they had been children, she had strived for his approval and longed for his encouragement.

He doesn't see, she thought, disappointed. *He doesn't understand that right now is exactly when I need him to help me be strong, to be sure of what I'm doing. . . .*

She sighed deeply and said, "I'll think about—everything, Dev. But I am going, and I'm going to be the best doctor I can."

He turned her around to face him. Searching her face, he cradled it in one hand, then bent and lightly brushed her lips with his.

All kinds of noise broke the silence. The front door banged open, and the loud voices of three men, all talking at once, rang through the foyer like great jangling bells. Suddenly a voice drawled from the door of the drawing room, "Hey, Doc—Dr. Duvall—would you—?"

Dev and Cheney didn't exactly jump apart, but they were startled and moved away from each other. Shiloh Irons stood at the door. He looked from Dev's grim face to Cheney's blushing one and went on. "Guess I'm interrupting something, huh?"

"Yes," Dev said shortly.

"No," Cheney said in confusion. "I mean—what do you want, Mr. Irons?"

"Shiloh. Umm, well, I've got a little scratch on my arm, and I thought a doc might should take a look at it." Shiloh grinned, evidently enjoying Cheney's discomfort.

"I don't have time right now, Irons," Dev said almost rudely, striding toward the foyer. "And it's *Dr.* Buchanan." Reaching the door, he looked up at Shiloh Irons for a moment with challenge in his dark eyes; then he turned back to Cheney. "I'm going now, Cheney. I'll be back tomorrow, to go to the ship with you."

"Pardon me, Dr. Buchanan," Shiloh said with exaggerated courtesy, swerving to avoid Dev as he barreled through the door, "I wasn't asking *you* to look at my arm. I was talking to the other doc."

Cheney felt as if bees were buzzing in her brain; she was trying to absorb everything that had happened between her and Dev in the last few minutes. "What? Oh yes, Shiloh, I can look at—what did you say? Your arm?"

Outside, in the foyer, Cheney could hear Dev saying goodbye to her father and Mr. Jack, and then she heard the front door open and close. Her father's and Mr. Jack's voices faded as they drifted down the hall to Richard's study.

"You all right, ma'am?" Shiloh asked quietly.

"Well, of course I'm all right," Cheney said with irritation. "Just—give me a minute, will you? There's something I need to—to think about. . . ." She turned to look out the window again.

"Sure. I'll just go down to your father's study. No hurry." With one last look at the tense line of Cheney's back, he left and went to join Richard and Mr. Jack.

Alone in the quiet, comforting room, Cheney thought for a few moments about Dev Buchanan. Never once, in all the hours she had spent thinking of Dev and trying to analyze her feelings for him, had she considered marrying him. It seemed so far beyond what she felt, so many steps past where they stood in their relationship.

Not impossible, she thought, *just not possible right now*. Then she took a deep breath and decided to go see about Shiloh Irons. She would think about Dev Buchanan later. Right now she had work to do.

Cheney left the drawing room, crossed the foyer, and walked down the other hall to her father's study. The door was closed, and voices and laughter emanated from it; Shiloh and Richard and Mr. Jack were still talking horseflesh. She smiled and went in.

"Now, Mr. Irons, what's this about a scratch on your arm?" Three faces turned questioningly to her. Shiloh Irons lazed in a big armchair between Richard and Mr. Jack, but they rose when she entered.

"Well, you see, I got a little—scratch last night." Shiloh spoke with more awkwardness than Cheney had heard from him yet. "That big fella in the alley—he had a knife, you know—and I tried to stitch it up last night, but I couldn't, you see—"

Cheney's face grew darker as he stumbled along. "Do you mean to tell me that you were *stabbed* last night?" She covered the room in a few long, impatient strides, asking as she approached, "Where? Did you say your arm?"

"Yes, ma'am," he said, shifting uncomfortably from one foot to the other under the scrutiny of the three. "And it's my right arm, see, and I couldn't stitch it up with my left hand 'cause I'm right-handed. Usually," he added ruefully.

Slowly Cheney pulled up the sleeve of his shirt; a ragged, awkward bandage stained with blood covered the entire forearm. Richard Duvall's eyes widened with consternation.

Mr. Jack said casually, "Yep. That there's definitely whut I'd call a scratch whut needs a stitch." He clapped his hat on his head and turned to Richard Duvall. "By your leave, Mr. Richard. I'll be

dipped if you need me here to do no sewin'." He turned and nodded to Cheney, then left, mumbling, "'Course, like I ain't done
as much nor more sewin' up folks an' horses than she has, and
what is a fine lady like a dorter o' Miss Irene's doin' stitchin' up
cuts and blood an' innards an' all? Ain't no unnerstannin' it. . . .'"

The tension broke and Shiloh smiled at Cheney; then he
gently removed her hand from his sleeve so that the sleeve fell
back down and covered the gory bandage. "It's not that bad," he
assured her, absently rubbing the V scar beside his eye. "Been
banged in the head harder and hurt worse."

Richard gazed at him gravely, and turned to Cheney. "Get
your bag, and I'll go get some hot water."

"No, sir," Shiloh said. "I'll go get the hot water, Mr. Duvall."
He winked at Cheney. "I'm the nurse, right?"

"Yes, Shiloh, we need hot water." Her answer was automatic
and unthinking. She was staring at Shiloh's arm. *My fault, all my
fault*, she thought. *I shouldn't have been so stubborn—*

Richard Duvall's voice was as soft as new-fallen snow.
"Cheney, dear," he said, breaking into her introspection, "I don't
imagine that hauling you around bodily last night was easy for
Mr. Irons. And he never said one word to any of us—or to Dev—
about being hurt. Don't you think it's time *we* took care of *him*?"

Cheney shook herself and with stricken eyes said, "Forgive
me, Shiloh. I—I—of course Father can get the water; you just sit
down and take off that bandage, if you can. I'll go get my bag."

She turned and left the room, her hurried footsteps clattering on the stairs. Shiloh seemed awkward and embarrassed, but
Richard Duvall clapped him heartily on the shoulder. "Wait'll you
see this. I should have been a nurse myself; I'm so good at boiling
water." Slowly he walked out of the room, his cane tapping across
the hardwood floor of the foyer and fading down the hall.

Shiloh sat down and obediently started unwrapping the
bandage. *Hate all this fuss—wish I could've taken care of it myself.
But it sure is tough stitchin' yourself up, especially left-handed.* He

winced a little as the bandage stuck to his arm. Raising his eyes to the door where Richard Duvall had left, Shiloh thought, *Good man. And he's so grateful for me bringing the doc home and all—it'll be good for him to do something for me.*

Resolutely he clenched his jaw and tugged at the sticky bandage. The ragged gash tore open again and started bleeding freely. He was looking around, trying to find something to staunch it, when he heard Cheney's step on the stairs. Relieved, he clamped the dirty bandage back on.

Cheney marched into the room holding a doctor's bag and a stack of small white towels. Walking quickly over to Shiloh, she shoved aside some books and glasses on the low table in front of his chair and sat down on it. Glancing at his arm she asked, "Bleeding again, is it?"

"Yeah," he said sheepishly and grinned, "and I couldn't find a decent place in this whole room to bleed." Cheney reached over and moved his hand and the bandage off the wound, then clapped a clean linen towel over it.

"Hold that," she ordered.

"Yes, ma'am," he replied obediently and pushed down on the clean towel. He was struck by the contrast between the confused girl of a few minutes ago and the matter-of-fact doctor who was now giving him orders.

As Cheney rummaged in her bag, Shiloh surveyed the room. One wall was lined with books, floor to ceiling. In front of that wall was a huge, shiny mahogany desk with an orderly stack of papers on it and a small, plain lamp. A leather wing chair was neatly drawn up to it. On the far wall, flanking the door, were two massive portraits. One depicted Irene Duvall in a long, sweeping green gown, standing by a short Corinthian column that held a vase of red roses. The other showed Cheney in a riding habit, holding the reins of a black Arabian horse beside her. Both portraits were excellent likenesses and expertly done. The wall opposite the door consisted of a set of floor-to-ceiling

French doors opening into a small, manicured garden. The sunlight through the glass warmed Cheney's hair into auburn fire as she bent over her bag.

"I'm going to swab it out with this," Cheney said briskly, "and it's going to hurt." She turned up a brown bottle into another clean towel and a yellowish liquid gurgled out. Her hands were steady, but her heart thudded. She was afraid she wouldn't do this right—and Shiloh would immediately know if she faltered.

Shiloh made a face. "Carbolic acid. Hurts. I swabbed it out last night."

"Good," Cheney said approvingly. He moved the towel away from the wound; blood welled up and immediately ran in rivulets down both sides of his arm, dripping onto the thick Persian carpet beneath their feet. "Uh-oh," Shiloh muttered, leaning forward to look at the floor as Cheney slapped the towel with the carbolic acid on his arm and raked up and down the long wound.

Richard Duvall appeared at the door, carefully balancing a large steaming pot in one hand, leaning on his cane with the other, and painstakingly making his way with his eyes on the pan. "She hurting you, Shiloh?" he asked.

"No, sir, but I'm bleeding on this nice carpet, I'm afraid," he said, dismayed. He wriggled around, trying to locate where the drops of blood had fallen.

"Be still!" Cheney snapped, turning the rag over and dragging it over his arm again.

"But, ma'am," he protested, "I'm bleeding—"

"On the carpet. Yes, we know, Shiloh, and we don't care. So be quiet and be still!" To his great relief, she threw a clean towel beneath his chair. Then she lifted the towel on his arm and peered at the wound with satisfaction. The free flow of blood had loosened the swelling somewhat, and the edges of the torn flesh appeared more elastic. Shiloh's whole forearm was yellow from the carbolic acid and the gash looked black, but the bleeding had eased.

Richard Duvall carefully set the steaming pot down beside Cheney and sank into the chair next to Shiloh. From her lap Cheney picked up a small needle, some catgut rolled into a small ball, and a pair of bandage scissors and threw them into the steaming water, then grabbed her bag and removed some narrow strips of linen and laid them aside. Next she poured a little of the carbolic acid into the water, pulled some long tongs out of her bag, and dipped the tips into the water, swirling them around.

Her father and Shiloh were watching her silently, and the attention made her very nervous. Taking three deep breaths—Dev had taught her to do this when she stuttered badly—Cheney made a deep, conscious effort to calm herself.

She fished the items out of the water with the tongs and laid them on a clean bandage by her side. Taking a small, cobalt-blue bottle out of her bag, she handed it to Shiloh as she bent closer to examine the wound. "Take two teaspoons of this."

Shiloh winked at Cheney's father, who seemed amused. "Uh, yes, ma'am, Dr. Duvall. Got a teaspoon on you?"

Cheney's eyes flashed with exasperation. "Oh, for heaven's sake, just drink some!" Scrutinizing the wound, she frowned, stood up, pulled the table she was sitting on close to him, and laid a clean towel along the large, overstuffed arm of the chair.

"Now, put your arm on that, Shiloh," she ordered. "And Father, pull your chair close and put your hand right *here*." She laid her father's hand on top of Shiloh's arm, above the wound. "Don't let him wriggle anymore."

She picked up the brown bottle of carbolic acid solution, poured a small amount in her hands, and rubbed them together; her long, slender hands turned the same dark yellow color as Shiloh's arm. He sipped from the blue bottle and smiled at her, nodding encouragingly.

Cheney picked up the needle and the catgut and deftly threaded the needle, saying, "Take another drink of the laudanum, please. This is going to take a lot of stitches."

"Yep," Shiloh agreed cheerfully, took another pull from the blue bottle, and squinted down at his arm. "You a gambling man, Mr. Duvall?"

Cheney took a deep breath and bent over Shiloh's arm. She inserted the needle in his flesh on one side of the wound, pulled the needle through, and reinserted it on the other side. Richard Duvall frowned darkly and looked up at Irons' face. The nurse was looking at Richard, mild inquiry on his face.

"What do you mean?" Richard asked.

"Betcha that's going to take at least forty stitches," Shiloh answered, a challenge in his voice.

Cheney pulled the catgut through both sides of the wound, leaving a three-inch tail on one side and the long thread with the needle on the other. Deftly she looped the thread and made a knot, pulling the lips of the cut together tightly, then picked up the bandage scissors and cut the long threads short. Picking up the needle, she began again. Her hands were steady, her face expressionless; no tension or worry showed. But a light sheen of perspiration glistened on her brow.

Richard Duvall frowned again as he scrutinized Shiloh's arm. "Nope. Thirty stitches," he said succinctly. "Five-dollar gold piece."

"Done."

Cheney was working swiftly, her head bent, and gave no sign of hearing the conversation. Without looking up, still stitching and tying quickly, she asked in a quiet, half-mocking tone, "Aren't you afraid I'll throw the b-bet for my father, Shiloh?"

Stutters when she's nervous. A small voice in Shiloh's head tucked the bit of information away. "No, Doc," he said gently. "I don't think you'd do that."

Richard Duvall shrugged. "Owe it to you anyway, Irons. Five-dollar gold piece is what I won on you when you put that fellow down in Jersey. But don't tell Irene."

Shiloh grinned and the two men talked quietly as Cheney stitched. She worked quickly and competently and soon had the wound stitched up to the deepest part, where it gaped open widely, and she knew that pulling the two sides together with the catgut would hurt as much as the needle did. For the first time she glanced up at Shiloh. He was talking casually to her father, but he turned to her slightly and winked. Undaunted, she dropped her eyes to the open wound, inserted the needle, and resumed stitching.

"Sure are doing a good job on that, Doc," Shiloh said. "That why you decided to be a doctor? 'Cause you can sew so good?"

Her head down, Cheney smiled to herself. "Hardly."

"No? Why then?" Shiloh's voice was casual, but Cheney could sense that the question—or rather, her answer to the question— was somehow important to him.

Hope I can stitch and talk at the same time, Cheney thought desperately. *I surely don't want him to know this is only the second time I've done this.* "Well, Shiloh," she said, working quickly, "it's kind of hard to explain. I wasn't one of those people—like Dev— who dreamed of being a doctor from childhood. I was just curious, and always liked my studies, and—"

"Was very intelligent," Richard said proudly.

"Anyway, I was—restless, and didn't exactly want—what most women want—"

"She means," Richard said, still with a tinge of pride in his voice, "that the idea of being married bored her silly. We didn't have the faintest notion what we were going to do with her."

"Oh, Father," Cheney said, embarrassed. Her heart pounded as she worked, trying to stitch as carefully and as fast as she could. "I thought about teaching," she continued, "but somehow that didn't seem quite right. Then Dev wrote me from England, telling me how wonderful medical school was. One line at the end of his letter caught my eye: 'Cheney, you should be a doctor.'"

The warm April sunlight streamed into the quiet room. The three sat silently for a few minutes, and Cheney kept working. To her dismay, a drop of sweat from her forehead fell on Shiloh's hand as she was right in the middle of a stitch. He reached over with his left hand, picked up a clean towel by Cheney's side, and wiped her forehead casually. A slight smile crossed her face and she went on. "And somehow, suddenly, it struck me that it was so obvious, and so simple—I even felt a little silly that I hadn't thought of it before. *I should be a doctor!* As soon as I read it, something inside me said, 'It's the truth!'"

"The Lord told you that, Cheney," Richard said, a little sadly. "It was awfully hard for me to face it at first, but now I know that's what He means for you to be."

"Can't ask for much more of a recommendation than that!" Shiloh said.

An hour later, Cheney was almost through. Shiloh and her father were still talking, Shiloh's voice never wavering or slurring from the laudanum. *Sounds as if he's at a tea party,* Cheney thought wearily as she was finishing the last few stitches. *And I feel as if I've been run over by a train!*

There was a soft sound at the door, and Richard and Shiloh turned their heads in that direction, but Cheney didn't hear it and kept working. Irene Duvall crossed the room and Richard said anxiously, "No, dear, don't—"

She stopped directly behind her daughter, staring wide-eyed at Shiloh's arm. Cheney sensed her nearness and smelled the sweet scent but didn't look up. In a strained tone Irene said, "Mr. Irons! What—how—you're hurt!"

Richard didn't try to rise, his arm gently but firmly still on Shiloh's. "It's all right, dear. Perhaps you'd better go upstairs. Cheney is taking very good care of him." Duvall's voice was quiet but firm.

Shiloh's arm now looked worse than ever, if that was possible. It was swollen, the skin stretched and stained a lurid dark yellow from the antiseptic, with a neat tight row of black catgut stitching running through it. Cheney knotted the last stitch and sighed with relief.

Irene looked horrified but she exclaimed softly, "My goodness, Cheney! What lovely stitches! From the condition of your needlepoint I never would have guessed you could do such a wonderful row of stitching!"

Comical surprise spread over the men's faces. Cheney sat up, stretched her back, and smiled at them. "Oh, my goodness, Father," she said. "Mother just came from attending her thirteenth or fourteenth childbirth! Did you really think she would swoon at a row of stitches?"

Richard was still staring at Irene as she smiled at him warmly. "Well, no childbirth yet," she said, gracefully pulling out a hatpin and taking off her hat. "Tansy's having a hard time; it's her first, you know." She handed Richard his cane. "Please come with me to the kitchen, and I'll get you some cool lemonade." Her husband rose obediently, and she took his arm as the two made their way to the door.

"Forty-three!" Shiloh called triumphantly.

Cheney's father winked over his shoulder. "Five-dollar gold piece," he nodded. At Irene's questioning look, he patted her tiny hand. "Don't ask, darling," he said with a sigh. "I know *you* wouldn't swoon, but *I* might when you got through lecturing me."

The two disappeared through the door, and Cheney and Shiloh stared at each other for a moment. Then Shiloh rose and handed her the bottle of laudanum. "Thanks, Doc—I mean, Dr. Duvall. Good job. Never had better stitchin' up." Then he began to pick up the litter of bottles, needles, and bandages.

Cheney stood up and protested, "You don't have to do that. Why don't you rest and I'll—"

"Nope," he said, busily rolling up unused catgut. "I'm fine. And it's my job. You've done yours, and now I'm going to do mine."

Cheney narrowed her eyes as she watched him cleaning up. His movements were deft and economical—even though he was using his left hand—his footing was steady, and his voice was strong and lazy at the same time, as it always seemed to be. She shrugged. "All right, if you feel like it."

She started to leave, but turned halfway to the door. "Um— would you—do you—feel like going to the ship with me?" It was difficult for Cheney to ask him for help, and she stared out the big French windows. "I'd—appreciate it if you would help me do what I was going to do yesterday before—before—"

"Sure. Matter of fact, Mr. Jack's prob'ly waiting out front right now. I asked him to take me down to the docks after he got back with Miss Irene."

"Oh. All right, I'll just go get ready." Cheney swirled around and left the room. Shiloh picked up the pan of water, gasped with pain, and quickly set it down again. Frowning at it, he set his jaw and picked the vessel up again, then left the room whistling through tightly clenched teeth "When Johnny Comes Marching Home."

⁂

An hour later Cheney rushed out of the house and down the walk. It seemed to have taken forever to wash the yellow stain from her hands. Shiloh waited by the carriage, stroking one of the beautiful black horses—with his left hand—and talking to Mr. Jack. When she reached the two she asked briskly, "Are we ready to go?"

Mr. Jack turned and snatched off his hat. "Oh, no big hurry, Miss Cheney," he began as Shiloh walked around to help her into the carriage, then climb in himself, "seein' as how we been standin' here a hour or two, worryin' that you might be a-havin' trouble with that silly bonnet." Mr. Jack folded up the steps. "Or if you couldn't find a parysol to match your dress." He slammed the door and headed for the front of the carriage. "Or whatever turrible problem was keepin' you!" He clacked his tongue twice at the horses and they started off.

Cheney giggled and Shiloh smiled. "You *are* quite a dresser, Doc," he told her. She still wore the plain cotton blouse and a navy blue skirt. The diamonds and sapphires sparkled at her throat, and she had put on a wide-brimmed straw hat with a diamond pin and thrown a navy silk mantle around her shoulders. She had even managed to find a navy blue reticule and plain white silk parasol.

"All through medical school I dressed like an old-maid schoolteacher," she said defensively, "so when I graduated, my mother gave me an entire new wardrobe as a gift. And—and—I like nice clothes! Whoever made the rule that women doctors have to be dowdy?"

"Easy, easy," Shiloh said, laughing and putting his hands up in defense. "I like the way you dress. It's pretty."

His simple, sincere compliment flustered Cheney a little, and she stared out the window, murmuring, "Well—thank you." They rode along in silence for a while, and when she turned back, she saw that Shiloh Irons was sound asleep.

⁂

By the time they returned that night, Cheney had fallen asleep in the back of the carriage, lying down on her right side on the hard seat, her head cushioned on her hat. Mr. Jack opened the door and for once was speechless. He had known Cheney all her life, and he had never seen her so still.

"What?" Cheney sat upright and blinked at Mr. Jack. "Oh, we're home," she said sleepily. "Thank you, Mr. Jack. It's been a long day."

She stumbled out of the carriage and stood still, staring up at the full, bright moon. It lit her face with a bluish, unearthly light. Mr. Jack was speechless at the sight. The moonlight on her strong face made her look like a beautiful distant ghost.

"Good night," she said and yawned, walking slowly toward the dark house, "and thank you, Mr. Jack."

Still staring and a little abashed, he whispered, "Yer welcome."

Cheney entered the house and saw one dim light at the top of the stairs, coming from her room. Holding the banister tiredly, she walked slowly up, kicking her heeled shoes off on the second and third steps so the noise wouldn't wake her parents.

Silently she reached the door of her bedroom. Two trunks stood outside the door, lined up like soldiers. Inside, the gas lamp with the pink tasseled shade burned with a soft rose light. Her mother, auburn hair glowing like a halo around her head, was kneeling in front of one trunk, carefully arranging parasols and tiny silk purses on top of a neatly folded cream-colored satin dress. Her father sat on a low embroidered footstool, cane on the floor beside him. Clumsily he folded a simple muslin dress and laid it on top of the almost-full trunk in front of him. He picked up the top tray, which was full of brooches, brushes, combs, cameos, and tiny colored bottles, and gently set it in the trunk. Tenderly he touched a few of the glittering things, then closed the dome top.

Tears stung Cheney's eyes, but she blinked them back. "I'm home," she said softly.

Her parents turned in unison, surprised at her silent entrance. "Good," her father said. "And you're all packed." He picked up his cane and stood up stiffly, with obvious pain. Walking over to Cheney, leaning very heavily on his cane, he kissed her and said in his gentle, deep voice, "I love you, daughter."

Her mother was right behind him, smiling. "Good night, Cheney. I love you, too."

Cheney stood motionless for a few moments, watching them as they crossed the hall and disappeared into their bedroom and quietly shut the door. One shining tear rolled down her cheek and she whispered, "I love you, too."

Then, wearily, she stumbled to the bed and threw herself across it. In less than five minutes she was sound asleep.

4

A Time to Keep Silence and a Time to Speak

"... and so they finally decided on Daffodil."

Devlin Buchanan's normally somber face was alight with amusement as he made this pronouncement. Tansy had finally had her baby at five o'clock that morning, May 1, after thirty-six hours of labor. Dev had then rushed to the Duvall home just in time to have breakfast with them. Now he and Cheney and her parents were on the way to the dock of the S.S. *Continental*. It was time for Cheney's voyage to begin.

"Oh, dear," Irene Duvall responded with genteel distress. "Daffodil ..."

Irene's mother—Rose Cheney—had named all her female slaves with flower names. Dally had been named Dahlia at her birth and had been called Dally two minutes afterward and from then on. For some reason Dally had chosen to carry on this tradition. All her daughters had been named after flowers, and their birth names had lasted about as long as Dally's.

Richard Duvall's fine gray eyes sparkled. "Daffodil, hmm. . . . Does this mean—?"

"Daffy!" Cheney could keep still no longer.

"No," Dev said with mock gravity. "Dilly."

Richard and Cheney laughed and Irene looked out the window, her trim shoulders shaking. Dimples showed for a second on Dev's face. "So," he continued, his dark eyes gleaming, "does this mean it's Dally's daughter Dilly?"

"No," Richard struggled for a sober face. "It's Dilly's grandma Dally."

"Stop it, you two!" Irene scolded, but she couldn't keep a straight face and a girlish giggle escaped, which widened Richard Duvall's grin.

"Yes, Miss Irene," Dev said obediently. "But I've been wondering something. I know Tansy's real name is Pansy—but what is Rissy's name?" Cheney and her father immediately burst into laughter; Irene tried once more to scold them but she again failed and began to laugh. Dev looked at each of them blankly.

Finally Cheney recovered enough to reply. "Well, Rissy's name is Iris, which is Dally's favorite flower, so Dally insisted they call her Iris and not, umm—corrupt it, you see—" Cheney was having a hard time keeping her voice under control.

"So she brought the baby to the house, naturally, and talked about her all day—" Richard continued.

"I just couldn't imagine . . ." Irene said in wonder.

"So Mr. Jack—Mr. Jack—" Cheney was almost gasping.

"Cheney, don't!" Irene tried to say sternly.

"What I wanna know is, Miss Dally," came a perfect imitation of Mr. Jack from Richard Duvall's lips, "why ye keep a-callin' that there byooteeful leetle girl Arse?"

The Duvalls dissolved in laughter again, and this time even Dev laughed out loud. Irene gave up her attempts at discipline, her cheeks coloring prettily as she laughed. Cheney warmed at the look of pure enjoyment on her father's face. It was not from the story, which of course they all knew well, except Dev. Richard Duvall was watching his wife's amusement with what Cheney could only call pure joy. *Dev and I don't look at each other like that.* The thought flitted briefly through Cheney's mind, but she tucked it away to consider seriously later. She had other things to worry about now.

"*Herald*! Get your *New York Herald*, right here! *Herald*!" a young boy's voice called out incessantly.

"You, boy!" Mr. Jack yelled. "You get yer *Noo York Hurld* outter the street!" The carriage jolted past a very young boy standing in the middle of the muddy street, a vacant expression on his face, waving copies of the newspaper at passersby. He looked cold, and Irene Duvall looked sad.

Cheney smiled at Mr. Jack's voice, but then she sighed deeply. Dev glanced sharply at her, the faintest glimmer of hope showing on his chiseled face. "I read that article yesterday, Cheney. Are you having second thoughts?"

"No," she said shortly, her thick brows drawing down in a sign of temper that Dev recognized.

Her father cleared his throat and brought his cane upright in front of him, both of his long, slender hands resting on the carved handle. "Good," he said vehemently, "because I personally believe that article was written by an ignorant, gossiping fool!"

Yesterday's *New York Herald* had featured a lengthy and emotional article condemning Asa Mercer and his Belles. Some of the column was dark implication and some was outright accusation—and all of it was extremely damaging. Asa Mercer had told Cheney and Shiloh last night as they worked in the infirmary that almost eighty of the ladies had canceled that day.

"Sir?" Dev asked, a little taken aback at the heat in Richard Duvall's words. "You are so certain of this Mr. Mercer and his—propriety?"

Cheney was a bit surprised herself; although her father and mother had been supportive of her decision, she had not expected such a staunch defense of Asa Mercer from her parents. She had, in fact, hoped fervently that they hadn't seen the article at all.

"Asa Mercer is a hardworking, honest young man who believes in what he is doing, which is trying to better the lot of the men in Washington Territory. And that is exactly what he should be doing, considering he is a member of the territorial legislature and actually has a commission from the governor of Washington to—to—well, to bring nice ladies to the territory!" Irene Duvall nodded firmly in agreement, and this in itself was enough to render Cheney speechless for a moment.

"But, sir," Dev said, "I didn't know all that! How did you find out?"

"Of course I had Mr. Mercer thoroughly investigated as soon as Cheney told us of this position she was offered," Richard answered with satisfaction, and Cheney's surprised gaze turned from her mother to him. "Asa Mercer's reputation and record are as clean as Dally's kitchen!"

"So it's spotless," Dev nodded, "just like Rissy's kitchen." A ghost smile flitted across his face at the memory of his housekeeper's real name. Irene Duvall noticed it and was glad. She had always felt that Devlin was too sober and serious; anything that lightened his life eased her burden for him.

"Well, Father," Cheney said a little huffily, "I didn't know all of this either! About Mr. Mercer, I mean. He never told me everything about himself—or about your little 'investigation,' either!"

Richard Duvall smiled at his daughter with a world of love and care in his eyes. "Cheney," he said softly, "except for your mother, you are the most precious thing in this world to me. As long as the Lord allows me to be on this earth with the two of you, I'm going to protect you as much as I possibly can. So I found out all I could about Mr. Mercer, and I was very glad for you when I got such a wonderful report on him."

Visibly softening at his words, Cheney said, "I'm sorry, Father. I didn't mean to fuss; as usual, you've done exactly the right thing."

"Speaking of that," Dev commented with deceptive casualness to Richard Duvall, "you and Miss Irene seem to have come to terms with this rather unorthodox situation with Cheney's nurse."

Now Cheney turned her ire on him. "Just being a woman doctor places me outside the realm of certain social niceties,

Dev," she said spiritedly. "You know that, and Mother and Father have come to understand it."

"Well, just because we understand it doesn't mean that we're happy about it, Cheney dear," Irene said gently. "Your father and I did discuss the propriety of your traveling with Mr. Irons." Cheney's eyes were fixed on her mother with mute pleading, and Irene smiled faintly and went on. "But since you are traveling with more than one hundred other ladies, there would seem to be no end to the chaperones available."

"Besides," Richard went on, speaking pointedly to Dev, "I have come to believe Shiloh Irons is an honorable man, and I happen to be *certain* that Cheney is honorable. Irene and I have been blessed with a daughter who has never given us a moment's trouble on that account."

"I know that, sir," Dev said quietly. "I'm just concerned about Cheney, too." He glanced meaningfully to Cheney, who blushed a little and looked out the carriage window. Richard and Irene exchanged glances. They knew, of course, that Dev had proposed to Cheney yesterday. Dev would never have presumed to ask Cheney until he had spoken to Richard first. Both of her parents had been fairly certain they knew what Cheney would say, and they had been right.

A breath of spring was strong in the air on that morning. The wind still blew chilly and briny as they neared the sea. But the sunlight on that first day of May held a promise of warm days to come; it seemed a brighter, more cheerful yellow than the bleak and shadowed sun of winter.

Soon the sounds of the horses and carriage wheels echoed hollowly on rough planking. They had reached the dock of the S.S. *Continental*. Mr. Jack slowed the carriage and came to a halt as the loud babble of hundreds of voices rose around them.

"My goodness! What a crush!" Cheney exclaimed as she stepped down. The pier was a mass of people, packed closely together all the way to the gangplank. Mr. Jack had been forced to stop almost at the entrance of the pier.

Squinting her eyes, Cheney searched the crowd for Asa Mercer. "I don't see Mr. Mercer—"

"There's Irons," Dev said evenly.

Immediately Cheney saw the tall nurse coming toward them. He loomed head and shoulders above everyone and was taking long, confident strides up the dock, and the crowd seemed to dissipate in front of him. Behind him, feminine eyes followed; and so did Asa Mercer, who was obliged to shuffle and tap people on the shoulders and excuse himself to get through.

"Hullo, everyone," Shiloh grinned and nodded slightly to the ladies. "Come to see Miss Cheney off?"

"Yes, and to say goodbye to you, too." Irene smiled, opening her parasol with a graceful motion and laying it on her shoulder. Its blue fabric shaded her face delicately and echoed the royal blue velvet of her cape.

Breathlessly Asa Mercer reached the group, exclaiming, "Dr. Duvall! And these must be your parents! And who's this? I'm so glad you're early!" He reached up and smoothed the familiar cowlick, which perkily sprang right up again.

Cheney smiled and made all the introductions. Her father shook Asa Mercer's hand. "It's a great pleasure to meet you, Mr. Mercer. I hear good things about you, and I'm very proud that you chose my daughter to be your ladies' doctor."

Mercer's boyish face lit up like an August dawn, and he pumped Richard's hand enthusiastically. "Why, thank you, sir," he beamed. "Believe me, I'm very proud to have her aboard. And thank you, too, for your confidence in me. I know you must have seen the article." His face became woebegone.

"We're all very sorry about that, Mr. Mercer," Irene Duvall said softly, holding out her hand, "and we hope you won't be too distressed or discouraged."

Asa took her hand, his gentle brown eyes mirroring his appreciation and gratitude. "Mrs. Duvall," he said, bending to kiss her hand, "I can see that Dr. Duvall comes by her charm and her beauty honestly."

Cheney's mother flushed with pleasure at this young man's obvious sincerity and smiled to herself as everyone completed their greetings. Cheney herself was a little taken aback, as she often was at compliments, especially when she was compared to her mother. Petite, delicate, Irene Duvall was, in Cheney's eyes, the very essence of beauty; Cheney saw herself as an outsized, coltish copy with the look but not the grace.

Asa Mercer made one of his now-familiar midcourse corrections. "Well, it turns out that we'll be sailing on time, at noon! They found one of the missing coal stokers dead in an alley, and they never found the other one, but Captain Weldon told me they just now got two more stokers, so we'll still have the meeting with the ladies at two o'clock, in the Grand Salon."

"Saints preserve us!" Mr. Jack's voice was uncharacteristically loud, and he shook his head grimly as he grasped the import of Asa Mercer's words. Shiloh Irons' face grew very grave; everyone else looked at Asa in varying degrees of confusion.

"Yes, you see," Asa continued eagerly, "when it came time for the seamen to report back from shore leave, two coal stokers were missing. So they sent the first mate and a couple of the sailors to drag them back. But they found one of them—a big brute—dead in an alley, and there was the body of a young girl, too. They think he killed her and then somebody killed him!"

Cheney's green eyes suddenly widened and shot to Shiloh Irons, who was watching the group grimly. *Somehow,* she thought erratically, *he seems so young, but now he looks so old. . . .*

Irene Duvall's eyes were fixed on Shiloh. Her face was as white as parchment and set in a tragic expression. Devlin Buchanan's lips drew together in a tight line as he glanced sharply at Shiloh, who met his gaze unflinchingly. Dev then nodded slightly, and Shiloh nodded back almost imperceptibly. Dev's eyes, dark and unreadable, focused out on the distant sea.

Shiloh's gaze went to Richard Duvall; he met the older man's eyes squarely. But now Shiloh's sky-blue eyes had lost some of their luster and warmth. Quietly Richard Duvall said, "I didn't know of this."

"No, sir," Shiloh said wearily, and he slowly dropped his gaze.

Asa Mercer didn't understand these exchanges, but he did see that Irene Duvall was in great distress. "Oh no!" he burst out with childlike regret. "I'm so sorry, Mrs. Duvall! And Miss Cheney! Of course, I shouldn't have—"

"It's all right, Mr. Mercer," Cheney said clearly. "All of us here have b-been faced with the specter of death before, and I assure you my mother and I are not going to have the vapors." Her words were assertive, but as she said them, Cheney glanced worriedly at her mother.

Irene Duvall's face was pale, and one tiny hand clung to her husband's arm. She was still looking at Shiloh Irons, who stood with his shoulders slumped, staring at the ground. Then she spoke, and her voice was satin-sheathed steel. "Yes, Mr. Mercer. Men die, and sometimes it seems an untimely, tragic thing. But sometimes it is simply because their time has come, and God in His wisdom takes them from this earth."

Slowly Shiloh raised his head, and his face lit with something like hope as he smiled at the understanding, forgiveness, and healing in her voice.

"That's right, son." The very timber of Richard Duvall's deep, quiet voice warmed the hearts of everyone present as he quoted: "'To every thing there is a season, and a time to every purpose under heaven: A time to be born, and a time to die. . . .'" He sighed deeply, but with no trace of reproach, and if possible his voice became even gentler. "You and I have seen a lot of men die, and we wondered if it really was their time. But sometimes there is no other choice. . . ."

The small group stood frozen in a soundless tableau. Even Asa Mercer was quiet. Obviously there was a story here that he was not privy to, but he felt it was not his place to intrude on these people—this family, as they seemed to be—as they exchanged such intense words and glances. Mercer was no fool; he could sense the invisible bands of strength that seemed to flow around and somehow bind these people, right down to the coachman.

Now loud grunts sounded from that coachman, behind everyone at the back of the carriage, as he wrestled the first of Cheney's four huge trunks out of the storage compartment. Mercer blinked. "I'd better get some of the shore gang for those," he said, and dashed off.

A long sigh seemed to run through the little group. Richard Duvall, his wife holding tightly to his arm, stepped closer to Shiloh. "Walk over here with us, Shiloh. My wife and I would like to talk with you for a moment. It seems that we're more in your debt than we knew." Again Shiloh's face lit up as they turned and walked a little distance off, talking quietly.

Dev laid his hand lightly on Cheney's shoulder; she was so deep in reverie that the movement startled her. "Cheney," he said softly, "I realize that the last few minutes have been a shock to you, and I'm sorry. But the time is getting short, so I want you to pay attention to me, please."

Her face troubled, Cheney began, "Dev, about yesterday—"

"No, Cheney," Dev interrupted, his voice gentle. "Yesterday is gone and today is for parting, though not with sorrow." A rare smile spread across his face and the dimples danced for a brief moment. "I love you, Cheney, and I'll miss you."

The simple words brought tears to her eyes. In confusion she threw her arms around him and hugged him tightly, just as she had done so often as a child. In a ragged whisper she said, "I—I'll miss you, too, Dev, and—and—I—I—"

Shiloh Irons' lazy voice broke in on their goodbyes: "Well, Doc, the gang's all here."

Cheney pushed away from Dev and wheeled around. Shiloh was standing by her trunks with two dock workers. A little apart from the carriage, Richard Duvall gazed toward heaven and began humming. Irene Duvall busily closed her parasol and hung it around her wrist.

"I think it should be Dr. Duvall, Nurse Irons," Dev said stiffly.

"Yes, sir, Dr. Buchanan!" Shiloh replied. The two workers each hefted a trunk; Mr. Jack wrestled one, and Shiloh bent down and lifted the fourth one easily. "Just four trunks," he drawled impudently. "Not bad at all, ma'am. Don't worry about us; we'll be all right." They started making their way through the crowd.

Cheney looked murderous, but immediately her face grew alarmed. "No, Shiloh, you idiot!" she called after him. "Stop it! I refuse to stitch up that arm again!" But he ignored her, unconcernedly parting the Red Sea of humanity again as he strolled along with the huge trunk.

Dev sighed in exasperation and pecked Cheney on the cheek brusquely. "Goodbye, Cheney, and good luck." Then he stalked to the carriage and planted one shiny black boot on the bottom carriage step, waiting for the Duvalls to say their farewells.

Irene kissed Cheney and held her close. "I love you so much, dear. God be with you." Her voice was steady, but one large shiny tear slipped down her cheek as she pulled back, her lips trembling as she smiled at Cheney.

"I love you, Mother," Cheney whispered, "very much."

Then her father enveloped her in his familiar, infinitely comforting embrace, and a horrible lump welled up in Cheney's throat. Afraid to speak, she clung to him wordlessly. Richard Duvall murmured softly, "Cheney, no matter what happens, never forget that your heavenly Father will protect you, just like I try to, only—He'll never fail you, and He's always there, right with you."

She leaned back and looked into his eyes, her own suspiciously moist. "I wish I—was like you, Father. It's—not the same for me, you know. You've always been so close to God, and I—I've never quite . . ."

Cheney had been raised in church—the Duvalls were faithful Presbyterians—and she knew lots of facts about God. She believed that Jesus Christ was the Son of God and had, in fact, asked Jesus to be her Savior when she was very young. But her faith was nothing like her parents'. They seemed to walk, talk, and live with God in a way that Cheney had never really understood.

Now as her father looked down at her gravely, she struggled to fight back the tears. "I know, Cheney, and your mother and I have worried because you don't seem to be able to completely surrender your life to Jesus, even though," he smiled gently, "you do seem to have a speaking acquaintance with Him. But I believe the day will come when you'll not only understand what it is to live with Him as your Lord, but also come to see it as the most precious gift we have: the wonderful life He provides for us, every single day of our lives."

Cheney again buried her face in his scratchy wool coat, and he hugged her tightly, murmuring, "I love you, Cheney, and I'll miss you terribly. But I'm not afraid, because I know that God is with you!"

Cheney breathed in the clean, spicy scent of her father's clothes, her eyes closed, and she managed to smile. Pulling back, she looked into her father's gentle eyes and whispered, "I love you, Father!"

Cheney turned, her eyes blinded with unshed tears, and almost ran into Mr. Jack. Stubbornly he blocked her way, fidgeting with his hat and looking awkward. Impulsively Cheney threw her arms around him and kissed his leathery cheek; he smelled like horse liniment and carbolic soap. "Goodbye, Mr. Jack! Take good care of Mother and Father and Romulus and Remus while I'm gone!" she said, suddenly feeling adventurous and light-hearted, eager to begin this voyage.

At that moment the ship's whistle sounded a deep, booming warning for passengers to board and an "All Ashore" to non-passengers on the ship. Mr. Jack had been completely taken aback when Cheney hugged him; but the long call of the ship's whistle gave him time to recover, and he said indignantly, "As if I ain't never took care o' Mister Richard and Miss Irene and them two fancy-pants horses, of which"—he took a breath and, as if to enumerate, placed one gnarled forefinger on one little finger—"some ladies orter be a-seein' to takin' care o' themselfs, an'"—now he extended one strong brown hand to someone behind Cheney—"here's wishin' you the best, Mr. Arns."

"Shiloh," Shiloh chided gently as he appeared at Cheney's side and shook Mr. Jack's hand.

"Yes, sir, Mr. Shiloh, an' don't let this lady be a-runnin' in public, whiles yer a-watchin' out for her, an' she do freckle without one o' them silly parysols." He clapped his hat on his head and started stalking to the carriage. "Or one o' them big bonnets, if she can keep it on whiles she's a-runnin' about. . . ."

"I'll do my best," Shiloh said as Cheney, blushing and laughing, turned and waved her final goodbye.

PART TWO

Songs
in the Night

Where is God my maker,
who giveth songs in the night?

Job 35:10

5

One Hundred Petticoats

"First, this scow gets overloaded with petticoats," Bull Lynch grumbled, "and now them there six thousand boxes."

"That's right, Bull." Beans Lowery nodded vigorously in agreement. "Six thousand."

Beans had a tendency to repeat whatever Bull Lynch said; he thought Bull was a real smart man. And Beans knew what he was talking about. He'd gotten his own name from a man who once told him, "You don't have beans between your ears, Lowery!" Willie Lowery had taken this for a compliment on his native intelligence—that he had sense enough not to let stuff like beans clutter up his head. So he had started calling himself Beans.

The reason for Bull Lynch's nickname was obvious. He was a huge man—six feet tall, with a thick torso and legs, hands like two hams, and a neck so thick it seemed to disappear into his broad shoulders. He had black hair and sharp hazel eyes. His features would have been handsome; but his expression was sneering and rather sly, and he was missing a front tooth.

Beans was short but stocky and muscular, with wiry red hair and freckles. His expression was permanently vacant, his pale blue eyes blank; it had been an intellectual strain for him to learn the mechanics of stoking the coal in the huge furnaces of the S.S. *Continental*. But Bull had eagerly helped him learn, and Beans thought with satisfaction that now he could stoke coal twice as fast and work twice as hard as Bull did when they worked together.

Now the two were idling away the time on the bridge of the ship. The *Continental* had been scheduled to get under way at noon, but it was already one o'clock and they were still at the dock. A late shipment had arrived and was just beginning to be loaded. Below Bull and Beans, the wharf groaned under the weight of several tons of pig iron and four hundred six-by-three-by-three-foot boxes that looked like coffins.

"Whaddya think's in them there boxes?" Bull Lowery asked.

"Dunno," Beans answered solemnly. "What do *you* think's in them there boxes, Bull?"

"Dunno." They watched in silence for a while, leaning on the topside rail. Voices drifted up to them from the stateroom deck directly below them.

On the stateroom deck, at the head of the gangplank, Captain Cyrus Weldon stood talking to a company agent named Siddle. Bull couldn't see the men in the sheltered deck below him, but he certainly knew his captain's voice, which now grew loud in anger. Bull could picture the gruff, impatient man of fifty-five. Thick, bushy gray hair. Ferocious muttonchop whiskers. He'd been a sailor since he was fifteen, Bull had heard, and loved and knew the sea well.

Bull leaned precariously over the rail to catch the words, and Beans watched him. Then Beans leaned far over the rail, too, though his eyes were fixed on Lynch in bewilderment. "What are we doin' now, Bull?"

"Shut up and listen!" Bull growled.

"Golly, both at the same time?" Beans asked in distress.

Bull gave him a vengeful look and Lowery kept quiet.

"You listen to me, Siddle!" Captain Weldon was bellowing. "No, don't listen—you look! Look at that waterline! This is going to overload us, and you know it!"

At these words, Bull looked at Beans in alarm, and Beans' face mirrored his, although Beans didn't understand why they were getting scared.

"Yes, I understand what you're saying, Captain Weldon," a timid voice answered, "but—but—"

"What, man? Speak up!" Captain Weldon thundered.

"Well, Captain, would you, er—like to go—er, explain this to Mr. Bingham and Mr. Lloyd?" Captain Weldon cursed, and Siddle spoke again. "I thought you might reconsider, Captain. Mr. Bingham and Mr. Lloyd would, I think, be singularly displeased if this problem were presented to them."

Mr. Bingham and Mr. Lloyd were the owners of the S.S. *Continental* and four other steamers. At ten o'clock that morning, Weldon had received a message from the company offices that an overflow shipment from the S.S. *Navarre*—another Bingham-Lloyd steamer—would be loaded onto the *Continental*. No explanation had been given, so now Captain Weldon demanded, "Why does my ship have to carry the overload? I've got passengers, man, and the *Navarre*'s a freighter!"

Theodore Siddle adjusted the glasses that sat precariously on his small nose. "Well, Captain, as I understand it, you have had over one hundred passenger cancellations in the last two days, have you not? And the *Navarre* can now steam around the Horn with only a stop in Rio de Janeiro, instead of having to drop at Havana and Aspinwall."

"Black bilge water!" Weldon shouted with the wave of a burly arm. "Whatever made you people think that you can just substitute several tons of pig iron for one hundred petticoats!" Theodore Siddle winced, but Weldon was warming up now and he continued. "And my hold is going to be chock-full with that pig iron, so those blasted boxes of widgets or whatever will have to go in the crew hold, and I'll have to stick all of the crew in steerage! Black bilge water!" he shouted again.

Bull looked at Beans with malicious anticipation and whispered, "Steerage!"

Stoutly Beans agreed, "Yeah, steerage! What about it?"

Theodore Siddle was standing quietly, waiting for Captain Weldon to work it out. *Owners are the real captains, after all,* Siddle thought with a mental shrug. *The rest of us are just passengers—and Weldon knows it.*

Captain Weldon watched the dock workers struggling with the boxes and dourly considered his position. The owners obviously did not realize that the *Continental* would be overloaded—and Weldon knew from long experience with the sea that they didn't want to know. If he insisted on facing them down, he just might lose his job. There were a lot of would-be luxury steamer captains roaming New York.

"All right," he gruffly relented, "but just this, and no more!"

"Of course," Siddle replied cordially. Weldon turned to leave, but Siddle stopped him with quiet words that gave the captain an even stronger sense of foreboding. "Captain Weldon, I am to turn this manifest over to you personally. In other words, no one else is to know what this—shipment is."

Six feet above them, Bull Lynch leaned over even farther to listen. He was very curious about those boxes. Beans Lowery leaned over, too, and asked, "What's a manifest, Bull?"

"Shut up, Beans!" Bull grunted in a low, menacing tone. "I'm tryin' to hear what's in them boxes!"

"Widgets. Captain said they was widgets," Beans explained patiently. Bull just made a chopping motion, and Beans again shut up.

At the agent's words, Captain Weldon turned sharply to search Theodore Siddle's face, and what he saw there made him turn with sudden suspicion to study the boxes the men were loading. All of them were of the same size and appearance, and none had an emblem or stamp. Two men carried some of the boxes, and four men were required to carry others. Frowning, Weldon snatched the manifest from Siddle's hands and scanned it quickly. His bushy gray eyebrows shot up and he looked back at Siddle with exasperation. "Dangerous stuff! What am I supposed to do with it when we reach Aspinwall?"

Mr. Siddle nervously shuffled some more papers. "A gentleman from Pinkerton's will meet you there and take charge of the, ah—cargo. Here is his name on the Aspinwall bill of lading." He handed the rest of the papers to Captain Weldon with evident relief. "Frankly, Captain, I am glad that these, er—uh—goods are off my hands. Good-day, sir." He tipped his brown bowler and started down the gangplank, dodging four gasping dock workers as they started struggling up the steep ramp with one of the boxes.

One of the men carrying the "coffin" glanced up and grinned; Bull Lynch and Beans Lowery were still draped over the bridge rail, obviously trying to hear what the captain was saying. Captain Weldon noted the direction of the dock worker's gaze; he shot out onto the gangplank and looked up. "You two men—who is that?" he bellowed. The two men disappeared from his view. "Who the devil? Get down here—now!" Captain Weldon thundered. The rail stayed deserted.

With muttered oaths, the captain started toward the bridge to see who had been eavesdropping on his conversation, but at that moment he heard a woman's voice call softly from the dock below. "Captain! May I speak to you for a moment, please?"

Captain Weldon looked back down the gangplank as a woman and two small children began to ascend it. *What now?* Weldon thought in exasperation. *All the passengers have been loaded for two hours, and the All Ashore's been long sounded! Those people—where's that blasted purser?*

"Littlejohn!" Weldon roared. "Stateroom deck, gangplank!"

Douglas Littlejohn appeared magically within a few seconds, hurrying around the curve of the stateroom deck. With a curt nod Weldon indicated the woman and children struggling up the gangplank, and then the two went down to meet the latecomers.

Above them, Bull Lynch's huge head rose slowly and furtively above the bridge railing. Beside him Beans Lowery popped up. He looked around in wonder. "Have we seen any of them widgets yet, Bull?"

Bull Lynch reached up with one meaty hand, and Beans Lowery suddenly disappeared.

⚜

Cheney and Shiloh had boarded the ship as the warning whistle sounded at eleven that morning. "Let's check the infirmary, Shiloh," Cheney said, "and then I'm going to freshen up for the meeting with the ladies at two." Together they had double-checked the infirmary to make sure everything was secured—especially the quinine water that Mr. Jack had fetched from the apothecary's yesterday. Then they had separated to go to their cabins.

Nervously Cheney washed her face and smoothed her hair. The next half hour she spent worrying about how to proceed with Shiloh Irons. *I've got to talk to him,* Cheney thought apprehensively, *about—about—that night. And that man that Shiloh—that Shiloh—*

Her mind shied away from the memory, the vision, and the facts. Finally she straightened her shoulders and chided herself. "I haven't even thanked him," she said aloud, and then forced herself to go on. "And he killed him. Shiloh killed that man, and I have to talk to him about it." Cheney knew her voice sounded strained and shock-ridden, but somehow saying the words out loud helped to clear her mind and steel her resolve.

Cheney's stateroom, the infirmary, and Shiloh's stateroom were all meant to be a family suite; they had internal connecting doors. Cheney went across the infirmary and knocked on the door to Shiloh's room. He immediately opened it and looked at Cheney with mild inquiry. "Yes, ma'am? What can I do for you?"

"Please, Shiloh, come in the infirmary for a moment. I need to talk to you." Shiloh came in—stooping through the door, as he had to do throughout the ship—and sat down on one of the tiny bunks. He and Mr. Jack had dismantled them so they wouldn't be in the usual bottom-top bunk arrangement. Cheney sat on the other bunk.

"I want to thank you, Shiloh," she said in a clear, strong voice, "for saving my life."

He shrugged and his gaze idly went around the small, sterile infirmary. "Sure," he answered simply. "Forget it."

"Well, that's—why I need to talk to you, Shiloh. I won't forget it, ever. And n-now—after what Mr. Mercer s-said—that y-you—that you—" Cheney just couldn't go on. *Stupid stammer,* she thought angrily.

Shiloh listened to her gravely and sat quietly for a moment after her voice faltered and stopped. "This is kinda hard for both of us, Doc. I don't much want to talk about it. Do you?"

Cheney thought hard, then sighed. "Not really, no. But I had to thank you, and I—would like to ask you just a couple of questions."

"Fair enough."

"I know that—man had a knife, so I know it was self-defense, wasn't it, Shiloh?"

"Yes," he answered firmly, then shrugged. "He didn't give me much choice. I tried to just—fight him off, but he wouldn't give up. It made me real mad, but . . ." His voice trailed off as he shifted uncomfortably on the tiny bunk, his eyes again searching the room. "I've—well, I've got a bad temper, Doc, and it gets away with me sometimes. But that's not how it happened in the alley. That big fella just—didn't give me no choice. He was trying to kill me."

"All right," Cheney said, taking a deep breath. "Now, what about that girl? Mr. Mercer said something about a girl they found in the alley, and—I was just wondering if—"

"No," Shiloh said, watching Cheney carefully. "I don't know nothing about that girl. I was just on my way to the ship, you know, mindin' my own business, and I saw them dragging you into the alley, so I just ran after the three of you as fast as I could. I never saw no girl. Did you?"

"No," Cheney said with a little shudder, "but it could've been me."

"I know," he said mildly, "and that's why I don't feel quite so bad about that fella losing the fight."

Cheney smiled very slightly. "Believe me, Shiloh, if my father thinks you did the right thing, you don't have anything to worry about. He's the most—honorable and honest man I've ever known."

"I kinda thought the same thing of him, Doc," Shiloh agreed warmly.

"But I noticed that my mother and father were just as shocked as I was, out there on the pier," she went on doggedly. "Why didn't you tell my father—and the police?" Cheney asked the question with obvious reluctance.

"I didn't want to tell your father because it would have put the same burden on him that it did on me. And after I'd known him for about five minutes I—realized that I just didn't want him to have to make that decision."

"I don't understand," Cheney said, her brow furrowed.

"Don't you, ma'am?" Shiloh asked very softly. "Think about what happened. I was bleeding, you know, and I was already on my way to the ship—and to a doctor. I thought, anyway. I didn't know you—I mean, I didn't know the lady in the alley—I mean—"

"I know what you mean," Cheney smiled. "We had widespread problems with identification that night. Go on."

"Yeah, we did. Anyway, when I found out it was you, and after I got you home and all, and met your parents—" Shiloh stopped and seemed to force himself to speak the words. "I didn't want to drag you to the police to explain what happened. And I didn't want your father to be a party to that decision; it would've been too hard for him."

Realization washed over Cheney as Shiloh completed the picture of that awful night. *Of course,* she thought humbly, *he didn't want me to go through that! The police—so humiliating, degrading to even talk about those two men—and Father would have been torn to pieces trying to do the right thing—and I, wandering around on the docks by myself like an idiot!*

"Don't wander around on the docks by yourself no more, ma'am." Shiloh surprised her by echoing her thoughts. "All right? It'd sure make both our lives a lot simpler."

Cheney opened her mouth for a tart reply but was interrupted by a knock at the door. "Dr. Duvall?" a male voice inquired.

Cheney opened the door. A blond-haired man with cold blue eyes stood in the hall. Elegantly slim and immaculately dressed in a white uniform, he was obviously some sort of ship's officer. "I'm Douglas Littlejohn, ship's purser," he said, nodding slightly to her and Shiloh. "Mr. Mercer has a problem with one of the ladies, Dr. Duvall, and requests your assistance." He had an efficient, no-nonsense air, and Cheney immediately picked up a medical bag. "No need for that, Dr. Duvall. It isn't a medical emergency. Come with me, please."

Cheney followed him around the stateroom deck, with Shiloh close behind. Littlejohn led them to the gangplank, then stepped back wordlessly. Asa Mercer stood about halfway down the ramp talking with a weary-looking woman and her two children.

"But, Mrs. Terrell," Mercer was saying with evident distress, "it's just not *possible* for me to be personally responsible for paying your passage." His youthful face twisted with anxiety. "I'm so sorry, but you do see, don't you, that if I paid your way, it would be extremely unfair to the other ladies? Some of them have had tremendous hardships, too, and they've had to pay their own way. And also—it just won't look—it wouldn't be—"

The woman literally seemed to wilt. "No, it wouldn't be proper. I see." Martha Jane Terrell at twenty-six years of age was still pretty, but the last few years had evidently been difficult, for she looked haggard and workworn. Her face should have been heart-shaped but was now too thin, so her high cheekbones were starkly outlined above the deep hollows of her cheeks and the strong line of her jaw. Her face was dwarfed by unusually dark blue eyes and paled by jet-black hair. A red-haired boy stood sturdily by her, his arms crossed. Peeping around her skirts was a tiny girl with enormous dark eyes framed by glossy black ringlets.

The children were dressed in plain gray wool clothing, and Mrs. Terrell in black. *In mourning,* Shiloh observed. *Probably the war.* He noticed that Mrs. Terrell wore only a thin black shawl to protect her from the raw sea wind, and her thin shoulders trembled slightly with cold. One pitifully small, worn valise lay on the gangplank at her feet.

"Excuse me, Mr. Mercer. Mrs. Terrell?" Cheney and Shiloh came forward, much to Asa's relief, and Cheney took Martha Jane Terrell's hand. Speaking in calm, reassuring tones, she introduced herself and Shiloh and then gently asked Mrs. Terrell what the problem was.

"My daughter got sick on the way here from Missouri. I had to take us off the train for two days in Columbus. It took all my money to pay for a hotel room, Dr. Duvall," Mrs. Terrell said, resolutely lifting her chin. "We had our rail tickets to New York left, and that's all. So we're here, and I've been—I asked . . ."

She faltered and grew quiet, her face working to cover any display of self-pity. The last year, since her husband had died, had been hard on Mrs. Terrell, Cheney would learn, but the woman had always been a strong, proud woman who rarely cried or admitted weakness. This situation was shameful and embarrassing, but she was determined to be strong, not piteous.

Watching Mrs. Terrell's obvious struggle to control her shame and embarrassment, Cheney felt a surge of sympathy. She knew what it was like to make yourself be strong when all you wanted to do was dissolve in tears.

Cheney turned to Asa Mercer. "I will be responsible for the Terrells' fare," she said decisively. "Make the arrangements with Mr. Littlejohn, please." Asa Mercer looked as if Cheney had given *him* a present, and he whirled and dashed up the gangplank to where the purser stood.

"Oh, thank you, Dr. Duvall," Martha Jane Terrell murmured, again extending to Cheney her work-roughened hand. "Of course, I'll—look at this as a loan, and I'll—pay you back as soon as I can."

"Yes, it is a loan, Mrs. Terrell," Cheney agreed briskly as she shook her hand, "and after you get settled in Seattle, we can talk about how you can pay me back."

Cheney's detached tone had the effect of placing Martha Jane Terrell on the level of a business partner instead of burdening the woman with gratitude for charity. Shiloh thought, *For a rich girl, the doc's learning fast.*

"Now," Cheney went on, looking around the docks, "where are all of your trunks? Shiloh can get them for you."

. . . but she still has a lot to learn, Shiloh finished his thought with a rueful glance at the single, shabby piece of luggage on the dock.

Martha Jane Terrell was a wise woman, and she had instantly perceived that the evidently wealthy and rather impulsive Dr. Duvall knew nothing of what it meant to be poor. *She is compassionate and generous, though,* Martha Jane thought, *and she's going to be more embarrassed by this little social situation than I am.* So Mrs. Terrell turned to Shiloh and said gracefully, "Thank you, Mr. Irons, but it won't be necessary for you to help with our luggage." She smiled warmly down at the small boy by her side. "My son Stony has been in charge of that since we left Branson, and he can take care of it."

Stony grinned up at her and picked up the battered valise.

Cheney was instantly mortified as she realized her error, and for a moment she simply couldn't think of anything to say. Mrs. Terrell turned to her and smiled unselfconsciously. "Now, Dr. Duvall, would it be possible for my children and me to come on board and rest somewhere for a while until they find a place to put us?"

Shiloh said, "Well, there's some things in the infirmary that I think these younguns need to see. Isn't that right, Doc?"

Gratefully Cheney agreed, saying, "Yes, come with us." But as she and Shiloh led the Terrells to the infirmary, Cheney was chiding herself, *Well, that has to go right at the top of the list of dumb things I've done! And she was worried about me being embarrassed! So of the two of us, who was more generous?*

Cheney sighed and Shiloh, walking behind her, knew very well what she was thinking. "Doc," he said in a low tone only she could hear, "that was real generous of you."

※

"Why, yes. Ah do have a problem," the woman drawled in a voice as soft as peach fuzz. "Ah'm allergic to the cat. And ah don't think he likes me much, either."

It was two o'clock, and all of Mercer's Belles were gathered in the ship's Grand Salon, which was aptly named. From the promenade deck one descended a shallow, fan-shaped marble staircase into the long room that served as both a meeting place and a ballroom. A luxurious red carpet flowed up to a marble dais, where Asa Mercer stood to address the ladies. Behind Mercer was a gleaming grand piano and a golden harp. Cheney and Shiloh had arrived before anyone else and had seated themselves at the back by the marble staircase.

Now Mercer asked in a bewildered voice, "Cat? What cat, Miss Jakes?"

"Hers," the woman answered shortly, pointing to a pretty young lady sitting quietly a few feet from her. Cheney was a little jarred at the softness of the woman's voice. From the complaining passenger's appearance, Cheney had expected a loud, brash, and wordy person. *She's still Jezebel, even with that southern accent as thick as honey,* Cheney thought. *Jezebel Jakes.*

Ever since arriving on the ship, Cheney had been fighting against an old habit of mentally tagging people with nicknames. She had done it for years, almost without thinking, and for a long time she had defended the practice as a way of remembering names. But in medical school she had found that this didn't help her at all; in fact, it had the opposite effect. Her mind would stubbornly recall the titles she had assigned to people and refuse to bring to recollection their proper names. And Cheney had dubbed this woman as "Jezebel" the moment she had set eyes on her back on the dock.

Miss Jakes was about thirty, short and full-figured, with bright henna-red hair. Her dress and mantle were an unremarkable navy blue, but it was the woman's face Cheney had noticed more, because it appeared rather hard. Also, she wore rouge and bright red lip paint, which was generally considered unsuitable for nice ladies.

Now the young woman that Miss Jakes had pointed to spoke up in a quiet, calm voice. "I'm sorry, Mr. Mercer," she said. "It seems that my cat Rex and Miss Jakes took a dislike to each other."

"Quite all right, Miss Stephens," Mercer said soothingly. Then turning to Miss Jakes, he went on. "We will rearrange the stateroom assignments as soon as possible. Please see me after this meeting and we'll talk to the purser to see what we can do." Miss Jakes nodded with satisfaction.

"Does anyone else have problems with the stateroom arrangements? No? All right, then. I've spoken to each of you, I think, but now I want to welcome you all and tell you exactly how this trip has come about. Last year, I came to New York and advertised for women to come to Washington Territory. We need teachers badly—"

"And wives, I hope!" A short, stocky, country-looking older woman spoke out unabashedly, and Mercer grinned at her.

"Yes, Miss Barlow, most definitely! So, last year, I took eleven ladies, and every one was teaching—and married—within a year."

A murmur of excitement ran through the room, and Miss Jakes spoke up again. "And, Mr. Mercer, do you need a wife, too?"

Mercer blushed, but retained his composure. "Let's just say, Miss Jakes, that I'm not married—but I hope to be someday."

"Really?" Miss Jakes drawled, glancing mischievously at a companion by her side. "Then you can call me Georgia." She pronounced it "Jaw-juh."

Covertly looking to Shiloh Irons beside her, Cheney tried to gauge his reactions. In this lavishly decorated room filled with more than one hundred women, he stood out like an orange in an apple crate. But he didn't seem to feel uncomfortable; he leaned back in the plump red velvet chair, long legs crossed in front of him. There was an unfocused benign expression on his face. He seemed to see all the women and yet not really notice anyone in particular.

" . . . and if any of you, at any time, change your mind," Mercer was saying, "you'll be returned to New York as soon as possible. Now, do you have any questions?"

"Oh yes, Mr. Mercer, Mr. Mercer!" a young woman squealed, waving a lace handkerchief. "Where are we going?"

Several of the ladies burst into laughter, and Mercer immediately rescued the pretty young girl. "Now, ladies, please! Of course, Miss Van Buren wants to know our exact route and the ports of call, isn't that correct?"

The Porcelain Doll (Cheney thought resignedly) indignantly looked around the room and said, "Of course that's what I meant! The route and the ports where we'll call!"

Cheney and Shiloh exchanged furtive grins. Cheney had noticed this young girl and her family on the docks, too. One harassed-looking gentleman had stood with six women—all identical porcelain dolls. The mother had clear blue eyes, perfect skin, and silver hair. She was surrounded by five daughters, all with blond ringlets, tiny waists, and high giggles. *This one must be the youngest,* Cheney thought. *At least, she is the shortest. I wonder why they would send the youngest instead of the oldest one on a trip like this?*

Asa Mercer's boyish face lit up as he addressed the pretty girl. "Well, Miss Van Buren, after we get under way from New York, we'll reach Cuba in eighteen days. We'll stay in Havana for one night, then go on to Aspinwall, in Panama. From Aspinwall we'll take a four-hour train ride to Panama City and stay there two nights. Then we'll sail from Panama City to Realejo, Nicaragua, and we'll—call at that port," he said gallantly, "for one night. From there we'll go straight to Seattle, and that'll take about thirty days."

Miss Van Buren had gotten lost after Havana, and she looked helplessly up at Asa Mercer with innocent, dewy blue eyes. "Oh, dear," she sighed, "I just don't—"

"It's all right, Miss Van Buren," Asa Mercer said hastily, and looked around the room. "I have a map, and all of you are welcome to come look at it when we get through here."

"Well, Mr. Mercer, I'm sure we all want to look at your map," a cool, mocking voice said, "but right now we don't seem to be going anywhere. I assume we are leaving New York today?" The woman who spoke with such disdain was tall and slender, and she wore a dress of the palest blue. Her hair was almost white and gleamed with a silvery sheen; she had a very pale, fine complexion.

I've got to stop this, Cheney thought despairingly. *If I keep labeling these women, I'll never remember their names. But I can't help it, she does look like—*

Shiloh Irons leaned over and whispered, "Ice Queen."

At that moment the S.S. *Continental* vibrated slightly. A great creaking noise lasted for long moments, and then the ship began to move in long, gentle undulations.

Mercer's Belles were on their way to Seattle.

6

First Night

"Mr. Drake," Cheney asked with interest, "do you travel for business or pleasure?"

They were seated at the captain's table for dinner that first night at sea, and Powell Drake was directly across from Cheney. She was curious about this man. He was handsome and virile-looking, with a powerful build, strong features, and thick silver-looking hair. But his dark eyes were shielded and his manner was distant, even cold. He seemed to isolate himself from his surroundings with great deliberation and determination.

Drake speared a fat boiled shrimp with a darting motion and looked up to meet Cheney's eyes. She felt as if she were looking at a statue's eyes, not a man's.

"Neither, Dr. Duvall," he answered in a colorless voice. "And do you consider your trip business or pleasure?"

"I'm fortunate, because it's both," she said, nodding at Asa Mercer, who beamed at her. "Of course, I intend to work, but being on the *Continental* is like taking a wonderful vacation!" The shrimp appetizer was one of Cheney's favorites; she, too, took a bite as she quickly surveyed her other table companions.

She had been seated to the left of Captain Cyrus Weldon, with Shiloh at her side, directly across from Asa Mercer. First Officer Bryce Carstairs sat opposite the captain at the other end of the table. He was thirty years old, about five-ten, with dark hair and an obviously permanent tan. His blue eyes had that far-reaching quality often seen in seamen, and they had crinkles at the corners from narrowing his eyes against a thousand suns. Cheney noticed that her praise of the ship was pleasing to the first officer, and she even thought she saw a smile lurking beneath Captain Weldon's bushy whiskers.

"Thank you, ma'am," the captain said in his gruff voice. "And don't forget the Captain's Ball, which will be on Saturday the sixteenth, in two weeks. I'll expect you to be there, Miss Duvall." Captain Weldon perversely refused to call her "Doctor," but Cheney didn't mind. Weldon's manner might be brusque and demanding, but she sensed that he meant no disrespect in his treatment of her.

Smiling brilliantly at Captain Weldon she teased, "I'll be honored to, Captain Weldon, since you've invited me personally. This must mean you intend to take the first dance, and I thank you."

Weldon's eyes rose from his plate to meet Cheney's and she was surprised to see the gleam of humor in them. "Hrmph!" he grunted. "Be glad to!" With relish he speared a huge shrimp and stuck it in his mouth, watching Cheney appreciatively as she laughed.

All of the men had varying degrees of admiration in their eyes as they looked at Cheney. Her dress was of dark velvet, the fabric so rich that it looked almost black, but in the light it glowed a deep forest-green. She had managed to pile her hair on top of her head and secure it with an emerald comb, but undisciplined strands had escaped and fallen to her shoulders and down her back in long, curly wisps. In the subdued light of the gas chandeliers, her auburn hair looked dark with occasional glints of red fire, and the skin of her shoulders and face gleamed like fine ivory coral.

"Yes, the ladies love the Captain's Ball," Mercer agreed. "You'll love it!" His eyes sparkled as he spoke. Other guests around the table picked up the conversation about the ball, that is, except Powell Drake, who seemed intent on appeasing his appetite. He ate four shrimp in a calculated manner, taking a sip of white wine between each bite. Shiloh, too, seemed to be enjoying the meal and had finished six huge shrimp in exactly six bites, while Cheney delicately dissected hers into tiny bites as required by ladies in public. Politely chewing on a morsel so small it was really only a brief taste sensation, she glanced around the dining room.

In one corner of the room, Martha Jane Terrell sat with her children. Mrs. Terrell caught Cheney's eye and smiled at her with obvious gratitude.

Georgia Jakes was seated close to the captain's table. Cheney noted Miss Jakes' décolletage, which was cut lower than the rest of the women's but was not *quite* indecent. Miss Jakes was talking incessantly to Sybil Warfield, a pale, sharp-faced woman, who seemed to be listening avidly. Seated with them was another woman with red hair and a strong, rather horsy face—Cheney couldn't remember her name—and across from her sat Arlene Tate.

Cheney had felt sorry for Arlene, who was rather plump and painfully shy. But now Cheney looked at her with real concern. She wasn't shrinking with shyness; she looked very ill. Even as Cheney debated whether to go over to her, the girl abruptly put her hand to her mouth and rushed toward the door.

Cheney watched her with sympathy; she herself was not feeling too well. Pushing her plate away with a few shrimp left, she gave her attention to the conversation at her table. Captain Weldon was speaking in his usual blunt way as he addressed Asa Mercer. "I'm here to take care of the problems, Mercer," he said. "If you have any, let me know."

"None so far, I'm glad to say."

"What about the colored woman?" Carstairs asked pointedly.

Mercer looked at him with unfeigned naiveté. "Miss DuQuesne? She hasn't caused any problems."

Cheney was surprised; she hadn't noticed any colored women in the meeting. Mercer's and Carstairs' eyes were focused on a point beyond her left shoulder, and curiosity got the better of her. Turning to glance quickly, she found herself staring at an exotic mulatto woman.

Tani DuQuesne was as tall as Cheney and very slim, with a delicate coffee-and-cream complexion. Her face was slender, with high cheekbones and a straight aquiline nose. Her three table companions talked vivaciously among themselves. Tani ate and drank with slow, graceful movements, speaking to no one.

"Littlejohn said two women refused to share a stateroom with her," Carstairs said to Mercer.

"Well, then, it seems to me that we have two other ladies making a little trouble, not Miss DuQuesne," Mercer answered earnestly.

"That's right, Carstairs," the captain grunted. "That woman's money's the same color as everyone else's. And the stateroom situation doesn't really matter; we've got plenty of empty ones this trip."

Mercer's face fell at the mention of the last-minute cancellations he had received. Captain Weldon took a long swallow of wine as his eyes rested on Mercer, then went on. "I don't blame you for it, Mercer. I don't know why you want to steam around with all these females for three months, but I've seen that your passengers aren't a bunch of hooligans and hurdy-gurdy girls like that newspaper tried to say."

Deadpan, Shiloh broke in. "The hooligans and hurdy-gurdy girls are the ones who canceled."

Light laughter rippled around the table, and then Carstairs shrugged. "Well, we made up for the lost revenues from the cancellations, anyway. Special last-minute cargo."

Captain Weldon shot the first officer a black look and abruptly changed the subject. A congenial discussion of the Belles and their backgrounds soon involved all except Powell Drake, who sat silently sipping his wine, and Cheney. She tried to join in the conversation, but she didn't really want to talk. She had been feeling worse and worse as the meal progressed. Her stomach was rolling, and a mysterious loud roaring was beginning to sound in her ears.

Suddenly a bowl of hot bouillabaisse was set in front of her by a smooth-faced young steward. Cheney stared at the spicy-smelling red stew; eleven different kinds of fish pieces floated in it, along with baby clams. A cold sweat broke out on her forehead and she swallowed several times, fighting back overwhelming nausea.

Captain Weldon, the perennial hardy sailor, grinned at Cheney's downcast, pale face. "Oysters in aspic tomorrow, Miss Duvall. My favorite."

Cheney put her hand to her mouth and took a deep, shuddering breath. Out of the corner of her eye she could see Shiloh's knowing and sympathetic face. Cheney gritted her teeth and swallowed bitter bile. "Gentlemen," she murmured weakly, "I'm afraid you're going to have to excuse me . . ." Unsteadily she stood up, and Shiloh rose with her.

"I'll take you back to your cabin, Dr. Duvall," he offered gently.

"No!" Cheney gasped. She was fighting with every ounce of her will not to be sick yet. "I'll—see you in the morning. Goodnight . . ." Her words faded as she hurried out of the dining room, noticing that several other people were leaving at the same time, their faces turned to various hues of green.

⁂

"Doc? Miss Cheney? You all right?" Shiloh tapped very lightly on Cheney's door. It was almost noon on Saturday morning, and he had seen no sign of Cheney since she had left the dining room the previous night. He knew she was seasick, and he was very sympathetic, even though he himself didn't appear to be afflicted. This malady seemed to choose its victims with illogical and malicious whimsy.

"Go away." Cheney's voice was weak and shaky.

Shiloh warned, "I'm comin' in, ma'am. I've got a steward with me. It's time for morning rounds, and he's got keys."

"Oh, all right then, come on in."

Cheney lay on the bottom bunk, still in the gorgeous velvet dress. She had thrown up as soon as she reached her stateroom, and countless times throughout the night. Too weak to change clothes and too sick to care, she had just dropped her wide hoop underskirt to the floor and fallen onto the tiny bunk. Pulling the chamberpot up close, she hadn't moved all night except to lean over the bunk when she was sick.

"This is Joed. He's been helpin' me this morning," Shiloh said cheerfully. He gestured toward a young steward who seemed to be about fifteen years old. He was a thin, nondescript boy with brown hair and brown eyes, dressed in a crisp white double-breasted jacket at least a size too large for him.

"Good morning, Joed," Cheney said, coughing a little. "I wish we had met under better circumstances."

"Very nice to meet you, Dr. Duvall," the young man answered, already scooping up the chamberpot and going out the door. His voice was very soft and gentle, and he had an air of seriousness much beyond his years.

"What have you been doing? Emptying chamberpots?" Cheney meant to be droll, but she sounded petulant.

"Yep," Shiloh answered easily. "Not much else you can do for seasick ladies. I've been up since dawn, making the rounds with Joed, and a lot of them are sick. We've only gotten around to about half so far."

Cheney straightened a little and tried to smooth down her soiled, wrinkled dress, sighing deeply. She had known, of course, that seasickness among the ladies would be inevitable, but not once had it occurred to her that *she* might be subject to it. Naturally, she noted with some annoyance, Shiloh seemed as robust as ever!

"I'm going to make rounds, too," she told him stubbornly. "There is one thing we can do that may help a little." She looked up at Shiloh, who awkwardly stepped over the crinoline lying on the floor, a series of concentric wire circles sewn onto a huge circular white cotton underskirt. Cheney ignored it, and Shiloh politely tried to.

"I brought a lot of chamomile; it's in the infirmary. If you and Joed can get some hot water down here, I'd like to make chamomile tea and take it around to the ladies who are sick. The one thing that can make this—this—*affliction*," she spat out the word, "complicated is dehydration. They have to drink as much liquid as possible."

"You're right about that." Shiloh was thoughtful and stepped toward the door. "And I don't know nothin' about the tea. But if you think it'll help, we're gonna have a big pot of it in a hurry. There's a couple of ladies I'm a mite worried about—"

"Are you worried about me, Doctor?" A low voice sounded from the door. Georgia Jakes stood there, vibrant in a green-and-yellow plaid dress and a perky little bonnet with yellow and black feathers. Cheney struggled to control her feelings of jealousy and anger. She was jealous because this Jezebel looked disgustingly healthy and rosy, and she was angry because the woman was evidently talking to Shiloh, not her.

Shiloh looked amused; he stepped forward and took Georgia Jakes' outstretched hand. "No, ma'am, I don't see no reason to worry about you," he said, shaking her hand vigorously, "and I'm Nurse Irons. This is Dr. Duvall." He gestured to Cheney, who felt like a soiled little rag doll as she slumped on the bunk.

"Oh dear!" Miss Jakes drawled in her syrupy voice. "I seem to have made a mistake, Nurse Irons. So sorry." She nodded curtly to Cheney. "Anyway, what I came for is to ask if you might just peek in on my roommate. She kept me up all night"—she yawned prettily, patting her rouged mouth with one black-gloved hand—"and it was just no fun at all!"

"Be glad to check on her, Miss Jakes. Sorry I didn't get to your cabin this morning, but—"

"Oh, that's quite all right, Nurse Irons, and please call me Georgia." Then she added in intimate tones, "You can come any ol' time!"

Cheney rolled her eyes and sighed loudly.

"Well, I really must go," Georgia went on without glancing at Cheney. "It's stateroom 68. Don't forget, Nurse Irons." She disappeared from the doorway without acknowledging Cheney.

Shiloh turned back to Cheney with an amused expression on his face, but she was not amused in the least. "Yes, be shuah and remembah that, Nuss Irons," Cheney drawled, mocking the woman's thick accent. "Stateroom 68." She got up and waved him toward the door. "Go away. I'm going to clean up and get dressed. You go find Joed and get some big pots of hot water and figure out how to get them down here and cart them around."

"All right, ma'am," he said, and stepped outside. "Stateroom 68, was it?"

Cheney slammed the door on his grinning face.

❦

Sybil Warfield emerged from stateroom 101 holding a lantern burning very low. She turned right, passed the door to Purser Douglas Littlejohn's stateroom, and disappeared down the dark, narrow stairwell at the stern of the ship. The stairwell was not marked "private," but it was clearly intended for the use of the captain, the first officer, and the purser, whose cabins were in a line across the stern of the stateroom deck.

At dinner the previous night Sybil had sat next to Georgia, who talked a lot. The woman was a foolish gossip, but one thing she had drawled on about interested Sybil. Georgia had mentioned a mysterious cargo locked away in the crew's quarters. Evidently the crew was quartered on the steerage deck, which had resulted in a lot of problems for the women in steerage, so rumors and gossip were running rampant among Mercer's Belles.

Sybil bypassed the entrance off the stairwell to Deck C, which was the steerage deck, and continued down into the bowels of the ship. Stepping out of the narrow stairwell, she faced a dark, narrow hallway. Without hesitation she started forward.

The cargo hold was cool and the air felt wet; she could hear the sea much more clearly down here. When she reached the end of the hallway she stopped and peered cautiously left, then right. Two men were standing to her right, next to the huge oak door of the crew quarters. A lantern set on the floor beside them cast a strange amber halo around their black figures.

Sybil blew out the light in her lantern and set it down. Silently she stepped around the corner and walked toward the two men. The large man was standing with his back to her, blocking her view of the smaller one. Sybil, a small, thin, quiet figure in black, stepped up close behind the two without their even knowing she was there.

"You aren't really going to be stupid enough to break that lock, are you?" she asked with evident interest.

The larger of the two whirled around with a quickness that belied his bulk. His face was a study in comic surprise. The shorter, stout man jumped straight up and yelped.

The big man recovered like lightning and stepped dangerously close to Sybil, looming over her like a black shadow. He grinned and a row of large, very white teeth gleamed ferally, punctuated by a black gap right in front. "Passengers ain't supposed to be down here, ma'am," he said in a low menacing tone. He took one small step closer, actually stepping on the hem of Sybil's dress. "But then again, I might just ask you to stay a little longer," he threatened.

"Yes, I'd like that," Sybil said, looking at him blankly. "But get off my dress, you big lout! Step back right now, or I'm going to shoot you in the gut."

The man's eyes went down to Sybil's waist, where she held a small derringer. It was trained right on his belly. He took a slow step back, holding his hands up in conciliation. "Sorry, ma'am," he sullenly muttered. "You just shouldn'a snuck up on us like that."

Sybil was still holding the derringer, but she relaxed her stance just a bit. "Who are you two? What are your names?"

"I'm Bull Lynch, an' this here is Beans Lowery," the large man answered sullenly.

"We're coal stokers," Beans announced proudly.

"Oh, really?" Sybil snorted. "I never would have guessed!" Both men were solid black, completely coated with sooty dust except for their eyeballs and teeth. Both were naked to the waist, and Beans Lowery held a black coal shovel.

"Yeah, an' we were just gettin' ready to go into our quarters here, ma'am," Bull said expansively, his eyes on the gun, "when you scairt us."

"Scairt me good!" Beans commented eagerly.

"No, you weren't going to your quarters," Sybil answered calmly. "You were getting ready to break that padlock and steal some of the cargo that's stored inside."

Bull's eyes narrowed as he stared at Sybil Warfield. "What are you doin' down here, lady? And whaddya know about what's stored in there?" He jerked his thumb toward the door of the crew quarters.

"I don't know much about what's in there," she answered. The gun was still pointed their way, and Sybil's voice was calm and cool. "But I do know this. If you break that padlock with that"—she motioned with the gun toward the coal shovel Beans held, and he held it up, grinning—"they're going to know someone broke in, Mr. Lynch; and whatever it is, they're going to conduct a search for it. So what were you going to do? Steal it and stick it in your pocket?"

"Well, o' course not!" Beans said disgustedly. "Widgets won't fit in your pockets! I'm gonna hide mine in my sea chest!"

"Shut up, Beans," Bull said absently. Then he said to Sybil in a crafty tone, "And is that what you're doin' here, lady? Come down to give us a hand, help us out?"

"That's right, Mr. Lynch." Sybil nodded graciously, as if they were at a soiree. "My name is Sybil Warfield. I'm here to help you out, because you obviously need help—and *I* need what's in that locked room. We're all going to work together. Do you understand?"

"Yeah, I understand, Miss Warfield—" Bull began.

"I don't!" Beans said.

"—but how exactly are you gonna help us out?" Bull finished, ignoring Beans, who looked hurt. Bull eyed the woman up and down. Sibyl Warfield was in her early twenties—not quite pretty, but not ugly, either. Her face was sharp, her nose long, straight, and pointed, and her eyes were a cold, pale blue. The planes of her face were stark and jutting, giving her an angular appearance, but her frame was small and delicate. Bull was sure he could more than span her waist with his hands, and he thought with a sneer that one hand would easily go around her long, thin neck. He met her cold stare again and went on. "I don't hardly think we need you to break that lock."

Sybil Warfield smiled and shook her head, saying, "Tch, tch," like a schoolmarm. "I told you, Bull," she said with insulting patience, "remember? We're not going to break the lock. First we're going to find out exactly what's in that room. Then we're going to take it and hide it until we get to Panama. And no one's going to know that we did it, and no one's going to find it. If you do what I say, you just might get away with it instead of having to toss the goods overboard to keep the searchers from finding it after they realize someone on the ship has stolen it!"

Her tone had grown ugly, and Bull suddenly understood exactly how dumb his plan had been. He and Beans had intended to break into the room to find out what was in the boxes. Then, Bull had thought vaguely, he would take a couple of days to figure out how to steal whatever it was and hide it. But it hadn't occurred to him that once the padlock was broken, the officers would know someone was after the cargo and that snake Littlejohn would probably post a manned guard on it.

Light broke on Beans Lowery's face. "Hey, yeah! If we toss it overboard instead o' hidin' it, no one'd ever find it, Bull!"

"Course not, you idiot!" Bull snapped, "but neither would we!"

"Oh yeah," Beans said, and then he frowned deeply, thinking some more.

Sybil Warfield was amused. "I thought all men were dumb," she said, "but you, Mr. Lowery, take the cake!"

Beans' face brightened. "Why, thank you, ma'am! An' you can call me Beans. 'Cause I don't have to worry 'bout no beans between *my* ears."

"Yes, Beans, I can see that." Sybil looked up at Bull Lynch and, with a deliberate movement, slipped the gun into a hidden pocket in her skirt. Bull relaxed, and Sybil walked closer to the door to inspect the padlock.

The door to the crew quarters was of solid oak, but it had never had a lock. A new six-inch hasp of thick metal had been bolted to the outside of the door. The slot fit over a staple that was an inch in diameter, and a three-inch padlock hung on the staple. "Well, it looks like we can't take off the hasp without tearing up the door," Sybil said, almost to herself. "Where did this padlock come from?" she asked Bull, inspecting it. The padlock was plain except for the number 413 stamped on it.

"Purser," Bull said curtly. "He keeps up with all the keys an' locks and all that junk."

Sybil thought for a moment. She had seen padlocks just like this all over the ship—on the lockers on the bridge and on the small rooms in odd corners of the ship that were obviously used for storage. "He must have a lot of these padlocks on hand," she said to Bull. "Do you know where they are?"

Bull shook his head negatively, but Beans spoke up. "Yes, ma'am. There's a whole box of 'em in the engine room, locked up with the coal stokers' stuff. I seen 'em last time Mr. Littlejohn let me in there to git me a new shovel. Bull broke his an' took mine," he added mournfully.

Bull grinned and rippled his muscles; he figured he was the only man alive that could actually bend up a coal shovel until it was unusable. But he'd had to grab Beans' shovel and pretend he'd been working when the chief engineer suddenly came into the engine room.

"Well, that's just wonderful, Beans," Sybil said, and Beans' black face beamed. "Now, do you two know exactly what's in here?"

"Yep—" Beans started to say, but when Bull gave him a black look he finished, "Nope?"

"Beans, will you just let me talk a minute?" Bull said impatiently. "Nope. We just know that it's a buncha boxes shaped like coffins, and the captain didn't like havin' them on board, and they must be something good 'cause I don't never remember *no* cargo bein' locked up like this." He motioned down the long cargo hold. Stacked as far as the eye could see were boxes, tools, implements, iron, and the hundreds of other normal things that made up a cargo on a steamer bound for Panama.

"All right," Sybil said thoughtfully. "Now you two listen to me. Get me another padlock, and get one that's numbered in the four hundreds."

Beans said helpfully, "Well, here's one right here, ma'am. Number"—he squinted at the padlock on the door—"413!"

"Not *that* one, Beans," Sybil said, speaking very slowly; "get me one that looks just like it, with a key in it. Maybe you can find one that has the number 423 or 433. All right?"

"Yes, ma'am!" Beans agreed, but Sybil looked doubtfully at Bull.

"We'll get the padlock all right," Bull growled, "even if I don't understand what you want it for. But I got a question. What are we gonna do when we get in there, lady? There's about six thousand boxes in there!"

"Six thousand," Beans nodded.

"Where's the manifest?" Sybil asked curtly.

"Purser's got it," Bull answered sullenly. "He's in charge of all the papers and things." He shrugged his massive shoulders. "Guess they're all in his cabin. Ain't no offices or nothin' on the ship, and ain't no place to fool with papers on the bridge. Captain don't like papers."

Sybil's eyes grew hard and calculating. Crossing her arms, she stared out thoughtfully across the cargo hold. Beans thought she looked real smart, and he crossed his arms like her and looked down the hold, too. Bull rolled his eyes but stood silently.

"All right. You two meet me back here on Friday night, at this same time, and it's"—she picked up a watch hanging from an ornate chatelaine's pin at her waist—"ten-thirty. Be here at ten-thirty next Friday night with a new padlock and key. Do you understand?"

"Yeah," Bull growled, "and you don't have to bring that gun."

"Yeah," Beans grunted in a poor imitation of Bull's snarl, "but you hafta bring that watch, else we won't know what time we're s'posed to come down here."

7

Back and Forth

"Mister," a child's voice said tremulously, "my mommy's sick."

Powell Drake had emerged from his sumptuous stateroom and started down the long hall to the stairs in the middle of the stateroom deck. He had seen the little girl standing outside of one of the staterooms, but he had walked past without even glancing at her. Now, at the sound of her voice, he stopped and turned around.

Pretty little thing, he thought with a sigh, remembering that he had seen her with her mother the first night of the voyage. *Must be about three years old.*

Actually she was almost four, but Kelvey Terrell was small for her age. She had shiny black ringlets that fell below her shoulders, and large, liquid dark eyes with thick black lashes.

"I'm sorry," he said stiffly. "I'll go get the doctor."

The stateroom door opened, and a young boy stepped halfway out. "No, sir," he said firmly. "Shiloh will come when he can, thanks. C'mon, Kelvey."

He started to pull the little girl back into the stateroom, and she began to cry a little. "I don't wanna go back in there! Mommy's sick, an' I'm scared!" she said piteously.

Impatiently Drake stalked back down the hall. "What's your name?" he asked the redheaded boy.

"Stony Terrell, sir," the little boy said. He took a step backward, still holding his sister's arm tightly. *That boy looks as if he's scared of me!* Drake thought with a start. Suddenly he envisioned himself stalking down the hall, practically growling, so he slowed his pace and tried to remember exactly how one speaks to children without frightening them half to death.

Reaching them, he squatted down so that he was eye level to Stony Terrell. The little girl was so tiny, she looked like a walking baby doll. "Let me talk to your mother for a minute, all right?" he coaxed. To his ears, the words sounded forced—it amazed Drake that he simply didn't know how to speak civilly anymore—but he must have done something right because both of the children suddenly, visibly relaxed. Stony peered at him speculatively for a moment, then relented, stepping back into the stateroom.

Powell Drake walked in and looked around the room. It was scrupulously clean. There was absolutely no litter of any kind—no clothing, no toiletries, no personal articles anywhere. *Something . . . missing . . . what is it?* Drake thought bemusedly. Shadowy images of warm rooms where children laughed began to creep to the edges of his mind, and Drake slammed a mental door, but not before he realized there was not one toy in the room. This was Monday, May 4; the *Continental* had been at sea for three nights and two days. *What have these children been doing for the last few days?* he wondered.

Martha Jane Terrell lay on the bottom bunk. Her face was as white as the cotton sheets she lay on, and blue veins showed in her eyelids. *She looks like a skeleton,* he thought. *Wonder if she's asleep . . . or unconscious?* "Mrs. Terrell?" he whispered, but the pale woman didn't stir.

"I brushed her hair," Stony said with pride. The black hair was indeed smooth and neat on her pillow, and obviously the boy had kept her very clean. Her face and hands were white and freshly washed.

Drake turned abruptly. "Come with me, children. Now." Persistent stirrings of old memories made his voice harsh.

Kelvey Terrell looked up at him and whispered, "Is my mommy dead?"

Immediately Drake knelt again and grabbed the little girl's hands. She flinched, and Stony took a step forward, his face scared and defensive at the same time.

"Oh no, Kelvey," Drake said with obvious pain in his voice. Stony stopped and the little girl looked at him with huge, dark, frightened eyes. "Of course she's not dead. I'm sorry I scared you. I—I—haven't talked to anyone but grownups for so long, I've forgotten that sometimes men can be scary to children."

"You sure can," Kelvey nodded vigorously.

A smile came over Drake's face, and he was again amazed at himself. It had been so long since he smiled that the skin on his face actually felt stretched. "Well, I promise I won't scare you anymore. Let's go up to the top of the ship, and I'll find the doctor and ask her to check on your mother. But she's going to be all right. I'm sure she's just seasick."

Actually he wasn't too sure about Mrs. Terrell's condition; she looked very ill indeed. But he knew he couldn't do anything about that, and there was no point in alarming the children. Besides, he had confidence in the young Dr. Duvall and her huge nurse. Both seemed intelligent and capable, even though Dr. Duvall had been a bit under the weather herself.

Stony looked at the still form of his mother on the bed. "I can't leave, Mister. I gotta take care of my mother."

At that moment, Shiloh Irons appeared at the door. He looked around the room with a lightning-quick glance and stepped inside, moving fast. He was standing behind Kelvey before Drake could even move, and he loomed threateningly over the older man, who was still kneeling and holding Kelvey's hands.

"Drake?" the nurse said in a cool tone, "what're you doing in here?" His eyes looked like blue ice.

Slowly Drake came to his feet, his gaze never wavering from Shiloh's cold eyes. "Relax, Irons," he said. "The little girl just asked me to help her mother." He spoke in his normal aloof manner, and Kelvey looked up at him, obviously puzzled. Stony was watching Shiloh with veneration in his blue eyes.

Shiloh looked down at Kelvey. "That right, Kelvey? Did you ask Mr. Drake for some help?"

"Yes, Shiloh," Kelvey nodded, and slipped her tiny hand into Drake's big one. He didn't look down, but his eyes were startled for a moment; then they softened. He swallowed hard and tightened his grip on the little girl's hand just a little. "He's nice," Kelvey went on decisively, "and he smells good." Drake smiled, and Stony looked at Shiloh with a wary but hopeful gaze.

Shiloh's penetrating gaze searched Drake's face for a few tense moments, and Drake wondered with some irritation why he wanted this young nurse's approval. But his face remained expressionless as he met Shiloh's eyes squarely. "You know," Shiloh finally murmured softly, "I think you're right, Kelvey. He does smell all right."

Stony relaxed visibly. He didn't understand the double meaning of Shiloh's words, but he sensed that the current between the two men had turned from hostile to benevolent, and he knew that Shiloh had decided Powell Drake was okay.

"Mr. Drake said he was gonna take us up to the top of the ship. The promenade deck," he informed Shiloh with great superiority. "Do you think Mom would care?" He glanced toward his mother with anxiety.

"No, I think it'd be good if you two got out of here and let her sleep for a while," Shiloh answered. "And here, I borrowed these from a little girl that's staying on another deck."

Shiloh held out two worn children's books to Stony. He took them without even a glance; he was looking up at Shiloh speculatively and said absently, "You mean she's in steerage." Stony's gaze went all the way down to Shiloh's boots and slowly back up to his amused blue eyes. "How in tarnation tall are you, Shiloh?" He was craning his neck to squint up at the tall nurse.

Drake, no small man himself, was looking up at Shiloh, too. "Yeah, Shiloh, how in tarnation did you get to be so tall?"

Shiloh looked back down at Stony. "How tall do you think I am?"

"Oh, 'bout ten feet," Stony said confidently.

Shiloh laughed. Powell Drake didn't, but his eyes reflected quiet humor. "What's so funny, Irons? I thought you were about ten feet tall, too. Especially when you came swooping in here a while ago."

"Sorry, Mr. Drake," Shiloh shrugged. "And I'm—uh—five-sixteen. It's just that I've been the only one that's been in to take care of these younguns, and it just shook me up for a minute to see you in here."

His voice held no reproof, but Drake felt guilty for some reason. "I see," he said stiffly. "But I'm going to help take care of them now. They're more interesting than most of the adults I've met on this ship."

He sounded exasperated, and Shiloh knew why. A lot of the women on the ship had targeted the obviously wealthy Powell Drake. Shiloh had noticed that the man spent very little time socializing and seemed impatient when he was thrown into a situation with the ladies. He usually chose to sit by himself in the dining room—when he could escape the females who invariably flitted around him.

Shiloh looked down at Kelvey and Stony with affection. "Well, I've gotta admit that Stony and Kelvey are pretty interesting people." The children lit up like two bright little lamps. "Okay, why don't you all get out of here? I'm going to check on your mother, and I'll come up to the promenade deck to see you later."

Without another word, Stony scooted out of the room; they could hear his loud whoops echoing down the narrow hall. Kelvey started out the door, too, and Drake said, "Looks as if I'd better move fast," and he was gone.

Quickly and efficiently Shiloh checked Martha Jane Terrell's pulse and listened to her heartbeat with the new flexible stethoscope Cheney had given him. To Shiloh's relief, her heart sounded stronger; it had been weak and erratic when she first got seasick. *Doc was right,* he thought as he put the stethoscope back in his bag. *All she needed was a little medicine and a lot of rest.*

Martha Jane was still sleeping soundly from the dose of laudanum Shiloh had given her last night, so he decided to just let her sleep. He left quietly and made his way to Cheney's cabin.

"Doc! Get up!" he called cheerfully, knocking loudly on Cheney's door. It was flung open immediately, and Cheney stood before him.

"Be quiet! You're going to wake up the whole deck!"

"You're better," he observed, nonchalantly leaning against the doorjamb. Shiloh's head touched the top of the jamb; the doors to the staterooms were just a little over six feet high. Luckily, the ceilings were seven feet.

"Yes, I do feel better," Cheney sighed, "but I don't know if I'm completely back to normal. I still feel a little—queasy."

"Well, you look better, Doc. You look pretty." Cheney was wearing a simple white blouse and black skirt with a crisp white apron. Today her cheeks had a little color in them, and her eyes were brighter.

Shiloh's simple, honest compliments always flustered Cheney, and she turned to grab her medical bag. "Let's go," she said briskly, "I want to check on Mrs. Terrell."

"Just came from there. She's sleeping, and her heart and pulse are more regular, so I just let her sleep. I think she's gonna be all right in a few days."

"Oh, thank heavens," Cheney sighed. "I've been really worried about her."

Cheney had, in fact, slowed her own recovery in worrying about the other women who were seasick. She felt horribly guilty that she still had not been able to see all of them. Shiloh and

Joed had worked about twenty hours a day checking on the sick women, but Cheney had been able to work only an hour or two here and there before she became so ill she'd have to return to her stateroom. But she did feel better this morning and was determined to visit every one of Mercer's Belles, even if she had to stop and throw up in every nook and cranny of the ship.

"All right," she told Shiloh. "Let me see that diagram of the stateroom deck." They looked at the illustration of the staterooms labeled with all the ladies' names, and Shiloh explained in what order he had been going up and down the halls to visit each of them.

As they talked, Joed appeared around the corner with his metal bus cart, a wheeled table with two shelves that held two steaming pots of hot water, a large teapot, and stacks of teacups. Cheney's chamomile tea had, indeed, seemed to help some of the seasick ladies, and Shiloh and Joed had begun serving it to all of them twice a day, once in the mornings and once in the afternoons. Shiloh and Cheney greeted Joed warmly and decided to start with the cabins down the hall, across the deck's central corridor.

"Miss Winston-Smythe and Miss Alexander," Shiloh announced gravely as they reached the first door. "The Ice Queen and the Queen of Hearts," he added under his breath as Cheney knocked. The door was opened by the Ice Queen.

"Come in, Doctor," Allegra Winston-Smythe said in her cool voice, a haughty expression on her aristocratic features. Her eyes were a light, icy blue, and she wore a pale green dress. Even the air around her seemed chilly. She stepped back, and Cheney entered the stateroom.

Her roommate was Enid Alexander, and Cheney had never in her life seen such a beautiful woman. Jet-black hair streamed over her shoulders down to her waist, shining like polished onyx. Perfectly shaped eyebrows winged over dark blue, almost violet-colored eyes. Her nose was small, her mouth wide and full in the middle, her complexion was pale and translucent. "I'm Enid Alexander," she said in a voice as warm as Allegra's was cold. Rising, she steadied herself on the bedpost and extended a slender hand. "I'm very pleased to meet you, Dr. Duvall. Please excuse our disarray; both of us have been ill."

"Yes, I can see that, Miss Alexander. Please sit down." Cheney looked at the woman with a critical eye; she was much too thin, and very pale, and when Cheney shook her hand she felt its iciness. "I think I'd better give you a thorough examination," Cheney said.

"Oh no, Dr. Duvall," Enid protested, "I'm fine, except for a little seasickness. This isn't the first time I've been on a ship, and I was seasick before. There's nothing to do but wait it out."

Shiloh came in holding a steaming cup of tea and set it down on a small table by Miss Alexander. "C'mon, Enid," he said coaxingly, "let the doc look at you. How are you gonna have the energy to break all the men's hearts if you get sicker?"

"Behave yourself, Shiloh," she smiled, looking up at him through long black lashes. "I'm just pining away because you broke my heart." Cheney saw that this exchange was an old joke between her nurse and Miss Alexander; and she also noticed a particularly frosty expression on Allegra Winston-Smythe's face. But Miss Winston-Smythe thanked them politely as they left.

Cheney, Shiloh, and Joed visited several more staterooms before being interrupted by Asa Mercer, who came dashing down the hall toward them. "Oh, Dr. Duvall," he exclaimed, anxiety seaming his face, "please come with me! You've got to come check on Miss Van Buren! She's really sick!"

He turned and hurried down the hallway, and Cheney followed slowly. Her knees were trembling from weakness, and the ship's up-and-down movements made her feel as if she were falling down all the time. Shiloh had stayed close beside her, as he had all morning, regulating his long stride to her uncertain steps.

"She must've eaten thirty-seven more bonbons last night," Shiloh remarked.

"Please tell me you're joking," Cheney sighed. Her stomach rebelled furiously at the thought.

"Maybe not thirty-seven, but she's got this huge box of them, and they already made her sick once," Shiloh shrugged.

"Twice," Joed murmured in disgust as he pushed the cart behind them. "Miss Stephens said it made *her* sicker just to watch Holly Van Buren cram 'em in her mouth. And Annie told her that. Sorry, Dr. Duvall."

Loud groans were emanating from the open door of the stateroom into which Asa Mercer had vanished. When they reached the doorway, Mercer was kneeling by the bottom bunk, holding Holly Van Buren's hand. She wore a frilly bedjacket with rows and rows of lace underneath her little pointed chin. Her face was pale and stricken, but her blue eyes were surprisingly clear. They were, in fact, wide open and round, just like her pink mouth. "Oooohhh," she groaned loudly. "OOOOOhhhhh, I feel *terrible*!" Mercer anxiously stroked the plump little pink hand and spoke to her soothingly.

Cheney walked over to the bed. "Please excuse me, Mr. Mercer. I want to examine her."

She sat down on the edge of the bunk, and Shiloh appeared beside her with her doctor's bag. Holly Van Buren's eyes went up to him and she moaned, "Ooohh, Nurse Irons, I feel so bad!" Unconsciously her hand went up to her hair, which was parted in the middle and cascaded down both sides of her face in perfect ringlets. Her heart sounded strong and steady. *Wonder how she managed to find the time away from her bonbons to wrap her hair last night and arrange it this morning?* Cheney thought disgustedly.

Because he was standing behind her, Cheney couldn't see Shiloh's face. But she heard the irony in his voice as he answered the girl, who was looking up at him with piteous blue eyes, "Well, that's strange, Holly, because you look just fine."

"Do you really think so, Shiloh?" she asked in her normal coquette's voice, but when he didn't answer she quickly began moaning again.

Cheney picked up the girl's hand, put a finger on her wrist, and looked at her watch. For thirty seconds she checked Holly's pulse; then, still looking at her watch and holding the girl's wrist, she checked her respiration for thirty seconds. It was customary to check patients' respiration without their knowledge so that self-consciousness wouldn't alter their breathing patterns. *If this exquisite little Porcelain Doll knew I was checking her respiration, she'd probably suddenly have very shallow breathing,* Cheney thought.

But Holly Van Buren's pulse and respiration were normal, and Cheney stood up. "You're going to be fine, Miss Van Buren," she said evenly. "But I'm afraid I'm going to have to put you on a bland diet for the next week. No meat, no potatoes, no bread, and most certainly no candy! Here, have some chamomile tea."

Now genuine groaning emanated from the bottom bunk, but Cheney turned her attention to the top bunk, where she found her green eyes strangely mirrored by the unblinking green eyes of a huge black cat. He was sitting up there watching her with the typical contemptuous curiosity that felines display for the human race. The surprised doctor and the supercilious animal stared at each other for long moments. Then the cat seemed to finish sizing up Cheney and started delicately washing one large black paw.

"This is Rex," Shiloh grinned, "and this is Miss Stephens." He was holding the hand of the woman who lay so quietly on the top bunk, and he began to take her pulse. Cheney remembered the modestly pretty lady who had apologized because her cat hadn't liked Georgia Jakes. *Rex has good taste,* Cheney thought rather cattily herself.

Annie Stephens' face was lined with suffering and her complexion was rather greenish at the moment, but she seemed composed. Her hair was a light ash-brown, and she would not have been a woman one noticed at all except for her exceptional eyes; they were a rich brown color and very expressive.

"Please, call me Annie," she murmured to Cheney. Shiloh let go of her hand and she pulled it back shyly, nervously stroking the huge cat's long, shining black fur. He started purring so loudly that everyone in the room could hear it; then he quit washing his paw to stare at Cheney again.

"Your cat is absolutely beautiful," Cheney declared. "I haven't been around cats much. May I pet him?"

"Oh, I don't mind a bit, Dr. Duvall. The trick is to find out whether Rex minds." Annie's voice was weak, but it was a lovely, calm voice. Cheney smiled and hesitantly extended her hand to Rex. He studied the hand disdainfully for a moment; then, to Cheney's surprise, he stuck his massive head under it for her to stroke. His fur felt luxurious and thick, and she exclaimed at its softness.

"He likes you, Doc," Shiloh said with amusement. "You oughtta be honored. He's a real snob, you know."

"Does he like you?" Cheney asked curiously.

"Much to my surprise, he does," Annie answered with a smile. "Shiloh wools him around like a puppy, and he doesn't seem to mind. Maybe it's good for him. No one's ever played with him before."

Cheney became a little distracted; Asa Mercer had knelt by Miss Van Buren again and was making sympathetic let-me-help-you noises as he gave her a cup of tea. Evidently she was so weak that she required him to help her sit up to take the tiny sips.

Cheney returned her attention to Annie and said, "You look very weak. Please drink some of this tea, if you can, and try to rest. We'll be back later to check on you."

Joed appeared beside her with a cup of tea, and Cheney handed it to the young woman. She struggled to sit up, and Shiloh unobtrusively adjusted her pillow so she would be more

comfortable, but again the woman looked distressed at his attentions. Suddenly Shiloh reached out with his left hand, grabbed
Rex by the stomach, flipped him over, and shook him furiously.
Instantly, Rex grabbed Shiloh's forearm with his front paws, bit
his hand, and savagely kicked with his huge back paws. Shiloh
looked at Annie and laughed; her eyes lit up as the cat attacked
Shiloh's arm with typical carnivorous enjoyment.

"Now, Dr. Duvall," Annie said with quiet humor, all traces of
embarrassment gone, "you see why no one's ever played with Rex."

"Yes, I do! And Shiloh, stop that right now, because I don't
want to put twenty or thirty stitches in your *left* arm, too!"
How does he do it? Cheney thought enviously. *Every room, every
woman—he relaxes them, and—and—just makes them feel better!*

Shiloh made a little face at Cheney but started extricating
himself from the cat's grip. Annie, her curiosity obviously piqued
by Cheney's comment, glanced at Shiloh's right arm, but as usual
he wore a long-sleeved shirt. His arm was healing nicely, but it
still looked lurid and gory, with all the black stitches. It was always carbolic-acid yellow, too, because Cheney insisted that he
pour the antiseptic on it after he made rounds.

Cheney, Shiloh, and Joed said their goodbyes to Annie, Rex,
and Holly Van Buren. Asa Mercer was still on one knee beside
Holly's bunk. "I'm going to help Miss Van Buren finish her tea,"
he said, looking up at the three. "I'll come check with you later."

"You might just glance at Miss Stephens, too, Mr. Mercer,"
Shiloh said easily. "Tough to manage on the top bunk." But Mercer was already distracted by Miss Van Buren's low moaning in
between sips of the tea, so the three left the stateroom.

"Wonder if all five—no, six, counting the mama—have their
own fainting couches?" Shiloh mused when they were back in
the hallway. "You know, one in every room, in case of swooning
emergencies. . . ."

Joed ducked his head. Cheney had seen him hide smiles from
her before, and she had fleetingly wondered why. But now there

was only one thing she was worried about—getting back to her cabin before she got sick.

"I'm—I'm—going to go back to my stateroom for a moment," Cheney said. "You two go ahead, and I'll catch up with you."

"Doc, why don't you just rest now? Me and Joed can finish making the rounds."

Cheney, already hurrying across the hall, turned her head and flatly said "No!" as she disappeared into her stateroom.

"Stubborn female, ain't she?" Shiloh remarked idly to Joed as they pushed the creaky cart to the next stateroom.

The young man grinned up at him. "Yeah, she is. Can't imagine why she won't mind you, Shiloh."

"That's 'cause she's kinda like Rex," he answered, grinning down at the boy as he knocked on the stateroom door. "She tolerates me, even likes me a little, but there's no way she's ever gonna mind me. Here she comes now."

For the next two hours Cheney, Shiloh, and Joed went from stateroom to stateroom, serving the fragrant tea to the ladies. Periodically Joed would go for more hot water, and at regular intervals Cheney would return to her stateroom to get sick. Then with teeth-gritting determination she would reemerge, find the cart in the hallway, and start again. Her face grew white and strained, with dark smudges under her eyes, and Shiloh became concerned about her. But no matter what he said nor how much he cajoled her, she wouldn't quit.

The women's faces and names became a confusing blur in Cheney's mind; only a few stood out in her memory. Tani DuQuesne, the exotic mulatto woman, drank the tea gratefully, but courteously let Cheney and Shiloh know that others were more in need of their attentions than she.

Arlene Tate, the chubby young girl who had been the first to get seasick, was still very ill. Georgia Jakes was her roommate, and Miss Jakes had left Arlene on the top bunk without bothering to put the chamberpot up with her. *I'd like to take a chamberpot and dump it on Jezebel Jakes' henna-red head!* Cheney thought savagely as she cleaned Arlene up. The girl grew so agitated when Joed and Shiloh came in that Cheney had to shoo them away and tend to Arlene herself.

The last stateroom they visited was that of Sybil Warfield and Lydia Thornton. "Saved the most fun for last, Doc," Shiloh told Cheney. "I call them Back and Forth."

Shiloh always told Cheney some little anecdote about the ladies they were about to visit, or gave them a nickname. Cheney suspected this was primarily to help her remember them; he was already on a first-name basis with all of them. *Except Miss Allegra Winston-Smythe,* Cheney reflected. *She's a really good Ice Queen if she can freeze Shiloh.*

Mentally shaking herself, she looked up at Shiloh and asked, "Back and Forth? Which is which?"

"You'll see."

The thin, angular woman who answered their knock at the door obviously wasn't ill. "Come in, Shiloh," she said. "And I know who you are, Dr. Duvall. I'm Sybil Warfield." She shook hands with Cheney, one up-and-down jerk. The twenty-two-year-old woman had a terse, businesslike manner that seemed incongruous with her small and delicate frame. Her voice was low-pitched, but not particularly pleasing because it was devoid of emotion and inflection—as was her expression.

Her cabin mate, Lydia Thornton, two years younger than Sybil, sat up in the bottom bunk as they entered the room. At first glance her resemblance to her roommate was remarkable. The women were built much the same—small, with wasp waists—and they both had brown hair and brown eyes. But Lydia Thornton's expressions and mannerisms were vivacious and animated—even though she was plainly ill—and her voice had the rich, fluid quality of a fine singer. "I'm so pleased to meet you, Dr. Duvall," she said, "and I'm so sorry to hear that you've been seasick, too. Horrible, isn't it? Do you feel better now, or are you just being a martyr?"

"Oh! Well, I am feeling better, thank you," Cheney said, a little startled because none of the other ladies had thought to inquire about *her* health. She sat down on the edge of Lydia's bunk and wondered fleetingly about Lydia's outfit; she wore a puce-green nightdress with a scarlet bedjacket. But Irene Duvall had instilled in Cheney a well-bred distaste for questioning people's choice of clothing, so she resolutely made herself stop staring and focus on Lydia's face. "How are you feeling, Miss Thornton?"

"Oh, I'm much better, thank you!" Lydia declared.

"Talk of martyrs," Sybil remarked. "You don't feel any better, and you know it."

"You're right," Lydia smiled, "but it's just so tiresome when you tell how you really feel."

"Well, stop lying," Sybil said triumphantly. "You'd certainly fuss at me if you caught me at it!"

"Yes, I would," Lydia agreed. "But would you let me talk to Dr. Duvall for a minute, please? I promise I won't tell any more lies!"

"Hmph," Sybil sniffed, "as if you ever did."

Lydia rolled her eyes and looked back to Cheney. "I wondered if you'd help me, Dr. Duvall. There are two things I need."

Joed appeared with a cup of the aromatic tea, which Lydia took gratefully. "Oh, thank you, Joed! And how are you today? Tired as usual of taking care of all us horrible women? And how is your brother?" Cheney marveled again at this woman; no one else had bothered to ask the unobtrusive steward's name—much less inquire about his well-being. Cheney herself didn't know he had a brother on board.

"You're not horrible, Miss Lydia," Joed replied solemnly, "and my brother's fine. He asked me to tell you hello, and he's going to come see you when he can."

"Oh, good, and you come with him, if you can, Joed," Lydia said with obvious pleasure. "Now, what was I—?"

"You were going to ask Dr. Duvall for a basic medical guide and for a list of the ladies' names that are sick," Sybil answered with a tinge of impatience. She got a cup of tea from Joed, too, and sat down at the tiny table by the door.

"Oh yes," Lydia said, turning her wan face back to Cheney. "Could you—do you have those two things? It's very important!"

"Well—I don't know—" Cheney said in confusion, glancing up at Shiloh.

"What do you want them for, Lydia?" Shiloh asked mischievously. "A medical guide? Haven't me and Joed been taking good enough care of you?"

"Oh, Lydia's got some fool notion that she's going to have to doctor those poor, unsuspecting Indians she's going to hunt down and preach to!" Sybil answered. "And I just know that, sick as she is, she'll stay up all night and pray for every one of these fool women by name if you give her that list!"

"That's right, Sybil," Lydia said mischievously. "I'm tired of staying up all night and praying just for you!"

"Lot of good that's doing you," Sybil shot back.

"Oh, it may not be doing *me* any good," Lydia answered with sudden softness, "but it surely will do you good, Sybil. One day, you'll see."

Cheney, who had listened to this exchange with quiet amusement, darted a glance at Sybil to see her reaction, and Cheney could have sworn that she saw a ghost of a smile on Sybil Warfield's sharp face. Turning back to Lydia, she asked, "You're going to do what, now, Miss Thornton? Preach to Indians?"

"I'm a missionary, Dr. Duvall," Lydia said with pride, "and I'm going to the Rogue Indian settlement as soon as I get to Washington. They're very primitive, you know, and all of their camps' living conditions are backward, and—I was hoping you could recommend some sort of basic medical guide that might help me."

"I don't know of one offhand, but I'll be glad to find out for you."

"Oh, thank you! Now, what about the list?"

"You're a singleminded lady, aren't you?" Cheney said. "I don't know that I can help you with that. At this point, Joed and Shiloh know a lot more about all the ladies than I do, since I've been ill myself."

"Here, Miss Lydia," Joed said quietly, coming through the door with a piece of paper. "This is the diagram of the stateroom deck, with all the ladies' names on it. I've put X's by the ladies who are sick."

"That's perfect! Thank you, Joed!" Lydia's vibrant voice contrasted dramatically with her pale and tired face. "But—you don't need this?"

"No, ma'am," Joed said quietly. "I've had it memorized for two days, so you're welcome to it."

"Wish I was that smart," Shiloh remarked as Joed went back out in the hall. "I'm still squinting at that picture to try and find my way around."

"Just knock on any door, Shiloh," Lydia teased. "Whoever the lady is, she'll be glad to see you." She and Shiloh smiled at each other as if they had known each other for a long time.

"Oh, Lydia, quit flirting with him," Sybil fussed; but Cheney was beginning to hear an almost indiscernible undertone of affection when Sybil talked to Lydia, a tone quite different from the one she used to address everyone else. "Shiloh's probably a heathen, just like me."

"My favorite kinds of people," Lydia said softly.

8

Earth and Air,
Water and Fire

Bull Lynch stood up from the rough plank table, one of two that served as dining tables in what was called the common area of Deck C, the steerage deck. Wiping the beer from his mouth, Bull told Beans, "I'm gonna ask Miss Katherine to come have a drink with us." He turned and walked to the entrance of the hall that led down to her cubicle and yelled, "Kat! Come out here! I got something for you!" Then he snickered.

Beans protested, "Aw, leave her alone, Bull. I don't think she likes you very much."

With a threat in his voice Bull yelled again, "Katherine! Don't make me come get you!"

Katherine Dailey couldn't run into a cozy, private state-room and shut the door to get away from Bull Lynch. Although steerage on the S.S. *Continental* was not nearly as dreary as on some other ships, it still was a completely different world from Deck B, the stateroom deck. Katherine had never seen it, but she pictured it: cool, clean, ladies laughing and talking with silvery sounds, nice gentlemen who took off their tall beaver hats and bowed to everyone they greeted, glittering ballrooms and a luxurious dining room, and brisk walks in the clean sea air on the wide promenade deck.

Her vivid mental pictures were actually very close to the reality, but that didn't make them any more accessible to Katherine.

She was in steerage. And steerage meant a single long room with the engine room at the stern end, the common area in the middle, and four rows of double bunks running to the bow. The only concession to privacy were curtains that formed a small cubicle around each two sets of bunks, which were never politely assigned by a purser in immaculate whites. Anyone just slept anywhere, until the inevitable pecking order defined how much space you would have, and where.

Katherine huddled in the corner of a top bunk, trying to blink back the frightened tears in her doe-brown eyes. She was only seventeen years old, and all alone in the world. After working two years as a scullery maid in Boston, she had managed to scrape up enough to buy a steerage passage to Seattle, hoping to get a better-paying job as a maid or servant in a new, clean territory. Kat was a pretty girl, with lovely ash-brown hair, rosy cheeks and red lips, and Bull Lynch had treated her as his possession since the first day of the trip.

She slipped off the bunk and Drusilla Myers, a strong country woman from Maine who bunked below her, muttered, "Don't go out there, Kat. You shouldn't have to put up with the likes o' him."

But Katherine knew that Drusilla was afraid of Bull; even as she spoke those defiant words, she lowered her head so as not to meet Katherine's eyes.

"I might as well go," Katherine whispered, "or he'll just come get me, like he did before." She shuddered a little at the memory of Bull grabbing her ankle to haul her down from her bunk. Stopping to pull the curtain aside, Katherine looked back half-hopefully at Drusilla, but the older woman only sighed without looking up.

Kat walked down the hall to the common area; Bull reached up and threw a meaty arm around her waist. Wincing, she sat down obediently on the plank seat and looked pleadingly at Beans Lowery. He grinned unselfconsciously and said, "You don't like him, do you, Miss Katherine? I done told him an' told him, but—"

Bull banged a thick mug down in front of Katherine. "Drink this, girl. Maybe it'll loosen you up! Let's have some fun!" He sat down by her and threw his heavy arm around her shoulder. She tried to pull away, but he savagely pulled her close and picked up the beer. "Here, girl, sit still! Drink this!" He shoved the ale to her mouth, and it banged her lips hard. She cried out and put her hand to her mouth; her teeth had cut the inside of her lip. A drop of blood appeared at the corner of her mouth, and tears welled up in her eyes.

"This how you have fun? Bustin' pretty ladies in the mouth?" The mocking drawl made Bull whirl around on the seat. Shiloh Irons stood at the head of the long table. His cold blue eyes were fixed on Bull Lynch as he set two books down and stepped back into a loose but alert stance.

"I don't know who you are, Pretty Boy," Bull snarled, "but this ain't none o' your business. And you better leave now before I make you sorry you busted in."

Bull had turned to face the tall blond man directly, which meant that Katherine was free of Lynch's steely grip. Her hand to her mouth, her eyes wide and tearful, she jumped up and disappeared down the hall. Lynch turned to grab her, and swiped at thin air. "Now look what you done!" He got up and started after the girl.

Shiloh Irons stepped squarely in front of him. "I want you to sit down and finish your beer and leave the lady alone," he said in a quietly dangerous tone, his nostrils flaring whitely.

The coal stoker didn't appear to notice the danger signal. "And what if I don't wanna do that, Pretty Boy?" he sneered.

"Then," Shiloh said deliberately, "I'm going to make you."

Bull was stunned. Shiloh's calm statement sounded absurd to the burly stoker. He had never been bested in a fight, and this rangy young man didn't look like any kind of a threat. Although he was taller than Bull, Bull was much broader and at least twice as muscular.

And yet the man didn't even seem nervous; in fact, he looked a little—well, a little regretful, like he was sorry for Bull, or something. This so outraged the coal stoker that it seemed as if he looked up at Shiloh through a red mist.

"You, Lynch! Vere are you? Get to de engine room, now!" The voice of Lars Johanssen sobered Bull up quickly. Bull wasn't exactly afraid of the engine room chief, but he knew that Johanssen wouldn't mind banging him on the head with a coal shovel to keep him in line. He had seen Johanssen do it to other men, and if they fought back they ended up in the brig for assaulting an officer. Bull didn't want to be locked up in the tiny brig for who knows how long.

"*Now,* I said!" Johanssen roared. He was a big, barrel-chested Swede.

Bull's dark eyes glinted as he stared at Shiloh Irons. "I'm gonna get you, Pretty Boy. You just name the time an' the place. We'll see who makes who do what." He wheeled and stalked toward the engine room, followed by Beans and Johanssen.

Shiloh caught his breath; he felt as if something was beating the inside of his temples with fire hammers. *Handled that pretty well, I think,* he told himself. *Wanted to beat his brains out, but he probably doesn't have any to beat out anyway.*

Bull was cursing under his breath as he entered the steamy, noisy engine room. The last shift was clearing out, and Johanssen disappeared up the stairs to document the shift change and the coal usage. Beans watched Bull warily, skipping out of his way as he paced the floor, muttering and swearing.

As soon as they had the engine room to themselves, Bull picked up one of the coal shovels, opened the small door to one of the furnaces, and tossed the shovel in with all his might. Beans' mouth opened in a round O. "Whadja do that for, Bull?" he gasped. "Now I gotta call somebody to git me another shovel again! An' I'm gonna git in trouble!"

"Shut up, Beans," Bull growled. "Mr. Johanssen!" he yelled up the stairs. "Get the key to the storage! Shovel missing!" Then he turned around to Beans and muttered, "We gotta get in the storeroom, remember? Miss Sybil needs a new padlock."

Johanssen came down the stairs and looked suspiciously around the engine room. "Vere's de udder shovel, Lynch? It was here a minute ago."

Beans said, "Bull opened the coal door—" Then he made a loud whooshing sound, because Bull clapped him on the back so hard it forced the air out of his lungs. Beans' eyes opened wide and he gaped like a fish, his mouth opening and closing soundlessly.

"Bug on your back, Beans," Bull said carelessly. "Dunno, Chief. Only three shovels here I can see."

Lars Johanssen was a busy man with more things to worry about than a missing coal shovel and the antics of two idiots. He immediately went to fetch the key from Douglas Littlejohn, who meticulously recorded the loss of the coal shovel. Then the engine room chief returned to unlock the small storage room for Lynch. Johanssen ran back upstairs for a moment, made a couple of notes on his report. When he came back down to lock the storage room, Bull Lynch had a new coal shovel and a smile on his face.

❦

"Now I understand why you have to be so careful with laudanum. I've been floating around without caring about anything for—how long is it now, Dr. Duvall? My goodness, what day is it?" Martha Jane Terrell asked in consternation.

Cheney's mouth tightened imperceptibly as she finished doing up the two dozen tiny jet buttons on the back of Martha Jane's black cotton dress. "It's Saturday, Mrs. Terrell, the ninth.

We've—I've been giving you the laudanum for over a week. Your heart was so erratic, and you needed the rest—"

Whirling around to look up at Cheney, Martha Jane's face showed distress and regret for a moment; then she smoothed out her features quickly. "I didn't mean to criticize you, Dr. Duvall. I did need the rest, very badly, and you and I both know that I wouldn't have been able to rest unless you had prescribed the laudanum for me. Thank you."

Cheney relaxed as she realized that both she and Martha Jane were laboring to present a strong and unemotional front to each other. "You're welcome," Cheney said, "but Shiloh is the one who's done most of the work. I've been ill myself, so I know how very tiring it can be. You look much better."

"Thank you," Martha Jane said formally, "and now I'd also like to thank you again for making this trip possible for me and the children. And for the lovely stateroom! It really wasn't necessary, you know; we could have stayed in steerage—"

"Please, Mrs. Terrell," Cheney cut her off in embarrassment, "you have to stop thanking me every time you regain consciousness! All right? Please! Let's just—talk for once!"

A bare hint of mischief showed on Martha Jane's gaunt face. "All right. Let's go find the children, and they can thank you."

"Mrs. Terrell—!"

"Really, let's go up to the promenade deck. I want to get some fresh air, and I can't wait to see the children." Martha Jane picked up her black shawl and she and Cheney left the stateroom. "But there is one more thing I want to tell you. I'm a seamstress—a good one—and I'd like to offer my services to you if you should need any repairs or other work on your clothes. I won't say thank you again, but it would make me feel better if I could do something for you."

"You don't have to do that, Mrs. Terrell. I—it's—I—"

"Dr. Duvall," Martha Jane retorted with mock sternness, "I believe it is as difficult for you to receive thanks as it is for me to give them. You're right. Let's just stop being so exquisitely polite to each other."

"Yes, let's," Cheney said with relief. The two women reached the promenade deck, and Martha Jane stopped at the rail for a moment, breathing deeply of the warm sea air, her face upturned to the sun and her dark blue eyes squinting in the bright light. Cheney saw the beginnings of crow's-feet at the corners of Mrs. Terrell's eyes and wondered if they came from stress or simply from the eyestrain of sewing tiny stitches for hours on end—something Cheney heartily despised.

"So you're a seamstress? Well, I think that's wonderful," Cheney told her as they strolled around the wide deck toward the stern of the ship. "I can't sew one stitch, unless it's in human skin!" As soon as the words were out of her mouth, Cheney regretted them; she had found that some people didn't appreciate medical humor.

But Martha Jane laughed, and Cheney thought the woman looked much prettier and younger when she did. "That's good, considering what you do for a living! But I'll stick to satins and silks, thanks."

The two women talked companionably as they walked to the ship's fantail, where Shiloh had taken the children. They liked to perch on this small platform that overhung the rear of the ship and watch for dolphins in the wake.

"Mama! Mama! Look, Kelvey, it's Mama!" Stony Terrell started whooping wildly. He was standing on the fantail, and Powell Drake was sitting composedly in a long frock coat and tall beaver hat, holding on to the little boy's legs. Now Stony leaped into thin air and steamed full ahead toward his mother, followed by Kelvey, who had been sitting close by Drake.

Stony barreled into his mother, almost knocking her down, and then clung to her knees, his thin arms encircling her black skirt. Then Kelvey reached her and did the same. Martha Jane laughed, "Well! It's about time you children paid some attention to me!" This made both the children start laughing and protesting and yanking on her skirt, telling her all sorts of things in loud, happy voices.

Powell Drake walked up to them and stood stiffly by Cheney, clearing his throat. "Dr. Duvall," he said and bowed very slightly, "I haven't had the pleasure of meeting the children's mother. Would you introduce us, please?" His voice was crisp and formal; Cheney nodded back and echoed his tone.

"Certainly, Mr. Drake. Martha Jane Terrell, may I present—"

But Cheney's attempt at satisfying the demands of courtesy were futile because the children were making so much noise introducing Drake themselves, their high voices competing for their mother's attention: ". . . reads us books" . . . "dolphins from the fantail" . . . "Sir Somebody Drake, you know, and he's a sea dog" . . . and finally, when Stony had to stop for breath, Kelvey shouted triumphantly, "And, Mommy, he smells so good!"

Cheney saw a flicker of amusement in Powell Drake's eyes, but he said nothing. Martha Jane looked up at the man with warm humor and said, "Very nice to meet you, Mr. Drake. I appreciate your taking such good care of the children while I was sick. But where is Shiloh?"

"He's playin' poker," Stony announced proudly. "But he wouldn't let us come with him."

Cheney murmured in exasperation, "Well, I wonder why-ever not?"

"'Cause I'm too young to go in the Gentlemen's Salon," Stony carefully explained, "and 'cause Kelvey's a girl. Anyways, Mr. Drake said he'd rather play with us than lose a bunch of money at poker, so we've been out here playing pirates! Mr. Drake's a great pirate!"

"That so?" Drake commented, looking down at Stony with no visible trace of humor. "Then I think I *will* go join that poker game." Touching the brim of his beaver hat in a curt gesture,

Drake wheeled and left the four behind as he stalked across the deck to the Gentlemen's Salon.

Cheney and Martha Jane glanced at each other in mutual surprise at Drake's brusque exit. Stony said, "Aw, don't pay any attention to him when he talks like that, Mama. Most of the time he's real nice, you know. When he talks like that is when I think he remembers he's not happy." Stony's blue eyes looked after the man thoughtfully.

"Well, for heaven's—" Martha Jane looked down at her son in bewilderment. "What makes you think he's not happy, Stony?"

"'Cause, Mama," Stony explained with great patience, "when he talks like that, it sounds like you when you talk about Pa."

❧

Powell Drake entered the Gentlemen's Salon and ordered a whiskey at the tiny, gleaming bar. Downing it in one swallow, he put the glass down and ordered another, then turned to the table off to the right where three men were engaged in a lively game of poker.

It was Shiloh Irons' deal; he expertly shuffled the cards and looked up at Drake standing at the bar. "Younguns all right, Drake?"

"Yes. Their mother is evidently feeling better. She and Dr. Duvall came up to the fantail, so I came in here." As soon as he said the words, Drake knew he sounded cold and unreasonably disgruntled, and in exasperation he tossed off the other drink.

Grinning up at him, Shiloh shuffled the cards again. "Why don't you bring that money over here? Might as well let me win it from you as give it to that bartender."

"Believe I will," Drake replied in a more reasonable tone, taking the fourth chair at the table. "But I'm not a charity case, Irons. I take my poker very seriously."

"What a surprise," Shiloh said blandly, and a ghost of a smile flitted over Powell Drake's lips.

For three hours Shiloh, Drake, First Officer Bryce Carstairs, and another passenger named Jeff Withers played poker. Shiloh was an erratic player, sometimes making outrageous bluffs and winning, sometimes losing, sometimes folding unexpectedly, playing with quiet good humor whether he won or lost.

Powell Drake was true to his word. He played methodically and studiously, going with the odds. Shiloh observed that he played poker the same way he did everything else: carefully distancing himself from the game and the players. *Except the younguns,* Shiloh thought. *Seems to be the only soft spot he's got—Stony and Kelvey.*

Bryce Carstairs was a fair poker player, betting small and never taking chances. Shiloh got the idea that playing poker with the passengers might be an unwritten duty for the officers of the S.S. *Continental* when there weren't enough men for a good table. Carstairs watched Jeff Withers' every move, not with hostility but with an openly displayed keenness. *Making sure the nice passengers don't get ate up by the card shark,* Shiloh thought as he observed Carstairs watching Withers.

Jeff Withers was a nice-looking man of about thirty who wore fine clothes—not as expensive as Powell Drake's, but a little more dandified. He had wavy blond hair, blue eyes, and a ready smile. A large diamond ring on his pinkie finger winked gaily as the cards performed acrobatics in his well-manicured hands. During the course of the polite, low-stakes game, he played with unabashed superiority and won the modest pot, all the time acknowledging Bryce Carstairs' narrow-eyed gaze with amusement.

Bryce Carstairs and Drake excused themselves, and Shiloh and Jeff Withers remained at the table. Shiloh idly shuffled cards and eyed Withers, who leaned back in his chair and lit a cigar.

"You're not a bad poker player, Irons," Withers said expansively, "but you're a better fighter." He took the slim, fragrant cigar out of his mouth and studied it with exaggerated casualness. "Looks like neither of us is going to make any money at what we're doing right now. Gamblers don't get rich on ship's officers"—he stuck the cigar back in his mouth and grinned around it at Shiloh—"and nurses don't bring home fighter's winnings."

"True," Shiloh shrugged over the soft slaps of the cards he shuffled and stacked, "but nurses don't get their noses broke every Saturday night."

Withers took a long drag from the cigar, then blew out a long, thin column of smoke. "I happen to know you never got your nose broken, Irons, because that very subject came up between me and a friend of mine before your last fight. It was a real mystery to us how a thin, patrician nose like yours never got broken. I figured it was just because you happen to be one of the fastest I've seen, both at punching and ducking."

A half smile came over Shiloh's face as he cut the cards to the ace of spades. "Yeah, well, I worked real hard. 'Specially on the ducking part. You interested in fightin'?"

Withers stood up and pushed his chair close to the table, finished a drink that had been at his side for the entire two hours, and grinned amiably at Shiloh. "Not fighting, Mr. Irons. Just watching and winning. You interested in winning?"

"Maybe."

"Then," Withers said as he stuck the cigar in his mouth and turned to leave the salon, "I'll be in touch."

Shiloh sat and shuffled cards for a long time.

❧

The sea gently rocked the steamship as she sturdily plowed south. The days were slowly growing warmer, everyone had noticed. The breezes on the open walkways were more caressing, less cold and briny, than they had been; the passengers could feel the first gentle touch of the tropics' fingers, and they began to look forward to reaching Havana in another ten days. Even the sea seemed warmer, the waves less impatient and more languid. The indigo-blue night sky was spangled with thousands and thousands of stars that seemed to twinkle lazily and sleepily.

Lydia Thornton breathed deeply of the night air, closing her eyes and tilting her head back with sentient pleasure at the smell of the sea and the warm, moist air on her cheeks. Lydia was an aesthetic woman; she derived a tangible, physical pleasure from smells and sounds and touch sensations. The ocean green-smell, the muted low roar of the ship's paddle heartbeats, the rough wet feel of the wooden railing beneath her fingers gave her as much enjoyment as the beautiful music she made when she sang or played the piano.

With a sigh, Lydia opened her eyes and returned to her state-room. Pausing to take a deep breath, she opened the door and smiled warmly, "Oh, Sybil, it smells so good out there tonight! I'm so glad I can finally go outside again!"

Sybil Warfield was peering into a mirror mounted on the tiny dressing table, expertly arranging her hair on top of her head. She spoke to Lydia's reflection in the mirror in front of her instead of turning around. "Smells so good? What does that mean? Don't most people go outside to see instead of smell?"

"I don't know . . . I didn't notice what it looks like. I mean, it's dark, isn't it?" Lydia's brow furrowed; this wasn't the first time people had commented on some visual beauty that she hadn't noticed. It rather mystified her, considering that her other senses—especially her hearing—seemed so extremely sensitive, almost overdeveloped.

"Not that dark. The nights are getting shorter, warmer. In fact, it's so nice, I think I'll go for a walk," Sybil announced in a businesslike tone. "I know how much you love to be alone."

Her tone, though not warm, held no rancor; but Lydia gave her a guilty glance. "It's—all right, Sybil—don't go on my account—"

Rising from the dressing table, Sybil picked up a light shawl and opened the door. "My dear Lydia, do you imagine that I want to stay here and watch you on a night like this? Hardly! I'm going topside. You can have your praying party all by yourself. Goodnight. Don't wait up, *Mother*," she said mockingly, closing the door firmly behind her.

Lydia smiled to herself as she changed into her nightclothes. *Why in the world does she have to cover her kindness with that rudeness? Silly—she knows how much I like to be alone—too much, I suppose. . . .* Pulling the single chair up to the tiny table by the door, Lydia got the kerosene lantern and her Bible and sat down, the lantern casting a faint glow on her face as she eagerly turned the big book's pages.

Sybil walked soundlessly around the stateroom deck to a line of deck chairs that mutely faced the sea. Settling herself in one of them, she checked her watch. It was a blue night, not a black night, and her sharp eyes had quickly adjusted to the dimness. *Five after ten. I'll give it an hour; then I'll see if she's asleep.*

Lying back in the chair, pulling the shawl close, Sybil's thoughts ticked as methodically as the big watch at her waist. *It's going to work. No one will get hurt, and I'll get what I want, and no one will know.* Over and over Sybil visualized the events to come; the stars winked benignly, the sea rolled sweetly, and the ship hummed, but it was all wasted on the woman who sat alone in the navy-blue night.

With a start, she looked around. *Fell asleep,* she thought groggily, and pulled her watch up to look at it with sleep-ladened eyes. *Almost eleven-thirty.* Quietly she rose and returned to the stateroom.

She fit the key into the lock and opened it with a tiny snick that sounded loud in the silent, dark hallway. With satisfaction she noted that no light showed under the purser's door. Silently she pushed the stateroom door open and breathed a sigh of satisfaction. Lydia was still seated at the tiny table by the door. Her head was down on her arms, and her dark hair spilled over the sleeves of her white cotton nightgown and the Bible underneath. She had fallen asleep again as she prayed. Still weak from seasickness, Lydia had done this for the past three nights.

Sybil closed the door behind her and leaned against it, breathing erratically. Taking a deep, long breath, she set her jaw in a steel line, then took two steps to the table. Deliberately she reached out, picked up the kerosene lantern, and walked over to the bunks. She went down on one knee, her movements soundless and slow, and carefully set the lantern on the floor. A corner of the blanket hung down from the bottom bunk. Sybil tugged on it until a good bit of it lay flat on the floor, laid the kerosene lantern down on top of it on its side, then stood and took a step back to watch. Behind her, Lydia's breathing was slow and regular.

It seemed like a long, long time to Sybil, but actually it took only a few minutes for some of the kerosene to leak out of the bottom of the lantern and catch the blanket on fire. Even so, she made herself stand still and calm until a good blaze was going, staring critically at the flickers of flame, judging when it was serious enough to keep people busy for a little while. Then she opened the stateroom door and screamed, "Fire! Help! Fire!"

Lydia jolted upright, her eyes wide and staring. Sybil ran to the purser's door and beat on it, screaming hysterically. In just seconds, Douglas Littlejohn flung open the door and, without even glancing at Sybil, ran into the next stateroom. Unmistakable flame reflections danced in the hall outside the cabin's open door.

Like a shadow, Sybil slipped into the purser's room, leaving the door standing a little ajar. No lamps were lit. But the purser's cabin, like the other two officers' cabins at the stern of the ship, had windows in the rear walls, so the room was filled with the same blue-gray dimness as the deck.

Sybil had managed to catch one glimpse of the purser's stateroom earlier that day as Littlejohn came out, and she had noted the desk and papers under the window at the right corner of the room. Gliding silently over to the desk, she took one nervous glance over her shoulder. A confusion of shouts, calls, and screams sounded in the hallway outside.

In the dim room Sybil smiled a little and turned back to the desk. Taking a box of matches out of her pocket, she struck one and saw three neat stacks of papers methodically centered on the desk. One appeared to contain inventory lists and supply counts. Another consisted of the passenger lists, stateroom diagrams, and crew shifts and assignments. The last stack of papers was what Sybil was looking for.

Willing herself to be calm, she blew out the match, laid it carefully on the desk in front of her, and lit another one. Her eyes searched the top paper of the third stack, then another, then another.

The calls and cries outside sounded as frantic as ever, and for a moment her mind flirted with panic: *What if I've burned the ship down! What if Lydia—oh, this is ridiculous.* Impatiently she focused on the papers in front of her. *We're in the middle of the ocean. Should be enough water to put out a few little sparks.*

At the bottom of the stack she found the manifest for the last shipment. Methodically she blew out the match, laid it down, and lit another. Her hands were steady; the small, bright flame unwavering.

Her eyes flew over the manifest; she knew she couldn't steal it, because it would be missed. Carefully she studied the paper with its strange symbols and abbreviations, and then she saw one item that made her eyes gleam with satisfaction. And lying under the manifest, as she anticipated, was the paper she needed. It was a meticulously hand-drawn diagram of the stacks of boxes in the crew quarters, and each box was labeled with a single capital letter.

Sybil chose another diagram out of the stack—one that evidently showed where and how a quantity of boxes of wine were stacked—blew out the match, and again laid it down carefully. She shoved the diagram of the wine cases under the manifest of the cargo in the crew hold. Then she picked up her three matches. Carefully she folded up the cold matches in the piece of paper with the drawings of the boxes on it and stuck it down the front of her dress.

Silently hurrying to the door, she furtively looked out. People were hurrying back and forth to her stateroom door with buckets of water, and other women and men were milling about in confusion. With a start, Sybil saw the strained white face of Powell Drake, his normal bland expression replaced by stark, frozen shock. "Dr. Duvall! Dr. Duvall!" a woman screamed hysterically. Sybil figured that she had a few more minutes of confusion before she was in any danger of discovery.

She hurried back to the desk, preparing to search the drawers, when a silver glint on the wall caught her eye. Almost laughing when she realized what it was, she walked over to a board that was mounted on the wall. Dozens of tiny nails stuck out of it in four rows, and from the nails hung tiny, identical keys. Another match revealed that each nail had a label and each key had a number stamped on it. Taking a key stamped "433" out of her pocket, she substituted it for the key that was stamped "413" and that hung on a nail with an obviously new label, "Crew Quarters."

Slipping back to the door, she peered through again. It was quieter, but several of the passengers were still walking around the hall, talking in anxiety-ridden voices. No officers were in sight.

Sybil watched for just a moment, then slipped back out into the hallway through Purser Douglas Littlejohn's slightly open door. No one noticed her, and she stood silent and still, a small dark figure in the far corner of the hallway, for a long time.

9

Prayer Meeting, sans Prayers

". . . so this morning I want to ask forgiveness from each and every one of you. I foolishly endangered your lives, and I freely confess this sin to the Lord and to you . . . and ask forgiveness from Him and from you."

The silence in the room beat on Cheney's ears. Lydia Thornton stood alone on the dais in the Grand Salon, a slight wisp of a woman, her shoulders bent with grief and fatigue. The only trace of defensiveness she showed was that she stood with her arms crossed, holding a ridiculous bright purple shawl around her tightly. Her feverish gaze fell on every face, one by one, and she seemed to be silently imploring each person.

The quiet stretched on painfully, and Cheney shifted uncomfortably in her chair. There was a tension in the room, a hostility, an ugliness that was so tangible it left a sour taste of dread in her mouth. She glanced furtively at Shiloh, who was close by her in one of the sumptuous red velvet chairs. He sat bolt upright, his hands knotted into tight fists in his lap. He was more tense than Cheney had ever imagined he could be, and this unsettled her more than she wanted to admit to herself.

Captain Weldon had given Lydia permission the previous week to hold prayer meetings each Sunday morning—but this was no ordinary prayer meeting. This was more like a courtroom, with Lydia as the defendant, and the verdict was "guilty."

Many of the faces that Lydia searched so intensely were hostile and angry.

Powell Drake, in particular, was sitting close to the dais, his handsome features twisted in what Cheney thought was inordinate anger. Allegra Winston-Smythe looked disdainful and haughty. Sybil stood at the back of the room, her fists clenched at her sides, her face white and strained out of all proportion, with two marked spots of crimson high on her cheekbones. The first officer and the captain stood at the side of the dais; Bryce Carstairs' expression was murderous, but Captain Weldon looked as gruff as usual, no more and no less.

Lydia's glance lingered on some of the kinder faces in the room. Martha Jane Terrell's was sympathetic, and in some strange way the two children at her side displayed the identical adult look of concern and compassion. Tani DuQuesne's beautifully sculpted face remained impassive, but her dark eyes were soft as she met Lydia's gaze.

Annie Stephens and Holly Van Buren sat together. Annie seemed as if she were about to cry; Holly was looking at Shiloh, and beyond her, Asa Mercer was staring at Holly. To Cheney's surprise, Georgia Jakes' red lips were soft with sympathy, and as Cheney watched, Georgia unconsciously made a small, strange placating motion with her hands as she leaned forward in her seat.

"Hrmph," Captain Weldon grunted as he marched forward and mounted the dais to stand by Lydia. His stocky figure, suited in crisp navy blue, made Lydia look like a forlorn child in her mother's dress-up clothes. She wore a bright green dress with the purple shawl; and with angry frustration Cheney thought, *Whyever didn't I think of helping Lydia get dressed this morning— can't use her hands—*

"Miss Thornton, I'm sure everyone here knows that the fire last night was just a terrible accident, and now it's all over." Awkwardly Captain Weldon patted Lydia's thin shoulder with a thick-fingered hand and turned to address the crowd. "Now,

Miss Thornton has promised to obey the ten o'clock lantern cur-few, and I'm sure she'll be careful from here on. So let's just break it up until next Sunday, and Miss Thornton will have a prayer meeting then. We've had enough for today."

He tried to lighten the thick tension by adding, "And don't forget, everyone, the Captain's Ball is this Saturday night. You can come to the ball and have too much fun, then come to prayer meeting in the morning and repent."

No one laughed, and Captain Weldon glared out at the crowd. Asa Mercer stood up and cleared his throat. "Yes, we should all go now. Miss Thornton is obviously exhausted, and I think she's more than paid for—"

"She has not!" Powell Drake jumped up and spat out the words with a viciousness that made Lydia visibly flinch. "She has not paid enough! Don't you realize"—he turned and his furious gaze swept the crowd—"don't any of you people understand ex-actly what she did? She could've killed all of us! And the chil-dren! There are children here, and that idiot woman could've murdered the children in a stupid, careless—"

"Shut up, Drake." Shiloh's voice was low and dangerous as he slowly stood and walked toward the older man. Behind him, hardly realizing what she was doing, Cheney jumped up and fol-lowed Shiloh.

Drake turned toward Shiloh, his whole body stiff. "*You* shut up, Irons! What's the matter with you? She could've turned this ship into a flaming hell on the water! It's criminal!"

Murmurs and mutters swept the crowd, some assenting, some appalled, some frightened. Cheney noted quickly that a group of sailors and stokers were standing in the back of the room, most of whose faces were ugly with accusation. Mercer looked around with anxiety at the hostile crowd as he threaded his way forward.

Shiloh approached Drake and stood next to him, glaring down at the man, his face hard as flint. "If you don't shut up right now, Drake," he said in a menacing monotone, "I am going to shut you up—with great pleasure."

"You're just as stupid as she is, then," Drake spat recklessly, "and just as criminal!"

With horror, Cheney saw Shiloh's shoulder muscles bunch up, his fist clench, and his arm draw back slightly. *He's going to hit him—hurt him—break all the bones in his face*—Her incoherent, frantic thoughts all ran together. Cheney had reached Shiloh and afraid of what he would do, her hands shot out and grabbed his fist with both of hers. Like a viper striking in one blurred motion, Shiloh yanked his hand away, turned around, raised his white-knuckled fist, and struck out.

The blow stopped just short of Cheney's face.

The room echoed with loud gasps. Cheney, Shiloh, and Drake stood motionless in a strange tableau: the tall blond man, his handsome face twisted in ugly rage, his fist shaking slightly inches from Cheney's fearful face, and Drake directly behind Shiloh, his eyes widened in shock, his own hand frozen in what would have been a vain attempt to stop Shiloh's blow.

"Stay out of this, Doc," Shiloh muttered, his lips barely moving. Abruptly he dropped his hand and turned back to Drake.

"Stop . . . please stop—" Lydia broke in, her voice raw and full of pain. "He's right; I could have killed . . ."

Cheney ran to the dais and put her arm around Lydia's waist; the sobbing woman was visibly weakening, and she leaned helplessly on Cheney. Gently Cheney disengaged Lydia's crossed arms and held up her hands; both of them were shapeless white lumps of bandage.

"Look! She tried to beat the fire out with her own hands, Mr. Drake," Cheney cried angrily. "And to make it worse, some of the kerosene from the lantern got on them, and her hands were engulfed in flames! Is that enough punishment for you?"

"No!" Drake responded bitterly, and to Cheney's confusion, she saw tears in his eyes. Whether they were of sorrow or anger, she couldn't tell; his voice wasn't trembling, but it was full of pain. "It's not enough! She committed a crime, and she should be treated like any criminal! She could've killed the children!"

"Leave her alone! All of you!" A strangled cry sounded from the back of the hushed room, and Sybil Warfield put her hands to her mouth, her eyes dark and wild above them. Then she wheeled and literally ran out of the salon.

Shiloh's eyes burned with anger, his fists clenched; he never looked away from Powell's face. Drake didn't seem conscious of the danger in the young man beside him; but even standing up on the dais, Cheney could feel the barely controlled menace that radiated from Shiloh.

"Mr. Drake," Martha Jane broke in, her voice calm and assured, "you seem to be too overwrought by all this." She rose and walked to Drake as he watched her with uncomprehending, hostile eyes. In the silence her dress rustled softly, gently, as she moved. "And I realize you must be speaking of my children," she continued as she reached him and gently placed her hand on his arm, "but surely you see that they're all right? We're all safe, and now you *must* leave poor Miss Thornton alone. Will you come sit with me and the children, please? They're frightened."

Moments of silence passed as Drake stared down into the mildly inquiring face turned up to his. Then, slowly, Drake's shoulders loosened, the tense, bunched muscles of his jaw smoothed out, and his wild eyes grew steadier. Soon his face settled into the familiar remote expression, and with distant courtesy he answered, "Yes, I'll come sit with Kelvey and Stony, Mrs. Terrell. Thank you."

They walked back over to the children, and with no hesitation, Kelvey got up and offered her chair to Drake. When he was seated, she promptly climbed up in his lap. He looked startled for a moment, as he always did when the beautiful little girl so unselfconsciously showed her affection for him. Then he awkwardly pulled her a little closer to him, sighed deeply, and dropped his head.

Wordlessly, Captain Weldon turned his stern gaze to Shiloh, who still stood tautly, with clenched fists, staring at Drake. Shiloh took a deep, ragged breath, slowly unclenched his hands, then turned and abruptly walked out of the salon.

"All right, that's it—show's over, folks!" Captain Weldon boomed. "Everyone clear out!"

"Oh, please, Captain, couldn't we—I mean, couldn't I—just say a short prayer?" Lydia put her bandaged hand on the captain's arm and looked at him pleadingly. Cheney still stood by her, arm around Lydia's waist, feeling horribly self-conscious up in front of the crowd but determined to support Lydia both physically and figuratively.

"Well . . ." the captain muttered, glaring suspiciously around the room.

"Oh, please? I—wanted to have some music, but I can't play now, of course, since—" She looked helplessly down at the shapeless lumps of her hands and again pulled her shawl around to hide them. "But we could have just one prayer, couldn't we? I mean, that *is* why we're here."

"Oh, did y'all want some music?" Georgia asked. Cheney's nerves were still stretched thin from the tension of the scene, and Georgia Jakes' everlasting drawl made the arm around Lydia's waist tighten convulsively. Lydia looked up at Cheney with the ghost of a smile in her soft brown eyes.

Georgia rose and with great drama smoothed down her emerald-green dress, snapping open a fan with ornate Chinese illustrations on it. Waving it languidly in front of her face, she said in too-honeyed tones, "Well, I can play some music, all right? And maybe everybody can relax a little bit." Swaying toward the dais in a walk as deliberate as her voice, she continued fanning herself with exaggerated languor. "Good heavens, it's too hot in here, and there's too many people getting mad for anyone to pray. Why don't you sing, instead, Miss Thornton? Didn't Sybil tell me you can sing real pretty? An' we should do a duet today—our dresses match, hmmm? Of course, I haven't got a pretty purple shawl quite like that one. . . ."

"Purple?" Lydia repeated blankly as Cheney's mind shrank with dread and embarrassment. *What are you going to bang out on the piano, Jezebel Jakes? "Dixie?"*

To the surprise of everyone present, Georgia Jakes passed the gleaming grand piano, walked slowly over to the great gold harp, and looked around expectantly. Captain Weldon recovered from his astonishment and moved forward to unbolt the small piano stool from the floor behind the piano. He carried it over beside the harp, set it down, and knelt to loosen the harp from the floor braces that held it upright.

Georgia spread her wide skirts and sank gracefully down on the stool, eyeing the captain as he knelt on the floor by her. "Just what I love," she sighed loudly, "having a handsome man at my feet."

"Steam and strumpets!" Captain Weldon mumbled in embarrassment, his head down.

Small sounds of relieved laughter rippled around the room. A slight smile came even to Lydia's face, and she looked up at Cheney gratefully. "Thank you, Dr. Duvall, but I feel better now. Would you like to sit down? I think I *will* sing something with Miss Jakes."

"Call me Georgia," the other woman said, and her fingers swept over the strings of the harp as Captain Weldon rose and hurried off the dais. A fluid wave of sound rolled through the room. Twice more her hands moved over the strings, brushing them with an easy grace. Then she rested her hands in her lap and looked around the room with undisguised satisfaction.

Lydia stepped over to Georgia, bent and whispered something, then straightened and looked at the crowd, pleasure lighting her face. Georgia again raised her hands, and the rich music engulfed the crowd in warmth; then Lydia began to sing in contrasting cool notes that pleased the ear like distant sleigh bells in the first night snow:

When I survey the wondrous cross,
On which the Prince of glory died,
My richest gain I count but loss,
And pour contempt on all my pride.

Were the whole realm of nature mine,
That were a present far too small;
Love so amazing, so divine,
Demands my soul, my life, my all.

When Sybil ran out of the Grand Salon, she hurried around to the stern of the ship and furiously marched into the Gentlemen's Salon. It was open, as it always was during daylight hours, but no bartender was in sight. *Guess everyone's in that stinking Grand Salon,* Sybil thought in aimless fury. *How was I supposed to know that everyone would blame Lydia like this? It wasn't that bad! But her hands—*

Sybil violently shoved that picture out of her mind. Rebelliously, she pushed behind the bar and poured a huge amount of brandy into a balloon snifter. The amber liquid glug-glugged into the large glass, and the acrid alcohol smell rising up made Sybil's nostrils sting. Taking a gulp of the brandy, her watering eyes barely peeping over the wide mouth of the snifter, she saw Bull Lynch and Beans Lowery come through the door. Bull was grinning nastily at her, and Beans was looking around the small, elegant room with childlike curiosity.

Sybil slammed the glass down on the bar. "What are you doing here? Get out!"

Bull scowled, "*You* get out, Sybil. This here's the Gentlemen's Salon, ain't it? And we're gentlemen, and you ain't!"

"You're no more a gentleman than I am, Bull, and you don't belong here any more than I do. What do you want?"

Bull shrugged his heavy shoulders. "You were gonna come down to the cargo hold tonight to talk to us anyways. Figure this is as good a time as any, since ever'body's busy lynchin' that little girl in the Grand Salon." His voice fell into a snarl. "Wish they'd hang her from the yardarm! That fire coulda kilt us all—"

"You shut your stupid, stinking mouth, Bull!" Sybil snapped in a deadly tone. "Don't ever mention that again, do you hear me? Because if you do, you just might find my derringer interrupting your conversation again!"

"Uh-oh," Beans mumbled with dread.

"All right, all right," Bull said, stepping backward a little and holding up his grimy hands. "Calm down. All I wanna talk about anyways is the job. You got it figured out? What're we gonna do? How are we gonna—"

"I told you to shut up!" Sybil's eyes raked over Bull with contempt as she lifted the snifter and took another drink of the strong brandy. "You just come down to the cargo hold tonight, like I told you to. Stop trying to think, Bull. The strain might overload your pea brain."

Bull lowered his massive head just like his namesake would in a temper; he rounded the bar and grabbed Sybil's wrist. "You stop talkin' to me like that, woman!" he growled and jerked her wrist savagely. "I'm gettin' real tired of your smart mouth!" His black eyes bored into Sybil's and with satisfaction he noted a hint of fear.

"Bull—" Beans said timidly.

"Not now, Beans," Bull snarled.

"But, Bull—"

"What?"

"Hullo there—Bull, is it? Charming name. Fits you."

The familiar drawl of Shiloh Irons' voice made Bull's head snap up. "You!"

"Yep, me. Again. And I'm not in as good a mood this time as I was the last time I caught you manhandling a woman." Shiloh Irons was breathing raggedly; he was still wrought up from the scene in the Grand Salon. Instead of the cold disdain Bull had last seen, Shiloh's blue eyes held a reckless invitation to danger as he stared down at Bull. "In fact, I'm in a downright bad mood. Want to come outside and let me tell you about it?"

"Suits me, you sucker!" Bull snarled as he came around the bar.

"First we have to discuss this in a civilized manner, gentlemen," a coolly amused voice sounded from the door. "There are arrangements to be made, drinks to be drunk, bets to be placed before a good fight like this." Jeff Withers puffed on his cigar, stuck his hands into the pockets of his immaculate white pants, and leaned up against the door of the salon.

Shiloh whirled around, and the expression on his face was cold. "Stay out of this, Withers," he said. "This isn't for your entertainment."

Withers took the cigar out of his mouth and studied it carefully. "Oh no? Whose entertainment, then? Yours?"

Bull looked back and forth from Shiloh to Withers in uncomprehending impatience. "What's goin' on? Who're you, Fancy Pants? Get outta the way! I got somethin' to settle with Pretty Boy here!"

"He is kinda pretty, isn't he? It's a wonder he stayed that way, considering—"

"Considering what?" Sybil couldn't help but ask. She had finished the large brandy and was unconcernedly pouring herself another one.

"Considering, my dear lady," Withers continued with affected gallantry, "all the men that tried to uglify him."

"Had a cousin that got uglified once," Beans offered helpfully. "Turrible thing to wake up to in the mornin'."

"Shut up," Shiloh and Bull said in unison.

"My goodness, just look at all the men," Georgia Jakes said, appearing behind Jeff Withers. "May I come in? The party's over in the Grand Salon, so I thought I'd just come see what everybody's doing over here."

"Come on in," Sybil said recklessly, holding up the half-full snifter. "Party's just starting, and the drinks are on me. What'll you have?"

Jeff Withers moved out of the doorway and bowed slightly to Georgia as she swept past him. "Oh, just a tiny, tiny bit of sarsaparilla, I think," she said with cloying delicacy.

"No sarsaparilla here, Georgia dear, you'll have to go to the Ladies' Salon for that," Sybil said, her eyes glittering.

"Oh no," Georgia said hastily. "Then I'll just have whatever you're having, Sybil dear."

A loud squeal sounded from the doorway. "Ooh, Shiloh, there you are!" Holly Van Buren tripped into the now-crowded salon to stand by Shiloh, gazing up at him with adoring chinablue eyes. "You were so—so—scary in there!"

"Holly!" Asa Mercer called as his head popped into the doorway. "I don't think—Oh, Miss Warfield! Don't you think—and Miss Jakes, really, please think about what you're—"

"I'm leaving," Shiloh snapped. "Too much thinking going on in here. Sounds like I stumbled into the Ladies' Salon by accident." He disengaged his arm from Holly's plump little hand and headed toward the door.

"Ain't this the Gentemmen's Saloon?" Beans asked, turning a circle in confusion. "Did I git lost again?"

"We better get outta here, too," Bull announced. "C'mon, Beans, Cap'n will have our heads if he catches us up here."

"But, gentlemen," Withers protested, "first let me talk to you about something that is of mutual interest to all of us—"

"What does that mean, Mr. Fancy Pants?" Bull asked suspiciously.

"It means that you and Mr. Irons here could still beat each other to a pulp, just as you want to, and make some money from it, too," Withers said expansively. "Maybe a lot of money."

"Oh, my goodness!" Holly exclaimed with excitement, "can I listen?"

Shiloh stopped on his way out the door and turned to Jeff Withers resignedly. "Go ahead and talk, Withers. If I'm going to tangle with Mr. Bull here, I might as well get paid for it."

10

Captain Weldon's Ball

I never liked this thing, anyway, Cheney thought impatiently as she pulled the tomato-red satin dress from her trunk. *It makes my skin look a funny color.*

Grabbing her medical bag, she rummaged through it and brought out a small alligator case. Opening it, she chose a scalpel from the six that fit neatly in the velvet grooves. Tossing the bag and case aside, she grabbed the red gown and sat down on her bottom bunk, fumbling with the yards of shiny satin until she found the hem. Following the hem around several inches, running it inch by inch through her fingers, she finally grunted, "There!"

Pushing the blade of the scalpel through the material about six inches up from the hem, she brought it down in a smooth motion. It cut the material easily and cleanly, and Cheney looked at the tear with satisfaction. Then she threw the dress down, grabbed a crinoline that lay on her other side, and went through the same procedure, cutting it just below the last wire circle sewn into the creamy white satin.

Grabbing the dress and the crinoline, she rushed out of her stateroom and almost ran to the Terrells' cabin. She knocked on the door; Stony cracked it open and peered up at her with puzzled blue eyes. "Dr. Cheney! Why do you look so funny? You been running fast?"

The door opened wider, and Martha Jane said, "Stony, let Dr. Duvall in if—" Then she caught sight of the bundle of crimson and white satin that spilled out of Cheney's arms and down to the floor in a gleaming river. Martha Jane stopped in mid-sentence and stared.

"Here!" Cheney thrust the dress and the wide circle of white into Martha Jane's hands, and the startled woman took them automatically. "This dress has a tear in it, Martha Jane," she explained, talking rapidly and a little breathlessly, "and I was about to throw it away—"

Martha Jane's face grew horrified as she looked down at the rustling, rich satin in her hands. "Oh no, Dr. Duvall—!"

Stony, still standing in front of his mother and fingering the bright red material, exclaimed, "Cooee!"

"—because I don't like the stupid dress anyway; it makes me look, umm—orange," Cheney blundered on, "and I thought you might be able to sew it up and—and—use it. For the Captain's Ball tomorrow night, you know. If you can't—I mean, I'm embarrassed about giving you a dress that's torn, but—well, goodbye!"

Martha Jane leaned out of the door and called after her fleeing figure, "I'm not going to say thank you, Dr. Duvall!"

"You're not welcome, Mrs. Terrell!" Cheney returned as she sped back to her stateroom.

Shiloh stood in front of Cheney's stateroom, his hand poised to knock, as Cheney came down the hall. He looked at Cheney inquiringly as she reached the door. "What're you and Martha Jane yelling at each other about?"

"Nothing, just—nothing," Cheney answered hurriedly as she went into her stateroom and started putting the strewn articles back in her medical bag. Shiloh lounged against the doorway. "I'm just going to check on Arlene Tate and Enid Alexander," she sighed. "I wish Arlene would admit she's better, and I wish Enid would admit she's sick."

"I thought Arlene really was sick," Shiloh said with some surprise.

"Yes, she was more seasick than the rest of us, for a longer time. She's seemed a little better in the past few days, but she's so shy that she just stays in the cabin all the time, in bed. I'm going to try to talk her into getting up today and coming to the Captain's Ball tomorrow night."

"Why don't you go see her, and I'll go check on Enid?" Shiloh asked casually.

Cheney suspected that Shiloh really wanted to see Enid's cabin mate, Allegra Winston-Smythe. The attraction Shiloh had shown for the coldly elegant woman frustrated Cheney. She thought Miss Winston-Smythe was haughty and snobbish, not at all the kind of woman that Shiloh should be attracted to. "No, I'll go see Enid," Cheney amended, also too casually. "You go—oh no, that wouldn't work, would it?"

"I think Miss Tate might be terrified if I went and banged on her door," Shiloh grinned. The plump, bashful Miss Tate had never allowed Shiloh or Joed into her room.

"Oh, all right," Cheney shrugged. "I'll go see Arlene. But I think I need to see Enid, too. There's obviously something else wrong with her."

"Yeah, there is, but so far she won't let me get close to her at all," Shiloh said with some frustration. "Not even to take her pulse. Where's your other medical bag? I'm going to try again today to at least take her pulse and listen to her heart."

Cheney finished loading her medical bag, a fine black leather one that Dev had given her for a graduation present, with medicines, instruments, the alligator case with the scalpels, and a brand-new flexible stethoscope included. She had already owned one fully stocked bag, but everything Dev had given her was of first quality.

She started out the stateroom door, muttering, "The other bag's in the infirmary. Why don't you just keep it? You're the only one who uses it, anyway. I have this brand-new one. And go ahead and try to get Enid to let you examine her thoroughly," Cheney grumbled with ill-disguised impatience as she went down the hall. "That is, if you can tear your attention away from Miss Ice Queen long enough."

"The stethoscope, too?" Shiloh called down the hall.

"Yes, the stethoscope, too," Cheney called back without turning around.

"I won't say thanks, Doc!"

"You're not welcome!" Cheney yelled.

All that day until dinnertime Cheney visited every single one of Mercer's Belles that she could find to encourage them to come to the ball on Saturday night. She was concerned about the uneasiness and tenseness that had seemed to permeate the ship after the fire, and she thoroughly believed that a little relaxation and companionship would help everyone.

Most of the women were excited and planning to come anyway. With the ones who were reluctant, Cheney unashamedly pulled rank. As their doctor, she told them, she was prescribing dancing, some warm night air on the promenade deck, and some of Chef Martel Renaud's fresh orange-lemonade, which would be served only at the Captain's Ball.

Cheney slept well that night, as she had ever since she had gotten her "sea legs." Indeed, most everyone was easily lulled to sleep by the gentle motions of the *Continental* as she faithfully steamed toward the balmy Caribbean. Cheney slept heavily, dreamlessly, and awoke refreshed and excited about the night's festivities.

Early that morning Shiloh's familiar knock sounded on her stateroom door. "G'mornin', Doc! Let's go have breakfast!"

"No," Cheney said firmly. "I'm not coming out until tonight! I'm going to have a long, hot bath and spend all day pampering myself and getting ready!"

"Well, you have to open the door now, anyway," Shiloh said. "Your hot water's out here."

Cheney jumped up from the tiny dressing table, where she was laboring to brush out her long, thick hair, and opened the door. The young steward stood outside with the familiar galley cart, which held two immense pots of steaming water instead of the chamomile tea they had all carted around for so long. "Good morning, Dr. Duvall," he greeted her as he wheeled the cart inside Cheney's stateroom. There was just enough room to get it inside the door.

"Good morning, Joed," Cheney said gratefully. "Oh, thank you! Just leave the whole thing right there, and you can come back to get it later."

"All right, Dr. Duvall," the smooth-faced boy answered as he left the stateroom, "but it's Joel."

"What?" Cheney asked Shiloh as he leaned against the door and looked around the crowded stateroom with amusement. "Did he say Joel? Have I been calling him the wrong name all this time?"

"How in the world are you going to take a bath in here?" Shiloh asked curiously.

"Well—well—" Cheney sputtered, "I hardly think that's any of your business!" She maneuvered around the galley cart and shut the door on Shiloh's interested face. "Go away! I'll see you at the ball tonight!"

"But, Doc, I need your help!" he protested from the hall.

"Help to do what?"

A few moments of silence ensued, and Cheney thought Shiloh had just gone away. Then she heard him faintly (evidently he was going on down the hall) say, "Oh, never mind . . . I've got another idea."

Cheney shrugged, and turned to look at the pots of hot water with unmitigated joy.

❖

The Grand Salon of the S.S. *Continental* served also as the ballroom. A luxurious room, well-appointed and spacious, it was a source of great pride to Messrs. Bingham and Lloyd, who traveled periodically on the *Continental* just for fun, much as little boys play with their toy ships.

The walls gleamed with mahogany wainscoting up to three feet, topped by a creamy ivory wallpaper with a red velvet pattern. Huge mirrors with ornate silver frames were mounted every three feet along the walls to reflect the splendor of the room.

In the exact center of the room was an enormous silver chandelier that was the steward's nightmare to polish. It was four-tiered and hung so precariously low from the ten-foot ceiling that directly beneath had been placed a huge round ottoman of the same red velvet as the chairs. The ottoman had large scarlet buttons sunk so deeply in the plush that they almost disappeared.

The two hundred plush salon chairs were normally arranged in intimate groups of twos and threes; they seemed casually placed but were actually bolted down. Tonight, for the Captain's Ball, they had been bolted down along the walls. In addition, two long tables had been set up in front of the marble dais, leaving a space in the middle to mount the platform. Snowy white cloths covered the tables, and the cold gleam of highly polished silver tureens and bowls reflected the room as brilliantly as the mirrors on the walls.

On the dais, a man was softly playing bits and pieces of music on the piano; behind him, another talented sailor was tuning a violin. Standing by him was another sailor playing a wooden flute; the tentative, breathy notes of the instrument already sounded poignant and exotic, even though they were just random sounds floating on the warm night air. Lydia Thornton sat alone close to the dais, her eyes sparkling yet wistful as she watched the musicians warming up.

At the other end of the room, Captain Weldon stood with his three officers at the foot of the marble staircase, waiting to receive the guests. "I know there's over a hundred of 'em," Captain Weldon grunted, "but between the four of us, we're gonna dance with every single one—and that's an order!"

"Aye, aye, sir," First Officer Bryce Carstairs and Engine Room Chief Lars Johanssen said in unison.

"Except for Miss Thornton," Purser Douglas Littlejohn amended, nodding toward Lydia. "She doesn't wish to dance tonight since her hands are bandaged."

"Frankly, I'm surprised she would come at all," Carstairs commented in a faintly critical tone.

"Enough," Weldon warned. "That's exactly why I wanted Littlejohn to talk her into coming. Maybe everyone will dance, relax, see that she's no ogre and that the fire is best forgotten."

"Pardon me, Captain," Littlejohn said in a level tone, "but speaking of fights, do you really think this fight between the nurse and Lynch is wise?"

"Better than having Irons busting up my passengers, Littlejohn. I don't mind him banging Lynch around a little bit; Lynch can take care of himself."

"Ya, dis is true," Johanssen agreed. "An' if da nurse vill only hit Bull in de head, no one vill get hurt."

The unmistakable rustling of women's dresses sounded at the door, and the men looked up expectantly. "Well, men," the captain scowled with ill-disguised dread, "if they all looked as good as that, this wouldn't be such a chore." He moved forward to escort the women who had appeared at the top of the stairs, muttering, "Shut your mouth, Carstairs, and come help me, for Neptune's sake!"

Poised regally at the top of the shallow staircase was Cheney, holding her head high and wearing a satin turquoise dress finished with such a high sheen that light shimmers shot across it with every movement she made. Beside her was Martha Jane Terrell in a crimson gown with a breathtakingly wide skirt that made her waist look as if a man could span it with his hands and overlap his fingers. Captain Weldon was not sure he would have recognized her as the same tired, wan woman who had stood shivering on his gangplank a couple of weeks ago.

Martha Jane's children stood in front of her and close to Cheney. The skirt of little Kelvey's dress had been fashioned with five tiers of the same scarlet satin that her mother wore. Stony was dressed in knickers and a clean white shirt with a small black string tie. He looked rebellious and bored at the same time.

Beside them was a young girl who looked amazingly like the cameo she wore on a black velvet ribbon around her neck, Bryce Carstairs thought. Her shining brown hair had been fashioned in the popular "spaniel" style: parted down the middle, with masses of long ringlets over each ear. Blushing, her eyes downcast, she looked very young and innocent in a pale pink dress with a white lace overskirt.

"Miss Duvall, Mrs. Terrell, please come in," Captain Weldon said heartily, offering each woman a burly arm. "And I'm sorry, but I don't know you, young lady."

"Captain Weldon, this is Miss Arlene Tate. Miss Tate, this is Captain Weldon and First Officer Bryce Carstairs." Cheney made the introductions with gracious movements of a matching turquoise fan that hung from her wrist.

The group moved into the room, and Cheney quickly made her way over to where Lydia Thornton sat alone. "Lydia! I'm so sorry I couldn't get to your cabin in time for your dinner, but I got hopelessly tangled up with Arlene this afternoon."

It was impossible for Lydia to eat with her burned hands, so Cheney, Shiloh, and Sybil had been taking turns feeding her like a helpless infant. She sat with a bright pink shawl tightly crossed in front of her, hiding her hands, and Cheney saw with dismay that she was wearing a dress of a strange orange-yellow color that looked hideous with the shawl! Cheney couldn't imagine why a woman of Lydia's taste and intelligence wore such outlandish outfits, but again Cheney scolded herself for being critical and nitpicking.

"You mean *that's* little Arlene Tate?" Lydia was asking, her eyes wide. "Why, I didn't even recognize her! She's so—so—"

"Thin?" Cheney finished the sentence, her eyes sparkling. "Yes, poor little thing! She was so sick for so long! Then, when she started feeling better, she still didn't eat much. She just wouldn't come out of her stateroom at all, until tonight, and I was afraid I was going to have to drag her bodily."

"She looks so frightened! She must be terrified to go to the dining room by herself," Lydia said sympathetically.

"Oh, I hadn't thought of that," Cheney responded. "Her cabin mate is Georgia Jakes, and I know she never spends any time with her. I'll have to think of something. Arlene does look lovely, but I'm certainly not going to let her go without eating anymore."

"Maybe I can talk her into coming and eating with me for a few days," Lydia said thoughtfully. "I could use the help—as you well know—and I'd like to make friends with her. She looks so sweet. And what a lovely dress she's wearing!"

"Oh, that dress! That's why we got into such a mess today. I showed up at Arlene's door—I'd made her say she'd come to the ball tonight—and she burst into tears when I came in. Her dress was just falling off her!"

Cheney watched the girl affectionately. She was walking toward them, looking like a doe moving cautiously in the woods, when she caught her own reflection in one of the large mirrors on the wall. Stopping abruptly, a comically startled look came over her face as she gazed in wonder for a few moments at her own reflection. Then she blushed and again continued her way to Cheney and Lydia.

"I went and got Mrs. Terrell—Martha Jane," Cheney went on, "and she came and literally *sewed* Arlene into that dress, since she didn't have time to take it up properly. Thank heavens for Martha Jane!"

"Yes," Lydia said softly, "I certainly thank the Lord for Martha Jane Terrell!"

"For what?" Martha Jane demanded, approaching Cheney and Lydia with the children in tow.

"For last Sunday," Lydia answered matter-of-factly. When Martha Jane opened her mouth to protest modestly, Lydia went on, "Speaking of pretty dresses, Martha Jane, you look lovely! And Kelvey! You're so pretty, all the men are going to want to dance with you instead of us!"

"Today's my birthday," Kelvey announced solemnly, "and my mommy gave me this dress for my birthday."

Martha Jane threw an intensely grateful glance to Cheney, who blushed and said, "Well, happy birthday, Kelvey! And this must be your birthday party!"

"It is," she nodded eagerly, "and thank you for coming."

The music began as more people arrived. Powell Drake came striding in and promptly took up a solitary position at the other end of the long tables from where Lydia, Cheney, and Martha Jane sat. All week he had been avoiding the other passengers, sitting alone in the dining room and on the promenade deck for hours at a time, staring out to sea and curtly rebuffing every attempt to engage him in conversation. Once or twice he had played with the children, but even with them he had been distant and inattentive. Neither of them seemed to mind, however, and now both youngsters rushed over to corner him, their high, piping voices raised in excitement as they talked to him.

Asa Mercer entered with Holly Van Buren on one arm, a delicate pink blush on her cheeks as she searched the room eagerly, and Annie Stephens on the other arm, smiling faintly. Holly wore a china-blue dress that matched her eyes, and white ribbons fluttered from the gown everywhere. Annie looked demure in dove-gray satin with a delicate white fichu.

Sybil Warfield and Georgia Jakes entered together—a very unlikely pair. Sybil looked spare and rather severe in chocolate-brown velvet, the chatelaine's pin at her waist the only ornament; Georgia wore a bright green satin dress trimmed with glittering black jet and black velvet ribbon. Three black feathers were arranged in her brilliant red hair, held on by an impossibly large emerald and diamond hairpin.

Cheney turned to say something to Lydia, but Lydia was looking past her at Sybil and Georgia. Lydia raised her hand and waved, a welcoming smile on her face, but abruptly her face fell. Cheney glanced back to the entrance of the room and saw Sybil rushing to the other side of the room to sit by herself while Georgia sailed toward them.

"She's been ignoring me since the—fire," Lydia gulped. "I think she can't forgive me, and I hate it. We were just getting to be friends."

Cheney started to lecture Lydia on the unworthiness of her prickly roommate, but Captain Weldon arrived to claim Cheney for the first dance, as he had promised that first night in the dining room. Then Douglas Littlejohn claimed her, and then, to her delight, the jolly Engine Room Chief, Lars Johanssen, asked her to dance. He paid her extravagant compliments in staccato English and then proposed to her as he took her back to the group of women. She let him down easily, and he promptly claimed Arlene Tate for the next dance, his blue eyes twinkling merrily. Cheney heard him begin his routine again with Arlene, who blushed furiously but looked pleased.

Lydia sat talking to Annie Stephens and Martha Jane Terrell. Georgia Jakes was seated with them, but ignoring them as she searched the room with hawk's eyes.

Annie shrugged. "She's harmless, really. Just very young and pampered." As Cheney approached, the three women turned to watch Asa Mercer dancing with Holly Van Buren, who was giggling in a high-pitched voice.

Martha Jane sighed. "I remember what it was like to be that young and silly."

"Unfortunately, she's also making Mr. Mercer look silly," Lydia idly commented. "It'd be different if he was deliberately making a buffoon of himself, but she does flirt with him so." Lydia's shrewd gaze was fixed on Annie, whose beautiful brown eyes took on a thoughtful expression.

The dance ended. Asa Mercer bowed to Holly and tried to take her arm to escort her back to her companions, but the women could hear Holly plaintively insisting that he dance again with her. Cheney knew that even though Mercer was infatuated with Holly, he would never shirk his responsibilities to the other women. But now in Holly's insistent clutches, he looked rather like a helpless rabbit in a snare.

"Please excuse me, ladies," Annie said firmly and walked quickly to the dance floor where Holly and Asa stood. Laying her hand lightly on Holly's arm, she smiled and said something; like a petulant child, Holly flounced over to the long tables and picked up a crystal cup of orange-lemonade, glowering at Annie and Asa as they began to waltz.

Cheney was surprised at Annie's calm handling of the situation, but Lydia Thornton looked well satisfied with herself and the world in general. Jeff Withers appeared in spotless whites and asked Georgia to dance. She literally shot out of the chair to oblige.

Martha Jane smiled as she watched Asa and Annie, then roused herself as she caught sight of Powell Drake seated across the room. Kelvey sat in his lap, with Stony on the red carpet in front of him, playing some game with three rocks that he always carried in his pocket. "Speaking of looking silly," she said wryly, "I hope Mr. Drake doesn't cringe at the sight of my children these days. I think I'd better go fetch them." Hurriedly she worked her way through the dancers to the other side of the room.

There was a slight stir on the staircase as Shiloh came into the room with Allegra Winston-Smythe on one arm and Enid Alexander on the other. It was quite an entrance. Shiloh looked tall and immaculately groomed, although he was dressed simply in a white shirt with billowing full sleeves and his customary tan breeches tucked into shiny black knee boots. Miss Winston-

Smythe wore an icy mint green, while Enid Alexander looked dramatic in solid black. All over the room people turned to stare at the three.

Doesn't seem to notice the attention or really care, Cheney thought. *What exactly does he care about, I wonder? He's friendly, he cares about people . . . but while they immediately start trusting him, he's never really personal with them. Never says what he's really thinking. . . .*

Kelvey and Stony ran to Shiloh, calling loudly to him. Grabbing Kelvey, Shiloh swooped her up, turned circles with her high in the air, and said "Happy Birthday" in a loud voice. Her delighted giggles sounded above his singing and the music. Allegra stared at the children with mild distaste; Stony stopped directly in front of her, his hands on his hips, and said something. She merely looked around with impatient expectancy, as if she were looking for a butler to appear and remove the offending small object in front of her. Enid went straight to a chair and sat down, her face white and strained as she covered her mouth with a delicate black lace handkerchief and coughed slightly.

"Look," Lydia said softly, "they're dancing."

Cheney turned; Drake and Martha Jane were waltzing discreetly in the corner of the room. Drake waltzed expertly, but he held Martha Jane stiffly far away from him while his eyes focused on a point somewhere beyond her left shoulder. She was talking to him with an earnest expression on her face. Cheney looked curiously at Lydia. "You're not—upset, or angry with Mr. Drake?"

"Why, no, of course not," Lydia answered in surprise. "Everything he said was right, and the—strength of his reaction tells me that there's more to it than just the fire the other night. Something . . ." Her face grew thoughtful as she watched the couple dance, and then she gave a self-deprecating laugh. "Besides, Shiloh defended me really well, don't you think?"

"Well—" Cheney began, but was interrupted when Captain Weldon again appeared.

"I'm the captain of this ship, Miss Thornton," he growled, "and I could order you to dance with me, you know."

"Captain Weldon, you know very well that I'm not going to dance, but I thank you anyway. And thank you for making all your poor officers come over here and ask anyway, just to make me feel comfortable," Lydia added mischievously. "But it's really not necessary, you know. I'm fine, and I'm having such a good time."

"Hrmph!" Weldon grumbled. "Never been turned down so rudely with such politeness! Pardon me, ladies, I guess I'll go scare that poor little Tate girl into dancing with me! Who's she hiding behind now, I wonder?" He disappeared, his back stiff with determination.

Georgia Jakes appeared, slightly out of breath, and plumped herself down in the chair on Lydia's other side, fanning herself with an outrageously large black ostrich feather fan. Lydia welcomed her warmly, and Cheney managed to nod with some civility. Georgia's skill on the harp hadn't made Cheney like her much more than before, especially since she had seen Georgia and Sybil Thornton drinking in the Gentlemen's Salon twice in the past week.

Cheney turned to survey the dance floor. "There's Joed, dancing!" she exclaimed with delight. "I wonder who that is he's dancing with?" *Oh no,* she was thinking with agitation, *I don't think I've seen that girl before. . . . However could I have missed one of the women . . . ?*

"Oh, that's Kat," Lydia answered. "She's in steerage. Pretty little thing, isn't she?"

"Steerage?" Lydia could tell from Cheney's tone that she barely knew what the word meant.

"Yes. She's doing so well! Dancing, I mean. And that's Joel, not Joed. I don't know how Kat still has the energy," Lydia sighed, "considering that Shiloh probably yanked her arms out of their sockets all day today."

"Shiloh?" Cheney repeated in bewilderment.

"Yes, while Tani was teaching them to dance."

"Tani?" Cheney's voice was growing more and more astonished.

"This room must have terrible acoustics," Lydia said with a smile. "I keep hearing an echo."

"But—but—"

"You see, Shiloh came to my room at breakfast to help me, and Tani was there. She won't feed me, you know, because she was a slave and all and, well, it just makes her feel—you understand," Lydia explained matter-of-factly. "But she has this wonderful voice with a French accent—she's one-fourth French, from New Orleans, you know—"

"Lydia—" Cheney helplessly implored.

"I'm sorry, but I am trying to tell you. I just thought—you knew, I guess. Anyway, she was reading to me when Shiloh came and tried to bully me into teaching him to dance. Well, I didn't care how much he fussed; I am simply not going to dance! I told him that my hands hurt enough without him jerking on them, the big ape. So Tani said that she wouldn't dance with him either, because she was a slave, you know, and even though she doesn't like white men, she likes Shiloh, but she wouldn't dance for him like a—houri." Lydia recalled the word with obvious relish.

By now Cheney had been reduced to speechlessness; she simply looked at Lydia and shook her head slightly, as if to clear it.

Without expression, Lydia watched Powell Drake and Martha Jane dancing, and went on, "But Tani said that she was going to teach one of the girls in steerage to dance, and Shiloh could come, and he knew Kat anyway, because he already almost had to beat up Bull Lynch for bothering her twice before. So Tani spent the whole day teaching Shiloh and Kat how to dance." Lydia took a deep breath and added absently, "And personally, I'm glad that Shiloh's going to fight that Bull person fair and square. He sounds horrible, and probably he has it coming."

Cheney shook her head again, her large green eyes wide, unable to frame even one of the questions that were shouting in her mind after this story.

Powell Drake appeared in front of the ladies. Georgia straightened up in her chair and waved her fan in front of her face, her eyes coyly blinking up at him. "Why, hello there, Mr. Drake," she smiled up at him, languidly moving the fan in front of her face.

"Evening," he said curtly, his eyes on Lydia, who returned his gaze unflinchingly. Cheney felt familiar dread rising at the forbidding expression on Drake's face; then it increased tenfold as Shiloh appeared behind Drake, his eyes snapping.

"Miss Thornton—" Drake began.

"Drake—" Shiloh interrupted, and clapped a hand on his shoulder.

"Shiloh," Lydia said sternly, "it's all right. Yes, Mr. Drake?"

Drake paused, looked behind him at Shiloh, then turned back to Lydia and with obvious difficulty asked, "Would you do me the honor of dancing with me?" Behind Shiloh, Martha Jane appeared with a slight smile on her face.

"She doesn't want to dance, Drake," Shiloh warned. Cheney stood up; her nurse had that peculiar tension in his shoulders that Cheney had noticed a few days before. *His temper—he gets so angry so fast! Worries me . . . when his shoulders bunch up like that and the muscles start working in his jaw . . . somebody's about to get hurt.*

"Thank you, Shiloh," Lydia said graciously and stood up. "But I believe I will dance with Mr. Drake."

To everyone else's surprise, Lydia laid down her shawl, held out her bandaged hands, and danced off gracefully with Powell Drake, who looked grudgingly relieved. Cheney watched them for a moment. Lydia looked small and particularly frail with the huge white lumps at the ends of her arms. But Drake seemed to hold her with a surprising gentleness—though at his customary distance—and Lydia smiled up at him as he haltingly spoke to her.

Shiloh was watching them darkly, but Cheney didn't care how he felt at the moment. Stepping in front of him squarely, she demanded, "I want to talk to you about something."

For a few moments he stared at Lydia and Drake in silence, not acknowledging Cheney. Then he grinned down at her disarmingly, put his arm around her waist, held up her right hand, and swept her out onto the dance floor, all with the same swiftness he had displayed when he almost hit her at the prayer meeting. "Sure, Doc," he said gaily. "Having a good time?"

"I said I wanted to talk to you, not dance with you," Cheney said, her cheeks flushing a becoming pink.

"You don't want to dance with me?" Shiloh asked in genuine surprise. "Why not?"

He doesn't play right, Cheney thought with frustration. *He always just—just—says what he means!* "Never mind that," she said hastily. "What I wanted to talk to you about—"

"—is the fight," he finished for her.

"Yes. Whatever are you thinking of? You can't go and just—just—fight with someone!"

"Why not?" he asked innocently.

"Well—well—you can't! You're a nurse, for one thing! And your arm's not healed yet!" Cheney sputtered.

"I was a fighter before I was a nurse," he answered mildly, smiling and nodding at people as they swept around the floor. "'Course, I am a better nurse, but it sure doesn't pay as much as fighting."

"But—"

"And my arm—well, it just ups the odds, you know?" he explained earnestly. "So I made sure I told everyone how you had to spend hours sewing it up and all, and how much it hurts all the time."

"What? That's a lie!" Cheney said indignantly.

"No, it's not," Shiloh answered with such honest surprise that Cheney caught her breath.

"Oh," she said in a subdued tone. Cheney had taken the stitches out that Monday, two weeks after he was stabbed. It had healed well, and Cheney hadn't thought much more about it. Now she wondered, *What was I thinking of—or not thinking of? It was a serious wound—of course it must have hurt!* Not once in the last two weeks had Shiloh mentioned his arm. And he had certainly never complained of pain—but that didn't excuse Cheney's thoughtlessness. Her thoughts distracted and distressed her, and the couple danced for a while in silence.

Shiloh could read each thought passing over Cheney's face. *She hides things pretty well,* he thought. *You have to pay attention. This ship ain't much like Duvall Court or the University of Uppity-Ups . . . she's had to learn a lot in a hurry. Learns fast, though. . . .*

"So," Cheney said with an abrupt flash of triumph, "if you're still having pain, you certainly don't need to be fighting. Therefore, as your doctor, I forbid it!"

"Sorry, Doc," he shrugged, "but they're going to announce it at midnight. And, besides, my money's already down. I've gotta go through with it now."

"What!" Cheney exclaimed as the dance ended and they walked slowly back to her seat beside Lydia. "Do you mean to tell me that you bet on yourself?"

"'Course," Shiloh said easily as he seated her in her chair. He towered over the women as he stood beside them, and Cheney noticed that Georgia Jakes simpered up at Shiloh like a lovesick schoolgirl. "It's sorta like when you're runnin' for office," Shiloh continued in a mocking tone; "you always gotta vote for yourself." He winked at Lydia as Cheney started spluttering indignantly and unintelligibly, and then he went on inexorably. "Oh, but 'scuse me, I forgot, Doc. You wouldn't know about that, hmmm? Since you can't vote and all . . ." Lydia hid a smile, Georgia looked puzzled, and Cheney flushed as Shiloh made a gracious bow, then turned and slipped away.

11

Cargo Deck: Crew Quarters

"We gotta hurry, Beans," Bull Lynch warned. "They're gonna announce the fight at midnight at the captain's li'l soiree—" He pronounced it "SWA-ree," and Beans looked mystified. "—and we gotta make a showin'. Sybil said so."

It was ten minutes after ten. Beans and Bull had just finished their shift at the furnaces, hurried to steerage to grab Beans' seabag, and then scuttled furtively down the stairs to the cargo hold, the music from the ball faintly following them until they reached the bottom of the ship.

Bull reached into the seabag and brought out a kerosene lantern and lit it. Both men breathed a sigh of relief; the cargo hold was spooky in the wet, subterranean darkness. Now Bull held the lantern high to look at the worn, greasy piece of paper in his hand. "It's gonna take a while to do this right, so don't bug me with all your fool questions. Just do what I say, all right? I gotta think."

Beans was awed by this and obediently kept quiet.

"Now, Beans, you go get them four boxes of nails—oh no, I better go with you," Bull amended hastily. He dropped the seabag at the still-padlocked door of the crew quarters and started threading his way down the packed cargo hold.

Together they picked their way cautiously, Bull holding the lantern high in the clammy darkness. He was always more than a little jumpy in the cargo hold. The sounds of the sea were underwater mysteries here, echoing the murky songs of fish and sirens. Bull was determined to hurry as fast as he could to get this part of the plan over with.

"Here! Pick up these boxes. We gotta get four of 'em to the door of the quarters." He hefted two three-by-four-by-six-foot boxes of Duvall's sixteen-penny nails and staggered back toward the crew quarters' door, the lantern teetering precariously on top of his load.

"Wait, Bull!" Beans cried. "It's dark, an' I'm scairt!"

"Grab two o' them boxes and follow me," Bull gasped. Beans hefted two of the boxes. A sharp pain immediately shot across his back, but still he shuffled as fast as he could to get into the flickering amber light that surrounded Bull.

Dropping the boxes at the door with relief, Bull looked again at the paper in his hand. "Number two: Unlock the door. Put the padlock and key in your pocket." Sybil had written idiotically simple instructions on the piece of paper Bull held.

"Wisht I could read," Beans said enviously.

"Well, I cain't read too good," Bull admitted as he squinted at the paper. "But I just about got this here list mem'rized, like Sybil said. Should have," he added darkly. "She read it to me about a hunnert times, like I'm dumb or somethin'. And she drew me these little pitchers, just in case. Here, heft these here boxes inside." Bull obediently pocketed the "413" padlock and key and swung open the heavy door; then the two pulled the crates of nails and the seabag in after them.

They were faced with rows and rows of the blandly identical coffinlike boxes they had seen being loaded onto the ship. Beans looked around vacantly. He had little understanding of what they were doing and no conception of the problems involved.

But Bull did. He swung the door securely shut behind them and raised the lantern to study the paper again for long minutes. Beans got bored and went to sit on one of the boxes, kicking his feet and humming. Bull turned the paper upside down, squinted up at the room, turned the paper sideways, searched the room

again, and went on doing this for quite a while. Beans thought
Bull looked real smart.

"All right," Bull finally said, "I think I got it. First box oughtta
be over here. See? It's marked in red." Bull generously let Beans
look at the paper as they walked down a long row of boxes stacked
three high on both sides. On the paper Beans saw a bunch of big
squares, some of them with two smaller squares inside of them.
Each square was marked with unintelligible signs, and four of
the small squares inside the big squares were circled in broad red
ink strokes.

Down at the bottom of the paper was a series of tiny, meticulous pictures and arrows that interested Beans. As he scrutinized them carefully, a light began to dawn; Miss Sybil had
illustrated the instructions she had written, and Beans actually
understood some of the pictures, comprehending the actions
drawn. *Almost like readin'!* he thought to himself triumphantly.
He nodded sagely at the paper as Bull began to heave one of the
coffinlike boxes off the top of a stack of three. "Gimme a hand
here, wouldja? This thing's heavy," Bull grunted, and Beans hurriedly grabbed the box. They banged it down, then did the same
with the second box.

"This better be it," Bull muttered as he reached into the seabag and pulled out a crowbar. Roughly and impatiently he started
prying off the top. Beans stood behind, holding his breath. He
had no idea what was in the boxes, but it was fun to be getting
into them. Bull pushed back the top of the box and Beans leaned
over eagerly.

Inside were two smaller boxes. They, too, were absent of
markings. "Where's that piece o' paper, Beans?" Bull demanded,
and Beans shoved it into his hand, gazing at the two unremarkable boxes with disappointment in his blue eyes. Bull took one
look at the paper and began to pry the top off the crate on the
left. It popped off unexpectedly, and both men drew long gasps
of breath.

Gold!

The box was full of five-dollar gold pieces that gleamed so brightly they seemed to dim the lantern's light. For long moments Bull and Beans stared at the box with identical expressions of awe. The room was so quiet they heard the soft hiss of the gas burning in the lantern.

Anything I want! Bull thought, and licked his thick lips.

"Purtiest thing I ever did see," Beans whispered in wonder.

"We gotta get to work," Bull said. "Go get one of them boxes of nails, Beans." Bull spoke absently; he couldn't take his eyes off the gleaming vision before him.

Obediently Beans went and fetched the box. "Now, Beans," Bull said with superiority as he tore his eyes away from the box of gold, "I'm gonna explain to you what we gotta do. It's gonna be hard, but unless you get it, and get it right, I'm gonna have to do it all by myself and that'll take too long. You got it?"

Beans nodded earnestly. "I got it, Bull. I can do it. I'll help you."

"Here." Bull reached into Beans' seabag—which he had carefully packed with the items Sybil had specified—pulled out a large brass chamberpot and set it down firmly in front of Beans.

Beans looked at his companion doubtfully. "But, Bull, I don't gotta—"

"Just shut up, Beans," Bull growled. He had wondered for a long time if Sybil Warfield had gone insane when she told him over and over again to take the chamberpot, and then she had lost her temper several times trying to explain to him why he had to clean a chamberpot and haul it down here. He had finally begrudgingly decided to do as she told him. Now he suddenly understood what it was for, but he was still a little embarrassed as Beans looked at him so reproachfully.

"Just—shut up," he repeated, scowling. "This is what we gotta do, and you listen good. We gotta take them nails outta that box there, see? Put 'em into this empty—" Bull pointed.

"Chamberpot," Beans said mournfully.

"Then we gotta pour all the gold outta this box"—Bull pointed to the gold, then to the nail crate—"into that empty nail box."

"Yeah . . ." Beans said hesitantly. "An' then we—"

"Pour all the nails outta the—pot—into the gold box," Bull said with patience.

"I git it!" Beans shouted.

"Be quiet, Beans!" Bull hissed. "I know everybody's up there dancin', but we still don't wanna make too much noise. Remember, we don't want nobody to know we're doing this. Besides," he sighed heavily, "that ain't all we gotta do."

"It ain't?" Beans whispered.

"Nope," Bull said reluctantly, "we gotta do one more thing. We gotta cover the top of the gold with nails and cover the top of the nails with gold."

"Huh?" Beans said.

"Yeah, see, we gotta leave this here box here, and that there box out there, and this here box has gotta look like gold, and that there box has gotta look like nails," Bull explained, stabbing a black forefinger back and forth at the boxes.

"Hey—wait a minute—wait a minute—" Beans said, almost gasping with effort, his brow furrowed. Bull ignored him and started manhandling the crate of nails to empty it into the hated chamberpot. Grunting with the effort, he glared up at Beans, but Beans was staring off into space with a fervent blank gaze, gasping and gaping. "I git it! It's like them pitchers Miss Sybil drew! I really unnerstan', Bull!" he finally whispered laboriously, a broad white grin splitting his coal-blackened face.

"Good," Bull grunted, "'cause we gotta do this three times, and I don't wanna have to explain it to you every time. Help me, wouldja, Beans?"

Together the two men finished pouring the nails and gold back and forth. The complicated maneuvers fascinated Beans and delighted him because he actually understood what they were doing. He would have been happy to do it all night long.

Twice more they went to a box after Bull studied the diagram for a few minutes. The third time, they popped open one of the coffinlike boxes and looked in expectantly; again the contents took their breath away. This time, however, it wasn't the gleam of gold that did it. The box was full of guns—ominous-looking rifles stacked haphazardly right up to the rim.

"Boy oh boy oh boy oh—" Beans breathed. "Did we git the wrong box this time!" Eyes wide, he hurriedly began putting the top back on the crate.

Bull cursed loudly, ignoring Beans' shushes. "We better get the right one this time. It's gettin' late." Impatiently he searched the paper again and finally realized they did have the right stack of boxes; the one holding the gold was the one on top, not the second one under it. Quickly they replaced the top of the crate and looked into the one that had been sitting on top of it.

"Lemme do it by myself this time, Bull," Beans said proudly, "since I unnerstand how to do it, an' all. Wisht I could git a job doin' this all the time."

Bull rolled his eyes. "Beans, you won't hafta get a job ever again after we get to Panama. Go ahead and do it all by yourself," he said indulgently. "You're gettin' pretty good at it, an' I'm thinking about something on this here paper. . . ." While Beans expertly shuffled nails and gold, Bull looked at the paper for a while, then gazed speculatively at the other box beside the box of gold, chewing on his lower lip.

When Beans had finishing nailing the tops back on the crates, Bull said, "Looky here at the paper, Beans. Mr. Littlejohn wrote a G on these here four boxes we got into, right?"

"Yeah, right, a G's what I thought," Beans agreed bravely.

"And on that other box there, the one fulla guns, he wrote a F," Bull went on, obviously talking to himself.

"*Gun* starts with a F?" Beans asked in astonishment. "Seems like that'd make it F-un. . . ."

"No, ninny, *F* stands for—" A long silence ensued while Bull's mouth moved as he struggled to read the paper. Finally he gave up, but he didn't want Beans to know he couldn't read it. "*Fire,* a-course, since guns fire, y'know."

Beans nodded, "Yep. *F* stands for guns."

"And that there box—" Bull craftily looked down at the other innocent-looking crate beside the one Beans had just filled with nails and topped with gold. "That there box is labeled with a *D*.

"A *D*," Beans echoed.

"Yep. And Beans, you know what that stands for?" Beans opened his mouth to answer, but Bull ignored him. "Diamonds!"

"You think?" Beans asked eagerly.

Bull didn't answer; he was already prying off the top of the other crate, and he was hurrying. Inside, buried in a thick bed of wood shavings, was one small zinc can. Bull and Beans looked blankly at it, then at each other.

Bull picked up the can and turned it round and round. It was smooth, with no pry-off top; it would have to be opened with some kind of sharp tool. Impatiently, Bull looked at Sybil's watch—she had reluctantly loaned it to him for this job—and swore for a few minutes while Beans waited patiently. Finally he said, "Let's just stick this can in your seabag. We'll get it open later."

"But, Bull, are we gonna leave this here box empty? I don't think Miss Sybil would like that," Beans warned. Since he had grasped the concept of how they were covering their tracks, he felt like an expert.

"Miss Sybil ain't gonna know nothin' about this here can o' diamonds! You understand, Beans? Nothin'!"

"But, Bull, that ain't fair!" Beans protested.

"You don't worry about that, Beans," Bull snarled. "Her Majesty's gettin' two boxes of gold, and me and you are gettin' one apiece. I don't know how that skinny woman thinks she's gonna haul around two boxes like this anyways! Me and you are gonna have all we can carry when we get to Panama! Anyways, she's gonna have more gold than us, so we can have the diamonds."

Beans picked up the dully gleaming can and peered at it carefully, then shook it hard. "I don't hear nothin' that sounds like diamonds, Bull. You sure it's diamonds? It sounds like water, or somethin'."

"That's prob'ly diamond packin'," Bull said disdainfully.

"Oh yeah? Well, diamond packin' sure does stink." Beans set the can back down with a disgusted thump. "And what are we gonna do 'bout that empty box?"

"Just—just—put that stinkin' chamberpot in here," Bull said with inspiration, "and cover it up real good with the wood shavin's, just so's some of the metal shines through. That'll be good enough."

"All right, Bull," Beans sighed. He was disappointed that *he* hadn't had this brilliant idea.

"And we'll just stick this can in your sea chest 'til we get to Panama next week," Bull said indulgently. He was feeling particularly generous; besides, if somebody did find out that the cargo hold had been robbed—well, that would just be too bad. Bull would miss Beans when he got arrested.

"Oh, thanks, Bull!" Beans said gratefully.

The two men finished all their little chores, tidied up the room, and repacked their seabag. Then they took the boxes of nails—now filled mostly with gold—and replaced them just as they had found them in the cargo hold. Standing at the doorway of the crew quarters, Bull looked around with satisfaction. The mute coffinlike boxes looked exactly the same as when he and Beans had come in two hours ago. With great deliberation he took a padlock out of the seabag, squinted at it one more time to make sure that it was stamped "433," nodded, and with a click that sounded loud and final, locked the door to the crew quarters.

"We did it, Beans!" Bull said triumphantly as they left the cargo hold. "And we did good!"

They did good, except for one thing. The *D* did not stand for diamonds. It stood for DuPont, the major manufacturer of gunpowder in America. And the can in Beans' seabag certainly didn't have diamonds in it; it didn't even have gunpowder. It contained a thick, oozing oil, a new chemical that only a handful of chemists in the world dared experiment with, among them Alfred Nobel and LaMott DuPont. They called it nitroglycerin.

PART THREE

Shadow of the Almighty

He that dwelleth in the secret place of the most High shall abide under the shadow of the Almighty.

Psalm 91:1

12

A Matter of Fists

"The Iron Man and the Bull!"

Jeff Withers jumped up on the fantail and raised a glass of rich red wine as he yelled exultantly to the crowd of men milling around on the promenade deck. Shouts of agreement and acclamation followed, and Jeff tossed off the glass of wine as if it were cool spring water, licking his lips with appreciation.

Withers had found himself in a gambler's dream scene: men with money, restless and bored, and two opponents straining at the bit to fight. And no matter who stood or fell, Jeffrey Withers, for the first time in his life, was a sure winner; he had "promoted" the fight and would therefore take a generous cut from both of the fighters' cuts. At the last minute, in addition, he had placed an inordinately large bet with Powell Drake, and he was confident his man would win.

It was about time for the fighters to appear, and Jeff saw with a slight shock that Georgia Jakes and Sybil Warfield had joined the rowdy crowd of male passengers, ship's officers, seamen, stokers, stewards, and cooks, and that Dr. Duvall was also standing on the deck. Withers thought that probably every man on board the *Continental* was on the promenade deck that morning. But he had not expected to see any of Mercer's Belles; fighting was considered much too strenuous and vulgar a sport for ladies.

Well, I guess the lady doctor has to be here in case of injuries, he mused as he cupped his hands around a match and touched it to the end of one of his slim cigars. *And I guess I shouldn't be surprised at those other two by now.* He watched the women surreptitiously for a moment. Most of the men hadn't noticed them yet; they had glided onto the deck from the Ladies' Salon and seated themselves in two nearby deck chairs. *Strange pair,* Jeff thought with mild curiosity. *The Warfield woman's as tense as a dude gambler in short sleeves, and her southern cohort's as loose as a hurdy-gurdy girl on Saturday night.*

The fight was set to take place in a wide open space between the salons, directly in front of the fantail. The deckhands had created a ring for the fight—a square outlined by three strands of rope. Most of the chairs had been removed so the spectators had to stand, but no one complained; in fact, a holiday mood prevailed as the crowd milled around talking about the fight.

Cheney stood outside the Ladies' Salon, uncomfortable with the men's club atmosphere and disgusted with the whole thing; and when the two fighters came on deck, she almost went below to her stateroom. But she did not go, knowing that she had a personal stake in the affair. Shiloh was her nurse, and as she watched him bend and slip through the ropes, she thought, *Why couldn't I have found a nice young lady named Jane for a nurse? I feel like a fool half the time with him!* It was a feeling she'd struggled with since the first moment she'd seen the big man, and wearily realized it was a problem that would not go away.

A sudden cheer went up—mostly from the crew—and Cheney saw Bull Lynch bend through the ropes and step into the ring. He was barefoot and stripped to the waist, wearing a pair of black trousers cut off just above the knee. His grin pulled his lips back against his big teeth, a gapped half-moon against an olive-dark skin faintly shining with sweat. He raised his hands in a gesture of victory, and the motion caused the thick muscles in his back and chest to swell into prominence. Cheney had never seen such massive development on a man; his short neck joined into huge shoulders and arms.

Bull was pleased with himself and as Shiloh entered the ring, Lynch tilted his head back to study his opponent the way a butcher might measure an ox for a slaughterhouse sledging. His feral enjoyment sent a shiver down Cheney's spine.

The ship's third officer, a cheerful young redhead named O'Malley, stepped into the ring and held up his hands for silence, then announced, "For your entertainment this morning, we have arranged a sporting event—a boxing match. The rules will be simple. A knockdown constitutes a round. After each round the fighters will come together again in the center of the ring. If one of the fighters cannot come to scratch, he will be considered the loser. There will be no butting, kicking, biting, or gouging."

Cheney suddenly realized the import of what O'Malley was saying: the two men would fight until one of them was beaten into total unconsciousness! *Why, the whole point of this thing is to inflict a brain concussion!* She shook her head with revulsion—and some fear—for the bulky form of Bull Lynch was terrifying. His long, heavy arms gave him the look of a gorilla, and the sheer massiveness of the man made it evident where he got his nickname of "Bull"!

"In this corner," O'Malley called out, "at two hundred and twenty-nine pounds, we have Bull Lynch. In the other corner, at one hundred and ninety-two pounds, his opponent, Shiloh Irons. Gentlemen, come up!"

The two men came together as O'Malley slipped aside. Shiloh, when contrasted with Lynch, looked almost frail. But this first impression was deceptive, for Cheney's practiced eye took in the symmetry of the tall man. He, too, was barefoot and stripped to the waist, wearing a pair of thin cotton trousers. And there was not an ounce of surplus fat on Shiloh Irons' body. He was a man of loose and rough and durable parts, built like a machine intended for hard usage. He was long of arm and meaty of leg, with a chest that swelled and shoulders that had thick pads of muscle.

If Lynch reminded people of a bull, Shiloh Irons gave the impression of a great cat—clearly a fair match for the heavier man. But Cheney was staring at the raw-looking scar on Shiloh's right arm, wondering if it would take the stress of the fight. She knew of cases when a wound such as this had been reinjured and the results had been worse than the original injury.

Cheney had no more time to speculate, for Bull Lynch had thrown himself toward his opponent with a roar. It was a trick the stoker often used; he had discovered that the sudden shout would disconcert some men. But the ploy didn't work, for Shiloh merely grinned and turned to one side, allowing the huge form of Lynch to sail by. He made no attempt to hit Lynch, merely turned to keep his steady gaze on the other man as he whirled and came roaring in again.

This time the sheer animal strength of Bull's rush prevailed, and Shiloh could not avoid all the blows thrown at him. He parried most of them, but a thundering right caught him in the chest, and the force of it drove him back, sprawling onto the deck. A roar went up from Bull's supporters, but Shiloh was not seriously hurt. O'Malley announced, "The end of round one," and the two men stepped forward as soon as Shiloh rose to his feet.

"Next time it'll be your pretty face," Bull grinned.

As soon as the second round began, O'Malley stepped back, and Bull moved forward in a flat-footed fashion, throwing blows at Shiloh, but few of them landed. Shiloh was moving lightly, up on the balls of his feet; he bobbed and weaved, catching blows with his fists. Around and around the square they went, and finally Bull Lynch stopped and yelled, "Why don't you fight, you yellow—!"

It was the moment Shiloh had been waiting for. Planting his feet firmly, he threw a hard left hand directly into Lynch's mouth. The force of that blow began in Shiloh's right foot, ran up his leg and through his torso. The left fist shot out, connecting with Bull's mouth at the exact moment that Shiloh's arm was fully extended—and the result was an explosion! It was the blow of a professional fighter, delivered with all the experience of hundreds of fights. If the blow arrives a fraction short, the energy of the blow is dissipated. If it arrives too soon, it becomes a push. But this blow landed with all one hundred and ninety-two pounds of solid bone and muscle behind it. It was like being struck by a driving timber.

Lynch's head was driven back with the force of the blow, and then he crashed to the deck. A groan went up from his supporters, a cheer from the friends of Shiloh. Cheney shivered at the violence but thought, *Thank God it's over—and he didn't get hurt!* She could not imagine any man getting up after that sort of blow—but she failed to grasp the toughness of Bull Lynch.

The referee waited, his eyes carefully studying the fallen fighter. He had never seen a man take a harder blow, and he was as surprised as the rest of the crowd when Lynch rolled over and slowly crawled to his feet. "Round three," O'Malley announced as Lynch staggered to the center of the ring.

Shiloh thought, *He can take a punch. I'll have to be careful.* His right arm was throbbing from parrying blows, and he knew he would not be able to use it much. This bothered him, for it was with that right hand that he'd built his reputation as a fighter. Now, as the burly form of Lynch lumbered toward him, he backed away. He'd have to depend on speed and his left hand if he wanted to avoid being beaten senseless.

Lynch should have been unconscious on the floor. But he was a ferocious brute with bones like a grizzly's and an oxlike vitality. All his victories had come from this thick shield of bone and muscle, an insensitivity to injury. He was alive and stung and dangerous as he advanced toward Shiloh. "I'll kill you, Irons!" he muttered vehemently, his huge maul-like fists raised, ready to strike.

The fight went on for what seemed like hours to Cheney. Sometimes it was Lynch who was down, but the brute force of the stoker could not be denied, and Shiloh took punishment as well, being knocked off his feet several times. As Cheney watched, tense and rigid, she twisted her handkerchief to shreds and her jaw grew sore from clamping her teeth. *Why don't they stop it?* she thought, but she knew the fight wouldn't end until one man was beaten to a pulp.

Asa Mercer, too, was watching the scene with clenched jaw. He had attended a bullfight once, in Mexico, and what he was seeing reminded him of that spectacle—which he'd hated thoroughly. The bullfight had been a test of skill, he remembered, with the slim matador dressed in silk pitted against a massive bull. The matador had escaped charge after charge of the murderous horns by turning his body at the last possible instant, letting the tips sometimes graze his clothing. And it was like this with Shiloh and Lynch; Irons repeatedly survived disaster by moving his head slightly and allowing the killing fists of Lynch to slide by, sometimes scraping his skin, but never delivering the killing blow.

But the bull got him in the end, Mercer remembered, and he had a sudden, sickening vision of the bull's horn catching the slender matador in the groin and tossing him high into the air. Now as he watched he wanted to turn away, for he could see that both men were tiring. Sooner or later, Bull Lynch was sure to catch Shiloh Irons with a killing blow and turn him into a helpless victim to be chopped to bits.

Shiloh was feeling desperate, for he knew that he could not continue to stave off the rushes of the brute in front of him. *Got to nail him!* he thought numbly, and at that moment he tried a desperate strategy; he allowed one of Lynch's thundering rights to catch him high on the head. The blow was a disaster running down his spine, and it sent a roar through his head. Shiloh's eyes lost focus for an instant, and he stood there helpless.

Cheney uttered a brief wordless cry of fear; she could see that Shiloh was out on his feet. Others in the crowd groaned or cheered, depending on their favorite, and Captain Weldon muttered to the purser, "Mud and murder—he's got the lad!"

But Shiloh's head cleared just as Lynch came in, his bloody face wreathed in a grin of victory. He came on slowly now, seeing that at last he had a still target. Deliberately he planted his feet, drew back his right hand, and took dead aim at the face of his victim. He grunted as he threw himself forward—but the vicious blow was never delivered.

Shiloh had let Lynch set himself. But then, as the big man moved forward, Shiloh launched a terrible blow with his *right* hand. It was the first time he had used that hand, and Lynch was caught completely off guard, having decided that Shiloh could not use it.

Now the full force of the right caught Lynch coming in—which is what every fighter wants. *Get your man coming in,* Shiloh's old trainer had insisted, *and you'll nail him! You'll have your own weight—and his, too—when you hit him!*

The thundering right caught Lynch square in the mouth, striking a split second before his own blow landed. It drove his head back once more; he fell to the deck and lay still except for a twitching in his legs.

Shiloh was trembling with weariness, and the hurts probed at his body as he watched dully. *If he gets up—I'm whipped,* he thought. But Lynch didn't get up. When O'Malley came to the center of the ring, he took one look at the unconscious man, then smiled. "And the winner is—Shiloh Irons!"

Shiloh managed to move, but it was all he could do to get through the ropes. He was vaguely aware that hands were pounding his shoulders, but he could not make out the words that were shouted in his ear. Shrugging off the hands, he staggered out of the ring and moved almost blindly down the stairwell and along the corridor to his stateroom. Opening the door with swollen hands, he entered and slammed it with his foot—then fell across the bed. Real pain hit him then, and he knew he'd reinjured his right arm, but he could not move to stop the blood as it soaked the bedding. His chest was heaving deeply; he closed his eyes against the pain—and everything went black.

"Get off my foot, you great lout!"

"That was his head, dummy!"

"Grab his hand—I think I stepped on it!"

The four men carrying Bull Lynch to the infirmary were having a hard time of it, and Cheney winced at the thumping and crashing sounds behind her as they slowly made their way down the narrow stairwell. Finally they reached the infirmary and dumped Bull unceremoniously onto one of the narrow bunks. Anxiously Cheney lifted one of his swollen eyelids to show solid white. *Still unconscious—I hope Shiloh didn't put him into a coma.*

Abruptly Cheney straightened and looked around the infirmary. She had assumed that Shiloh would be here, cleaning and bandaging the cuts and scrapes on his face. With a start of apprehension she hurried across to the door that opened onto Shiloh's room, telling the men, "Please wait for just a minute—" She knocked loudly on the door, calling, "Shiloh? Are you all right?" Only silence answered her. Nervously Cheney fumbled with her keys and opened the door.

Shiloh lay face down on the bottom bunk, his long legs hanging awkwardly over the side. Cheney hurried over to the bed and saw a wide stain of blood under his right arm, joining a smaller stain under his face. Around the angry scar on his right arm the skin was a sickly deep blue color, and in two places the skin had split. Both painfully torn places were steadily seeping dark red blood.

"Oh no!" Cheney cried involuntarily, then steadied herself and hurried back into the infirmary. Mercer, Beans Lowery, and the two stout seamen who had carried Bull down from the promenade deck were standing at the door staring inside.

Cheney grabbed a thick white towel from a small table and ordered brusquely, "Come and bring Shiloh into the infirmary right now!"

The men followed her, picked up Shiloh and struggled through the door with his long form, and placed him on the empty bunk. His legs hung off the end, and for some reason this worried Cheney terribly. She frantically looked around the room for some way to prop up his feet. Suddenly she became aware of the men staring at her curiously, and she said, "Thank you—now please leave."

Hastily they beat a retreat, except for Mercer, who loitered by the door as Cheney quickly pulled a clean, white bibbed apron over her head and tied it behind her back. "Thank you, Mr. Mercer, for standing up for me with Captain Weldon. I just couldn't let them take Lynch back to his bunk below." Captain Weldon was one of the men who believed there was something scandalous about female doctors treating male patients.

"Of course you couldn't, Dr. Duvall," Mercer said. "You wouldn't be a good doctor if you didn't feel like that. Say, you could use some help. Can I get one of the women for you?"

"I guess not." Cheney loosened the towel on Shiloh's arm and cast a worried glance at the still form of Bull Lynch. "The only one I can think of is Lydia, but with her hands—"

"Nonsense," a businesslike voice sounded behind Mercer. "I thought you might need a pair of steady hands, Dr. Duvall, and I'll be glad to help."

Mercer turned with relief to face Martha Jane Terrell, who marched into the room, found and donned a clean apron.

Stony had entered the infirmary with his mother and now observed with relish, "Oooh! They're all bloody!"

"Stony, come out here; we'll go have our lunch." Powell Drake stood at the doorway. He was holding Kelvey, who was also craning her neck to look curiously at the two battered men.

"That would be a help, Mr. Drake," Martha Jane said with a warm smile as she shut the door behind them. Then she looked at Cheney, who had cushioned Shiloh's arm with clean towels and was gathering bandages, carbolic acid, and scissors. "I don't know much about nursing, but I can follow instructions, Dr. Duvall."

Cheney looked up and the slight stammer in her voice revealed the tension inside her. "I—I know what to do, Mrs. Terrell, but I'm a l-little flustered."

Martha Jane said gently, "Why don't you just tell me how they're hurt—then what I can to do help? And why don't you call me Martha Jane?"

Cheney was steadied by the calmness of the other woman and spoke with more confidence. "Lynch is unconscious and may be in a coma. We'll have to watch him very closely. He seems to be bleeding from one ear, and that can be very serious. If he wakes up but doesn't open his eyes, we need to try to rouse him. Ask him if he has any bad pain in his head. Right now, you can clean him up. Put this on every single cut."

Wrinkling her nose at the brown bottle that Cheney thrust out to her, Martha Jane asked, "What is it?"

"Carbolic acid. Use it to clean all the cuts—every place the skin is open. He'll get cold while you're doing it, so work as fast as you can. And put another blanket around him."

Obediently Martha Jane started applying the carbolic acid to the cuts and scrapes on Lynch's swollen face. Cheney turned her attention to Shiloh's arm, which was still bleeding. Placing her hand to his forehead, she found it was clammy and cool. *He's in shock,* she thought, and cast a worried glance at his still-bare, dangling feet while continuing to work on his arm.

Martha Jane picked up on the gesture. "Well, Mr. Lynch's skin is warm and dry." She laid down the carbolic acid and glanced around the room. She crossed the room to where the medical supplies were stored, untied one of the casks of quinine water and shoved it along the floor to the foot of Shiloh's bunk. Placing a pillow on it, she lifted Shiloh's bare feet one by one and placed them gently on top of the cask. Then she covered his feet with an extra towel and said, "That ought to do it."

"Thank you, Martha Jane," Cheney said, ducking her head and pressing a clean towel to Shiloh's arm.

Martha Jane looked at Cheney curiously. She had never been a woman to pry, but she thought, *Dr. Duvall seems to feel a little more for Shiloh than she does for most patients—but she sure doesn't want anyone to notice it!* Picking up the brown bottle again, her delicate nose wrinkled as she began to clean the blood from around Lynch's ear. . . .

Someone's groaning. Make them stop.

Stirring a little, Shiloh realized that the groans were coming from his throat, and he mentally groped around until he found out how to stop them. *Open my eyes. Need to see—won't open—what's the matter with them?*

He reached up in dreamy slow motion, and vaguely, from somewhere far off, the pain signals began to make noise. Shiloh groggily decided that when they got closer and louder, he was going to wake up, and it was going to hurt. Meanwhile, his hands had reached his face, but instead of delicately tracing his eyelids, he had soundly bashed himself in the mouth with the sore lumps at the ends of his arms. Laboriously he decided to put his arms back down.

"Be still," the red angel said softly.

Red angel? Shiloh thought in muddy confusion. *Who's that?*

Then he realized that in his mind's blurry eye, the voice belonged to a red angel because she was red-warm, not blue-cool, with hands and voice that made Shiloh see a bed of glowing coals in a campfire and hair that glowed like fire in the lantern light. . . .

"Drink this, Shiloh. Here, I'll help you."

"Laudanum . . ."

"Shhh, go to sleep now."

Slowly the warm red voice faded, the warm red liquid went down to his belly, and the warm red mist covered him like a heavy blanket as he drifted away. . . .

13

Havana

With identical weary sighs, Cheney and Martha Jane sank into two deck chaises on the port side of the ship, facing the eastern sea. A round orange halo heralded sunrise on the horizon. The wind was a strange mixture of cool, wet night air and warm, tropical day breeze, each separate and distinct, as was the light. Bright coral fingers of dawn pushed back the lingering darkness, and the sea began to glow with a rich azure hue.

"What a night!" Martha Jane exclaimed. "You can have this job back! I'd rather sew shrouds than be a nurse!"

"Well, I think you're a wonderful nurse," Cheney said gratefully.

"Nurse? Baby-sitter, you mean! Hmph! Worrying that that big ox might have brain damage—or a concussion! He doesn't have sense enough to have either!" Martha Jane's dark hair was mussed, and tiny sea droplets in the air made the loose wisps around her face curl becomingly.

"Martha Jane!" Cheney protested. "You know it scared both of us, with his ear bleeding like that! It was so bad, I was afraid everything in his head was coming out his ear!"

"In that case, there wouldn't have been anything coming out his ears," Martha Jane retorted with relish. "But yes, I admit I was relieved to see that Shiloh had only just about torn Bull Lynch's ear off instead."

Bull's right ear was almost split horizontally, and this had caused the bleeding that had worried Cheney. But that had turned out to be his worst injury—and one he had loudly and profanely complained about when he regained consciousness. His problem was not so much with the pain—Bull seemed to feel none after he had been out cold for several hours—but with the fact that the ear had swollen hideously and looked like a foreign object stuck on the side of his head.

Both women's eyes lit with appreciation as the sun appeared and quickly became a benevolent yellow globe in the sky. They couldn't see Havana yet, but they knew they must be close because the regular paddle-wheel heartbeat of the ship had slowed into a recognizable rhythm instead of an ever-present low roar. Cheney and Martha Jane sat in companionable silence, enjoying the warm welcome of the morning.

After a while, Martha Jane idly remarked, "I assume Shiloh is going to be all right, since you felt that we could leave him."

"Yes," Cheney sighed, "he's going to be all right, even though he looks a mess. It's a miracle he didn't go into complete shock from the beating he took and the hemorrhages on his arm. And unlike every patient I've ever seen, he actually seemed to improve during the night. Most sick or injured people are worse at night . . ."

Cheney's voice trailed off as she lapsed into a deep reverie. *He's been sleeping soundly for several hours,* she considered. *And that means he's going to want to get up today—and go stir something up in Havana, I imagine! How in the world am I going to keep him in—?*

"You were going to let me stay in bed all day, weren't you?" a muffled voice accused. "It's almost eight o'clock! Morning, ladies!" Shiloh appeared beside their deck chairs and squinted down at them.

His voice was muffled because his lips were swollen. One punch had driven his teeth through his bottom lip, producing a nasty puncture wound. A wide, raw gash marred his left cheekbone. He was squinting, not from the sun, but because of the conditions of his eyes. His left eye was only slightly swollen and bruised, but his right eye would not open at all; it was a round blue mound that stuck out farther than his forehead and the cheekbone below. Shiloh's right arm bulged above the tight bandage, and he was moving with painstaking deliberation.

"Shiloh," Cheney demanded sternly but with no real hope of success, "go back to bed!"

"And miss a beautiful morning in beautiful Havana?" He gestured grandly toward the now-visible land, then winced and grabbed his side.

"Thought so," Cheney said succinctly. "Ribs broken."

"Not broke," Shiloh drawled, "just bruised. And you bandaged me up real good, Doc! Except for my arm, which looks like a fat sausage."

"Yes, it does, but I can't help that!" Cheney retorted crossly. "You burst it open, and it hemorrhaged worse last night than when you got stabbed!"

"You got stabbed?" Martha Jane asked with interest.

"Yes, ma'am," Shiloh answered with relish. "Me and this guy were in an alley, see, and—"

"Where's Bull?" Cheney interrupted hastily.

"Wolfing down three breakfasts in the galley," a quiet voice answered. The young steward walked up to the table between Martha Jane's and Cheney's chairs and set down a large silver tray with a fitted silver cover.

"Oh, thank you, Joed!" Cheney exclaimed as the steward lifted the large silver top. The tray held an ornate silver tea service, heavy enough to stay balanced in this mild sea, and thick pottery mugs instead of china teacups. The spicy scent of tea wafted up as the steward deftly poured for Cheney, Martha Jane, and Shiloh, then proceeded to fix each cup as they liked their tea. Rich, buttery croissants lay on a small platter beside the teapot.

"You're welcome, ma'am. And it's Joel," the steward answered as he walked back toward the galley.

Rather abruptly Shiloh folded himself into a chaise beside Cheney. He gratefully sipped a cup of the steaming tea but refused a croissant. Cheney watched him with critical eyes. His swollen face had grown a shade paler, and the fact that he had stopped his ceaseless banter set off warning bells in Cheney's mind. *He's just like a child,* she thought dryly. *If he gets quiet, something's wrong.*

For some time the three watched as the ship moved steadily closer to Havana. Cheney and Martha Jane munched hungrily on the flaky pastries and talked idly about the passengers who began to appear, and about shopping in Havana (although this was mostly Cheney's subject), and about how wonderful it was to see and hear the raucous sea gulls after nineteen days at sea. All the while, Shiloh remained quiet and grew paler.

Jeff Withers appeared on deck, headed for the dining room. Shiloh hailed him and walked cautiously to meet him a few steps off. After a few exchanged words, Withers handed Shiloh a small handful of bills. When the two men parted, Withers slapped Shiloh lightly on the back. Cheney noted that Shiloh staggered slightly as he made his way back to the deck chair and lowered himself painfully into it. A muscle in his jaw worked convulsively, and Cheney realized how ill he was actually feeling.

"You're sick, aren't you?" she demanded.

Wordlessly and reluctantly, Shiloh nodded.

"That's *it,*" Cheney announced firmly as she rose and took Shiloh's left arm. "You're going back to bed right now. No nonsense, no jokes, no Iron Man. I'm the doctor, and I mean *now!*"

Shiloh remained still, swallowed hard, and muttered, "Need to talk to Mrs. Terrell first. Would you excuse us, please?"

Martha Jane looked at him curiously.

"No," Cheney answered, and politely but insistently pulled on his arm. She felt it tremble a bit in her hands.

For a few moments Shiloh sat staring blankly at the bluish-purple haze of Havana. Then with jerky movements he reached into his pocket and drew out the money Withers had given him. He counted out some of the bills, laboriously stood up, and placed them into Martha Jane's lap. "Not for you," he mumbled with some effort. Obviously he was choking back nausea by sheer will. "For the younguns. Side deal I made with Bull."

Martha Jane's eyes widened and she hastily picked up the money and held it out to Shiloh. "No! I mean, thank you, but—"

Cheney was surprised and curious, but concern for Shiloh took precedence. "Not now, Martha Jane. Just take the money and spend it on the children. Shiloh can explain later. Right now he's going to bed."

To Cheney's surprise, Shiloh obediently followed her to the infirmary and went straight to bed without further protest. Gratefully Cheney retired to her own stateroom to rest for a while.

She slept soundly and dreamlessly for what seemed like just a few hours. When she awoke, however, she found to her exasperation that Shiloh was gone, and only then did she realize that the ship's engines were silent. The S.S. *Continental* was in Havana—and so was Shiloh, most likely. Cheney decided to go ashore.

She had almost finished dressing when someone knocked on her door, and Cheney called out impatiently, "Who is it?"

"It's Joed, ma'am," the steward called softly. "Mr. Irons said you'd be awake by now, so it'd be all right to disturb you and give you a message. And to be sure and bring you a cup of coffee."

With a half-smile Cheney opened the door to Joed, who stood outside obediently holding a cup of strong, hot brew. "Thank you, Joed. How was Shiloh? *Where* is Shiloh?"

Joed recited the message in a singsong voice that told Cheney he was giving it word for word. "Mr. Irons feels fine, and he's gone ashore. You can't come ashore by yourself, so my brother and I would be happy to escort you. Mr. Irons will be at the Blue Parrot if you would like to speak to him."

"Yes, I *would* like to speak to him," Cheney said with an emphasis that made Joed's eyes widen with apprehension. "And I would be happy to be escorted by you and your brother. I haven't met him yet, you know."

"Sure you have, Dr. Duvall." Joed smiled as he turned to leave. "I'm going to go get him now. We'll meet you at the gangplank." He hurried down the passage, obviously excited to be going ashore. Cheney reflected that it was the first time she had seen the young steward act like a boy of fifteen instead of a grave man of thirty.

Cheney gathered a reticule and parasol and smoothed her hair into a semblance of order. Hurrying up to the promenade deck, she stopped in midstride as she neared the gangplank. Two identical stewards, dressed exactly alike and with the same expectant expressions, watched her. Joed and Joel were twins.

"Did you do this to me on purpose?" Cheney demanded with a smile as she sailed past them. Obediently they fell into step slightly behind her.

"No, ma'am," they answered in a duet.

"Happens a lot," one said with amusement.

"We're hardly ever together on the ship," the other said behind her.

"Just took you a little longer than usual to catch on," one said reflectively.

Cheney sighed and turned to the twin behind her to the left. "Well, we can work this out later. Right now, can you take me to the Blue Parrot, whatever that is?"

"Yes, ma'am," they both answered and moved forward in step to take the lead. Obviously they knew where they were going, and Cheney looked around curiously as the three hurried along.

Havana was a rich mixture of bright colors, wretched squalor, Spanish voices, hundreds of smells, and throngs of people. Here and there Cheney saw groups of Mercer's Belles. Lydia waved to her from a stall displaying a bewildering array of brightly colored shawls, and Cheney shuddered when she thought of the shawl Lydia was likely to pick. Holly Van Buren looked like an idiot riding a tiny burro led by a grinning Spaniard. She held a tiny parasol above her and was complaining loudly that the "mule" was "jouncing her too hard."

Joel and Joed turned down a side street, then another, and the babble of voices and noise of the dockside market faded into the distance. They crossed a wide, shady square, and on the far side Cheney saw Tani DuQuesne come out of a church. On her head she wore a beautiful black lace mantilla instead of the usual brightly colored tignon, and Cheney thought with some surprise that Tani must be Catholic.

With sure steps Joel and Joed led Cheney up a street off of the square, and Cheney began to hear the sounds of singing and guitars. Ahead of them she saw several native men lounging on a wide porch, some standing, some sitting. Outside the crude wooden building hung a sign with a beautifully painted blue parrot on it. The swinging doors unmistakably marked it as a cantina.

Joel and Joed hesitated and turned to look doubtfully at Cheney. With determination Cheney marched up to the swinging doors—much to the amusement of the male patrons outside—and swept through them, leaving them creaking loudly behind her. Once inside, she stopped and narrowed her eyes to adjust to the murky, smoky interior of the saloon.

Ignoring the curious stares of the men gathered around the bar, Cheney stood straight and still until her eyes adjusted. Then she began to search the room—and she soon spotted the tall form of Shiloh Irons standing in front of a round table at the rear of the cantina. His back was to her, and Cheney immediately headed straight for him.

Looks as if I got here just in time for all the fun! she thought with exasperation as she neared the table. Ahead was a tableau that told her the entire story.

Bull Lynch stood on the other side of the table, his back to the rough plank wall, facing Shiloh with a snarl. Even though his face was bruised and swollen, the high color told Cheney that he'd been drinking, probably a lot. Seated at the table on either side of him were Sybil Warfield and Georgia Jakes. Georgia's head lolled slightly—she was obviously drunk—but Sybil's dark eyes burned as she stared up at Shiloh, her lips tightly compressed. Her color was high, too, but she looked alert and determined.

On Cheney's left side, Asa Mercer was shuffling nervously, saying something inaudible, his hands held out in a placating manner. On the other side, Beans Lowery was a shadow on the wall, his blue eyes wide as he stared at his friend.

"Mr. Lynch, there's really no need to be angry," Mercer said nervously. "Mr. Irons is just here to help me escort these ladies back to the ship."

"I'm tired of looking at your ugly face every time I turn around!" Bull snarled at Shiloh, ignoring Mercer.

"I thought you said I was pretty," Shiloh drawled in a dangerously quiet voice. "And I'll be happy to remove my face from your presence, right now. Come along, ladies. Party's over."

Sybil's burning eyes turned toward Bull, who glanced down at her and then back to Shiloh. "Ladies ain't ready yet, Irons. But I'm ready. Know what I'm ready for?"

"Tell me."

"I'm ready"—Bull raised one great ham fist—"to do this"—he shook it menacingly at Shiloh—"to you!" With a grunt he crashed his fist into the rough plank behind him. It made a loud, thudding noise; then a crack appeared as the board splintered across. "Whaddya think about *that,* Mr. Iron Man?"

With a wolfish grin, Shiloh reached across his chest with his left hand, stuck it under his shirt, pulled out a large pistol, and shot the plank beside the one Bull had cracked. The gunshot was like a clap of thunder, and the cantina was deathly silent for long moments. Bull Lynch's muddy eyes grew big, and then he sank wordlessly into a chair.

❧

Martha Jane Terrell bent over the still forms of Stony and Kelvey. Then, seeing that they were breathing deeply in sleep, she turned and moved through the cabin door, closing it softly behind her. Making her way down the corridor, she ascended to the main deck and walked slowly toward the fantail of the ship. Few people were stirring, and she was aware that most of her fellow passengers had gone ashore for a night in Havana. She herself had chosen to stay aboard and enjoy the relative quietness of the vessel. She was a woman who liked silence, and the incessant activity and constant murmur of talk on shipboard had drawn her nerves thin.

Relieved to see no one else at the stern area of the promenade deck, she moved to the rail, placed her hands on it, and took a deep breath, soaking in the peace that lay over the ship. The *Continental* was moored to the dock, and across the way she could see the lights of Havana and hear the distant, tinny sound of music. The moon was a waning crescent, but the stars were bright, and the sea was barred with wavy reflections that moved constantly over the surface. The gentle waves made a sibilant chaffing on the side of the ship, and now, after days at sea, Martha Jane caught the smell of land—of mountains and fresh earth mixed with the exotic odors of the city.

What will I do in Seattle?

It was the thought that always lay below her conscious mind, a thought she kept firmly imprisoned like a dangerous man who must not be allowed freedom. One of the advantages of the loud, busy activity on board the ship was that she could tire herself out, and that kept the thought from forming. Now, however, as had happened several times at night when she was restless, the question popped into her mind as plainly as if it had been spoken aloud.

A woman with two children—no money, no skills. What man would want me? And if he did, would I want him?

Martha Jane's face as a rule was mild, gentle, and smooth, but now the planes hardened and she shook her head in a short, almost angry gesture of denial. She had been besieged with doubts about that part of the bargain—living with a man she didn't know, with a stranger. Now as she stood on the fantail she felt trapped by the inevitability of the matter. Asa Mercer and Dr. Duvall had allowed her to come, waiving serious objections, with the tacit understanding that she would be an asset to Mercer's Belles.

And the only way I can pay them back is—to marry. That was the bargain—and I can't stand the thought of it!

For a long time, she stood at the rail, struggling with the problem, growing more and more despondent. So absorbed was she in her dilemma that she failed to hear the sound of footsteps approaching; and when a voice spoke up very close to her, she started and uttered a small cry. Whirling, she held her hands out as if to protect herself from the tall man who stood there.

"Why—I'm sorry to have startled you, Mrs. Terrell—" Powell Drake blinked in surprise, adding, "I'm such a heavy-footed fellow I thought you must have heard me."

"Oh, I guess I was—" Martha Jane broke off, not wanting to confess her true thoughts, then smiled up at him. "The children went to sleep early, so I came up for some air before going to bed."

"You didn't want to go ashore? I'd have been glad to help with the children."

"Oh no, Mr. Drake!" She looked up at him, the starlight reflected in her eyes and the silver glow smoothed her cheeks. "You've done too much already. I—I don't know what the children and I would have done without you."

Powell gazed at her expressionlessly. "Would you like to sit down for a while? And would you please stop calling me Mr. Drake?"

Martha Jane laughed suddenly, the streak of humor that lay just below the surface of her placid character showing itself. "You're so formal, I'm not sure I can use your first name."

He smiled briefly, waited until she sat down on the edge of a cargo hatch, then nodded. "I know. I'm as pompous as a preacher. But you can call me Powell—and may I call you Martha?" When she nodded, he said suddenly, "That was my mother's name."

"Really?"

"Yes. She was a wonderful woman. But she died when I was sixteen." He looked out over the water and let the silence run on. "I think I might be different if she'd lived."

"How so?"

Drake shrugged. "Oh, more gentle, I think. She was a gentle woman, and somehow she was able to pass that along to others. People were more—more *graceful* after being around her. I could never understand how she did it." He hesitated, then turned to face her. "You remind me of her—very much."

Martha Jane flushed under his steady observation. She was not accustomed to many compliments, and somehow this one pleased her greatly. "What about the rest of your family?" She sat beside him as he began to speak of his father, who had been a stern man—one who loved his children but could not express his feelings. He spoke with affection of his two sisters and his brother, and then he abruptly stopped. "I'm becoming an old woman for talk!" he exclaimed with a rueful laugh. "Sorry to bore you to death with my family history."

"I wasn't bored."

She said it with such a simple sincerity that Powell glanced up at her, thinking, *She means exactly what she says—not like some women.* Aloud he said, "Well, turn about. Tell me about yourself."

Martha Jane hesitated. She had kept silent about herself so long that she found it difficult to speak, but finally she began to relate the details of her childhood. As she traced the days of her courtship and marriage with Jim Terrell, the slapping of the waves against the hull of the ship had a hypnotic effect, and she spoke more freely than she knew. Finally she said, "Jim was killed in the battle of Spotsylvania—" and then she glanced up, and he saw tears in her eyes.

"I'm sorry," Powell murmured. "You must have loved him very much."

"We loved each other. There was never anyone else, from the time we first fell in love."

Powell asked cautiously, "You don't think you could ever love another man?"

"Not like I loved Jim," she said simply; then after a few moments of silence, she added, "But I like to think that I have enough love for—another man. And that love would be good, too. But not the same, for what Jim and I had—well, I have my memories, and I have Stony and Kelvey."

He didn't speak for so long that she turned to look at him— and was shocked to see that his face was pale and his lips were contorted as if he were in terrible pain.

"Powell—what is it?" she asked in alarm. "Are you sick?"

He didn't answer, seemed not even to have heard her question. When she took his arm, she found it was tense as an iron bar, but his hands were trembling violently. He seemed to be short of air, for his breath came in short bursts, and Martha Jane thought, *It must be some sort of fever—but it's so sudden.*

"I—I was married once—and I had—I had two children, just like you!"

Martha Jane stared at the big man. The words seemed to have been forced from between his lips. She wanted to say something, but he seemed too far away. His eyes were wide open, and he suddenly clasped his hands together and swallowed convulsively. She waited, not knowing what to do, and finally he began to speak in spasmodic bursts, his voice choking at times so that he had to struggle for breath.

"My wife's name was—Caroline. We loved each other— I never thought—she'd go first. I was older—I thought I'd die before she did." He bent his head, and Martha Jane could hear his teeth grinding horribly. "Our boy's name—was Gerald. He was eight years old—so much like his mother. Our daughter— Sabrina—was six. She was—she was like me, they said. . . ."

Martha Jane sat frozen to stillness; she had never seen a man in such agony of spirit. Wordlessly, she waited for him to tell her more.

"I came home," he whispered, "and the house was on fire. I— ran inside, but the roof collapsed on me." A tremor ran through his body as if he'd taken a bullet, and he said hoarsely, "Caroline and the children—were on the second floor—they never had a chance!" Suddenly he choked back a sob, then threw his hands over his face, groaning, "Oh, God! Why didn't I die with them? What good am I without them!"

And then Powell Drake began to weep. Not softly and gently, but in great raspy sobs that racked his entire body. For years he'd kept this inside, never once speaking of the hell that lived in his breast, but now like a volcano the grief poured forth.

Without thinking of what she was doing, Martha Jane turned to him and threw her arms around his shoulders. "Maybe I can help," she murmured and pulled him to her breast. She doubted if he even heard her words. But there was such a helplessness in him that he came to her, and she held him as she would have held Stony or Kelvey. There was indeed something childlike and fragile in the big man as he clung to her, sobs still tearing through him.

Powell Drake was, Martha Jane saw, completely unaware of what was happening. His grief had eaten away at him for years, and only stern discipline had kept him going. Now he had simply collapsed, and all the pressures that had been building up for years burst through as he sobbed on her breast.

The lips of Martha Jane were broad and maternal as she held him, smoothing his hair and murmuring small sounds of comfort. She now understood what she had not—what no one understood—that this man for all his pride and strength was a broken man, a man crucified by loss. And she also knew some-how that what was happening to them would give her a caring and concern for Powell Drake that she had had for no man other than her husband.

Finally the choking sobs grew fainter, and the trembling of Drake's form lessened. Suddenly he pulled himself away from her and turned away. He pulled a handkerchief from his pocket, wiped his face, then cleared his throat.

"Sorry to be such—a baby," he muttered, and she saw that he was terribly ashamed—and she knew he must not be so.

"Powell—never be ashamed of your tears," she said with in-tensity. "If you don't weep for those you lose, that only proves you didn't love them."

He stared at her, his face swollen and a look of utter exhaus-tion scoring his features. For a long moment he gazed at her, and she feared that he might turn and walk away. But he didn't. He nodded slowly and, in a voice of wonder, whispered, "Why, that's right, isn't it? I never thought—"

Martha Jane's own experience had made her wise enough to know that Powell Drake had made a huge step out of the deadly grip of memory—but it was just a first step. "Tell me about them, Powell," she prompted. And when he began to speak haltingly about his loss, she breathed a sigh of relief.

He's going to be all right! she thought with a sudden sense of gladness. *I can help him—and he'll be a whole man again—and a good one!*

The two sat there for a long time, and as Powell Drake leaned back against the side of the bulkhead, he knew that something dark and deadly had left him. And as he looked at the smooth face of Martha Jane, who sat beside him quietly listening, he knew for the first time a ray of hope—hope that life could have joy and meaning again for him.

14

Guns, Gold, and Women

Traveling by ship tends to reduce life to its lowest common denominator. Each person's nature consists of two things: the sky and the sea. Each passenger is allotted an easily measured square of space that belongs to him or her; "lots of space" and "not much space" are no longer relative terms, but absolutes that can be expressed in terms of square feet. Food, drink, and other necessities exist in nonreproducible quantities.

Personal interaction, civic activities, and governmental institutions are all structured very simply: the ship is an absolute monarchy, with the captain at the top of the pyramid. Officers, crew, and passengers make up the lower tier of the pyramid, in varying configuration, depending upon the particular activity one is reflecting upon, but always the captain is at the top. To passengers and crew, organizationally speaking, the captain is the only man between them and their God.

Strange little cosmos, Cheney observed. *We don't usually think in terms of a limited universe like this. When we're on—earth—I guess you'd call it—there's no limit. Even when you're hungry, somewhere there is more food, and there is always water to drink; you just have to go where it is. You might live in a city of thousands of people and dislike all of them, but you can always go somewhere else to find another thousand or so to pick from.*

The *Continental* was two days out of Aspinwall, Panama. The thermometer inched uncomfortably upward during the day, but the nights were still cool and pleasant. This evening,

Cheney and Shiloh had decided to sit on the fantail for a while after dinner and enjoy the stars. There seemed to be many, many more stars visible at sea. The night sky was one vista that Cheney never tired of.

"What are you thinking about?" Shiloh asked. "You're smiling."

"About liking people," Cheney answered idly.

"I sure like you, Doc," Shiloh said easily. "You like me, don't you?"

Cheney glanced sharply at the man next to her, but his face was guileless. He wasn't flirting or being silly; as always he was simply and honestly stating his thoughts. Not for the first time, Shiloh's lack of pretension made Cheney conscious of the thousands of little prevarications and innuendoes that people use every day to communicate.

"Well—well—yes, I suppose I do like you, Shiloh," she answered haltingly. "And I'm glad you like me. But then, you like most everyone, don't you?"

"Most. Some more than others."

"Who?" Cheney was surprised at herself, asking such a Shiloh-style question.

"Mmm, Lydia. Martha Jane. Tani. Stony and Kelvey."

"What about Powell Drake? What do you think about him?"

An uncharacteristic shadow crossed Shiloh's face, but it soon cleared and he smiled to himself. "Didn't like him much at first. Thought he was uppity, and then when he was so ugly to Lydia I wanted to punch him out. But Lydia made me change my mind about him."

"How in the world did she do that? If anyone needs to know how to make you change that stubborn mind of yours, it's me!" Cheney teased.

"Just ask Lydia. I think she could talk the wind out of blowing, if she wanted to. Of course, she does have a direct line to God, and that gives her a little edge. Anyway, she told me that

I was 'taking up a reproach against my neighbor,' and to stop it. So I did."

"What in the world does that mean—'taking up a reproach against your neighbor'?"

"It means that Drake offended Lydia, not me, but I took it upon myself to get sore about it. Lydia forgave him, but I didn't—in fact, if you want to get particular, my forgiveness was beside the point anyway. I never should've took offense in the first place, and it was Lydia's place to forgive. See?"

Shiloh waited for a thoughtful nod from Cheney, then went on. "So after I gave it some thought, I sorta—well—adjusted my thinking about Powell Drake. He's not so bad, especially in the last few days."

"Yes, he has changed, hasn't he? And I think it has something to do with Martha Jane."

"Looks to me like they're falling in love." Shiloh turned to look at Cheney, his head cocked slightly. There was no moon, but the muted luminescence of starlight made his hair look silvery-white. "But then, what does a roughneck like me know about love?"

Cheney didn't want to talk about love. The subject reminded her of Devlin Buchanan, and thinking about Dev made her feel restless and unsure of herself, so she abruptly changed the subject. "What was that side deal you made with Bull Lynch? The reason you gave Martha Jane money?"

"Oh, it was just a little—agreement we reached. I didn't really want to fight Bull very much, 'cause it hurts to fight," Shiloh said ruefully. "But he told me if I'd fight him and I won, he'd bring the whole engine-room crew to Lydia's prayer meetings. I knew she'd like that, so I agreed, and I also decided I'd give part of my cut to Lydia, for her missionary work, and Martha Jane, for Stony and Kelvey."

He made a dismissing gesture with one still-swollen hand. "I always give part of my money to things like that. Used to give it to the orphanage where I grew up . . . so then I decided that Stony and Kelvey and Lydia's Indians could use it just as much as them orphans."

"But that's almost like—tithing. Are you—religious, Shiloh?"

"Everyone's religious, Doc, just about different things. I give my money to things like that because it's a good investment. I always get my money back, and more, no matter what. Never fails."

Cheney digested this for a few moments. She had tithed ever since she was a little girl, but it was different for her. *We have—well, lots of money, I guess, she thought awkwardly, so it's no—trouble to give ten percent.*

"Strange about Lydia and Sybil, isn't it?"

Shiloh's question jolted Cheney out of her reverie.

"What? Oh yes, it is. They seemed to be finding a way to—fit together, I guess you'd say, at first. But not now. Guess they're just too different."

"That's not the reason, I don't think. Lydia could get along with anyone, sinner or saint," Shiloh observed. "Sybil's the one that's gone off half-cocked." Now Shiloh went into a brown study and Cheney watched the varying expressions on his face as he thought.

After a few moments he half-shrugged and went on. "Can't say I know what's on Sybil's mind, but she reminds me of some gamblers I've seen. Can be pretty sensible men—calculating and kinda cold, but sensible. Then a glint of gold hits their eye, and they decide to throw everything in the pot—everything. They get to where they can't think of nothing else, and then they get reckless—and usually dangerous."

How does he know all these things? Cheney thought as he spoke. *How in the world does he just step inside people's heads and understand them and know what they're doing and thinking? I've never been able to do that—probably never will.*

"You know, you're really a good nurse, Shiloh," Cheney told him with some awkwardness. "You've done a good job."

Even in the semidarkness Cheney could see the gentle amusement in Shiloh's light blue eyes as he turned to face her. "Thanks, Doc. You've done a good job, too. Much better'n I expected," he added slyly.

"Well, thanks—I think," Cheney retorted, but without heat. She knew now that Shiloh often made outrageous comments like that just to ease her discomfort when she was embarrassed or unsure of herself.

The gentle tropical breeze was changing. It had picked up into a fretful wind that tossed Cheney's hair and blew wispy dark clouds across the panorama of the stars. Cheney and Shiloh sat in companionable silence for a while, watching the subtle changes in their simple world. There were strange warm drafts in the stiff breeze, and sometimes it felt like tiny particles were carried in it. Cheney lifted her face and sniffed. The wind even smelled different. *I wonder—storm coming?* she thought.

"Wonder if there's a storm coming," Shiloh murmured.

❖

"Hurricane," Captain Weldon announced succinctly.

"What?" First Officer Carstairs yelped, then snapped his head around to look, as if the hurricane might be lurking in the corner of the wheelhouse. "You mean there's a hurricane coming, sir?"

"Didn't say that," Weldon grunted absently. His shrewd eyes were watching the steersman as he maneuvered the great ship's wheel. He studied the compass and the barometer, he looked up at the sky, he scrutinized the water.

Carstairs knew better than to question him any further. *If Captain Weldon wants to tell me about a hurricane, he will,* he sighed to himself. *If he doesn't, he won't.*

The nearer they steamed to Panama, the more restless and temperamental the sea got. The wind blew strong, but it carried no rain. The sky looked strange—not clouded, but still a uniform dirty gray, as if the sky itself had changed colors.

It was seven o'clock in the morning when Panama finally appeared as a thin, jagged black line on the horizon. Captain Weldon was glad they'd make landfall early. *She's wallowing like a number-ten washtub,* he scowled to himself. *Be glad to get all this freight off my ship. Guns, gold, and women! Just asking for trouble!*

Captain Weldon finally coaxed the S.S. *Continental* into Panama Bay at eleven o'clock. He had gotten impatient with the seamen and with the ship itself and had taken the wheel at ten o'clock. The sea was not in a fury, the waves were not huge, and the wind was not a gale. But still the elements seemed irritated and aggravated; the sea slapped the *Continental* back and forth peevishly and the wind gusted strong, sometimes from three different directions.

"Get Mercer up here," Captain Weldon barked. "And bring me Littlejohn." Carstairs hurried to obey, and soon he returned with Asa Mercer and the purser.

"Mercer, you're going to have problems on that railroad," Weldon announced authoritatively. "But you can't stay on board. I'm getting my ship out of this ruckus as soon as we're unloaded."

Mercer ran his hand through his hair, then turned a little circle as he scanned all the wheelhouse windows. "What problems, do you think?" he asked, his youthful face drawn with anxiety.

"I think there's been a hurricane through here in the last couple of days," Weldon said in a gentler tone. "Railroad might be torn up. There's a good hotel in Aspinwall, the Paradise. Bingham-Lloyd's hotel, actually. The *Conqueror*'s not due in to Panama City for three days. You might want to consider staying in the hotel for the night to get your bearings."

"Maybe, if it's still standing. The wharf looks good, doesn't it? Maybe—"

"See all those new boards in the pier?" the captain pointed out.

"Hmmm, yes, I do." Mercer sighed deeply. "Well, thank you for the advice, Captain Weldon. Thank you for all of your help. You've made this part of the trip a pleasure."

"Hrmph," Weldon growled. "It was my ship, not me. And the *Conqueror*'s her sister ship. Ought to be just like this one. And Captain Drury's a good seaman." Mercer took this as his dismissal and left the wheelhouse to find Cheney and Shiloh.

"Littlejohn," the captain ordered, "find that man as soon as we dock. You know the one I mean."

"Yes, sir," Littlejohn said smoothly. "The Pinkerton man who's responsible for the special cargo. I will, sir, and I'll arrange for the crew to give the stevedores a hand unloading."

"All the crew," Weldon ordered. "And tell 'em to hurry."

❧

As the *Continental* jerked and jolted her way closer to the docks, Max Townsend stood on the pier in the gritty, hot wind and watched. He was a plain man, of average height, and his nondescript features had come in handy on many jobs he'd done for the Pinkerton National Detective Agency. He looked like Everyman—a clerk this day, a hack driver the next, a cowboy another. Now, his light-olive complexion was deeply tanned by the Panama sun, and this made his even teeth look very white below a thin dark moustache. With his dark brown hair and his flashing dark eyes, he looked like a native. No one paid him any mind as he stood with arms crossed, a grim expression on his face, and waited for the ship to dock.

When the gangplank lowered, however, Townsend was the first one to ascend, and he was met halfway by Purser Douglas Littlejohn. "I'm Max Townsend, Pinkerton's. I believe you have my cargo on board." He handed the purser his copy of the shipping order, and Littlejohn meticulously studied it, glancing up at Townsend from time to time.

"Yes, sir," Littlejohn answered. "And I'm getting your cargo unloaded first. I've got the entire crew detailed for cargo handling, so we can be under way as soon as possible."

"Don't blame you," Townsend commented, glancing around at the disheveled port. "And I'm glad your crew is unloading, because things here are in a bit of disarray. Hurricane came through two days ago."

"I thought so," Littlejohn answered.

Townsend looked at him curiously, but he was in too much of a hurry for polite conversation. "Can your men load my cargo directly onto the train? I don't want it sitting out here on the docks."

"No, sir, I'm afraid not. Captain Weldon is in a hurry."

"I'll pay them double eagles if they'll do double time," Townsend offered. He held up a fifty-dollar bill as if to illustrate, then casually tucked it into the purser's jacket pocket.

Purser Douglas Littlejohn smiled coolly. "Mr. Townsend, you just bought yourself all the stevedores you need."

❧

From the stateroom deck, Cheney, Shiloh, and Tani DuQuesne watched the feverish activity on the Aspinwall docks. Even under the best of circumstances, Aspinwall was noisy and crowded and confused when the ships docked, but today it was pure chaos. The wind blew visible but unidentifiable pieces of litter in crazy circles. People shouted and catcalled in Spanish and English at high volume. Assorted wreckage was haphazardly piled everywhere—splintered lumber, big balls of tangled seaweed, shells, broken bottles, tree limbs. Men were scurrying up and down the gangplank with cargo from the *Continental,* their hair and clothing flapping wildly in the sudden gusts of wind.

Asa Mercer came running around the deck and skidded to a stop, colliding with Tani as he did. "Oh no!" he cried, an appalled look on his face. "Miss DuQuesne! Please forgive me!"

Tani's head had jerked around when Mercer jostled her, a mutinous look on her delicate features. But she softened a little when she saw the woeful look on his face, and merely nodded her head with a queenly gesture of acceptance before turning back to watch the docks.

"I'm glad I found you two," Mercer gasped to Cheney and Shiloh. "Please help me get word to all of the women that we're going to the Paradise Hotel tonight. I want all of us to stay together, but if any of us should somehow get separated, we should go to the hotel immediately."

"What about our luggage?" Cheney asked with concern.

"Can't leave those seventy-four fancy dresses behind," Shiloh commented, and Cheney made a face at him. Tani secretly smiled.

"If you two think you can herd the women—oh, dear, no, I didn't actually mean *that,* Miss DuQuesne." Again Mercer was mortified.

Tani stood motionless for a moment, her back to the group. Then she slowly turned and said in her low, rich voice with the staccato Creole French accent, "Mr. Mercer, I have decided that you are basically a good man and that you have no secret intentions of enslaving me or anyone else. So please do not feel that you must keep apologizing to me. It is unnecessary."

Cheney and Shiloh smiled, but Mercer just looked relieved. He bowed a little to the young woman as he continued. "Well, anyway, I thought I would attend to the luggage—somehow—if you two would make sure the ladies all get to the hotel."

Shiloh said, "I better help you, Mercer. The doc can get Powell Drake and Jeff Withers to help her take care of the ladies. It looks like"—he gestured widely to the crowded, confused docks—"you're going to have a problem getting porters."

"Then I'll carry them myself," Mercer stated firmly, and Cheney believed that he would, one by one, if he had to. "But—if you don't mind, Cheney—"

"Mr. Mercer," Tani interrupted, lifting a slender, long-fingered hand, "I will come with you. I can help you."

Mercer's eyebrows shot up. Tani had excellent manners, but she normally kept her distance from all white people and their problems. "But how—how—?" Mercer stammered as he paced two steps past her, then back.

"I speak Spanish. I will know whom to ask what, and how to find out where the hotel is, and how to get the porters who will not steal from us."

Cheney and Mercer looked surprised. Shiloh already knew how extremely well educated Tani was; now he looked at her approvingly. It was a big step for her to offer to help.

"Thank you very kindly," Mercer said formally, offering Tani his arm. "I accept your offer with pleasure, Miss DuQuesne."

For long moments the young ex-slave stared at Mercer's proffered arm, and instinctively Mercer stood still and relaxed, waiting. Finally Tani took his arm with an elegant gesture, and the two walked toward the gangplank.

⁂

Bull Lynch and Beans Lowery had been detailed to unload the shipment of Duvall's tools, plows, and building supplies first onto the Aspinwall docks and then onto the train siding at the bow end of the ship. Bull and Beans were unloading from the stern gangplank after a crew had unloaded the cargo from the crew quarters.

Bull smirked as he hefted the box of nails that actually was filled three-fourths full with shiny gold. *Littlejohn's doin' me a favor,* he thought with triumph. *Right nice of him to order me to unload this here gold.* Behind him, Beans huffed noisily with another box.

"This here gold sure is heavy," he grunted loudly.

"Beans!" Bull hissed over his shoulder, eyeing the purser as he stood watching a few yards off. "If you never understood the word 'shut up,' then do it now!"

"Whatcha mean by that, Bull?" Beans asked, his brow wrinkling.

Bull placed the box on the dock, slightly off to the side of a line of plows, and Beans did the same with his. Littlejohn looked around, glanced down at his papers, and called, "That's about it! When you get through here, go help Officer Carstairs' group!"

"Yessir!" Bull and Beans yelled in unison. Littlejohn turned on his heel and paced off down the docks. Bull let out a deep breath.

"Might as well go get them there shovels," Beans sighed, hitching up his breeches.

"Forget the shovels. Go get the can of diamonds and come right back out here, Beans. We're leaving now with our gold and diamonds." Bull glanced furtively around him. Seamen and natives were everywhere, but the one man who knew what they were supposed to be doing had just walked off.

Beans looked at Bull doubtfully but turned and went up the stern gangplank. A few minutes later he appeared again with his seabag slung over his back.

"No, Beans," Bull growled. "Not the seabag! It'll look funny!"

Beans leaned sideways and let the bag fall to the dock, then stepped back and studied it with a mystified expression. "What's funny-lookin' about it, Bull? I don't see nobody laughin' at it."

Bull shook his head and gave up. "All right, but you gotta carry it—and one box. How you gonna do that?"

"Dunno," Beans said happily, slinging the bag over his shoulder again. But either by instinct or chance, his arm went through the loop closure so his hands were free. Beans shrugged and bent to pick up the box. "All right. Where're we goin'?"

"Gorgona for a few days," Bull said with superiority. Sybil had told him how to do this. "Then back here, then back to

Havana." He bent and picked up another box, looking longingly at the other two. With a slight shrug he turned and started laboring up the pier, and Beans followed.

"But, Bull, if we gotta come back here, why don't we just stay here? This here box and bag's heavy!"

"Because—oh, never mind, Beans," Bull snapped with exasperation. "Just follow me. And don't say nothin' to nobody! If somebody stops us to ask us a question, you let me talk! You hear?"

"Sure, Bull," Beans answered, a hurt expression on his face. "You ain't mad at me afore I even do it, are you?"

In spite of himself, Bull laughed. "No, I ain't mad. Just don't do it. Keep quiet."

They walked slowly up the pier, Bull with exaggerated casualness and Beans with genuine casualness because he didn't understand what they were doing anyway. No one stopped them; no one even looked at them.

Just before they reached the wide wharf that led to the Aspinwall streets, they saw Asa Mercer and Tani DuQuesne. Tani was speaking rapidly to a big Spanish man, who was smiling broadly and nodding. Under his breath Bull muttered, "Woulda liked to've gotten friendly with that colored girl. Purtiest colored I ever saw."

Beans looked curiously at Tani and then glanced at Bull. For a fleeting moment, an expression of disgust shadowed his pale blue eyes, but then he lowered his face as if he were ashamed and walked on in silence beside Bull.

15

Train Ride to the End of the World

"He says that no one has wished to go to Panama City since El Diablo came through. I believe that 'El Diablo' must refer to the hurricane, Mr. Mercer, and not the actual devil himself. So he doesn't know if the railroad is passable or not."

The faintest flicker of amusement showed in Tani DuQuesne's dark eyes as she translated for the railroad conductor. He was a small, handsome man with an affable grin, obviously proud of his blue-striped engineer's cap. An impressive amount of gold oak leaves and braid had been added to it.

"Ask him how long the journey usually takes. And call me Asa."

Tani nodded and spoke to the engineer, then turned to Mercer. "Four hours, if it does not rain, if there is no unloading at Cruces—and if there are no banditos."

"Banditos!" The exclamation came from Mercer and was followed by a sharp gasp from Cheney, a small groan from Annie Stephens, and a loud screech from Holly Van Buren. Shiloh merely crossed his arms and looked grim.

Asa Mercer gazed around at the small group that surrounded the engineer, who began to pick his very large, very even white teeth with a small splinter of wood. "Well, we have to go," Mercer told them decisively. "Since the Paradise Hotel was blown all to h—paradise," he amended hastily, "there's simply no other place to house one hundred people. I'm sorry, ladies, but there doesn't seem to be any alternative."

Cheney straightened her shoulders. "No, of course there isn't. We'd have to go tomorrow, anyway—whether or not the train can get through. So Shiloh and I will help the ladies board, and you and Tani can go ahead and tell the porters to load the luggage."

"Thank you, Dr. Duvall," Mercer said as he smiled warmly at her. "Once again I'm thankful that you and Shiloh are here. You've both been more help than I ever knew I'd need."

"I'll help, too," Holly said petulantly. "I can tell a silly ol' porter what to do as well as anyone!" Grabbing Mercer's arm, she almost—but not quite—made a face at Tani DuQuesne, who ignored her with such eloquence that Holly's delicate cheeks blushed pink.

Gently, Mercer led her down the track to the next car, murmuring, "No, thank you, Holly, I need Tani to help me because she can speak Spanish. Why don't we go ahead and find you a nice seat on the train?"

"As if he doesn't have enough problems without dealing with that little minx!" Annie Stephens said with uncharacteristic fierceness, her brown eyes flashing.

Shiloh winked at Cheney and included Tani with a glance. "Why, Annie, you look just like Rex, with your fur all on end and your teeth all sharp and pointed!"

"Shiloh!" Cheney snapped.

"I don't care what I look like," Annie retorted, her color high. "Poor Asa! In fact, I guess I can help the most by keeping Holly out of trouble and out of Asa's hair, even if I have to sit on her to do it! I'm going to go get Rex right now!" She marched off toward the nearby dock where Rex lay in his box, seemingly oblivious to all the human folly surrounding him.

"She's so shy—how could you tease her like that?" Cheney demanded, looking up at Shiloh accusingly.

"She's not shy," Shiloh answered with obvious surprise. "She's just kinda quiet. Most of the time."

Tani said something in a low voice to the engineer and then went to meet Mercer, who was climbing down from the passenger car where he had deposited Holly. The engineer gave Shiloh and Cheney a wide smile, pulled on the bill of his elaborate cap, then climbed up into the engine compartment. Within a few seconds three loud, long whistles sounded.

"We're boarding, Doc," Shiloh said, appraising the group of women restlessly milling about on the dock nearby. "Let's go start 'herding women,' like Asa said."

◈

Before the Panama Railroad was built, travelers wishing to cross the Isthmus of Panama had been obliged to follow the Chagres River to Panama City on native barges. The journey had been dirty, dangerous, and long—four days of negotiating a tiny river through dense jungle. The only village between Aspinwall and Panama City along the river was Gorgona, and it was barely more than a collection of shanties and huts.

Finally, with American gold, the railroad had been built from Aspinwall to Panama City. The wharves at Aspinwall had been built to accommodate even the largest of steamers comfortably, and the town had been enlarged with American money and American travelers.

The railroad ran as close to the piers as was possible without actually being over the sea, and sidings had been built close to each wide pier leading right up to the tracks for ease of loading. The farthest siding was only about fifty feet from the dock. A car would simply be pulled to a siding and left there for loading while the engine either pulled another car to another siding or waited to maneuver on the same siding.

The *Continental* was the only ship at the docks when they arrived, and Max Townsend's special cargo had been unloaded from the ship and reloaded on two boxcars in record time. The rest of the shipment bound for Panama City had been methodically placed on the docks and was still being loaded onto the train.

Max Townsend crossed his arms and looked critically around one boxcar loaded with the cargo he was escorting. The crates had been neatly stacked from floor to ceiling with barely a seam showing. *Not a chance of looking inside,* he thought with a mental shrug. *All I can do is to count the crates and make sure I've got the right number.* Quickly he tallied the crates in this boxcar and then in the second one: exactly four hundred.

Swinging down from the second boxcar, Townsend looked curiously at a petite woman who stood closely observing while some men loaded a shipment onto the next car back. *Tools and plows? Kind of a funny cargo for a woman to be overseeing.* As he watched, the woman wheeled around abruptly and started walking down the line toward Max. Casually he leaned back against the boxcar and began to roll a cigarette, his eyes averted.

The steely faced woman passed Max without a second glance; he looked just like the hundreds of other natives crowding the docks. Something about her made an impression on Townsend, though, and after she had gotten two boxcars past him, he threw down his barely smoked cigarette and followed her.

Sybil Warfield certainly did not notice the man loitering by one of the hundreds of train cars. Too many things were on her mind for her to pay attention to one more porter wasting time on the docks. She had just barely found the Duvall shipment before it disappeared into one of the anonymous boxcars. *Only two boxes of nails—but no one seemed to notice two missing. No one around counting or checking a shipping order or ticking off a manifest. So for now at least, my gold is safe,* Sybil thought. Somehow the thought gave her no satisfaction or peace.

Walking quickly, she soon reached the passenger cars and unobtrusively rejoined the crowd of women waiting to board. No one had noticed she had been gone. Within half an hour, Mercer's group had filled the first two passenger cars, and Sybil made sure she was not on the same car as Lydia. After an inexplicable half-hour delay, a long whistle sounded, and the train began to slowly chug its way south.

Aspinwall was by no means a large city. The jungle could easily be seen from the docks, looming close over the town as if it were longing to devour the tiny buildings and streets. And the train had barely gathered speed before they were plunged into gray-green murk. The dense tangle of leaves and vines looked like a solid wall just a few feet from the train windows. The temperature seemed to drop a few degrees, but the humidity climbed rapidly as they rattled along.

"Not much of a view," Cheney commented to Shiloh, who sat next to her.

"From what I heard, they literally chopped a tunnel in the jungle for the train," he shrugged. "You won't see any panoramic vistas of tropical beauty. But at least it's a straight tunnel, straight through to Panama City."

"Odd that you should call it a tunnel," Tani's low voice said from the seat behind them. "The natives call it the Tunnel of Death."

"What?" Cheney gasped and turned around to face the mulatto girl. "Why?"

"Because many Panamanian men died clearing the way for this railroad," she answered in a distant voice, her dark eyes unreadable. "The overseers drove them until they could work no more—in all kinds of weather, whether they were sick or not, through bogs and thickets and undergrowth full of insects and snakes." Her beautiful face remained impassive as she stared out the train window at the solid green outside.

"Snakes!" Shiloh repeated in a strange, tight voice. Cheney glanced at him curiously and realized that until this moment she had never seen a tinge of fear for anything or any man in her nurse's eyes.

"Snakes?" he repeated in a calmer tone, turning to look at Tani himself. She didn't comment, merely glanced at him for a moment and then looked back out at the "Tunnel of Death."

Cheney and Shiloh turned back and began to talk in low tones about Asa Mercer and his two particular Belles: Annie Stephens and Holly Van Buren. Asa was seated in the first seat of the car, with Annie beside him. Behind them was Rex, his box splendidly occupying its own seat, and behind Rex were Cheney and Shiloh.

"Wasn't that just the cleverest trick you ever saw?" Cheney whispered with amusement. "Keeping Rex beside her until Holly settled down, then maneuvering Asa into the seat and putting Rex behind so Holly couldn't even get that close."

"Why, Doc, are you accusing that modest little woman of plotting to entrap poor Asa?" Shiloh teased.

"No, I'm accusing her of *rescuing* poor Asa from that blond-ringleted bundle of bows!" Cheney replied, nodding at Holly, who sat across the aisle and one seat back from Asa and Annie. The young girl was positively glowering at the back of their heads, which were close together in conversation.

Holly flounced restlessly, turning around to scan the seats behind with a pouting look on her face. Like a child, she knelt in her seat, placed her hands on the back of it, and strained to see through the gloom to the back of the car. Even as Cheney and Shiloh watched, her eyes lit up, her hand went up to plump the fat, shiny ringlets, and she pinched her cheeks with tiny little tweezing gestures of thumb and forefinger. "Uh-oh," Shiloh muttered, "looks like she's found another victim."

Mystified, Cheney turned to look around the passenger car. She had thought that only Mercer's Belles occupied this car and the next. Powell Drake and Jeff Withers had seats in the car behind, with the Terrells and Lydia and the rest of the ladies.

But there was, in fact, a man sitting by himself on the very back seat of the car, staring noncommittally out the window. Cheney turned back and fervently hoped that Holly—and the rest of the women surrounding the poor, unsuspecting train traveler— would behave themselves.

The train jolted along roughly through the jungle for about an hour, then abruptly screeched to a stop. Their dashing engineer didn't like to slow decorously to a halt, and consequently their arrival into the shabby little village of Cruces had the effect of a horse that decided to stop stock-still during a dead gallop.

Asa jumped up and hurried back to Shiloh and Cheney. "Would you please go check on the ladies in the other car? I'm going to ask the engineer if we can just continue on instead of taking a break here. I really don't want the ladies to get off the train and get scattered. It's late already."

Cheney and Shiloh agreed and threaded their way through to the second car. It was crowded and hot, like the first, but the women were fairly comfortable and seemed to be in good spirits. Though the jungle outside the windows was alien and somewhat frightening, the train ride provided a refreshing change from the ship.

As they were coming back up the aisle from the rear of the car, they were stopped by Lydia as she held out a still-bandaged hand. Cheney saw with exasperated affection that Lydia was wearing the shawl she had bought in Havana—black, yellow, and purple squares—with a green-and-brown striped dress. Lydia asked, "Sybil's up there, in your car, isn't she, Dr. Duvall?"

Reluctantly Cheney answered, "Yes, she is, Lydia, and she's fine." Sybil and Georgia Jakes were sitting together toward the back of the car, and Cheney was fairly sure they were nipping from Georgia's silver flask of brandy.

"Well, I'm coming up there. I haven't been able to talk to her much lately, and right now she's a captive audience." Lydia smiled.

Lydia's upturned face was endearingly eager, and Cheney took it upon herself to disappoint Lydia instead of allowing Sybil to hurt her. "No, Lydia, I don't think that would be a very good idea. We really need you to stay back here, on this car. Martha Jane is a good—well, leader for the women, but she's so busy with the children. I'm sure Mr. Mercer would appreciate it if you'd stay on this car." Everything Cheney said was true, and Lydia knew it, but her face fell a little just the same as she agreed with Cheney.

Shiloh and Cheney returned to their car just as the train began to move again. As before, it began to pick up speed almost immediately, and with difficulty Cheney led the way to their seats. Once she staggered hard against a seat, and Shiloh, walking close behind her, reached out and grabbed her with both hands to steady her. The warm touch of his big hands spanning her slender waist confused and unsettled Cheney, and as they moved up the aisle, Shiloh didn't remove them but continued to support her.

Goodness—this is—really—but I guess it's better than sprawling into the aisle, or onto someone's lap. When they took their places, Shiloh's face was expressionless, but Cheney's cheeks were a deep shade of pink.

Bull and Beans simply walked off the docks with the two boxes of gold and their "can of diamonds."

They labored with the heavy boxes straight through the small town, without even a curious glance from the natives. They had seen the gringos do stranger things than almost kill themselves carrying something they didn't need anyway.

At the edge of town, just in front of the treeline, stood the inevitable cantina. Outside it were three small burros, their simple rope halters looped over a small bush. Bull walked up to one of the burros, bent down to grab the rope with one finger, and led the gentle animal toward the darkness of the jungle. Beans was astounded but did the same without question. They were both too out of breath to talk.

When they reached the cover of the thick treeline, Bull dropped the box and stood for a while, panting, and again Beans did the same. After a few minutes they hoisted their boxes onto the burros' backs, tied them on with some rope Beans had in his seabag, and began to move along the treeline behind the last huts and shanties of the town, following the narrow path that separated the town from the jungle to the west. Soon they found the spot where the tiny Chagres River trickled out of the jungle to join the sea. Then Bull, Beans, and the two burros disappeared into the dark green depths of Panama.

"Tell me again where we're goin', Bull," Beans pleaded. "An' why!"

Bull had caught his breath by now and decided to try once more to explain. "We're goin' to walk right alongside this here river to a little town called Gorgona, Beans. We're gonna hide there a coupla days, 'til all them fancy women and Sybil and Asa Mercer steam outta Panama City on the *Conqueror*. Then we're gonna go back to Aspinwall and catch the next steamer to Havana." Bull relented enough to turn back and grin at Beans. "And when we get to Havana, we're gonna spend all this here gold."

"They ain't goin' to Gor-Gor—that there town you said? The train tracks is just over there a few miles," Beans said, his brow wrinkling with the effort of picturing the terrain.

"Nope. Train don't go to Gorgona. River does."

Beans shrugged and began to talk to his burro. After another half hour he had named his animal Eenie and Bull's Meenie and had been carrying on a normal—for Beans—conversation with them.

The jungle was dark and dank by the sluggish little river, which at times narrowed to almost a creek. It was deep, however, and sometimes there were strange, furtive splashings in it that always made Bull jump. Rustles and crackles sounded in the dense vegetation near them.

Most of the time they couldn't see the sun because the tall trees leaned over the river and, where it was narrowest, actually met in a roof over their heads. The canopy made for relatively easy going because the undergrowth didn't grow thick in the perpetual shade. Bull was happy about this. He hadn't thought to get a machete, and impenetrable thickets began where the sun reached the jungle floor just a few feet from the narrow path by the river's side.

"Bull, can we please stop for a few minutes?" Beans pleaded. "We been walkin' 'bout ten hours, and Eenie and Meenie is thirsty." They had reached a pretty little spot by the river where deep green moss, instead of thick mud, grew underfoot.

"Beans, we only been walkin' about three hours," Bull argued, "and I don't give a dead river rat about them mules."

At that moment they heard three long train whistles far off to the north. Bull nodded with satisfaction. "Train's leavin' Aspinwall. We're all right—nobody's stayin' to search all them fool women. Sure, Beans, we can stop for a few minutes."

Bull threw himself to the ground. Beans led the burros to the river. Then he snatched his floppy hat off his head, lay prone on the moss to fill it up with water, and drank thirstily. He tried putting it back on his head, but the wide brim flopped straight down over his eyes and ears, water running down his face.

"If you don't look like a fool, Beans," Bull sneered, but he was in a good mood now. The train and all the people connected with this gold were on their way to Panama City.

Beans decided to put his wet hat back in his seabag. He opened the seabag, and immediately his head jerked back convulsively. "Golly!" he sputtered, his eyes watering at the smell. "Bull! Looky here! This here can o' diamonds is leakin'!"

Reaching armpit deep into the long canvas bag, Beans maneuvered out his arm and then the can of diamonds.

It was covered with some kind of thick, smelly ooze.

With a disgusted look on his face, Beans wiped his hand on the clean moss, then went and washed in the river. Bull looked curiously at the can where Beans had set it down, and even as he was studying it, a faint but unmistakable red smoke began to trickle out of it in thin, delicate wisps. The smell made Bull's eyes water, too.

Beans came back from the river and opened his mouth in a round O when he saw the unremarkable can with the fantastic red smoke coming out of it. "Bull, I ain't carryin' that thing no more. It looks kinda funny, with that devil smoke and all. And besides, it stinks to kingdom come!"

Bull hesitated for only a moment. He still thought this might be a can of diamonds, but then again it might not, because there were lots of things in this world that Bull thought he understood, but it turned out he really didn't. Besides, it did stink.

"Aw, just toss it in the river, Beans," he said. "I don't wanna carry it, neither. Don't need it anyway," he muttered to himself. "Got enough gold to choke a goat."

His eyes cut over to the box on Beans' burro. And suddenly Bull had hard thoughts for a long while about his friend Beans.

❈

After they left Cruces, the train sped steadily southward down the Isthmus of Panama. There were no turns or bends or curves in this railroad, only a straight swath cut through the jungle to Panama City. Cruces had been the only stop along the way, and it was just a collection of about twenty small buildings and huts. The solid wall of green outside the window never varied and their speed never lessened—until they came once more to a screaming, crunching halt.

When they recovered from the jolt, the ladies began to talk in high anxious voices, straining to look ahead. Shiloh's eyes narrowed as he turned to Cheney and ordered in a low voice, "Stand up and tell the women to keep calm and stay in their seats. Talk to them for a few minutes. I'll go on up with Asa and see what's happened." Tani stood up to join him, and Shiloh almost stopped her, but then he relented and signaled for her to come.

Nervously Cheney stood up as Shiloh, Tani, and Asa left the car. She noticed that the man in the back of the train also got off and started toward the engine, and behind him Powell Drake came striding by, his long frock coat and tall beaver hat incongruous against the wild background. "Ladies, l-ladies," she called over the din. "Everyone please be quiet and listen to me. . . ."

The men who had left the train to investigate their unexpected stop had no need even to talk to the engineer. Immediately ahead of them was a clearing in the jungle—if it could be called that. It looked more like God had reached down with a huge hand and simply crushed the vegetation down flat. A rough circle had been hewn in the jungle, and the railroad tracks simply disappeared under about three feet of mangled trees and vegetation.

An aerial view would have shown the astounded observers that the hurricane had indiscriminately inflicted high wind damage in the jungle all along the coast, and then the line of damage had narrowed and become more intense. As it blew inland the hurricane had whirled itself into a tornado that beat down this circle of jungle. Then the tornado had moved off in an arrow-straight path on the other side of the clearing for about a hundred yards, where it had leaped above the jungle floor and rejoined the wild sky above.

The engineer lounged above them, deigning to descend from his small kingdom, as Tani and the four men reached the door of the engine room. Deliberately he pulled a wood splinter from a small stash in the gold braid circling his cap, picked his teeth for a moment, then motioned to the devastation that began just a few inches from the shiny cowcatcher of his engine. "El Diablo," he said simply.

Tani showed no emotion as she surveyed the scene. Shiloh crossed his arms and grunted softly, Asa Mercer ran his hand over his cowlick, and Powell Drake's jaw clenched. The stranger spoke up quietly. "Mr. Mercer, my name is Max Townsend, and I need to speak to you. I would appreciate it if you would stay, too, Mr. Irons. You, sir—" he turned to Drake and asked, "are you Powell Drake?"

"Yes, I am," Drake answered sturdily. "And who—?"

Max Townsend held up a hand in a polite but authoritative gesture of interruption. "I would appreciate it if you'd stay, too, Mr. Drake. But I won't explain until Miss DuQuesne returns to the train."

Tani's eyes flashed defiance as her head turned slowly to the stranger. She opened her mouth to reply, but Mercer stepped slightly closer to her and said sharply, "Mr. Townsend, I will not allow you to speak to Miss DuQuesne—"

Again Townsend broke in with polite insistence and addressed Tani directly. "Ma'am, I can assure you that this has nothing to do with your race or social status. Forgive me for being blunt, but this train and the people on it are in danger, and I need to speak to these men before we address all the ladies. So I ask you to please excuse us."

His tone was in no way condescending and Tani recognized grim honesty in the way Townsend spoke. Nodding to the men with a graceful gesture, she turned and glided back to the passenger car.

All eyes turned toward Townsend, who began speaking without preamble. "I know who you are," he said, "because the women around me talked about all of you. Now *you* need to know that there is a large shipment of gold, guns, and explosives on board this train. I am responsible for their delivery to a man named Zaldivar in Panama City. Obviously, Zaldivar is not going to receive his shipment tonight," Townsend continued dryly, "and he is going to be extremely disappointed."

He hesitated for a moment, searching the faces of the men before him. Each of them was listening carefully and patiently, and Townsend nodded to himself with approval. "There is a very good chance that Zaldivar will send his guerrillas to—ah— inquire about the delay. There is also a very good chance that one or some of them will shoot before they 'inquire.' But what I really fear will happen is that they may decide that we can clear the track."

"What do you mean?" Mercer asked, his youthful face twisted with anxiety.

"I mean, they might see this as a whole trainload of slave labor—women and children included. These people are not— ah—your usual businessmen."

He looked up at the violet-colored evening sky and shrugged. "There's also the chance that other banditos may try to rob the train; they would have no qualms whatsoever about shooting any of us. And if they decided to steal the explosives on board—well, that may be the worst thing of all."

"Why? Why couldn't we just stay on the train tonight and let them have your guns and powder?" Drake demanded in a hard voice.

"Because, Mr. Drake," Townsend quietly answered, "it's not gunpowder. It's nitroglycerin."

All of the men looked at Townsend blankly, and he sighed deeply. He'd hoped he wouldn't have to try to describe nitroglycerin, because he didn't understand it very well himself. Everyone was ignorant about nitroglycerin, even Alfred Nobel, who invented it. But that fact didn't make Max Townsend feel any less responsible for these people, and it didn't excuse him from blame. Escorting this shipment was his job, and he had freely accepted it.

"Nitroglycerin," he pronounced the word slowly. "It's a new chemical explosive in a thick liquid form. And if even one of the canisters on board this train explodes, that"—he indicated the devastation of the jungle ahead with a sharp nod of his head—"will be the result, only with a circumference much, much larger."

Wordlessly, the four men stared at the three-foot-high pile of dirt, vegetation, and large trees covering the railroad tracks for about a hundred yards. But before they could even frame questions to ask, they heard an unearthly crash followed by a deafening roar. Behind them, to the north, a huge black cloud with flashes of orange fire rose to the heavens, eclipsing the entire landscape with unnatural dark.

The roar seemed to go on and on, and the earth shook fearfully. Asa Mercer fell sprawling to the ground. Powell Drake slowly, inevitably sank to one knee. Shiloh and Townsend instinctively held themselves upright by grabbing on to the train.

All of them thought they were witnessing the very end of the world.

16

The Terror by Night

"Fire."

The word, so simply and quietly spoken by Max Townsend to Shiloh, Asa Mercer, and Powell Drake, threatened to release once more the tightly leashed fear in the men.

Forty minutes had passed since the horrendous explosion. It had taken that long for the three men to restore the terrified group of women to some semblance of order. Finally they had come back outside to decide what to do, and by unspoken agreement, Max Townsend had been included in their little group. As it turned out, there was no reason to call a meeting—no discussion was necessary and there was no decision to be made—because of the single word Max Townsend had just uttered: *fire.*

"Just one spark from that explosion could turn even this soggy jungle into an inferno." All of them looked anxiously northwest, in the direction of the explosion. "There's no smoke or any sign yet," Townsend went on. "I've been watching. But it doesn't matter. We have to get away from here just as fast as we can."

Asa Mercer wasted no more time. "I'll take the first car. Shiloh, come with me; I know Dr. Duvall needs your help. Drake, will you take the second car?"

"Yes—but what do I tell the women?"

Asa had already started down the line to the first passenger car. Over his shoulder he answered, "Tell them the truth, that there might be a fire. Tell them that we're walking to Panama City."

❧

The journey was a nightmare from beginning to end. The first hundred yards alone took them almost two hours to negotiate. Crossing the sea of debris left by the tornado was like trying to wade through a three-foot-high pile of kindling. Many of the women got scratches and bruises, in addition to those they had sustained in the blind rush of panic that ensued in the passenger cars after the explosion.

Cheney rushed from woman to woman, trying desperately to make sure no one was seriously injured. But the men insisted that they move everyone on, so all she could do was look the women over as the ragged group moved in single file down the railroad tracks.

After she had attended to the women as best she could, Cheney decided to find Shiloh, who was leading the group with Max Townsend. Instead of threading her way through the strung-out group of women, she left the railroad tracks and quickly made her way to the front of the line on the narrow side path, close to the treeline.

She had almost caught up with Shiloh and Townsend and was about to call out to them when Shiloh happened to look back. He saw Cheney hurrying along, so close to the jungle that branches from straggly trees brushed her, and the look on his face turned into anger with a hint of fear. "Cheney, no—!" he called in a harsh voice—then leaped off the track toward her, grabbed her arm, and roughly hauled her back up onto the track.

Cheney looked frantically around and behind her. From the intensity of Shiloh's reaction, she figured that at the very least there must be a jungle cat stalking a few feet behind her—perhaps a painted native with a large spear. But there was nothing except the wall of jungle, and Cheney looked up at Shiloh impatiently.

"What in the world is the matter? You scared me to death!" They continued to walk along, Shiloh holding Cheney's arm too tightly, and she pried his grip loose with her other hand. Max Townsend glanced at the two and tactfully walked a little ahead of them.

"Don't walk that close to the jungle."

"Do you think you might have just *suggested* that to me? You didn't have to haul me up here—"

"Sorry." Shiloh's voice had a note of strain that Cheney had never heard before, and she anxiously searched his face. His jaw was rigid, and his eyes constantly searched the ground around his feet and to either side. She could feel the tension emanating from him—a total change from his usual casual demeanor.

"What's wrong, Shiloh?" she asked with sudden concern and a tinge of fear.

"Nothing," he answered shortly, his eyes on the ground in front. "You just don't need to be sashaying around in the jungle like that. Might be snakes."

"I wasn't sashaying, and I wasn't in the jungle," Cheney couldn't help but snap back. "And I never saw a snake."

Shiloh shrugged impatiently. "Don't matter. Looks snaky."

Cheney walked beside him in silence for a while, struggling to understand what was wrong with Shiloh. *Wonder if he's angry with me for something else—no, that's not it. We haven't had a fight in days.* She stole another appraising glance at Shiloh's face. *He really is frightened—of snakes. Odd. I didn't think he was afraid of anything. But he still didn't have to treat me like that. . . .*

Finally, unable to solve the puzzles in her mind, Cheney simply cleared her throat and began the conversation she had come for in the first place. "Shiloh, I need you to help me with something. We need to get the women better organized. Asa and I are struggling to keep walking among all of them, but they're strung out for what seems like miles. I thought you and I could go back and group them into pairs, to walk together, and each person could take some responsibility for her partner."

She glanced up at a rare glimpse of sky showing through the towering canopy of trees. "It's going to be dark soon, and we don't need any of the women lagging far behind. They're all on their feet, but some of them are in trauma-induced shock, and they might just wander off into the jungle if they aren't watched and helped along."

"Real good idea, Doc," Shiloh said in a more natural voice. For the first time since the explosion, he looked at her and smiled, and she was surprised at her own relief. "Let's go," he told her.

Soon the women were walking closely together in pairs. Shiloh seemed to have set aside his mysterious fears for the moment; and when he moved among the ladies, they smiled wearily at him and seemed to cheer up a little. Annie Stephens sighed in gratitude when he offered to carry the box out of which Rex glared resentfully because of the jostling he was getting.

But the journey was still hard and dangerous, and it grew more and more difficult as the hours wore on. Night overtook them suddenly, and they stopped briefly to light the lanterns they had taken from the train.

Asa came down the line, his face pale and drawn, his slender shoulders sagging; he could barely hold the heavy lantern upright. Cheney, struggling to carry her medical bag, understood all too well how he felt. But she could also tell that she was holding up better than Asa, whose energies seemed to run in short bursts. *He just doesn't have the stamina. He's really going to have a hard time of it,* she thought with the helpless sympathy she had felt all too many times in the last few hours.

Indeed, the journey quickly and cruelly delineated between those with strong constitutions and those who were frail. Allegra Winston-Smythe seemed distant and unaffected by the distressing turn of events; she walked along with impatience, while her beautiful companion Enid Alexander struggled to keep up. Lydia

Thornton, walking close beside Arlene Tate, talked encouragingly to the young girl but kept a watchful eye on Enid as well.

Georgia Jakes swaggered along, seemingly untouched by any of the hardships of the walk, prattling on in her now familiar boisterous drawl and swinging the small bag of "valuables" she had insisted on carrying with her.

Sybil walked stiffly beside her, staring straight ahead, a rough bandage on her forehead. She had fallen during the panic after the explosion and cut her head badly; Cheney knew it was going to leave an ugly scar. Since then, Sybil had seemed oblivious to everyone and everything around her, Cheney thought in wonder as the unlikely pair made their way along the tracks.

Powell Drake had assigned himself to walk with Martha Jane and the children and now marched powerfully on with little Kelvey on his shoulders. Cheney was concerned about Martha Jane's pale face, but she trudged determinedly forward, holding Stony's hand. The little boy was uncharacteristically quiet.

Even the Porcelain Doll looked a little cracked after a few hours in the jungle. Her perky ringlets had long since wilted, her flawless complexion was marred by scratches, and her flirtatious flouncing had long since given way to a sober walk. She and her walking partner Annie Stephens seemed to have little to say to each other.

Finally as they stopped for a short rest, Cheney wearily sank to the track and looked around her at the exhausted faces. The past few hours had been brutal for everyone.

But somehow, I've done pretty well, haven't I? Much better than I ever thought I would.

Suddenly it was clear to Cheney that although she had managed to obtain the sheepskin that proclaimed her a doctor, up to now she had never been really certain that she was one—a true physician, a healer of body and mind and spirit. *But in the last few hours, that's what I've been. I've really taken care of people, no matter if the hurt was a cut, or fear, or confusion, or just the need for reassurance from someone calm, someone capable, someone who knows exactly what to do. Someone like me!*

As she sat on the railroad tracks in the middle of a tangled jungle, a slender form in tattered clothes, her head bowed, Cheney made a silent vow to Asa Mercer and to each person in his charge: *I can take care of you, and I promise I will, to the very best of my ability. I'll walk farther than you. I'll carry more burdens than you, and I swear I'll keep looking for ways to make this journey easier for each of you. I won't quit until every last one of you is safe in Seattle.*

And so they marched on through the jungle, deep into the night. By the time they finally reached Panama City, they were bruised, scratched, frightened, covered with insect bites and stings—and fatigued almost to the point of unconsciousness. A couple of the women—and Asa Mercer—were on the edge of collapse.

"We're alive," Cheney said gently to Asa as they wearily followed Max Townsend down a quiet, deserted street toward a hotel he had told them about. "And no one's seriously hurt. Thank God."

"Yes," he said in a voice so faint and weary it was barely audible. "Thank God."

❧

"Señorita Doctora?" The pounding on the door and the heavily accented voice grew more insistent. "Señorita Doctora? You are in this room? Señorita—"

The door flew open, and the young hotel clerk stared at the sight of the woman—hair clouded about her face and falling in a tangle over both shoulders and down her back, her green eyes heavy with sleep. Her clothes were dirty, and the hem of the once-exquisite green satin skirt was shredded in filthy tatters about her slender bare feet. Heedless of his scrutiny, she yawned delicately. "I'm Dr. Duvall. What is it?"

The man recovered his smooth manner and bowed slightly. "They have brought a man here, Señorita Doctora. He is badly hurt, and he is a gringo. The man that owns the *punta*—he thinks perhaps you lost him."

"I lost him?" Cheney repeated blankly. Her body might have been standing up and walking around, but her mind was still struggling to come fully out of sleep. "But—oh, never mind, you said he's hurt? I'm coming, just wait."

The door slammed in the clerk's face, and he was afraid to disobey Cheney's tone of command, so he stood in the exact spot until she opened it a few moments later. She almost knocked him down as she rushed out the door.

"Eh—this way, Señorita Doctora," he said nervously as he skittered out of harm's way. Cheney's room was on the second floor of the hotel, which was a plain, square box of a building with smaller square boxes inside for rooms. The clerk led Cheney down the stairs and along a hallway to a room exactly like hers: a plain cubicle with an iron bed, a small table made of beautiful dark wood, and a large crucifix carved out of the same wood and hung over the bed on the whitewashed wall. To the right was a single small window with white curtains that stirred delicately with the morning's cool breeze.

Muted yellow light poured through the window and fell softly on the bed; but even that gentle tropical morning didn't soften the vision of the man who lay face down on the clean white cotton bedcover. He was stripped to the waist, and his back was a deep, painful red. Here and there large blisters were forming. The hair had been burned off the back of his head in a strangely neat circle that began behind his ears and went up to the crown, and the sensitive skin of the open area was already fully blistered. Coarse black hair still covered the top and sides of his head.

The moment Cheney set eyes on the man, she drew in a sharp breath; the clerk nodded with satisfaction when he saw that Cheney knew him. And she did, only too well. It was Bull Lynch!

"Find my nurse, right now!" she ordered, and her voice made the clerk jump in the silence of the room. Already she was at the small table laying out medical instruments and bottles. "He's a tall gringo, long blond hair, long legs, handsome. Find him and tell him Cheney said to come right now." She turned her back on the man and immediately forgot him.

The young man turned and ran down the hall once again to do the imperious young senorita's bidding. As he ran he thought frantically, *Women! Who can understand them? How do I know a "handsome" gringo when I see one? They all look alike to me.*

An hour later Cheney and Shiloh sent for Lydia, who came immediately. Before Cheney could ask, Lydia began to boss them. "Go down the street three doorways," she told them as she practically shoved them out into the hall. "There's a nice little cantina, and they'll give you these wonderful little fried pastries called *sopaipillas* and good hot coffee. Go on! I know how to take care of someone who's been burned."

"Your burns were worse than his, Lydia," Shiloh grunted, pulling insistently on Cheney's arm, "so don't feel too sorry for him."

Cheney was still a little hesitant. "Are you sure you don't mind staying with him?" She glanced worriedly at Bull as Lydia firmly began to close the door. "He can be a difficult patient, to say the least, and he's not much of a gentleman—"

"Take all the time you want, Dr. Duvall." A mischievous smile lit Lydia's features. "I'm going to read the Bible to him, to keep him company."

Within ten minutes Shiloh and Cheney sat on low benches at a rough plank table in the cantina, licking honey off their fingers and filling up the hollows in the crusty golden bread with more. "Do you think he caused the explosion?" Cheney asked, her mouth full and a drop of honey slowly sliding down her chin.

Absently Shiloh reached over and wiped the drop of honey off with one finger as he shook his head. "Couldn't be. What would a pug like Bull be doing with nitroglycerin? It's—"

"I might be able to answer that question." Max Townsend appeared in the doorway into the small room. Cheney and Shiloh were the lone patrons; even the young girl who had served them had disappeared.

With a gracious nod of assent from Cheney—her mouth was still full—Townsend smiled slightly and sat down on the rough bench beside her and across from Shiloh.

"I expect Shiloh's told you about me? Thought so," he nodded, sparing her from interrupting her eating to talk. "Anyway, your charred friend back at the hotel almost certainly stole the nitro from the *Continental*."

"But he's just a coal stoker," Shiloh argued, "and not a very smart one, either. How—why—?"

"I don't know how or why—yet, but it's the only possible explanation. I happen to know for certain that there is no other nitroglycerin in Panama right now—not a drop, except what was brought in yesterday on your steamer. The only logical explanation is that it was stolen by someone aboard your ship and that it detonated while they were carting it around out in the jungle. Who could it have been but this Bull?"

Cheney was shocked to realize that they had docked in Aspinwall only yesterday—it seemed to her that they had been out in the jungle for days. The thought distracted her for a few moments, but Shiloh continued the conversation.

"I see your point," he finally relented, "and you must be right—I can't think of another explanation."

Townsend nodded, leaned back, and crossed his arms. "Well, Mr. Bull Lynch has presented me with a problem. I'm personally responsible for that shipment, and I have the power to make all decisions relating to it." He spoke matter-of-factly, without bravado, and Shiloh nodded in understanding.

"Lynch needs to be taken to San Francisco," Townsend continued. "I believe he committed a crime, and that crime was executed on the *Continental*—which for legal purposes is considered American soil. Good thing for him, too—if he was left to Panamanian justice, he'd be swinging from some tree this minute. But the crime was committed against Bingham-Lloyd, Limited, because they were the owners of record at the time."

Cheney and Shiloh registered identical surprise. "Bingham-Lloyd?" Shiloh asked. "The same company that owns the *Continental* and the *Conqueror*?"

"The same Mr. Bingham and Mr. Lloyd," Townsend nodded with ill-disguised amusement.

"But why would they be shipping guns and explosives to a jungle guerrilla in Panama?"

Townsend waved a brown hand in a global gesture. "I think you've seen how much money comes into Aspinwall and through Panama. There are certain plans to build a canal through Panama, which would increase the shipping traffic—and therefore the money—immensely. Bingham-Lloyd, Limited, would own a large interest in this canal."

Townsend looked around and dropped his voice lower, even though they still appeared to be alone. "The present Panamanian government is a guerrilla organization just like Zaldivar's, headed by a man named Montenegro, who stormed the governor's mansion about a year ago and named himself governor. There is one critical difference in the two organizations, however, and this explains Bingham-Lloyd's sponsorship. Montenegro opposes plans to build a canal in Panama, and Zaldivar supports it completely."

The light of comprehension dawned on Cheney's and Shiloh's faces. "How in this world did Bull Lynch get involved with all that?" Cheney murmured, mystified.

There was a slight sound at the door, and the three looked up to see Lydia walking quickly toward their table in the back corner. "Cheney, Shiloh, there's something I have to tell you."

She glanced at Max Townsend vacantly for a moment, then recognition dawned. She seemed to have no time for gracious manners, however, because she went on in an urgent tone. "Sybil came to try to see Bull, but I wouldn't let her. We—argued—" Lydia's voice grew troubled and her delicate lips twisted with sadness. "Oh, never mind how it happened. Sybil finally told me that she knew Bull had a friend with him out in the jungle, someone named Beans Lowery. She seems sure of it, and she insists he might be hurt. She thinks Bull probably just left him out there to die."

A loaded silence fell over the group as Lydia finished her story, and Cheney and Shiloh exchanged troubled glances. Cheney could barely remember Bull's shadow, his redheaded friend Beans. But Shiloh had been around him some, down in steerage, when Bull wasn't around, and Shiloh liked the cheerful, sturdy Beans Lowery.

"Doesn't matter to you three who it is, does it—or even if he's dead?" Max Townsend asked as he shrewdly studied the faces of his companions. "Because he probably is. Bull was a lucky man, and odds aren't good that there'd be two men that lucky in the same place at the same time."

No one even bothered to answer him, and Townsend didn't expect it. He knew that people like these couldn't just walk away from the possibility—however remote—that a man might be lying injured out in the jungle. A faint smile turned up the corners of his thin mouth as he began. "I talked to the man who brought Bull in on his *punta*—that's a little boat. I've got to go back to the scene of the explosion, anyway, to make sure that nothing's slowly smoldering out there and to conduct an investigation, so I'll—"

"I'm going," Cheney announced firmly, her eyes already beginning to flash green fire as she looked at Shiloh. He began to look stubborn, too, and opened his mouth, but they were interrupted by Lydia's soft voice.

"Dr. Duvall, you can't go. You have to let Shiloh do this." She put her heavily bandaged hand on Cheney's shoulder, which was stiff with resentment.

"I'm the doctor," she replied shortly. Her eyes never left Shiloh's face. "He's—there's a reason—he . . . I have to go," she faltered.

She knows I'm scared, Shiloh thought suddenly. *Scared of the snakes.* The hackles on the back of his neck rose, but he grimly pushed away the fear that loomed large and dark in his mind. "No, Cheney. I'm going," he said tautly.

The pressure on Cheney's shoulder grew a little more insistent. "Think about it, Dr. Duvall," Lydia said gently. "They may have to carry him—maybe a long way. And you need to be here, to take care of Bull and the rest of us. Shiloh's a good nurse, but right now we need a doctor around here."

Cheney tore her gaze away from Shiloh to look up at Lydia. "But you don't understand," she said with intensity. "Shiloh can't—"

Abruptly Shiloh stood up. "Yes, I can, Doc," he answered, and his voice was steady. "I have to. But thanks anyway."

He turned to Townsend, who rose, and drawled, "Let's go find that man with the fancy-soundin' boat. See you later, Doc—Lydia." Both men started toward the door, talking in low voices.

"Shiloh," Lydia called after him, and he stopped and turned. "Tread on the lion! Don't forget!"

The familiar easy grin lit Shiloh's face. "I'm treadin', right now! Thanks, Lydia!" He and Townsend disappeared through the cantina door.

"What was that all about?" Cheney asked.

"Hmm? Oh, it's a psalm. I'll show it to you sometime. Now, let's get back to the hotel—I need to see if I can find Sybil."

"Who'd you leave Bull with?" Cheney asked, dragging her mind back to her present responsibilities.

"Georgia."

Cheney laughed with joy. "You mean to tell me that all in the space of a single morning, Bull's had to deal with me doctoring him, Shiloh nursing him, you reading the Bible to him—and now Georgia Jakes?"

"Yes," Lydia answered, her eyes sparkling. "When I left, Georgia was asking him to help her pick out a ribbon to trim her hat with. She had bought lots and lots of ribbon, and she told him they were going to discuss them all. At great length."

Cheney and Lydia decided they were not in such a hurry to relieve Georgia, after all, and Cheney went to her room to rest. She fell asleep immediately, but her sleep was troubled with dreams, mostly scenes from the arduous trek the day before. She had slept for several hours, however, when again a knock at her door roused her. This time she started awake immediately, and she recognized the voice as Powell Drake's.

"Dr. Duvall? May I speak with you a moment, please?"

Immediately Cheney went to open the door. Drake's face was haggard, and his voice was rough with fatigue. "I hate to disturb you—I know you need your rest—but—please . . ." His words trailed off as he struggled to control his visible anguish.

"Come in, Mr. Drake, and tell me what's the matter while I get my medical bag in order." She turned her back to him, giving him time to collect himself, and aimlessly rummaged around in her perfectly ordered medical bag. Hearing him take a tentative step inside the room, she asked quietly, "Is it one of the children?"

"Yes, it's Stony," he answered, and now his voice was more controlled. "He got a little fever last night, not long after we arrived. I—I—helped Martha Jane with him, because she was so very tired, you know, but she didn't want to disturb you, so I've been—"

"You haven't slept? All night? And you didn't come get me?" Abruptly Cheney stopped reproaching him. She could see he was tortured enough by his own thoughts. "It's all right, Mr. Drake. Let's go."

He led her just down the hall from her own room to a slightly larger one that held two of the small iron beds. Kelvey lay in one, sleeping soundly, and Stony lay in the other. He looked much smaller than he did when he was up running around.

Martha Jane, who was sitting on the edge of the bed holding in her hand a cool wet cloth with which she'd wiped Stony's face, stood up quickly when Cheney came in. Cheney leaned over to lay her hand on Stony's forehead, which was hot and dry. Slowly his eyes opened, and he looked up at her with a weak smile. "Hi, Dr. Cheney. Am I sick?"

"Yes, you are, and I want you to stop it right now." Cheney smiled gaily down at him, but she was troubled. *Doesn't look good. Fever's too high, and the whites of his eyes are a little yellow—jaundice—?*

"That's the kind of doctor I am, you know, the bossy kind," she went on as she examined him. "I just visit all my patients and tell them to quit fooling around and get well, and the ones who don't do it are in big trouble."

He giggled, just a little, at Cheney's foolishness, and she continued to tease him as she probed and checked. Martha Jane watched silently on the other side of the bed. Cheney was almost as concerned about her as she was about Stony. Martha Jane was so drawn and pale that she looked half dead.

Stony was clearly exhausted by the time Cheney finished. But he was resting comfortably and his breathing was even, and Cheney thought that his fever might have cooled a little. She whispered simple instructions to Martha Jane and then ordered her to get some sleep, too, or soon she would be bedridden herself. Then Cheney went out in the hall and told Powell Drake the same thing. Finally she went back to her room to wait for Shiloh.

For a while Cheney paced in her room, restless and unable to settle down. The hours dragged on interminably, and she finally decided to go find Lydia. She went up and down the halls, talking idly to some of the women and listening to their ills. Mercer's

Belles, needless to say, overflowed the small hotel, and they were all going casually from room to room, as if they were at a party at a large estate. All of them were ragged, disheveled, bruised, scratched, and stung, but most of the fear and shock had worn off with rest and food.

Eventually Cheney found Lydia sitting in her room with the door open, looking out the window and singing softly. Cheney stopped in the doorway, motionless. The song was hauntingly beautiful, in a minor key that Lydia's low, strong voice expressed perfectly.

> *Surely, surely, He delivers me from the snare;*
> *No pestilence may come nigh, for He guards me;*
> *I fear not the terror by night,*
> *Nor for the arrow that flieth by day,*
> *For He guards me.*
>
> *A thousand fell at my side,*
> *Ten thousand at my right hand,*
> *But the destruction came to naught when it came by me,*
> *For He guards me.*
>
> *No evil befalls me, no plague dare come nigh,*
> *His angels have charge over me,*
> *I tread upon the lion, upon the adder I tread,*
> *For He guards me.*

The last clear note faded away, and Cheney said quietly, "Lydia, that's one of the most beautiful songs I've ever heard!"

She looked up at Cheney, her eyes shining with pleasure. "Oh, hello, Cheney, and thank you. Come in, please." She patted the bed, signaling Cheney to sit down.

"That—that was a *song*," Cheney commented, somewhat confused. "What you said to Shiloh, about treading on the lion. I thought you said it was a *psalm*."

"I did. It is. That's what the song is based on, Psalm 91, and that's the psalm Shiloh and I were talking about. I read it to him earlier today."

"Umm—my Bible is on the train, in my luggage. Would you mind if I read yours? I'd—I guess I'm just curious."

Lydia smiled and motioned to a large, worn Bible that lay on the small table. It was already open to Psalm 91, and Cheney's eyes immediately fell on verse 13. "Thou shalt tread upon the lion and adder: the young lion and the dragon shalt thou trample under foot."

"He can't help it, you know," Lydia said matter-of-factly. "A bully at the orphanage put a snake down his shirt when he was young. It bit him several times, and he got very sick and almost died. He's been fighting a horrible fear of them all his life."

Cheney dropped her eyes. "I'm—rather ashamed of myself, because he didn't confide in me, you see. I've just kind of—nosed around and—and—well, it's just that he doesn't know that I know."

"Yes, he does," Lydia said calmly.

At that moment the topic of their conversation appeared at Lydia's door. Shiloh was dirty, his breeches torn, his boots muddy, and there were bloody scratches on his arms and face. But his blue eyes shone as he said simply, "We found him! He's alive."

Cheney jumped up and ran up to him. She put her hands on his chest and searched his face. "You're all right?" she whispered.

He smiled down at her as he put his arms around her waist. "Now," he answered, "I'm just fine."

PART FOUR

He Divideth the Sea

Thus saith the Lord, which giveth the sun for a light by day, and the ordinances of the moon and of the stars for a light by night, which divideth the sea when the waves thereof roar; The Lord of hosts is his name.

Jeremiah 31:35

17

Vomito Negro

"The *Conqueror* may be the *Continental*'s sister ship—but they sure aren't twin sisters, are they?" Shiloh remarked.

"No, they certainly aren't. What does that mean, anyway—'sister ship'?" Cheney asked.

"Two ships, built at the same time, from the same plans. Captain Weldon told me the *Continental* was built in San Francisco and the *Conqueror* in New York. For their maiden voyages, they both sailed around the Horn at the same time. The *Conqueror* reached San Francisco one day after the *Continental* reached New York."

They were standing at the rail of the *Conqueror*'s stateroom deck and watching the dock workers as they snaked a long line from the nearby railroad to the ship with luggage and cargo.

Cheney had been surprised to see that some of the workers were native women. They were dressed in riotously colored clothes, some of them simple squares of fabric wrapped around them and then tied. Most of them were barefoot. They walked with unconscious grace, large bags and boxes on their heads, their slender, lithe arms making a lovely arc as they steadied their burdens.

"Well, I'll have to admit," Cheney confessed to Shiloh, continuing their conversation. "I liked the *Continental* better."

"Can't argue with that," he answered.

The two of them had already taken a short tour of the two top decks and had learned that, although the deck layout of the *Conqueror* was identical to that of the *Continental*, the resemblance ended there. Where the *Continental* seemed warm, sumptuous, and full of light, the *Conqueror* felt cold, impersonal, and spare. The officers and seamen kept their heads down and their conversations short, and wore somber navy blue instead of the whites that Cheney now realized were so attractive.

Cheney and Shiloh had also discovered that this ship offered no Ladies' and Gentlemen's Salons. The corresponding rooms on the *Conqueror*'s promenade deck were padlocked and posted with stern signs, warning: "Storage. Keep Out." Cheney was curious to see how this ship's Grand Salon compared with the luxurious chamber on the *Continental*. She would find out soon enough, because Mercer's Belles were scheduled to meet Captain Drury there momentarily.

"Look!" Shiloh pointed to the docks. Cheney saw Max Townsend hurrying toward the ship with a large valise. Shiloh yelled down to him, "What's the hurry, Townsend? Thousand guerrillas after you?"

Townsend shaded his eyes and looked up, his white teeth flashing in a smile. "Not so far! You got Bull?"

"Yep! He's full of it, too!"

Townsend pointed to the gangplank, and Shiloh and Cheney went down to meet him.

Townsend had disappeared the second day of their stay in Panama City; Shiloh had speculated that he had gone to meet Zaldivar to make arrangements for transfer of the cargo. Shiloh was probably right, for later that day their train had steamed triumphantly into the city, engineered by a man Cheney assumed was one of Zaldivar's guerrillas—a silent man with a bristling black moustache, cold black eyes, a new rifle, and two thick, heavy bandoliers that crossed on his chest. He had made no explanations and answered no questions, just climbed down from the engine cab, joined a group of about a dozen men embarking from the first passenger car and silently walked off with them in the direction of the jungle.

Cheney had noted that two of the train's boxcars were missing. She had been very happy that the infamous nitroglycerin was nowhere in Panama City. And she had been overjoyed to see her luggage again.

"We wondered if you were hanging from a tree out there somewhere," Shiloh said as he and Townsend shook hands. "Glad to see you made it."

"Thanks. Made it fine, under the circumstances. You say you got Bull Lynch and the other one? They're on board?"

"Yeah," Shiloh answered shortly.

Townsend gave him a curious look but merely said, "Thanks for taking care of that for me. Technically he's my responsibility, but I just couldn't get back to the city any sooner. Anyway, I need to talk to the captain. Any idea where he is?"

"We're about to have a meeting with him in the Grand Salon. Why don't you come along?"

Cheney and Shiloh escorted Max to his stateroom to leave his valise. Then the three went up to the Grand Salon, Asa Mercer joining them on the way. They descended a fan-shaped marble staircase identical to the one on the *Continental,* but the *Conqueror*'s Grand Salon was outfitted with dull green carpeting and chairs—no mirrors, no piano or harp, and no warmth. Captain Drury was already there, pacing in front of the staircase.

As the *Conqueror* and the *Continental* were two sides of a coin, so were Captain Charles Drury and Captain Cyrus Weldon. Captain Drury was tall, spare, and dour, with sparse silver hair framing a sharply angled face. His eyes were gray and piercing, his mouth a straight line. He somehow managed to be much more polite than Captain Weldon, though less courteous.

Introductions were made and everyone sat down in a group of chairs unbolted from the floor and drawn up in a loose circle. Cheney began the conversation promptly. "Captain Drury, our group has several problems, and we requested this meeting with you both to inform you of them and to ask your assistance."

She paused, but Drury only nodded shortly, so Cheney swallowed hard and went on. "First of all, may we consult with your purser about our cabin assignments? For one thing, my nurse and I had a family suite on the *Continental,* with the middle room serving as an infirmary. We need this same arrangement made, if possible—"

Drury held up a strong, long-fingered hand. "I have no purser, Dr. Duvall. I attend to all the financial affairs of the ship. Your group has fifty-four staterooms reserved for them, and you may assign them as you wish. Please just give me the names of the persons assigned to each stateroom."

"Thank you, Captain," Cheney answered in a formal tone that matched his. "Now, we have thirteen women and one young boy who have contracted some sort of fever and are seriously ill. As the physician on board, I would like to request that we stock extra supplies of fresh fruit—also soup stock and light foods that people with high fevers might be able to eat. We may need a lot of extra foods of this sort, especially if any of the crew should come down with this fever."

"Dr. Duvall, please allow me to assure you that there is no need for you to take on the burden of being the ship's doctor," Drury said in a steely voice that matched his eyes. "I attend to the officers and crew when they need it. And the *Conqueror* has been stocked with the correct allotment of foods for the amount of people on board and the length of the voyage that we are taking. If anyone wants or needs special foods, they are welcome to bring them aboard. But special diets and food preparation tailored to each person is simply not a service that we are able to provide."

"But—" Cheney began anxiously.

"It's all right, Dr. Duvall," Asa said with a tired gesture. "I'll send one of the stewards to the marketplace to stock up on fruit and other necessities. We can restock in Realejo." He was unusually pale and Cheney noticed a slight sheen of sweat on his forehead as he spoke. *Oh no,* she thought dismally, *not Asa, too!*

"Not my stewards, I'm afraid, Mr. Mercer. They have heavy duties when we are boarding and readying the ship for departure."

"It's all right; I'll go," Townsend offered. "I'll be glad to stock up on whatever you need, Dr. Duvall, if it can be found in Panama City. I owe you a debt for taking responsibility for my prisoners." He turned back to Captain Drury. "Which brings me to the reason I'm here, Captain. As you may know, I represent Pinkerton's Detective Agency. I have two prisoners that I must take to San Francisco. At present they are both under Dr. Duvall's care—one of them has serious burns and the other has two fractured legs and a head injury."

"You people must understand that this is neither a hospital ship nor a prison ship. The *Conqueror* will transport you to your destination as quickly as we can, with the most comfort we can afford—but we have no facilities for these special situations."

Townsend's dark eyes glinted for a moment; then his face returned to its usual passivity. "Captain Drury, I do understand you—perfectly," he nodded as he rose. "I'm not asking for any special consideration. As I said, I will take full responsibility for these prisoners. I merely wanted to apprise you of the situation. Now, if you will all excuse me—" With a sketch of a bow to Cheney, he turned and left the salon.

"Anything else I can help you with?" Captain Drury asked as he, too, rose.

"No, Captain, you've been such an enormous help already," Cheney answered in a sugary voice. The irony escaped Captain Drury, who smiled a tight smile that didn't reach his eyes; then he left the room.

Asa, Cheney, and Shiloh spoke for a few more minutes about supplies and cabin assignments. Some of the women started wandering into the salon and gathering in small groups, talking and glancing toward the three leaders, but they didn't approach them. Max Townsend returned for a list of supplies Cheney

needed, and disappeared again. Asa drooped in his chair, growing paler with each passing moment.

"Asa, I want you to go to your cabin right now," Cheney ordered. "You don't look well. I'm going to speak to the ladies for a
few minutes, then I'll be along to check on you."

Slowly and with obvious effort, Asa pushed himself out of
his chair. "No need, Cheney. I've got it, don't I? So I'll just get to
bed and rest. You make sure all the ladies are all right." He made
his way slowly out of the salon, unaware that Annie Stephens'
gentle brown eyes followed every step he took.

Cheney watched him go, too, her face lined with worry.
Then her expression cleared and she walked to the empty marble
dais. "Ladies, please listen," she called. Shiloh had followed her
and stood by her side, arms crossed. Every eye turned to them.
"You all know that several of the women are sick with a fever—"

"How many are sick now?" Georgia interrupted.

"Thirteen women and Stony Terrell," Cheney answered.

"Fourteen," Allegra Winston-Smythe called in a voice devoid
of inflection. "Enid's very sick."

Oh no! Cheney thought with dread. *This climate's been horrible for her consumption—she was already half dead.* The dark-
haired beauty who had been Allegra Winston-Smythe's cabin
mate had finally confided to Shiloh that she was really going to
Seattle for her health. But she had grown steadily weaker over
the course of the journey—and now this. *How many more will get
this horrible plague?* Cheney worried.

"All right," Cheney nodded. "She's never been very strong. I'll
see her as soon as I can. Now, you all know that Bull Lynch and
Beans Lowery are both hurt and that Shiloh and I have been caring for them. Please realize that all of this has put a very heavy
burden on us, but we're going to work as hard as we can to make
sure everyone is cared for."

"What kind of sickness is this, Dr. Duvall?" Annie asked anxiously. "How do you treat it?"

Cheney and Shiloh exchanged glances. His eyes were kind and strong, and Cheney took a deep breath. "I'm sorry; I just don't know. I've never seen a fever like this before, and I—I haven't found the c-cure or the t-treatment for it yet."

A low murmur ran around the room, and some of the eyes turned toward the dais were angry and full of suspicion. Holly Van Buren complained loudly, "Don't know what it is? What kind of a doctor—"

"*Vomito negro,*" Tani said in a calm voice that carried throughout the room. "That is what the natives call it—black vomit. We had it in New Orleans, many times. We called it yellow fever."

An anxious murmur ran through the room; many of the ladies had heard of yellow fever. And Cheney suddenly swallowed, searching her memory for what she had read about the disease. As far as she could remember, there was no known cure.

"You've seen this?" she asked Tani in hopeful desperation. "Can you tell us anything about it that will help?"

Tani shook her head mutely and lowered her eyes, refusing to say more. Cheney sighed and looked around the room, unflinchingly meeting all gazes directed at her. In a totally unconscious action she moved a few inches closer to Shiloh as she spoke to the women.

"Ladies, I need your help, and that's why I wanted to talk to you. Shiloh and I can only do so much, and right now what these sick people need is attention. They need to be bathed when their fever is high. They need to be encouraged to drink just as much liquid as they possibly can—including quinine water, which all of you need to drink. They need to be helped with chamberpots, and keeping themselves clean and their bedding dry and comfortable. I'm going to mix some medicines that they will need to take at least three times a day."

"I'll help," Annie and Lydia said simultaneously. The bandages were off now, but Lydia's hands still looked raw and painful. Several of the other women called out that their cabin mates were sick and that they would gladly take good care of them. Others asked Cheney to tell them what to do or call them anytime, day or night.

"Well," Georgia Jakes drawled, putting her hands on her hips and gazing around the room, "I'll help, too, and ya'll are gonna be grateful to me, I can tell you. I'll take care of that ol' Bull Lynch, so Dr. Duvall can help the ladies—and Stony. I'm the only one in this room that's mean enough to keep his paws off my skirts, anyway."

Murmurs of shock swept through the room; for some reason Shiloh noted that Tani's warm brown face drained of some of its color, and again she ducked her head.

"Well, if he feels good enough to be grabbing at you, Georgia, how much nursing does he need?" Miss Ordway, the little schoolteacher, asked.

"Oh, that's the fun part," Georgia answered, smiling sweetly. "I get to pour this stinking yellow stuff all over his back and that bald head. Stings him bad; he yelps like a stepped-on puppy."

Nervous laughter floated around the room, and Cheney could see that the ugly mood of a few minutes before was slowly dissipating. "Thank you, Georgia," Cheney nodded with sincerity. "You can joke about it if you like, but I happen to know that taking care of any sick person is difficult and demanding, and I appreciate you and your offer."

For the first time Cheney had ever seen, Georgia Jakes blushed at the compliment. The blush made her look younger and much prettier.

With a wide smile, Lydia volunteered, "I can take care of Beans Lowery, Dr. Duvall, if you'll just tell me what to do. I know it's mostly just sitting by his bed."

"Thank you, Lydia. If you'll stay for just a few minutes, I'll talk to you about it. Ladies, that's all I have to say, except for two things: thank you very much, each one, and please, above everything else—everyone pray. Pray for those who are sick and those of us who are taking care of them."

Two nights and three days passed that, to Cheney, seemed like a continual march up and down the dark, hot, subterranean hallways of Hades. It was midnight on Wednesday, June 3. Cheney was now stumbling blindly down the passageway from Enid Alexander's cabin, seeing demons in the dark corners of the unlit hallways, desperately aiming for the dim gray square ahead that was the door to the stateroom deck.

Wildly she fought back tears in her eyes and bile in her throat. *Crying won't help them, none of them!* she scolded herself bitterly. *And I don't have time to be sick! If I can just have—some air—clean air—not sickroom smells—*

Almost sobbing with relief, she rushed through the door and ran across the deck to sag helplessly against the deck railing, gulping in air as she buried her face in her folded arms.

"But, Allegra—" Shiloh's voice came to her ears, carried on the strong night wind. His tall form was about ten feet away, his back to her. He was facing the icily beautiful Allegra Winston-Smythe. Cheney knew Allegra hadn't seen her, either.

"No." Cheney could hear her cool voice only faintly. "I won't—I can't. I barely know her. We just happened to be cabin mates, that's all. I don't know anything about her, and I—I can't help her."

"Yes, you can," Shiloh argued. His voice sounded strained, with barely controlled anger. "You can be there for her, to talk to her, just to hold her hand. She doesn't have anyone, and she's—"

Cheney had moved closer to them, pulling herself along the deck railing in her weakness. "It doesn't matter now, Shiloh. Enid just died. She was alone."

Allegra's face was unearthly in the bright moonlight. She looked like a Greek statue carved of white marble. Her face never changed expression as she looked at Cheney; her only reaction was to put one slender white hand to her throat for a moment. Then she walked past Shiloh and Cheney like a lovely ghost in the night.

Shiloh had quickly turned at Cheney's voice, stunned by the words. As he looked at her, she felt nausea sweep over her, and dizziness, and weakness—all at the same time—her knees buckled, she sagged. Instantly, Shiloh swept her up in his arms. For long moments he held her, Cheney's arms instinctively thrown around his neck, his face close to hers, dark with worry, her eyelids drooping heavily, shadowing her eyes.

"Not you, Cheney," he murmured desperately. "Oh, God, please, no! Not you!"

"No—no—I'm fine—put me down," she whispered not very convincingly. Shiloh still held her tightly in his arms for a few moments, and Cheney closed her eyes, unable to meet his piercing gaze. Then he walked over to a deck chaise, lowered her into it with ease, and sat facing her on the one beside it.

"You're not sick." He swallowed with great relief, and Cheney stared at him. She could see that now he was embarrassed, and he settled back in the chaise, propping up his long legs with deliberate slowness, and put his hands behind his head. "I'm just now getting you broke in good," he drawled. "Don't want to have to start all over again with some other helpless doctor."

"Oh," she said in a small voice.

Slowly Shiloh brought his hands from behind his head. His right hand stole out; he took Cheney's cold one and held it, caressing it lightly to warm it. He was still looking negligently out to sea, his profile strong and shadowed strangely by the moon that traveled with the ship. "Sometimes a man gets something he can't stand to lose, Cheney. And I guess that's how I'm beginning to feel about you."

Cheney was so tired that she just ignored the possibilities and implications of Shiloh's words. Holding tightly to his hand, she relaxed in the chair, and simply enjoyed his nearness. They sat for a long time, and no other words passed between them.

As the days passed, four other women died, and twenty-four more came down with the fever. Two crewmen also became sick, and in spite of Captain Drury's initial coolness, he allowed Cheney to attend them. One of them died within twenty-four hours of contracting the fever.

That was the maddening aspect of this mysterious disease. Cheney's medicine seemed to help the symptoms a little, but nothing really reversed the progress of the fever, and there seemed to be no way to predict who would succumb. Sometimes the patients' vomit would turn black, and their skin would turn completely yellow, and then they would die. Others would toss with high fevers, develop a sickly jaundice, throw up repeatedly, and then suddenly begin to improve. Cheney could see no logic in it, and nothing she tried seemed to help the ones who died.

At the end of the first week, shy little Arlene Tate, who had kept off the weight she had lost and had slowly begun to emerge from her shell, died within hours.

Cheney left Arlene's cabin, closing the door softly behind her, hot tears welling up in her eyes. She swallowed hard, but now she couldn't force them back, and they spilled down her face in two continuous streams as she stumbled toward the infirmary.

She sat down on the ugly straight-backed chair—the ones in the *Conqueror*'s cabins didn't have the ruffled, overstuffed cushions that the *Continental*'s had—and stubbornly picked up her pocket watch. She stared at it, willing it to come into focus, ignoring her tears and the reason for them for a moment. Slowly the tiny numbers swam into view, and she smiled faintly. They were surrounded by twinkling little rubies and diamonds. Her father had given her the delicate gold watch and chain for her birthday two years ago.

Fatigue pulled at her, slowing down her usual quickness of thought. Then she sat up abruptly, thinking, *Stony—I've got* *to check on Stony. . . .*Then something in her mutinied, and she fought with the impulse to shove the thought away.

Almost hourly since the plague had grasped the ship, she had been forced to make hard decisions, and again and again she had to accept the flinty truth that one of her charges was not going to survive. Each death had been a wrenching, traumatic experience for Cheney, and more than once she had fled to her cabin and surrendered to a fit of weeping, pressing her face against the bedclothes to keep anyone from hearing her sobs.

I can't lose Stony, too! It's not fair—!

Her hands began to tremble and a sickness rose in her throat. Still, she forced herself to stand, to open her stateroom door, to move down the corridor to the stateroom where the boy lay. She found Martha Jane sitting in a straight chair beside the sick boy, her face pale and drawn, her thin hands clutching a wet cloth. "Powell has Kelvey," she said. Her sunken eyes were fixed on the face of her son, and she shook her head. "He—still hasn't come out of the coma, Cheney."

Something hot and bitter rose in Cheney's throat, but she tried to speak normally. "Sometimes it happens that way," she said, putting her hand on the woman's shoulder. "You go to my room and get a little rest—" She saw the resistance beginning to form in Martha Jane's weary eyes and urged, "Go on, now. We've got a long way to go with Stony, and you have to keep your strength up. I'll sit with him, and if he wakes up I'll send for you."

Martha Jane protested, but she was almost ready to collapse with fatigue, so she finally yielded to Cheney's urgings. As soon as she left the room, Cheney sat down abruptly on the chair and stared at the little boy's face, placing her hand on his forehead. He was hot to the touch, so she picked up Martha Jane's cloth and continued the work of sponging him with cool water to bring his fever down. He had lost so much weight that the sight of his emaciated body frightened her—and when she took his pulse, the faint, erratic beat made her catch her breath.

"Oh, God—don't let him die!"

It was a prayer she repeated many times for the next two hours; but as the hands on her watch wound inexorably around, she saw that the boy was losing ground. His vital signs were ebbing away, and there was *nothing* she could do about it.

In desperate frustration, she sank back into her chair and closed her eyes, trembling with anger at her own impotence. And suddenly, strangely, she was hearing her father's voice telling her, "Honey, I think you get more pleasure out of putting those things neatly in boxes than you do finding them. . . ."

He had been talking about the birds' eggs she'd collected as a girl. And he'd been exactly right. For hours she would work at putting together her collection trays, but she had never really enjoyed any of them until the box was filled, every compartment holding the proper egg.

Her father had also told her, when she was older, "You're not going to make everything in life come out as nice and neat as that collection of yours, Cheney." And he'd warned her more than once about her tendency simply to walk away from situations she couldn't handle as neatly as filling one of her trays: "You can't toss everything out the window that doesn't fit in with your little plan, Cheney."

Why am I thinking about all this now! she wondered as she sat in the chair beside the pale-faced boy. And then it came to her: this was one of those situations that could not be handled, tagged, and then cataloged neatly—not this sick child whom she'd learned to love!

"You're not going to make everything come out nice and neat. . . ."

Rebelliously she opened her eyes to push away the memories, then closed them again, unable to bear the sight of Stony's pitiful face. Now different words formed in her mind: *God— where are you in all this? Do you want this child to die—?*

She clamped her lips shut, but anger and fear combined in her heart so that she had to fight with all her strength to keep from crying aloud. Suddenly she knew that Stony was going to die and that none of her skills as a physician was going to save him. Never in her life had she felt so helpless.

A small sound came to her, and she opened her eyes. Stony was gagging. She had come to know that sound well—a death rattle, some called it. Stony was gasping for breath, and his thin body was arching with the terrible struggle.

And then Cheney could stand it no longer! She rushed blindly for the door, pulled it open—and nearly collided with Lydia.

"Cheney—what is it?" Lydia grasped Cheney with half-healed hands, ignoring the pain. "Is he worse?"

"He's—dying!" Cheney almost spat the words out. Then, when Lydia held on to her, she cried out, "Let me go, Lydia! I won't stay here and watch it—I can't!"

Lydia stared at the wild look in Cheney's eyes and suddenly threw her arms around the other woman, shoving her back inside the room. Whirling, she slammed the door, then turned to face Cheney. "You've got no choice, Dr. Duvall," she said firmly. "None of us have."

Cheney threw an agonized glance at Stony's writhing form and covered her face. Her breath came in short gasps as she half-sobbed, "What *good* will it do for me to stay and watch him die?"

"He's not dead yet. We can't give up—"

"Give up?" Cheney exploded with all the anger and frustration that had been building up over the past week. "Give up *what*? What good have I done him—or the others who died?"

"What good have you done those who *haven't* died?" Lydia countered. She looked very tiny next to Cheney, but there was a strength and power in her gaze as she continued. "Cheney, I've seen this coming—Shiloh and I have talked about it."

Taking a deep breath she said, "You care so much for people that you can't bear to lose them. It's like—like you lose a little of yourself when they die. That's the mark of a fine doctor, I believe—and of a fine Christian as well. But you can't let that stop you—can't let it tear you apart—"

"I've failed, Lydia—!"

"No! You haven't failed as long as you keep faith with your patients—and with God!"

Lydia stared at Cheney, then said more gently, "Cheney, God never promised we'd win every battle. No one ever does. But God's not keeping a score, tallying up so many wins, so many losses. He's only watching us for one thing—" She reached up and laid her hand gently on Cheney's cheek, saying, "The eyes of the LORD run to and fro throughout the whole earth to show Himself strong in the behalf of them whose heart is perfect toward Him."

Cheney blinked with shock, whispering, "That's my father's favorite scripture!"

"It's mine, too, Doctor."

Cheney thought of the many times her father had quoted that verse. And somehow, as she stood there uncertainly, the fear and anger began to leave her. She bowed her head, Lydia began to pray aloud, and Cheney began to pray silently as well. *Lord, I'm not able to help this child. I just can't make it all come out neatly, so I'm just going to have to stop trying. But I'm not going to run away! If he dies—I want to know I've done my best—and the rest is up to you!*

They remained still for long moments after Lydia finished praying. Finally Lydia opened her eyes and looked deep into Cheney's. Then a small smile came to her and she gave a satisfied nod at what she saw there. "Now then, Dr. Duvall," she whispered, "let's get to work. You *doctor,* and I'll *pray*—and we'll see what Almighty God can do!"

❦

Martha Jane awoke instantly as the knob turned, and she came off the bed as Cheney entered. "How is he?" she demanded.

Cheney walked over to her at once, her eyes glowing. She put her arms around the other woman and whispered, "He's out of the coma, Martha Jane! He's going to be all right."

Martha Jane stared at Cheney, tears forming in her eyes. "Thank you, Cheney," she said in a tight voice.

Cheney shook her head, and her voice was strong as she said, "No, Martha Jane, not me. The victory is God's. . . ."

Then she nodded slowly, adding almost to herself, "But if God had taken Stony, it would still have been a victory, wouldn't it?" Wonder was in her eyes, and she added, "It's the way we have to think about things, isn't it? God is in all of it!"

18

Murder at Sea

"This morning I want to talk to you about sickness and death—and life," Lydia told the group assembled in the Grand Salon. All of Mercer's Belles were there except for Tani, who was caring for Beans Lowery. Martha Jane Terrell and Powell Drake sat close together, holding hands, with Stony and Kelvey on either side of them. Stony was still thin and wan after his long ordeal, but his spirit was clearly back to normal; his eyes sparkled, and a sly grin kept stealing over his face.

Sybil Warfield sat at the very back of the room, her face ashen, her eyes haunted, her very person seeming to evoke an air of vulnerability.

"The Bible tells us in Hebrews that 'it is appointed unto men once to die,'" Lydia said softly. She stopped and looked around the room, letting the words sink in. "And we will, all of us, and none of us knows when or where or how. We've lost friends in the last two weeks. Their deaths seemed untimely and unfair, and we grieve terribly for our losses." Tears welled up in Lydia's eyes, resting momentarily before spilling down her cheeks, but her voice remained strong as she read:

"'But now is Christ risen from the dead, and become the firstfruits of them that slept. . . . For as in Adam all die, even so in Christ shall all be made alive.'" Lydia looked up from her worn Bible and her face shone as she continued.

"Between one of Adam's heartbeats and the next, our entire world changed. At one moment, the world held no ill for that first human—no animal would devour him, he never hungered, he needed no fire for warmth or light because he walked with God and looked upon His face.

"Then, in the next heartbeat, Adam knew that the thorns would now scratch him, the stones would bruise him, he would bleed—and he would die. We share this terrible legacy with him.

"But we also share Christ's legacy of eternal life. Our friends aren't dead—they now live with the same life that we'll know one day. A life that never ends, that is never shadowed by sickness or tragedy or accident or hunger—a glorious life forever and ever with Jesus!"

Yellow fever had taken a heavy toll on Mercer's Belles. Out of ninety-nine women who had trekked through the jungle (three women had chosen to return to New York with the *Continental*), thirty-eight had contracted the mysterious disease, and twenty-one had died. Fourteen of the *Conqueror*'s crew had also come down with the fever, but only two of them had died.

Cheney had almost worried herself to distraction trying to understand why the women's mortality rates were so high. Finally she had decided that most of the women who died had been very seasick on the beginning of the voyage, and they had never regained all their strength. That, and a newfound humility in accepting God's will, had finally put Cheney's worries more or less to rest. She knew she had done her best for them.

Tears were rolling down Sybil's cheeks as Lydia finished speaking and they stood to sing "Rock of Ages." She stayed seated, rigid and tense for a few moments; then she broke down, buried her face in her hands and sobbed, finally stumbling to her feet and rushing out of the salon. No one saw her leave except Lydia, who was facing the group as they sang. *I'll find her, Lord,* Lydia vowed, *and I won't let her run away or hide this time! Now I realize it's not me she's hiding from—it's you.*

As they finished the song and the group began to leave, Powell Drake walked up to the dais and whispered something to Lydia, who immediately held up her hands and called out, "Would everyone wait, please? Mr. Drake has asked to speak to you for a moment."

Everyone stopped at Lydia's words, most faces quite curious. The majority of the women had only caught glimpses of Powell Drake from time to time on the *Continental,* and some hadn't even realized he was on the *Conqueror.* "Is that Powell Drake?" Holly Van Buren asked Georgia, craning her neck to stare at the dais. "He's so skinny!"

"Does your voice have any volume but loud, sweetie?" Georgia asked, but Holly just blinked several times, uncomprehending.

"I—I—" Drake faltered, and then looked down at Lydia, who beamed up at him and said something in a low voice. Drake looked back up at the silent group, took a deep breath, and jumped right in. "I've asked Martha Jane Terrell to marry me!" he burst out. "And she said yes!" Then he practically jumped off the dais and returned to Martha Jane, who was blushing a deep pink but smiling happily.

Immediately women began to applaud and crowd around the two. Drake reached down to hoist little Kelvey into the air, and Stony pressed close as he grinned up at his mother.

"Lucky! No, not you, Mr. Drake; I mean Martha Jane!"

"How'd you manage it, Martha Jane?"

"Congratulations, dear! I'm so happy for you. And for you, children—"

"Does he have any brothers? Cousins? Uncles? Is his father still alive?"

The teasing and well-wishing went on for a long time. After a few moments, Drake handed Kelvey back to her mother and edged out of the chattering group of women toward the door. Shiloh met him with hand outstretched, and Drake looked extremely relieved to be in male company, if only for a moment.

"My congratulations, Drake," Shiloh said warmly, clasping Drake's hand with both of his. "And I mean it. You're both lucky, because it's obvious you were meant to be together."

"I—thank you, Irons." Drake swallowed hard and looked back at Martha Jane. She was still too thin, but her face was regaining its color and animation. To Drake she was the prettiest woman he'd ever seen. "But I'm the one who's really blessed. It's a miracle that God allowed me to have that woman—and those children. I'll tell you about it sometime."

"I'd like to hear it," Shiloh answered.

At that moment Asa Mercer and Annie Stephens walked by, deep in conversation. *Those two—maybe I'd better have a talk with Asa,* Shiloh thought. *He's real smart about women in one way, and real dumb about them in another.*

Cheney appeared at his side and tugged on his sleeve. "We're all going into Realejo this afternoon. Will you come with us? I'd like to see some part of this continent that's not in the middle of a hurricane, or in some dark cantina with people shooting big ugly guns, or dark, scary jungles, or—"

"I get your point." Shiloh held up a protesting hand. "I'll come." He couldn't help but grin down at Cheney; she looked like an excited little girl. Her green eyes sparkled, her hair curled becomingly around her face, and her simple sky-blue dress somehow made her look very young and innocent.

"Mind if I come with you?" Max Townsend asked as he joined them. "I'm tired of this ship, and those two pugs—especially Lynch. Guess Lowery isn't that bad, but Lynch—" He shrugged and everyone knew what he meant.

Townsend had put Bull in a stateroom on one side of him and Beans in the other, all three in a line down from Shiloh's cabin. Cheney had wanted to keep the two men close to the infirmary. Bull was almost well now, but had to be watched. The staterooms could be opened from the inside even when they were locked, and both Townsend and Shiloh had caught Bull down in steerage drinking beer and bothering the women. Angrily Shiloh had told Townsend, "Lynch is all right now; you can't hurt him! Let's either lock or tie him up. We need to do something!"

Townsend had answered dryly, "Technically, he's not even charged with anything right now. I don't have one shred of hard evidence against him, so I can't legally do anything like that. Hopefully, when Lowery gets well enough for me to ask him a few questions, he'll talk about his and Lynch's little foray into the jungle."

"And who's going to watch Bull?" Shiloh frowned.

"Have you met Nicholas Trent?" Townsend asked. "No? He was third officer until he fell off the mainmast in a storm about a year ago and broke his leg. He walks with a limp, and Captain Drury busted him to cook's helper—said he was too slow for a seaman. Anyway, Trent offered to keep an eye on Lynch instead of taking shore leave tomorrow. Miss DuQuesne has agreed to stay with Beans, and Trent said he'd check on them, too."

"Nicholas Trent seems like a good man," Townsend mused. He didn't exactly frown—his expressions were always too guarded—but Cheney and Shiloh could hear the displeasure in his voice. "It's a shame Captain Drury did that to him. He's too young and too smart to have someone hold him down and smother him like that."

"I don't want to hear anyone's problems now," Cheney declared. "Let's talk about it later. Right now I want to find the market. Let's go!"

"Uh-oh," Shiloh groaned. "We're in trouble! And you said Tani's not going to interpret for us? Then the Doc here is about to make some shopkeeper very rich and very happy!"

"I speak Spanish," Townsend remarked with amusement in his dark eyes. "I'll try to keep her from buying a nickel shawl for ten dollars."

Cheney sighed. "I'd pay ten dollars to get Lydia a pretty shawl. Why does she—?" Cheney broke off quickly. *I've got to forget these petty things! What does it matter what Lydia wears?* she scolded herself, but still a little voice inside her muttered, *Because she's a wonderful woman, and you don't like it when people laugh at her!*

"Might be a good idea, Doc," Shiloh agreed as he glanced across the room at Lydia's black, yellow, and purple shawl. "I don't much care to see people laughing at a lady like Lydia."

⧫

After the morning service, Sybil Warfield had rushed to her stateroom, thrown herself across the bed, and cried for a long time. When her sobs finally subsided, she sat up and wiped her face with savage movements.

I just can't! she had defiantly thought. *I won't give up that gold, God!* And immediately another voice had repeated its warning: *Let go, tell someone, give it up! God loves you and will forgive you! It's not worth this agony. Nothing is!*

No! I won't! she argued bitterly with herself as she splashed cold water on her face from the tiny washstand in her stateroom. *I'll keep it, and I'll never want for anything again!* Then she jumped up and recklessly started toward Bull's room. She felt as though she were hurrying straight toward hell, but she deliberately numbed the part of her mind that insistently tried to talk her out of the path she was choosing.

Bull opened the door to her knock and Sybil slipped inside. Before she could speak, he began to give her orders and threaten her.

"If you don't do what I say, Miss Sybil," Bull said with sarcastic politeness, "I'm gonna talk."

Sybil stood stiffly against the closed door of Bull's stateroom, her arms crossed protectively across her waist, her shoulders hunched tensely. Her face was pale and her eyes were dull and swollen. "No, I won't, Bull," she argued again. "I'll split the rest of the gold with you, but I won't bring you whiskey or help you—" She broke off and shook her head.

"What? What ain't you gonna help me do?" he demanded. Slowly he rose from his lounging position, where he'd been lying sideways across his bed, and walked deliberately toward Sybil and stood almost nose to nose with her. He was shirtless because, although his back was healing, he still had sores in places and the new skin was tender. He had shaved the rest of his hair off his head since the back half had been burned bald, and for some reason his huge, naked scalp made Bull look even more dangerous.

"I—I—won't help you—kill Beans! Or—hurt—that girl—"

"Let's take this one thing at a time," he growled in a deceptively calm voice. "First of all, Sybil, you *will* help me, 'cause you have to." He cocked his shiny head, a cruel smile on his face, forcing Sybil to drop her eyes against the brutality she saw.

"You're smart, and you sure didn't mind using them smarts when you wanted me and Beans to steal your gold, now did you? So you ain't gonna mind helpin' me right now, or—well, let's just say I won't take kindly to it if you don't." He reached out with a huge hand and lightly brushed the tips of his fingers across her slender neck.

Sybil shuddered with revulsion at his touch. *He's mad!* she thought as she looked helplessly into his black eyes, panic making her heart race. *He's gone completely insane. I thought nothing mattered to me anymore—but it does! I haven't gotten this bad—yet!*

"And you *will* help me kill Beans." He nodded slowly, as if it made perfect sense. "He ain't talked yet, but he will as soon as his brains get unscrambled. So far, they ain't got nothin' on me; they can't prove I did nothin'! That dumb Townsend don't even know the gold's gone! All he's ever asked me about is that explosion, and I don't know nothin' about all that!"

The words sounded rehearsed, and Sybil realized that they must have gone through his mind over and over until he could think of nothing else. His eyes, which had gone blank during his little speech, now lit on Sybil again with malignant intent.

"Anyways, Beans is sure gonna tell him 'bout the gold—and he'll tell 'em about you, too! Beans is getting better and better, and something's got to be done with him before that fancy woman doctor lets Townsend talk to him!"

"No! I—I can't! I won't!"

"Sybil," Bull growled, "you can—and you will. Go get me that whiskey, now, while everyone's gone. Then you go get that high yaller that's tendin' to Beans, and bring her in here.

"I need the drink first, 'cause he was my friend," he explained carefully to Sybil, who shuddered at his insane logic. "But I'll take care of him before they get back, and no one'll know it. They'll think that soft place on his head, where he got hit in the explosion, just went bad and he died. And then—me and that little colored girl's gonna have a drink. I tell you, I like that girl's looks—"

Sybil's eyes were wide with fear as Bull continued in a low, monotonous voice, leering at her. She reached behind her, fumbling wildly for the doorknob. Then she wrenched the door open and ran as fast as she could down the corridor. Behind her, she heard Bull step out into the corridor, laughing loudly.

Two doors down from Bull's cabin, Tani DuQuesne and Beans Lowery glanced at each other as Bull's laughter rang out, echoing hollowly in the relative quiet of the ship. Tani's sculpted face remained expressionless, but her eyes held an unmistakable hint of dread. Beans' face was blanched with fear, almost as white as the bandage that swathed the top of his head. Neither of them spoke until the laughter had faded and they heard Bull's door slam loudly.

"Mebbe—mebbe you better go, Miss Tani," Beans said weakly, his blue eyes clouded with anxiety. "Mebbe you better go find Mr. Nicholas again and stay with him 'til ever'body gits back."

"No, Beans," she answered calmly. "It's all right. You just rest, and I'm going to sit here and read to you until you go to sleep. Nicholas will be back soon, I'm sure." Tani picked up her book but didn't look at it. They fell silent again, both of them straining to hear any sound from the room down the hall.

"I'm scairt of Bull," Beans said in a quiet voice.

For a moment Tani didn't respond, and the silence in the room seemed heavy. Then she murmured, "Tell me about it, Beans."

"He was my friend. But then he left me, didn't he? Out there, after that big crash in the jungle?" His blue eyes searched Tani's face, and she nodded slightly. "Thought so," he sighed, closing his eyes and falling back on the pillow.

Again the room was quiet, and Tani thought Beans had gone to sleep. But his eyes opened again and he spoke as if he were telling a dream. "Bull came in here the other night, Miss Tani. He scairt me at first, but then when I seen it was Bull—I sorta thought everything was gonna be all right. He come over to the bed, and I looked up at him, and he leaned over me. He looked—funny—and then I got really scairt. He never said nothin'; he just leaned real close to me without sayin' nothin'!" He closed his eyes again as if he were exhausted.

Struggling to hold her voice calm, Tani asked, "What happened then, Beans?"

Without opening his eyes, Beans replied in a dull voice, "There were some noise out in the hall, and Bull went away. In a few minutes Mr. Shiloh come in."

Tani nodded with sympathy, even though Beans couldn't see her. She, too, was afraid of Bull Lynch. Twice now he had materialized in front of her like a demon, suddenly looming over her in the dark corridors of the ship as she went to different staterooms, helping to nurse the many women who had been sick. Neither time had he said a word; he had merely grabbed her around the waist with an iron grip, and started down the hall toward her stateroom, which was the last one of the row, and which had an empty one next to it.

Once she had managed to reach around him and slap him, hard, on his raw back. He had loosened his grip with a painful grunt, and she had run to her stateroom and locked it. The other time, Shiloh Irons had passed the head of the corridor, whistling softly. Bull had let go of her and shrunk back in the shadows, and she had run to join Shiloh without looking back.

A soft knock sounded at the door. Beans jumped, and even Tani started, then quickly smoothed her dress to cover the involuntary movement. "Miss DuQuesne, it's me, Nicholas Trent. I brought you some coffee and Beans some juice."

Tani rose gracefully and unlocked the door to admit the young sailor. He entered slowly, painstakingly balancing a tray so that his limp wouldn't spill the glass of juice and the steaming cup of coffee. Tani watched him with sympathy in her eyes, but she didn't offer to help him. She took her seat by Beans' bed and waited patiently for Nicholas to serve them.

He set the tray down and walked over to the bed, holding Beans' juice. "Thank you, Mr. Nicholas," he said gratefully, and struggled to sit upright. Trent bent over to help him, and Tani rose from her chair and moved out of the way.

Nicholas got Beans situated, then went back to the small table where the tray was. He glanced at Tani and said rather ungraciously, "Sit back down, Miss DuQuesne. I'll bring your coffee."

"All right, Mr. Trent," she murmured, and returned to her seat, watching the young man as he prepared her coffee. He was handsome, almost devilishly handsome. His hair was glossy black, and a thick lock of it fell rakishly over his forehead. His skin was almost the color of Tani's own, except it had the olive tinge of the Latin peoples instead of the walnut cast of her African heritage. His eyes were a startling dark blue. He was of average height, rather sturdily built, but his limp was pronounced.

"How old are you?" Tani asked suddenly.

He gave no sign of noticing her abruptness as he continued to fill the coffee cup and pour cream into it. "Nineteen," he answered as he turned and labored across the room to hand it to her. "Why?"

"I'm nineteen," she said as she accepted the coffee. "Thank you. We both look—older."

"Seen more, I guess," he shrugged. He watched Beans, who was slurping the fresh pineapple juice thirstily. "Looks to me like we've got a lot in common," he remarked idly to Tani.

"Oh?" Tani asked politely, in a distant tone.

He glanced at her with amusement. "Think I'm sweet-talking you?" He shrugged and slapped his bad leg. "You're not in any danger from me, Miss DuQuesne. I don't kid myself that I'm much of a prize."

Tani sipped her coffee, appraising him over her cup. *You didn't care before, about anyone, and their problems,* one part of her mind said coolly. *You walked away without a backward glance. What's happened to you? And are you better or worse?*

With graceful deliberation, she set her cup on the saucer and said, "You don't understand, I think. A girl like me hardly needs to worry about a man—what did you say?—talking sweet to me?" She allowed herself a small smile. "You may call me Tani. And I think that possibly you will be prized by a woman sometime."

Nicholas grinned at her, and his dark good looks confused her a little. Sternly she got a grip on herself as he went on. "Well, thanks, Tani—you can call me Nicholas. And what kind of a girl *are* you, anyway?"

She felt panicky for a moment at the blatant question; then she realized the young man really didn't know what she had been implying by the oblique reference to herself. He went on. "French? Spanish? You sure have a pretty accent."

"Don't she, though?" Beans beamed, as if he were personally responsible for Tani's voice, and she looked at him with affection. "She talks so purty, I want her to read to me all the time."

"Yeah, I bet that's nice, Beans," Nicholas nodded. "What do you read to him, Tani? The Bible?" He pointed to the large book on the floor by Tani's chair.

"No. I am Catholic," she said, and began to explain. "We believe that the priests—"

"I know," Nicholas shrugged. "I'm Catholic, too. My mother is anyway. She's Nicaraguan, and my father was white. See, I'm a half-breed like you."

Tani digested this information in silence for a few minutes, and Beans began to get restless. He struggled to change positions, and Nicholas moved to bend over the bed and help him. Tani stood up again.

Then suddenly the door flew open and slammed against the wall, and Sybil Warfield came flying into the room, her eyes wild and staring, her hair streaming. "We've got to get Beans out of here," she said hoarsely in a panic-stricken voice, and then turned to Tani. "You run! Now! Go hide!"

She grabbed Tani's arms, shook her for a moment, and whirled to face Nicholas, who had gripped her shoulder hard. "Help me! Oh, God, help me get him out of here!" she sobbed, grabbing the young sailor by the upper arms and staring up into his face.

"Lady, you just calm down—" Nicholas began.

"No! He might come! I went and got him the whiskey, and I drank with him, but I put laudanum in his! Right now he's out cold, but—" She jerked her head around, back and forth, crying desperately, first to Nicholas, then to Tani, and then to Beans. "But I don't know if he'll stay out or if he's coming right now! Don't you understand?"

"I understand, Sybil!" came a harsh shout from the open doorway, and Bull Lynch charged into the room. Spittle flew from his lips as they strained back in a snarl, and his eyes were dull with laudanum and loss of reason. He reached Nicholas Trent and knocked him sprawling with one careless blow from the back of his hand. Nicholas scrambled to get up, but Bull had reached Sybil, who stood frozen in mute terror.

Bull grabbed her by the front of her dress, tearing it, and shook her like rag doll. "You witch! You poisoned me!" He shook her again, and Tani heard Sybil's teeth rattling. "What'd you put in my whiskey, you witch? Come on! You're gonna drink it now, 'til you die, too!" Bull hauled Sybil toward the door, her dress ripping, her feet scrabbling along the wooden deck as she tried to get some toehold but failed.

Beans whimpered, tears running down his stricken face. Tani stayed motionless, holding her breath, her eyes wide with shock as she cowered against the wall. Nicholas Trent finally found his feet and yelled, "Let her go, Lynch! Why don't you come back here and face a man, instead of beating up women!" But he couldn't move fast enough to catch Lynch, who was striding along furiously, and Lynch either didn't hear him or didn't care.

Trent's face was twisted with pain, but he forced himself to run raggedly down the corridor. He moved past Sybil, who was being dragged along almost flat on the floor, and jumped on Bull's back. Lynch dropped Sybil, and she scrambled away, panting and whimpering. Bull roared again like a wild animal, the sound terrible with its fury and pain, and he crashed backward with all his strength. Trent's head banged against the corridor wall; for a moment everything went dark and Bull's roaring became muted.

Trent loosened his grip and fell to the floor, slumping along the wall. Dazedly, he looked up at Bull's head, his shining skull strange and gruesome, coming closer and closer until Trent felt fingers of steel around his throat. Bull shook him hard, once; then his fingers tightened and everything got darker. *Funny,* Nicholas thought dazedly. *Wasn't scared when I fell, either—dying doesn't scare me—*

Just before he passed out, he felt the death grip on his throat loosen. His lungs automatically sucked in air, and his vision began to clear. Bull had disappeared.

Trent shook his head, struggling to see clearly, and looked down the corridor past Sybil, who was a tiny lump of a shadow against the wall. A loud, regular noise was sounding just above her head, and Nicholas squinted with confusion at the blurred figures until they came into focus.

Shiloh Irons had Bull Lynch by the throat, shaking him like a floppy mop. Irons had one sinewed arm wedged against the wall for leverage; the other was working like a piston to slam Bull Lynch's shiny head against the wall methodically and furiously, again and again in a deadly rhythm.

Suddenly a woman appeared on Irons' other side. She looked small and frail and hopelessly vulnerable against his tall frame, which seemed to emanate deadly strength. But she put two white hands—Nicholas noticed that they were so white, so slender—on Irons' arm, lightly and tentatively, and said in a quiet voice, "That's enough, Shiloh. Stop now. That's enough."

As if she had thrown a huge switch, Irons grew still and dropped his hand as if he'd suddenly been burned. Bull Lynch slid painfully down, leaving a black shiny trail on the wall behind his head. His eyes were closed and his head lolled to one side, and Shiloh jumped back so Bull's legs wouldn't touch him as they sprawled limply across the narrow corridor.

⁂

At least Shiloh didn't kill Bull—this time, Cheney thought, dismayed at the mere idea of it. *Then again, I'm not so sure this man can be killed. He really is like a bull! All the things that have happened to him would have killed a normal man, but he just keeps getting up and charging around!*

Bull didn't even sustain a concussion from the vicious head-bashing Shiloh had given him. The tender skin on the back of his head had been scratched raw and bleeding, but within two days it had scabbed over and was beginning to heal once more.

Townsend had wanted to throw Bull into the brig, but Cheney had objected. The brig was a six-by-six room down in the cargo hold, cold and drafty and dark and smelling of brine. "If you have to put him there, do it," Cheney had wearily told Townsend and Shiloh, "but I'll have to go down there and check on him several times a day. He has open sores on his back and head." The two men had rejected that completely, so they left Bull in the stateroom and tried to keep a weary, tiresome watch over him.

Captain Drury had refused to allow shore leave in Realejo. When they docked, they had learned that the hurricane had passed this way, too, and that there was cholera in Realejo. The group had watched the city fade in the distance, dispirited at the fact that they faced another month at sea with no landfall.

Uneventful days wore on, and the weather was idyllic. The depression that had gripped everyone seemed to lift a little in the warmth of the sun, and the sea was a turquoise vision of calm. The moon waned, then disappeared, then smiled a thin smile on them again, and Cheney often stayed out on the deck late into the night to enjoy the stars and the soft, fragrant breeze.

Maybe the rest of the trip will be like this, she thought hopefully one night. *This isn't breathtakingly exciting, but it's—restful. And we've been through so much on this trip. I hope we can have some serenity, some peace, some time to stop and think.*

But her hopes were in vain, because exactly two weeks after the terrible scene in the hallway—on Sunday, June 28—the weather changed in the night, and the next morning they found Bull Lynch dead.

He was sprawled on the stairwell leading up from the staterooms to the promenade deck, a scalpel buried deep in his heart.

The scalpel was from Shiloh Irons' medical bag.

19

Now . . . in the Hour of Our Death

"So you're telling us, Dr. Duvall, that the scalpel we just saw sticking out of Bull Lynch's chest belonged to Mr. Irons here?"

Captain Drury's voice was cold and without inflection, but anger outlined his tall, lean form as he stood on the empty dais in the Grand Salon.

"Well—yes—" Cheney answered faintly. "I gave him the medical bag, you s-see—"

Shiloh stood at the foot of the dais, facing the people who were standing clumped in odd groups around the salon. Max Townsend was beside him, his face remote, and Asa Mercer on the other side, with a bleak countenance. Somehow, both men managed to communicate their support for Shiloh. Nevertheless, his face was grim.

Cheney dropped her eyes as she finished answering the captain's question. The salon seemed damp and dim as the *Conqueror* stirred restlessly in a gray, choppy sea.

"Cheney?" Shiloh's voice was quiet but insistent. "Tell him! Tell him that anyone could've taken that scalpel out of my bag!"

"What?" Cheney raised her eyes and struggled to clear her mind. "Oh yes, of course—" She turned slightly to face Captain Drury squarely, who loomed above all of them like a grand judge on the dais. "We don't lock the infirmary anymore, you see," she explained eagerly. "When so many women were sick, there were dozens of them going in there to get quinine water and fruit and towels and other things. The keys kept getting shuffled around, until I finally locked up the dangerous drugs in my stateroom and left the infirmary open. It's been that way the entire trip."

"I understand," Captain Drury said with an impatient nod. "Now, would you like to continue and tell me who stole the scalpel and killed this man? One of those women?" He made a sweeping gesture over the room, and below him the three men's faces grew darker as if by a signal. "Didn't you say, Dr. Duvall, that a *man—a man of great strength*—must have stabbed Lynch?"

Cheney whispered, "Yes, but—"

"Because the scalpel was buried so deeply—a full two inches past the blade?"

Cheney could no longer answer the questions, which were simply echoes of her own words. Captain Drury had called her to come look at Bull Lynch's body before they moved him. Lynch had been lying awkwardly on the stairs, his eyes staring blankly upward, his face frozen in vague surprise. Cheney had steeled herself and examined Lynch impassively. Now the clinically detached comments she had made to Captain Drury and the others as she worked were coming back to haunt her.

Can't believe I didn't see this coming! Cheney thought helplessly. She didn't know if she felt so desperate because she had carelessly implicated Shiloh—or because she was afraid that Shiloh really had killed Bull. Her head was beginning to ache painfully; she dropped her eyes again and rubbed her temples as they began to throb.

Georgia Jakes' sardonic drawl seemed to jolt many of the women out of their trancelike state as they stared at Shiloh Irons. "Well, *I'll* tell you something, Captain," she declared, taking a step forward and putting her hands on the ample curves of her hips. "That Bull Lynch made me mad enough to stab him with a skinny willow switch plenty of times! And I coulda done it, too, if I'd gotten just mad enough!"

"Madam, are you offering yourself as a suspect?" Captain Drury demanded.

"I ain't no madam, Captain," Georgia answered haughtily, "and I ain't no suspect—no more than Shiloh Irons should be!"

A low murmur of assent and approval ran through the crowd of women, and they unconsciously moved a little closer to Georgia Jakes. Soon small exclamations and indignant comments were forthcoming, and the volume of the voices began to rise. Even the stern, unmoving Captain Drury looked a little unsettled by the roomful of women, whose dark looks and righteous indignation were beginning to be directed toward *him*. Shiloh, Townsend, and Asa Mercer exchanged amused glances as the captain intoned in a voice much louder than his customary low rumble, "Mr. Townsend and I will conduct the rest of this investigation in private, ladies!

"Obviously, no one is going anywhere." The captain continued, casting a black look at Shiloh. "But I assure you I will find out the truth about this, and the guilty man will be confined to the brig until we reach San Francisco. In the meantime, please cooperate with us and give us any information that may be pertinent to Mr. Lynch's murder. Otherwise, just go about your business and allow us to go about ours!"

Drury stepped down and quickly walked through the crowd of women. Some of them swept their skirts disdainfully aside as he passed. Mercer joined the women, walking among them, and speaking in low, reassuring tones; Annie Stephens soon appeared at his side.

Shiloh watched Cheney as she hurried to a chair and sat down, ducking her head and massaging her temples. Without taking his eyes off her, he murmured to Townsend, "All right, Townsend. Go about your business like the captain said. Investigate."

Max Townsend took out a cigarette paper and a leather pouch of tobacco and with slow, precise movements began to roll a cigarette. Shiloh waited patiently, watching Cheney, as Townsend finished, smiling faintly with satisfaction at the almost-perfect cylinder. He stuck it in his mouth, lit a match with his thumbnail, and inhaled deeply. "You kill Lynch, Irons?" he asked as he squinted through the smoke to peruse the cigarette in his hand.

"Nope."

"Didn't think so. Investigation closed."

The two men were silent for a while, watching the women as they melted into small groups of twos and threes and then shifted to form other groups, their skirts swirling, their configuration constantly changing as if they were choreographed.

"Well, then, I got what you might call a rhetorical question, Townsend," Shiloh said, his eyes narrowed to blue slits. "If I didn't kill Lynch, who did?"

Townsend knew what to do with a rhetorical question; he didn't answer. He just drew deeply on his cigarette, blew out a long, delicate plume of smoke, and watched it float upward and disappear into the dimness of the ceiling far above.

❧

Over the next two days the sky slowly changed from a palette of watery blue-gray to shades of charcoal, almost black. The *Conqueror* tossed like a wood chip in a mutinous sea that boiled a murky green by day and showed only menacing white foam crests at night. Sudden squalls of rain would slash sideways across the deserted decks, then stop as abruptly as they had begun.

Meals were scant and tumultuous as the ship heaved in the sullen sea, and eating was a messy affair. Most of the women would go to the dining room, grab whatever food was available, then scurry back to their rooms to eat in private. Between meals,

Mercer's Belles gathered in staterooms, wandered the gloomy corridors, and occasionally braved the weather to gather in larger groups in the Grand Salon. They rarely ate in the dining room. Conversations generally revolved around the murder.

"For all their nosy questions," Georgia told Miss Ordway in a superior tone, "that huffy Captain Drury and that standoffish Max Townsend don't know any more than I know!"

"Which is?" Miss Ordway asked with amusement.

"That, number one," Georgia pronounced grandly, "Shiloh Irons didn't kill Bull Lynch! And number two, someone else did!"

"Excellent illustration of classical logic, Georgia dear," Miss Ordway remarked, her eyes sparkling.

After three days of weather-induced confinement, however, even talk of murder had worn thin, and everyone was bored and restless. During the long, dark afternoon, Cheney, Lydia, and Shiloh gathered in the infirmary on the pretense of imposing order in it.

Cheney had found herself seeking out Lydia often during the past few storm-tossed days, asking her to help with little tasks or to write down songs or just to talk about the Scripture passages she had been reading at night. She hadn't seen much of Shiloh, however, and in her own mind she found herself defending this state of affairs with needless vehemence. *I haven't been avoiding him—he's been spending a lot of time with Max Townsend, and I've been staying with Beans a lot.* But a sneaky little voice in her head chattered spitefully, *Yes, and you've been seeing a certain scene in your mind lately, haven't you? Or two scenes? One of Shiloh, in an alley—and one in a stairway—*

"I'm going to give Beans some laudanum," Cheney said too loudly and rather nonsensically in the quiet room. She was rolling bandages with obsessive neatness, while Lydia was needlessly polishing bottles until they shone like jewels. The only one not occupied was Shiloh, who was propped up on one of the bunks, idly watching them. He wasn't even pretending to have any work to do.

Lydia was standing next to Cheney at the small infirmary table. At Cheney's remark, Lydia looked up at her strangely. Only then did Cheney realize how idiotic her words sounded, and she threw down the bandage she had only half-rolled. It messed up her neat little rows of round linen strips, each cut exactly two inches wide, and that frustrated her further, but she just walked over to the small bunk across from Shiloh and sat down with an impatient flounce of her skirts. Shiloh looked faintly amused, and Cheney gave him a hard look.

"It's probably not a bad idea, Cheney," Lydia said in a soothing voice as she turned back to polish another already-shining bottle. "We're all on edge with this storm coming on, and—everything—"

"Like murders," Shiloh added helpfully, but Lydia ignored him and polished vigorously as she continued.

"Beans is a lot stronger, but he's frightened, you know," she said deliberately, "since Bull was killed. And his head still hurts him quite a bit. Some laudanum may do him good. I'll go with you, Cheney. Which one's the laudanum?"

"The blue one," Cheney answered. She moodily regarded Shiloh as he watched Lydia.

Lydia hesitated over the dozens of richly colored bottles in the rack on the table. Her hand stole to one, then another, and finally she picked up a dark brown one. "Is this it?" she murmured, almost to herself.

Shiloh sat up abruptly, and Cheney started to say something, but he interrupted her. His voice sounded too casual as he asked Lydia, "Would you hand me that red bottle while you're at it, Lydia?" He watched Lydia intently as she again tentatively picked up a bottle.

Walking over to Lydia, he gently took the bottle out of her hand. It was a bright, unmistakable green. She looked up at him, mystified, and he said gently, "Lydia, this bottle is green."

Cheney blurted out, "That explains it! Your clothes! You're color blind, Lydia!"

Shiloh turned to Cheney, but he hadn't been fast enough to quiet her outburst, and he just rolled his eyes upward.

"My clothes—?" Lydia repeated dumbly, and looked down at herself. She was wearing a dress the shade of pumpkin-orange, and had fastened a fichu of deep yellow over it. It was a horribly fascinating combination.

"My clothes?" Lydia asked again, and for some reason Cheney began to cry.

Lydia and Shiloh stared at Cheney as tears coursed down her cheeks. Lydia blinked several times. Then a small smile lit her face, and it grew into a mischievous grin. "Don't cry, Cheney," she urged. "I guess this means my clothes aren't light gray and dark gray, like I thought—but are they so bad they make you cry?"

They all laughed then, and soon Cheney began to explain to Lydia exactly what it meant to be color blind. For some reason, Lydia's face slowly lit up with joy at Cheney's words, and when Cheney stopped, Lydia jumped in, her face beaming, and said excitedly, "But—but this is wonderful!"

Shiloh and Cheney glanced at each other with concern, but Lydia went on impatiently, "Oh, not that I'm color blind, of course—but don't you see? It's made me—helped me—"

With a visible effort she made herself calm down enough to talk sensibly. "I've been praying for a way to communicate with Beans Lowery, you see, because he's like a man-child, and I just haven't been able to—reach him. But now—it's like when people talked about radiant colors, and I felt lost! Beans—he's lost, too—in a wilderness of unrecognizable words! Now I think I understand a little about how he feels, and how he thinks! I can't wait to tell him!"

Shiloh looked mystified, but a light dawned on Cheney's face. She'd spent a lot of time talking to Beans herself, and she knew he was a simple man who listened politely, understood little, and couldn't organize his thoughts enough to ask the right questions.

"I think I understand what you're saying, Lydia. I've wanted to talk to Beans about the Lord, too—you know, since that night in Stony's room—but I just couldn't figure out how to. But you have, haven't you?"

"Yes! I know exactly what to tell him!"

"Then let's go see him," Cheney said decisively. "Only let me pick out the bottles to take," she added seriously.

To her surprise, Lydia and Shiloh laughed, and Cheney was dismayed anew at her lack of sensitivity. But again Lydia made it all right: "Only if you'll help me with my clothes, Dr. Duvall. After I've talked to Beans."

The two women left the infirmary, chattering about clothes and Beans and colors. Shiloh was forgotten—ignored and alone in the infirmary. *That Lydia is some woman!* he thought, shaking his head. *Tell her she's color blind, and she starts thanking God! And the Doc—laughing one minute and crying the next!*

Shaking his head again, he decided to find Max Townsend in hopes of putting together an uncomplicated, unemotional, male-only card game.

⊷✠⊶

Lydia knocked once on Beans' door and then opened it. "Guess what, Beans?" she said, her eyes shining, as the two women came into the room.

"What?" Beans gamely asked. He was pale and thin, but his light blue eyes shone when Lydia and Cheney entered. He liked them, just as much as he did Tani and Georgia who had stayed with him for countless hours over the past few days. And he loved guessing games.

"I just found out I'm color blind," Lydia said gently and was going to continue, but Beans was ahead of her.

"Oh, that's nice, Miss Lydia," he said, scratching the heavy bandage on his head in bewilderment, but he looked at Lydia with anticipation. "Now, you guess what, Miss Lydia! No, never you mind, you can't guess nohow! I mem'rized a verse! From the Bible story you read me this mornin' 'bout that jailer man, and Paul and Silas."

Lydia's face glowed with pleasure. "Why, that's wonderful, Beans! What verse did you memorize?"

"'What must I do to be saved?'" Beans quoted proudly.

Lydia and Cheney glanced at each other, unsure how to react. Was Beans asking the question, or repeating meaningless words?

Beans looked from Lydia to Cheney, then back to Lydia, and patiently explained, "You see, Miss Lydia, it's kinda like a joke, you know? Only I never could git all the jokes people told me, and I git this one. See, I mem'rized the verse—but I unnerstan the question, too—so I'm askin' it at the same time."

His face was gentle and imploring as he quietly asked, "Miss Lydia, please tell me—what must I do to be saved?"

"Well, glory be!" Lydia exclaimed and sat back in her chair. She glanced at Cheney with joy in her eyes and then began to talk to Beans. She told the story of God's Son in simple, homey terms that Beans understood easily, and Cheney listened with delight as Lydia talked. *It's a paraphrase of the Bible, a perfect repetition of Bible verses—in Beans' language! It's—wonderful!*

When Lydia finished, Beans surprised them again. Without warning, and without hesitation, he bowed his head and prayed. "Jesus, please, sir, forgive me for all that I done bad," he said earnestly, "and please come into my heart to live, forever and ever. I love you, Jesus, sir, and thanks for everything!" Then Beans raised his head and grinned triumphantly at Lydia and Cheney.

The three talked and smiled and laughed for a time—Cheney wasn't certain for how long—when the door to Beans' room opened. They all looked up to see Sybil come silently into the room, shut the door behind her, and lean against it. She looked pale but determined, calmer than she had been for weeks.

"Lydia, I need to speak to you," Sybil said quietly. "No, don't leave, Dr. Duvall, please. I was going to get Mr. Mercer, but—maybe, since you're here, you're *supposed* to be here." Her words puzzled all of them, but they waited patiently.

Sybil straightened and moved closer to the bed to stand by Lydia. "I have a story to tell, a long one, and a complicated one. Don't be afraid, Beans," she told him as he stared up at her doubtfully, and for the first time her voice broke a little. "I'm—going to tell the truth, first to Lydia and Dr. Duvall. Then I'm going to tell Mr. Townsend, and I'm going to explain to him that you didn't do anything wrong—that Bull and I made you think you were doing something right."

Beans searched Sybil's face, uncomprehending but sympathetic, as she visibly struggled to maintain control. "But first, Lydia—" She turned to Lydia, who smiled at her, already reassuring her, and Sybil swallowed hard and held out her hand. "Lydia, would you pray for me?"

❦

The storm worsened steadily. The ship rolled back and forth constantly, with ominous creakings and groanings, and the wind roared above deck. Occasionally it would find the open stairwell and come screaming down the stateroom corridors like unseen banshees.

At ten o'clock that evening, Shiloh and Max Townsend sheepishly faced each other from their doorways. Neither was able to sleep, and they both had looked out of their staterooms at the same time. "Looks like a poker night to me," Shiloh grinned.

It was a strange nightmare game that grew more and more lurid as the minutes wore on. As Shiloh and Townsend shuffled and bid, the *Conqueror* began to heave back and forth in deeper and deeper troughs of sea, and the weak light from the kerosene lantern flickered eerily as it swung back and forth on its hook.

Several times it seemed as if the ship were almost perpendicular in the raging water, and the men's eyes met with the same unspoken question: will she founder or will she right herself?

It was midnight when the hammering started.

Shiloh had just raised on a pair of twos and taken five dollars of the Pinkerton man's hard-earned money when both looked up, startled by the noise.

"What the devil—!" Max Townsend exclaimed and looked upward as if he could see through to the top deck where the sound was coming from. "Sounds like a battering ram!"

"Hope we're not being broadsided," Shiloh joked, but his face was grim. Wood on wood, the rhythmic banging was definite and clearly separate from the monotonous moans of the ship. For a minute, perhaps, they listened, trying to identify the rather frightening sound.

Then a woman's scream of panic came to their ears, faint but definite, and a woman's shout—not a scream, but shouted words—sounded from down the corridor. Both men leaped to their feet.

Shiloh got to the door first and wrenched it open. The wind seemed to be lying in ambush, for it tore the handle out of his hands and banged the heavy door back against the stateroom wall. Shiloh looked blankly down at his feet, and in a moment Townsend did, too, as seawater washed down the hallways and sloshed crazily about their ankles.

As Shiloh started out into the hall, he heard Nicholas Trent's uneven tread on the stairwell. Trent came hurrying down the hallway and skidded to a stop when he saw Shiloh's tall form. "Help!" he shouted hoarsely, and Shiloh began to run. "They're going overboard!"

The ship heaved sharply to Shiloh's right, and a wave came crashing down the stairwell, washing Trent a few feet toward Shiloh. Then the young man struggled to his feet and fought his way back to the stairs.

"Wait!" Shiloh shouted as he pushed himself away from the walls, fighting the ship's maniacal tosses with all his strength, but Nicholas' form had already disappeared up the stairwell. Shiloh began to fight harder, Max Townsend a few feet behind him.

They seemed to run a long time through the shifting, turning tunnel of the corridor, but finally they reached the stairway and pushed themselves up it with both hands on the oak railings. Then Shiloh saw a woman's form at the top of the stairs, and immediately he recognized Cheney.

She, too, was holding with both hands to the railings, and even as he looked up, a wall of water beat against her. But her slender form held fast, and Shiloh took the stairs three at a time to reach her. Just as he reached her, she screamed, "I'm coming, Lydia! Hold on!" and tried to catapult herself out on the open deck.

Shiloh reached out with a long arm even as her feet left the deck, clasped her around the waist, and roughly pulled her back into the relative shelter of the stairwell, two steps down.

"Stay back, Cheney!" he shouted as he ran through the open doorway, and Max Townsend followed him. Cheney couldn't hear the words, but she looked up at him with unmistakable relief.

Shiloh took in the scene instantly. Two women were lying on the crazily tipping promenade deck of the *Conqueror,* about twenty feet on the starboard side of the stairwell entrance. The low side railing was gone all along the side of the deck, and one woman's feet hung off the side of the ship. She was stretched full length, one hand extended as far as she could reach. It was Tani DuQuesne.

Facing Tani, one hand outstretched and clasping Tani's in a tenuous grip, was Lydia Thornton. Her other arm was thrown about a wooden capstan with a fat rope coiled about it tightly. Her arm looked hopelessly slender against the wooden cylinder, and Shiloh winced as he thought of Lydia's still-raw hands desperately grasping the thick, rough rope.

The wooden ramming sound was a lifeboat that had lost its bowsprit moorings, and was being beaten against the sides of the ship. Even as Shiloh turned, the sea tore the boat loose and impatiently flung it out into the chaos.

Must have been why Nicholas was up here—fool women followed him, or just plain women's know-it-all, fix-it-all, Shiloh thought with fury. But he concentrated hard and turned his anger into physical strength, as he had done so many times when he fought men for money.

Shiloh moved back, past the stairwell, and away from the women, and for a moment Townsend was confused. But then he looked past Shiloh and caught sight of Nicholas, who was clinging to another capstan with one hand and trying to loosen the rope with the other.

The ship tipped starboard-upward and a wall of water rushed over to the side. Shiloh threw himself down and began to belly-crawl toward the capstan, and Townsend followed. They clung by finger- and toe-holds to the deck as the water rushed over them.

As the ship began its opposite roll, Nicholas threw them the rope. Shiloh grabbed it, tied it around his waist and pulled the knot secure, then rolled upright and pointed to Townsend, then to the capstan. Townsend jumped up with the ship's roll, ran to the rope, pulled himself to the capstan, and he and Nicholas fed the line out as Shiloh began to fight his way to the women.

Immediately the ship tilted starboard-up again, the waves crashed over the deck, and Shiloh threw himself prone. The backwash spun Lydia around sideways, but she kept her grip on both the capstan and Tani, though now she was stretched out as if on a cross. They had lost precious inches, and Tani's legs still hung over the side. She began to shout at Lydia, and the capricious wind picked up the words and tossed them to Shiloh.

"—killed—Lynch!" she screamed, and then repeated it, slowly and deliberately. "I—killed—Lynch." Lydia nodded understanding, and Tani seemed to throw all of her waning strength into screaming, "fell—on the knife—!"

Lydia, her face twisted with pain and sorrow, nodded and she shouted back, "Jesus—forgives—!"

Tani, her face hopeless, her grip inexorably loosening, began to shout to Lydia, and Shiloh caught some of the words as he desperately fought his way toward them.

"Holy—Mary, Mother—of God, pray for—"

"Tani!" Lydia shouted, "—Jesus!—forgives you—!"

Shiloh was getting nearer, though he was stopped by wave after wave rushing over them and the ship's tipping him back, away from the women. Lydia's hands were dark with blood, and then were washed clean, and then they darkened again as the blood flowed to cover both her hands and Tani's repeatedly.

With a supreme effort, Tani threw her other hand over her head and grabbed Lydia's, and Shiloh was close enough to hear Lydia sob gladly. But Tani couldn't see Shiloh as he drew tantalizingly near; the angle of his approach hid him from her. Slowly, to Lydia's and Shiloh's horror, Tani began to pry Lydia's bloody fingers loose from her grip on Tani's wrist.

"Holy—Jesus—" she shouted, whether to Lydia or to God, they never knew, "save us—me—now—in the hour of my—death—forgive me—Jesus—!"

Lydia's hand was free, and Tani disappeared.

❦

By mutual, unspoken consent, Shiloh and Cheney left the Grand Salon together. Lydia, Nicholas Trent, Max Townsend, Asa Mercer, and Captain Drury stayed behind in the salon, still talking in low, exhausted voices as they tried to sort out all that had happened. But Cheney and Shiloh had met each other's gaze across the room, excused themselves wearily, and walked out.

The morning was rainy and dreary, and the ship was still tossing around, but only slightly. Cheney and Shiloh climbed down the stairwell, looking curiously around it in the gray morning light, but instead of going down the corridor toward their staterooms they crossed to the door that led out onto the sheltered stateroom deck. Neither of them spoke.

Rain dripped dismally off the top of the deck. The waves were still high, but not whitecapping sharply. In unison they leaned against the railing, looking out sorrowfully at the uncaring ocean, both of them thinking of Tani DuQuesne.

"Did you think I killed him, Cheney?" Shiloh asked abruptly.

Cheney glanced sharply at him. To her surprise, his expression was one of pain. She looked back out to sea, her brow furrowed, and answered in a low voice. "Until I heard Lydia say— what Tani said—"

She made a curious, helpless gesture with one hand, and her voice shook a little as she went on. "Then I remembered that B-Bull had a bruise—on his forehead. He f-fell, face down, and they turned him over before I got there—I'm sorry, Shiloh!"

Shiloh's face darkened, and his eyes restlessly searched the foggy horizon. Taking a deep breath, Cheney reached out with a cold, trembling hand and took Shiloh's arm to turn him toward her. Reluctantly he faced her. His eyes—usually so clear, so full of gentle humor—were clouded with bitterness.

"Oh, Shiloh, you have to understand," Cheney pleaded, her face upturned to him and full of remorse, "I—I don't understand you, like you—you seem to just know me, so well! I—I—don't know what you're thinking, like you—do—"

She bit her lip hard as tears sprang to her eyes, and Shiloh's face suddenly became gentle. "Please, forgive me!" she whispered. "Please . . ."

Shiloh moved close to her, reached out, and gently grasped her upper arms. They were cold, and he massaged them lightly. "I forgive you, Cheney," he said simply, "and I promise, I'll never lie to you. I can't—because you know me better than you think—"

Cheney shivered, not from the cold, but in a strong reaction to his touch. She looked up at him, and she knew the strength of her feelings showed in her eyes. She couldn't seem to hide them or control them.

Shiloh's own eyes kindled as he stared at her, and he took a deep breath. Then he pulled her to him, and his lips met hers. Weakly, Cheney put her arms around his neck and pressed close to him, returning his kiss with a passion that frightened her. She couldn't make herself break away from him, and for long moments they clung together.

Finally Shiloh lifted his head and whispered hoarsely, "Cheney! Cheney—please—"

She was unable to speak for a moment. Then guilt, remorse, anger, and a hint of fear—all mixed together in a confusing dark shadow—swept over Cheney. Her heavy-lidded eyes opened wide, as if with recognition. She put her hands on his chest and pushed hard.

Shiloh was as solid as an old oak tree; her push made no impression on him. He looked at her, bewildered and lost, and in that unguarded moment she pounced. "Let go of me! What— what are we—I mean, what are you doing?"

Shiloh jumped a full three feet away from her. "What am I doing?" he repeated angrily. "I don't know! I must have been insane, attacking you that way—for *no reason!*"

"No reason!" she echoed illogically, but Shiloh flinched as if she'd cursed at him.

"Wait just a minute!" he demanded and again stepped close to her—but this time in anger. "I believe that you, Dr. Duvall, were guilty of kissing *me* while I was so busy attacking *you!*"

Cheney moved away from him, and paced for a few moments. "It doesn't make any difference, Shiloh," she said curtly as she came to stand in front of him, her shoulders tensed. "It's—It shouldn't have happened, and—it's—we're—it won't happen again!"

Shiloh's eyes grew stormy, the V scar beside his eye seeming to grow deeper as his face tightened. "What're you afraid of? What're you suddenly so high and mighty about, Dr. Duvall?"

Again he stepped close to her, and his stance was taut. "I'll tell you what's the matter with you! You want so much to be a good doctor—but you think that means you gotta be a man! And it's made you afraid to be a real woman!"

She glared up at him. "You don't understand anything!" she stormed. "That's ridiculous! You have no idea what I want or how I feel!"

With visible effort, Shiloh forced himself to calm down and relax his body. He smiled down at Cheney, but it was not like his usual warm, open grin; it was more like a wolf's grin at the sight of the rabbit in the snare. "You said just a minute ago that I can read your mind, Cheney, that I understand you too well?"

He paused for a moment, and abruptly Cheney's face closed, all emotion wiped clean, all passion and temper locked tightly shut. Shiloh narrowed his eyes and deliberately stepped backward, away from her.

"Y'know, I think I do understand you, Doctor," he muttered grimly. "Maybe I understand you too well. You don't have to put up that flinty wall, you know! Because I'm giving you my resignation—as of the minute we set foot in Seattle! That way, I won't be around to mess up your tidy little cubbyholes and pigeonholes where you put your feelings when you don't want to mess with 'em!" He stared at her for a long moment. "I'm going to the gold fields. And I hope there's not a woman there for forty miles around!"

20

End of a Voyage

Asa Mercer and Annie Stephens leaned against the railing of the stateroom deck as the *Conqueror* threaded her way through the clusters of ships docked in Seattle. The sky seemed to be made of masts, and the odor of raw earth and evergreens filled the air. The docks were lined with warehouses and as the ship glided into its slot, Asa pointed at the men lining the wharf. "Looks like we won't have to advertise," he smiled. "See all those fellows lined up for brides?"

Annie tilted her face toward him. "Don't you feel guilty, Asa?"

"Guilty? About what?"

"About robbing one of them of a wife."

Asa stared at her, his boyish face bewildered—then he realized she was teasing him again. It was part of his education, for he was basically a sober young man. Annie had told Cheney, "I'll have to take some of the stiffness out of him. He's as proper as a sixty-year-old deacon!"

Abruptly Asa pulled her close and kissed her firmly, then lifted his head and grinned. "No, I don't feel guilty. Let them go east and get their own brides!" She laughed at him, and he kept his arm around her waist, holding her close. When she protested that he was holding her too tightly, he merely squeezed her tighter, saying, "Might as well get used to it, Annie. I'm holding on to you real close for the rest of our lives."

Together they watched as the gangplank was lowered and the women disembarked. The crowd of men that had gathered parted slightly to let them pass.

"Don't you want to go with them to the hotel?" Annie asked.

"No, let them be escorted by all the fellows. I want you to see my house—your new home."

Annie beamed and squeezed his arms. "I can't believe I almost lost you to Holly Van Buren."

The reference to the blond girl embarrassed Asa considerably. "Oh, I don't think it was all that close," he mumbled.

Annie laughed at him, her eyes shining with fun. "She'd have had you jumping through hoops the rest of your life!"

They stood basking in each other's company, hardly aware of anyone else until Asa said, "Look, there's Lydia and Sybil."

Annie followed his gesture and watched the two women reach the end of the gangplank, where they were royally greeted by the mayor, a tall man who seemed to take charge of the two.

"I never thought Sybil would make it," Annie told him. "It's good that she and Lydia are going to stay together for a while."

"Do you think either of them will ever get married?"

"Sooner or later. Sybil needs lots of healing yet—and the young man who gets Lydia will have his hands full."

"She *is* a caution, isn't she," Asa agreed. "But she'll find just the right man—and he'll get a prize."

Allegra Winston-Smythe appeared, blinking a little in the sunlight. She appeared lovely and detached, as always, and the men gathered on the docks drew aside quietly as she passed. Guiltily they stole glances at her, but the coolness that surrounded her kept them at a distance. "You know, I never learned anything about her," Asa murmured as she disappeared into the crowds. "Did you?"

"No, nothing," Annie sighed. "I thought Allegra and Shiloh— but even he couldn't seem to—"

Asa's attention was distracted from Annie's observations about Allegra and Shiloh by the eye-catching procession that appeared on the gangplank. Annie followed his gaze, and a delighted smile appeared on her face.

"Beans," Georgia called over her shoulder, "you watch your silly self on this gangplank! You won't be doing anyone one bit of good if you fall and bust your noggin again!" She was wearing a white dress trimmed in black velvet. A clever black hat perched on her red hair, with a net veil that covered the top half of her face, and below it her lips were perfectly painted in a red cupid's bow. As she swayed down the gangplank, she lifted her wide skirts to show a flash of black netted ankle, and the men below whistled and catcalled.

Behind her, Beans Lowery moved slowly, looking dignified in a dark blue seaman's suit that Georgia had sweet-talked some unsuspecting sailor into giving up. He walked slowly, leaning heavily on two beautifully carved canes. One was topped with an eagle's head, one with a lion's head, and the rich reddish wood gleamed in the sunlight.

Georgia had bought the canes for Beans when the ship docked in San Francisco for three days, and he looked down at them with open pleasure as he walked. He had insisted on naming the canes Eenie and Meenie, for some reason he couldn't remember, but he was quite certain the explanation would come to him sooner or later.

"That's going to be some boardinghouse," Asa remarked with a smile. "Georgia as the proprietress and Beans as the handyman. Thank heavens they brought Kat in on this little venture—as young as she is, she does seem to have some sense."

"Don't be fooled by that slow drawl," Annie told him shrewdly. "Georgia Jakes has sense, more than a lot of women I've met." Behind Georgia and Beans came Katherine Dailey, the young servant girl from steerage. Bull had made her life miserable on the *Continental,* but Beans had become her friend on the *Conqueror.* Now she sternly charged three porters staggering behind her to be careful with Miss Jakes' trunks and hatboxes.

"Georgia's—changed, hasn't she?" Asa murmured.

"Oh yes, she has. She told Lydia that Beans treated her like a real lady, always had. Beans didn't care what she had been, only who she was *today*. And somehow that made her want to act like a lady."

Even as they talked, Georgia reached the crowd of boisterous men. But instead of coarsely responding to them as she might have once done, she walked proudly, with dignity, through the crowd without a backward glance. The men grinned with appreciation and doffed their hats to her as she passed.

"Tani . . ." Asa murmured softly to himself.

"They'll never forget her," Annie told him as the procession began their conspicuous way toward the city. "Georgia said she's going to name the boardinghouse 'DuQuesne House' so they would remember her every day."

"All that money she had," Asa sighed and shook his head. "And my first impulse was to find her *owner* to return it to *him*!"

Annie put her hand on his arm and drew closer to him as he went on bitterly. "I suppose that's exactly the kind of thing Tani faced every single day, again and again, from even good abolitionists like me!"

"Asa, you must stop punishing yourself for Tani. None of us could help what happened to her, and none of us—you especially—ever meant to harm her. Make the memory of her good, instead of painful. She obviously would have wanted it that way."

After Tani died, Asa had taken responsibility for disposing of her belongings as best he could. To his surprise, he had found a small chest of gold coins in Tani's spotless, impersonal stateroom. Inside her favorite book—a large anthology of British poets—was a letter, addressed in a schoolroom-perfect hand "To Whom It May Concern." After much agony of mind, Asa decided that it was his responsibility to open it.

The letter was dated June 5, a few days after the *Conqueror* had left Panama; and as Asa read, a lump of sorrow had formed in his throat:

As we leave Panama and I see the fever begin, it occurs to me that as a free woman I now have certain responsibilities. This does not concern family, for I have none. My father still lives, but he is also my former owner. After my mother died seven years ago, he kept me in his household, but he seemed to hate the sight of me. When the war ended, he gave me a large sum of money and told me to leave New Orleans and never return. I assure you, reader, that the gold belongs to me; and as you read, I am assured that this letter is serving as my Last Will and Testament.

To Georgia Jakes, I bequeath the sum of one hundred dollars. She is humble enough to see her own faults, strong enough to wish to correct them, and charitable enough to ask forgiveness for them. I forgave you, Georgia, then and now. You learned to see me as an equal, a woman talking to another woman, and that simple friendship was, to me, worth more than all treasure.

To Beans Lowery, I bequeath the sum of one hundred dollars. You treated me with unfailing respect and kindness, with absolutely no regard to my color, my physical attributes, my worldly wealth, or my social status. You simply liked me and respected me, Beans, and I wish you well!

To Our Lady of the Sea Church in Havana, I bequeath the sum of one hundred dollars.

An annotation dated June 30 said simply:

Whatever sums of money should remain after the above bequests, I bequeath to Lydia Thornton. You are color blind, Lydia, in all senses of the word, but I have rejoiced in this. Thank you, and God bless you.

There was no signatory, only Tani's name at the bottom of the page. Lydia had inherited almost two hundred dollars from Tani DuQuesne.

Annie smiled as she remembered the lovely, distant, elegant Tani DuQuesne, and Asa determined to put aside his regrets and do as Annie so wisely had said—to make Tani's memory one of warmth and beauty.

Abruptly Annie asked, "Asa, whatever happened to that young seaman—what was his name? The terrifically handsome one with the limp? I don't remember seeing him for the last few days—"

"Even though he was so terrifically handsome?" Asa repeated with mock sternness. "I don't think I'll tell you! You might just decide to go visit him, like you did for me so faithfully, when I was sick!"

Annie shushed him, but she looked pleased at Asa's warm teasing. He went on, "Guess I don't have to worry too much since you didn't seem to notice what happened to him. Max Townsend thumbed his nose at Captain Drury and snatched Nicholas Trent right out of his galley!"

Annie looked up at Asa, bewildered, and Asa laughed at the memory of Captain Drury's disapproval—and displeasure. "Townsend told me and Shiloh that he didn't particularly relish returning those two chests of gold to Zaldivar in Panama. Townsend seemed to think that the painful memory of those four boxes of nails might, as he put it, 'prejudice Zaldivar just a bit.' And at that point young Trent announced that he would consider taking it to Panama and explaining to Zaldivar what had happened, if Townsend was willing to pay."

Asa hesitated as Holly Van Buren appeared, her glossy blond ringlets bouncing and ribbons fluttering. Annie hadn't yet noticed Holly; Asa put his arm around the waist of his intended and turned her slightly away as he continued his story. Annie was listening with avid interest, and Asa took a deep breath of relief as he recalled the scene.

"Townsend told Trent that he was talking like a fool, that Zaldivar would probably hang his skinny—that is, hang him from the nearest coconut palm! Trent just laughed and told Townsend that there probably wouldn't be any danger since Zaldivar is Trent's uncle and he, Nicholas, was Zaldivar's favorite nephew!"

Annie laughed with delight, her eyes sparkling, and Asa watched her with undisguised admiration, solemnly reminding himself again how lucky he was. "As you know, Annie dear, Townsend got off the *Conqueror* in San Francisco, and Trent disembarked with him. Townsend swears that Nicholas Trent is going to be quite an addition to Pinkerton's!"

The morning began to wane into afternoon as Mercer's Belles slowly paraded down the gangplank to be absorbed into the bustling crowds of Seattle. Finally all the women had disembarked, and Asa said, "Let's go get your things. I'll find a carriage and take you for a tour."

"All right, Asa."

They gathered their luggage, and Asa summoned one of the crew to take the bags ashore—except for Rex in his box. Annie insisted on carrying him herself, as she had stubbornly done even through the jungles of Panama.

As they approached the gangplank, a voice stopped them. "Asa—Annie—!"

The pair turned to find Powell Drake and Martha Jane hurrying along to catch them, with Stony and Kelvey in tow. "Well, now, Powell," Asa grinned, "I've been meaning to talk to you about my fee."

"Fee?" Powell Drake stared at Mercer with astonishment, an uncomprehending look on his face. "What fee, Asa?"

"My fee for your bride, of course!" Asa and Annie laughed at the blank look on Powell's face, and Asa put his hand out. "Well, since I'm a bride stealer as well, I guess I'll have to let you off."

Drake smiled down at Martha Jane. "I think we'd better not tell those wild fellows I saw that we've kept a couple of women for ourselves. They might string us up."

"Where will you two be going?" Annie asked. "I hope you'll be staying here in Washington."

"We may do that," Drake nodded. "This is a good country for raising a family—lots of opportunity. . . ."

He paused to look down at Kelvey, who was pulling on his coattail. "Come on, Pa—let's go down there." She pointed a stubby little finger to Stony, who was running in wild circles through an unimpressed group of fat sea gulls. They fluttered around him lazily before settling back down to waddle along the dock, and Stony whooped loudly at them, his face beaming.

Martha Jane laughed at the title. "Pa Drake," she said, humor in her eyes. "Makes you sound like a patriarch."

They were moving toward the gangplank when Martha Jane looked back to see someone come on deck. "Dr. Duvall!" she called out. She was surprised when Cheney hesitated, seeming at first to turn to go the other way. Asa, too, called out, "Doctor, here we are!"

Cheney came slowly toward them, and her smile seemed tired to Martha Jane. She studied the young woman carefully as Asa said cheerfully, "Well, Doctor, we're here—end of the voyage. Now, we're having a celebration tonight, and I insist that you and Shiloh join us."

"I'm sorry, Asa, but we—I won't be able to come."

"What's that?" Mercer asked with surprise. "Why, you've just got to! I mean, hang it all, Cheney, you've been one of the best things about the trip!"

The others urged her, but Cheney only shook her head, saying, "I'm sorry."

Martha Jane said quickly to Powell, "Why don't you go find a carriage, dear. I want to speak to Dr. Duvall for a moment." She waited until the others were halfway down the gangplank before she asked, "What's wrong, Cheney?"

"Why—nothing's wrong," Cheney said, lifting her head. "I'm just too tired to go to a party."

Martha Jane stared at her, slowly shook her head, and said, "I'm no doctor, Cheney, but I hope I'm your friend. You've been so kind to me and the children. Can't you tell me about it?"

"Oh—it's nothing, Martha Jane," she said, trying to hide her misery. She cleared her throat, looked out at the forest of masts, and said, "Shiloh and I decided—to go our own ways."

After she spoke, she fell silent, her lips drawn into a pale line. She refused to meet the eyes of the other woman, adding, "I wish you and Mr. Drake the best, and—"

"Why did you decide to part?"

Cheney shook her head, and the gesture sent the curls tumbling. Her face was downcast, her eyes clouded. She had been withdrawn since her quarrel with Shiloh, and now she refused to let Martha Jane see how great the hurt was.

"It was a professional matter," she said brusquely, forcing a smile. "But I'll come to your wedding—when will it be?"

Martha Jane told her of the plans and made arrangements to see her on shore. But Martha Jane was unhappy about Cheney's situation and said so. "I'll be praying for you—and for Shiloh, too."

"Thank you."

Martha Jane quickly kissed her on the cheek and hurried down the gangplank. "She coming to the party?" Asa asked as Martha Jane reached him.

"No, she won't be there," Martha Jane replied quietly. When pressed she only said, "She's had a hard journey—and a disappointment."

"About Shiloh?" Powell Drake was watching Martha's face, and when he saw her surprise he shook his head. "I tried to get him to come—but he says he's off to the gold fields."

Asa stared at Drake. "I can't believe that! Not as close as he was to Dr. Duvall. I wonder what happened! Maybe we ought to find him and—"

"No, Asa." Annie took his arm, and her eyes were sad. "Some things we can't do—and I'm afraid this is one of them. Come along."

"Maybe they'll make it up," Asa said hopefully to Drake as they moved down the wharf.

Drake shook his head. "I doubt it," he said quietly. "They're both stubborn people—just the wrong kind to make things up. Too much pride—and I know quite a bit about that, Asa."

⚜

Cheney was sitting in a straight chair beside her window, staring down at the traffic passing on the street below. Two heavily loaded freight wagons clashed, locking their wheels; at once the two drivers came boiling off their seats and began pummeling each other. A crowd of men gathered, making a circle around the two as they rolled in the dust, kicking and striking out wildly.

Disgusted at the scene, Cheney started to rise, when she spotted Asa and Annie Mercer round the corner and head for the entrance of the Empire Hotel. She had attended their wedding two weeks earlier, just two days after Powell Drake and Martha Jane Terrell were married by the same minister.

They're coming to see me, she thought and rose quickly. Crossing over to the mirror, she stared dismally at the image. *You look as if you've been pulled through a knothole*, she thought grimly. She wet a cloth in the basin and pressed it against her face, then made a halfhearted attempt to pin her untidy hair. When the knock came, she crossed the room, put on a smile, and opened the door. "Why—it's you!" she said with as much animation as she could muster. "Come in."

"We've been shopping," Asa declared as they entered the small room. A rueful look crossed his smooth face. "I didn't know how much shopping a married man was tied to," he confessed.

"He's been a lamb, Cheney," Annie said proudly. "He's learned all my bad habits and loves me anyway! And Rex, too!"

"Except when he jumps on my head when I come in the house," Asa said woefully.

Then Annie told Cheney, "We've come to get you. Where's your coat?"

Cheney stared at Annie suspiciously. "What is it—another plot to show me off to the bachelors of Seattle?"

Asa flushed. "Oh, Dr. Duvall, it's not like that—!"

"Yes, it is," Annie rebuked him. Turning to Cheney she explained, "It's just a little luncheon in Asa's honor—for bringing the Belles to Seattle. But the bachelors will be there."

"Aren't they everywhere?" Cheney murmured. She shrugged. "All right, I'll go, but you two will have to protect me."

"You're driving them crazy," Asa grinned. "Good-looking woman, smart and educated. They pester the life out of Annie and me to bring you around."

Cheney fastened her hat, stepped to the door, and remarked wryly, "Every time I go out, I feel like a side of beef being looked over by a crowd of butchers."

Asa looked shocked at her choice of words, but Annie giggled. "It *is* a little like that, I suppose."

"What's the score?" Cheney inquired as they left her room and started down the hall. "Any single women left?"

"Not many," Asa replied proudly. "Georgia's turned down two proposals so far, you know! And Miss Ordway's teaching advanced students in that new year-round program she's always been so passionate about. She never made any pretense at wanting to get married, you know, not to me or to anyone else, but I'm still so glad she's here in Seattle."

"Holly Van Buren's getting married," Annie remarked with a teasing look at Asa, who looked at the ceiling with an exaggerated sigh. "To the richest man in Seattle. He's fifty-one years old and has gout," Annie announced with satisfaction. The couple's little game made Cheney smile wistfully at them.

They joined the large crowd in the banquet room, composed of most of Mercer's Belles and the men of Seattle. To Cheney's surprise, she enjoyed the affair. She wedged herself firmly between

Martha Jane and Annie, who kept the men at bay. The meal was good, but it was the brief ceremony afterward that pleased her most.

The mayor of Seattle made a speech and so did the territorial governor—all in praise of Asa Mercer. Then Asa rose, and to Cheney's surprise gave an excellent speech—though not eloquent, for he was not capable of that. Speaking simply and directly, he told the story of the trials of the young women and gave high praise to those who helped—especially to Dr. Cheney Duvall!

He ended by saying, "I'm sure we'd all like to hear a brief word from Dr. Duvall." Aghast, Cheney tried to shrink into her seat. But she could not disappear, of course, so she rose to speak briefly, making little of her own efforts but praising Asa Mercer and wishing the community well.

Finally it was over, and she fled to her room. For a while she sat by the window, but a restlessness stirred in her, so she put on a cloak and hat and left the hotel.

Turning toward the sea, she made her way to the wharf and for an hour walked back and forth. Her mind was numb, and she knew she should be thinking about her next move.

I'll have to go home, I suppose, she thought listlessly. The thought of going back East brought a heaviness, and she tried to shake off the feeling. *I might be able to get a place in one of the big hospitals. Now that I'm "famous."*

Her parents had sent her copies of the *New York Herald* article that dramatized her role in escorting Mercer's Belles to Seattle and made her out to be much more of a heroine than she had actually been. Remembering the righteously indignant article that had led to more than a hundred cancellations just before the Belles had left New York, Cheney thought, *At least they're consistent! Consistently misleading, misinformed, and generally incorrect!*

The sun was sinking into the waters, seeming to dissolve in golden waves. The smell of the sea pleased her, and as she walked along in the gathering darkness, she thought of the many times she'd stood at the railing and watched that same sun go down. Then she thought with sadness of Enid and Arlene, and Tani, and the others who had not survived the journey. Grief was sharp in her breast, for she had not learned how to mute it nor to exorcise the pain it brought.

She thought also of those who were now in a new land, beginning new lives. All of them had such high hopes, but she knew a feeling of despair as she thought, *Some of them will fail here—just as they failed in the East.*

A mere sliver of the curve of the sun was all that remained, and she turned to go back to her room. As she did, she saw a man approaching her, and impatience swept over her. When he came to stand in front of her, the sun was at his back, so she could not make out his features.

"Please—stand aside," she said coldly. When he didn't move, she demanded angrily, "Don't you have anything else to do but annoy women?"

And then Shiloh's voice touched her as he said, "I guess not."

At once Cheney blinked and peered up to see his face. He stepped aside and waited for her to speak. Now that he was out of the sun, she could see his features more clearly. He looked lean, and a trace of anger—or unhappiness—sharpened the angular planes of his face. Cheney was dismayed at the sudden feelings of relief that washed over her at the sight of him. To cover her emotion, she said in a tight voice, "I thought you were going to the gold fields."

He made a tall shape in the dusky shadows that were falling over the wharf, and he stirred his shoulders impatiently as he answered, "Found out I couldn't do it."

Cheney waited for him to speak, to explain his sudden appearance. A tinge of irritation hit her and she demanded, "Why not? Did you lose your stake in a poker game?"

The sea breeze, laden with its salty tang, pushed at them and lifted his hair, ruffling it so that it fell in chunks across his forehead. His eyes were almost hidden in the deep sockets, and his mouth made a thin slash, not at all the relaxed lips she was accustomed to.

"Well, why didn't you go?" Cheney demanded. Then, without waiting, she started to stride away.

"Wait—" His hand closed on her arm and held it tightly. She found herself being turned around, and when she was facing him, he said quietly, "Every step I took away from you—it seemed wrong."

Cheney stood very still, acutely aware of his powerful hands gripping her forearms, of his intensely masculine, deeply familiar presence. Somehow unable to move, she just waited helplessly. Then, when she saw that he was going to kiss her, she stiffened.

He ignored her reaction, lowered his head, and let his lips touch hers. She determined to keep herself stiff, to ignore the kiss—but discovered that she could not do it. He put his arms around her and drew her close, his lips insistent. Cheney put her hands on his chest—but found that she could not push him away. There was an intensity in Shiloh Irons that she'd never known in another man—and she found herself surrendering to his embrace.

I can't do this! she thought. But somehow her arms rose and she put her hands on his head, drawing him closer. She was aware of the hunger in his embrace, and knew that she had desires of her own. But somehow this did not shame her, and she pressed closer against him as he held her.

Finally he lifted his head and said hoarsely, "I know you only think of me as a nurse. But I'm telling you flat, Cheney, I'll never be able to think of you as just a doctor!"

"How—how—will you think of me?"

"As a lovely woman, the finest one I've ever known!"

Cheney suddenly felt weak, and she closed her eyes, leaning forward to rest her cheek on his chest. She could hear his heart beating steadily, and a sense of well-being swept over her.

"I don't think—I'd like it—if you thought of me only as a doctor," she murmured. For a time she clung to him—and then she pushed him away. Her hands were trembling as she tried to fix her hair. Finally she cleared her throat. "I missed you, Shiloh."

He grinned, saying, "That's good. Now when you get mad at me, I'll run off and let you get to missing me."

"Never mind that! Now, where have you been?"

The two of them stood talking as the last of the light faded. Only the flickering lanterns from the town and the ships broke the darkness. The wharf, which had seemed a lonely and forlorn place only a few minutes before, now seemed warm and safe to Dr. Cheney Duvall.

"Where will we go now, Doc?" Shiloh asked. "Go back East for another load of man-hungry females?"

"No! Once is enough!" Cheney laughed at her own vehemence. "We'll find a place," she said finally. "God will help us."

"You really believe that?"

"Yes!"

Shiloh leaned forward until he could see her eyes. They were bright with hope, and he nodded. "That'll be good enough for us, I expect."

They turned and began to walk down the wharf, speaking quietly and laughing from time to time. A sleek white cat that refused to belong to anyone except the wharfs of Seattle came silently out of an alley behind them as they passed. He sat down, washed one paw meticulously, then with unblinking yellow eyes watched the couple as they disappeared into the evergreen-scented darkness.

About the Author

Lynn Morris, daughter of popular historical novelist Gilbert Morris, is a recognized and talented writer in her own right. The first novel in this eight-book series was originally published in 1994, and it was an immediate bestseller (nearly half a million combined sales of the eight novels in the series). The author's careful background explorations of the historical setting, the medical customs of the late 1800s, and the training institutions finally being opened to women make for intriguing plots and dramatic tensions for the memorable character of Cheney Duvall.

Lynn has a grown daughter and lives near her parents in Alabama.